AMERICAN

HERO

ALSO BY LARRY BEINHART

No One Rides for Free
You Get What You Pay For
Foreign Exchange

AMERICAN

★ ★ ★ ★

HERO

LARRY
BEINHART

PANTHEON BOOKS NEW YORK

To my children--James Irving Beinhart and Anna Genevieve Beinhart--fortunate to be born in a rich and secure and remarkable country, as I was. May it stay that way. And to my wife--their mother--Gillian Farrell--an extraordinary woman.

There are those who feel that fact and fiction are significantly less distinguishable than they used to seem to be. They might say, as ABC Television did in its introduction to "The Heroes of Desert Storm":

"Tonight's film is based on true stories and interweaves news footage and dramatizations with actors and actual participants. To achieve realism no distinction is made among these elements."

AMERICAN
HERO

CHAPTER

* * *

ONE

He believed that he was Machiavelli incarnate. Political theoretician. Master intriguer. The most clever and the most ruthless man in the empire.

It was certainly true that it was an empire. In many ways the greatest the world had ever known though there was a prohibition against saying so in polite political society. In any case, it so far exceeded the sort of minor realm ruled by the Borgias, the meager reach of the Medici, the influence of any Italian city-state, that any such comparison was like comparing an elephant to an ant. It could only be compared, de facto, no matter what political-speak required people to say, to Rome when Rome was the very definition of empire.

And he was the kingmaker. The king might be crownless, but he was still the first in the land, armies at his command, billions to dispense, the power to create wealth or destroy life. The dreamer on the bed was the man who was advisor to the king. Which, in point of fact, was better than Master Niccolò Machiavelli, the man himself, had ever actually done.[1]

---

[1] Machiavelli was second chancellor and secretary of Florence from 1498 to 1512.

Although he was delirious—the effects of deadly disease, powerful drugs both violent and soporific, and fear: death was, after
all, imminent and known to be imminent—there was nothing
untrue about his thoughts. Though perhaps highly colored, a fancy-
dress version of reality, they were verifiable, accurate, real. He
would have had, and would have been entitled to have had, the
exact same thoughts at home, healthy, surrounded by family,
friends, sycophants, connivers, special pleaders, intriguers, followers, imitators, wannabes, power merchants, billionaires, at an
all-American Fourth-of-July-type barbecue—chicken and ribs and
watermelon, booze on ice and beer in the bucket.

"He's sleeping," the nurse said softly. She was not a pretty
nurse, but she was very clean and she was white. "He may wake
soon."

The guest looked at her questioningly.

"You can wait here," the nurse said, pointing at a chair by the
bed. "If you want," she added with some diffidence. This was not
a public hospital full of oppressive visiting regulations and rules,
where the doctors and even lowly nurses told the patients, their
family, friends, or patrons what to do and when to do it, and
expected to be obeyed.

"He was asking for me?" the guest asked.

"Yes," she said. "He said it was important. Very important.
But," she immediately added, "he didn't tell me anything more
than that," as if to reassure the visitor she knew no more than she
ought.

The visitor calculated. He was a very, very busy man. Very

He was frequently an envoy, though not an ambassador. Without a thorough
familiarity with the period, it is extremely difficult to make comparisons between
the power of his post and that of his spiritual heir. After the Medici regained power
in Florence, Machiavelli never held an important office again.

busy. About the busiest in the empire. Now. The man who was dying had been a friend. A colleague. A member of the same winning team. The visitor figured he could spare ten minutes. If the dreamer awoke and spoke, then it would be mission accomplished. If not, it was duty done and he could leave with conscience clear.

The patient's name was Lee Atwater.[2] He was dying of brain cancer.

This was a piece of irony so splendidly vicious that even his enemies thought it was in bad taste to chortle about it.[3] And his enemies hated him. He had made brilliant and devastating use of innuendo, half truth, and political distortion to exploit the malignancies of American society, especially racism.[4] Racism was always

---

[2]This is a work of fiction. Many public figures are named in the text. Politicians, celebrities, presidents, etc. Their actions as depicted here are absolutely figments of the author's imagination and should in no way be construed as "true" or even a "fictionalization of a truth that can be told no other way." Unless of course the reader has independent documentation that real actions are coincidental with these fictional ones. The same is true of the depiction of characters. The author has no knowledge of any real person mentioned in this book beyond what is in the public record, and even then he has chosen to treat that information very cavalierly—because this is a work of fiction.

[3]Atwater commented on it in his autobiography *Life,* written with Todd Brewster: "I recalled the maxim we had used in '88: 'Get inside the mind of your enemy.' Now cancer had used it on me."

[4]Democratic representative Pat Schroeder called him "the most evil man in America." Reverend Pat Roberston said, "Lee Atwater has used every dirty trick known to mankind." (William Greider, *Rolling Stone,* 1/12/89)

"Lee Atwater, his communications director Mark Goodin and Congressman Newt Gingrich . . . worked to spread a long-standing unsubstantiated rumor [of homosexuality] designed to humiliate new House Speaker Thomas Foley [as earlier he had been] "blamed for planting specious reports about the mental-health of Michael Dukakis."

"From his earliest days, Mr. Atwater displayed a skill in the use of racial messages and maneuvers, a crucial part of the effort by Southern Republicans to appeal to white voters." (Obituary, *New York Times,* 3/30/91)

effective, but it was dangerous to employ and required expert handling. It was not excessively egotistical for the dying man to feel that it was he himself who had made George Bush president in 1988. Before Atwater unleashed his campaign, Bush had been eighteen points down in the polls. Before Atwater engineered the media event in which Dan Rather was suckered into an attack on Georgie so that the vice president could lash back, Bush was a man with a reputation as a wimp. This was a man who couldn't speak a complete and coherent sentence unless it was pre-scripted, who was tainted by Iran-contra, and on and on, liability upon liability. With this crippled pony, this lame—if thoroughbred—nag, Atwater had won the biggest race in the world.

The seconds clicked by. There were gray clouds outside the window. Funeral weather, thought the visitor. It was less than a minute and he was already impatient. It was insane of him not to have brought his cellular phone up to the hospital room. Goddamn it, it was insane of him not to have brought his cellular phone and a couple of aides and a Portafax. If anyone would have understood, it would have been Lee, how precious time is to a busy, busy man.

Atwater thought on, dreamed on, of the man he had made king and whom he would leave behind to fend for himself. Although it was Bush who was president and Atwater who was the advisor—a dying one at that; and it was Bush who would go down in history, while Lee would be lucky to be much more than a footnote; and it was Bush who held power while Atwater could only suggest how it should be employed, one voice competing out of a cacaphonous chorus, Atwater still felt, frankly, rather patronizing about

---

Also, the *New York Times Magazine* (4/30/89) repeats a story in which Atwater always denied—that Atwater connived at getting a third-party candidate to use an anti-Semitic campaign against his main opponent, thus gaining the benefit without getting the backlash.

George. This is common in political consultants. As it is with lawyers about their clients, doctors about patients, agents about talent. They feel that the client is a product incapable of caring for itself, who has to be directed, instructed, cared for, protected. When the client does what it is told, it succeeds, thrives, survives. When it does not take advice, it makes a mess, it hurts itself, it creates more work for the handler, whatever the handler's title is.

There were a hundred different versions of that basic story floating through, sometimes zapping through, Atwater's mind. An entire assortment of images. He was Merlin, wand and cap and gown, to the presidential Arthur. Cus D'Amato to Mike Tyson. Brian Epstein to the Beatles. Livia to the emperor Tiberius. It was his mission not merely to have raised up the king but to protect him—lo, even from beyond the grave. Like a guardian angel. Something more than mortal. A spirit that could reach from the other side. A hand that held a fiery sword, like the archangel Gabriel, come down from heaven . . . In that, there was a sort of immortality. If he could do that, he was the most cunning of them all, slicker than death.

Enough of this, the man in the chair by the window thought. I've done my duty. Close to three minutes had passed. He got up to go.

Atwater had neither moved nor spoken. His message still buried in weariness and morphine. His visitor, passing the bed, looked down at the wasted body and bandaged head. Where once the creature below him had been full of exuberant vitality, clever, bullying, sharp-eyed and sharper-tongued, now the dullness was upon him, the emptying had begun. Atwater's hand, under the sheet, appeared clenched.

The visitor couldn't think of anything to say. Not to a recumbent form that neither spoke nor saw. He wasn't that kind of guy, who spoke to people in comas, saying, in that made-for-TV style,

"Yes, yes, he [or she] can hear me. I know they can." So, whatever Lee had summoned him for would have to wait until, later on, World Two, heaven or hell or Washington D.C. in the summertime, wherever dead politicos went this millennium. He nodded and turned to leave the room.

Inside Atwater the Merlin character arose. As if by magic, he reached beyond the dulled and sleeping senses—or perhaps opened the passage between sense and sensibility. Atwater got the message that his guest was here. "Jim," he whispered, "Jim."

James Baker, secretary of state, hand on the knob, stopped. He turned. Atwater's eyes were still closed, but his breathing was more urgent and his hand seem to move.

"Lee?"

"Ahhh," a groan, a grunt, a summons. Baker went to the bedside. Atwater's eyes suddenly opened. The old hawk looked out. Full of cunning and ego. "Listen," he said. "George . . ."

"George what . . ."

It seemed to Baker that he could see Atwater's thoughts like watchworks turning and meshing behind Atwater's eyes, and what he seemed to have thought was, I can speak my mind. Baker can't take it back to the office and use it against me, because, *cackle, cackle,* I'll be dead before he does. "George," Atwater said about the president, "is a wienie. Ambitious, conniving, vengeful, but still . . . And he's going to blow it, Jim. If he does . . ."

"What do you mean, blow it?"

"I mean in the polls," Atwater said as if Baker shouldn't have had to ask, as there was nothing else. "And if he doesn't do something about it, the reelection." It was hard, after Reagan, Reagan again, and then Bush/Quayle, smashing the opposition, to imagine that reelection could fail.

"Don't worry about it," Jim said, a bland reassurance. "We'll take care of it, Lee."

"That's my job. My mission." One hand reached out and clutched Baker, grabbed at his sleeve, held him, and pulled him closer. Atwater's breath was bad. Foul, fetid. Jesus Christ, Baker thought, why don't they brush his teeth or dose him with mouthwash or something. "I have a plan," Atwater said. The other hand, the near one, came out from under the covers where it had been visibly clenched. It held a half-crushed envelope. "If Georgie blows it, you open this. This is the surefire, ultimate election winner."

"Hey, thanks," Baker said politically. "I'll tell George. He'll be touched. You, in your condition—your thoughts are of him."

"Fuck that," Atwater said. "My thoughts are of winning. Remember that, Baker. There's only two things—winning and dying." He cackled. "Don't show it to him now. Don't you even look now. Wait . . ."

"For what?"

"Till you're in trouble and you need it."

"It's like a magic coin in a fairy tale or something like that?" Baker asked.

"Like that," Atwater said.

"Why can't I look now?"

"Because you'll think"—Atwater paused for a breath—"that it's insane. And it will frighten you. But it's so sane, and so logical, that you won't be able to resist it and you'll try it out too soon . . ."

"And so?"

"Then it may not work anymore."

"Like the goose that laid the golden egg or three wishes from the genie?"

"That powerful," Atwater said, appearing somewhat demented. He pushed the envelope into Baker's hands. Baker couldn't imagine what it could be. "It's beautiful. The president will love it. After you realize it's not insane. Not insane at all."

CHAPTER

* * *

TWO

I'm an authentic American hero. Really. That's what I am.

First, you start out with that I'm basically a little guy. I don't mean that I'm lacking in physical stature or I'm inadequate. I mean I'm kind of a regular guy. So there I am, a regular guy. Not out to change the world. Not out to be some kind of big shot. I got no ax to grind. I'm just a guy with a job to do and I try my best to do it. Well, what the job is, that's something else of course. I'm a dick. A gumshoe. A P.I. The stuff that dreams are made of. Books, TV, movies. What I'm trying to say, in a word, is—marketable. Get me?

The difference between me and them, the guys you usually see on the tube, is that I'm not a small-time loner working out of a shabby upstairs over some dry-cleaning plant or a playboy with a Lamborghini who's a detective just as another way to get his kicks. I work for a major corporation. Not Fortune 500, but not too far from it either. Our national headquarters is in Chicago. We have offices in twenty-two U.S. cities and in fourteen foreign countries. A business, you understand, like Wackenhutt or Pinkerton. Whatever a client needs, in the way of security, we do it. Alarm systems, armored cars, round-the-clock armed response, commercial guard services, we do it all. We have a sales-incentive system that runs through the whole company. Like if you decided you needed one of these many services that we do, I could make a commission by introducing you to it, even though what I am is an investigator.

I work here in Los Angeles. Hollywood sometimes. Sometimes in the Valley. Even East L.A.. Though not too much. We follow the money. So most of what we do, it's corporate. I've done work for Bank of America, Gulf Oil, Toshiba, Matsushita, Hitachi, Boeing, Kmart, all kinds of places. Do we do divorces? Sleazy keyhole peeking? You bet we do. But if I had to figure it, I would say that the lowest amount of money someone's going to be fighting over, if they come to us, it would probably be a million-dollar divorce. Look at it this way. Say you just want to put a tail on your spouse. That's round-the-clock, usually, because screwing knows no timetable. In fact, it is frequently active outside of your usual hours. I followed a guy one time, his wife thought he was an early-morning jogger. Four-thirty in the morning, he's out there, in his Yves St. Laurent coordinates and Asics Gel IIIs. This is so early it's like a moonlight run—what's that line?—"I'm so horny the crack of dawn better watch out." He comes home at six, six-thirty, jumps in the shower, then off to work. How far you think he runs? He runs about a quarter mile, that's how far he runs. His girlfriend, she's waiting for him on the corner. A maroon Dodge minivan, not chic at all, but functional. They do it in the van. Then she drives maybe half a mile away so he can jog back. Work up a sweat over the other sweat. Thoughtful. You'd be surprised how many divorces start with "I smelled the bitch on him."

I'm wandering. But I think you should have a picture of the kind of work I do, the kind of place I work for. I was talking about money. For example, in a divorce, you want to watch someone round-the-clock. We bill out, to the lawyers, at $60 an hour, per man, plus expenses. That's bare minimum—$2,880 per day, $20,160 a week, $86,400 for a thirty-day month. You could double that, easy. On a simple WSW. WSW is Who's Screwing Whom. So you understand that you don't spend that kind of money investigating a divorce where there's just a couple of hundred thousand in community property. You have to be talking about real money.

What do I get? About $22 an hour is what it works out to, with vacation time and sick leave. And we have a decent benefit package—medical, dental, and pension. I'm told it costs the company about 33 percent over our wages.

It's less than real cops make. But the working conditions are better. So is the company we keep.

The building I work in is a typical L.A. office building. A glass box with tinted windows, downtown. There's nothing to distinguish us from any other corporation. There really isn't. I used to keep a bourbon bottle full of tea in my desk drawer. As a joke, you know. So I could play it like a TV detective. I wouldn't have real booze there, in the office, even if we didn't have regular urinalysis. By the way, that's another service we offer. Complete drug screening for your entire work force, or any part there of, blood or urine. We test for alcohol, marijuana, all opiates, cocaine, barbital, amphetamine use. Full spectrum or targeted, it's your choice.

The office space is modular. Dividers, not walls. We got standard-issue desks, chairs, phones. Fluorescent lights. Not glamorous, but not seedy. The way I see it, this is an advantage. This is something your average Joe and Jane out there, they can relate to. It's very ordinariness is something refreshingly different.

Also, what I'm addressing here, right at the beginning, is the issue of credibility. Because this is an incredible story. An unbelievable story. I've been doing this ten, fifteen years. For the same company. I get photographed biannually. I'm bonded. You can take a look at our client list—top law firms, Fortune 500 companies, major studios and record companies.

I had just finished an investigation into securities theft for one of the major brokerages. I was catching up on my paperwork. Transcribing my handwritten notes to the company data base from the workstation at my desk.

Then Maggie Krebs walks in. Maggie is one of the ten most beautiful women in the world. That's official. Right out of *People* magazine. You know her as Magdalena Lazlo, movie star. I know her as Maggie Krebs, divorcée. I helped her get that divorce and keep her fortune.

Having that much high powered glamour walk into our drab offices is not unique, but it is unusual. A lot of stars are products of their handlers—makeup people and hairdressers, wardrobe and plastic surgeons. Products of our imagination in a way. But even offscreen and dressed down, Maggie has it. Everybody watched her, men and women, when she came down to my office.

"Hi-ya, Joe," she says. She looks me direct in the eye, gives me that smile, and that voice—you can read anything you want to into that voice—just the way she talked in Over the Line—and boom, you could knock me over with a toothpick. I don't let it show, but I figure she knows what that "Hi-ya, Joe," can do. How can she not know? It's her business, making strong men weak and weak men strong.

"Hi-ya, Maggie," I say. I speak low, slow, and level. Not because I think I'm John Wayne or something, but to keep my voice from squeaking like a fourteen-year-old's.

She looks around. Then she leans forward: "Joe, is there somewhere we can talk."

"We got a conference room," I say. I don't have to work so hard to talk, my voice and breathing are coming back under control.

"Hey, Joe," she says. "You got two bits?"

"Yeah."

"Then why don't you take me out and buy me a cup of Java?"

"Maggie, there isn't much that you could ask me that I wouldn't do."

Now let me explain a bit about this little piece of dialogue. First of all, it is verbatim. That's a gift I have, like a photographic memory, except I don't have it for the printed word, not at all, but I do have it for the spoken word. So that when I tell you through this story that so-and-so said one thing then them-and-such said another, it's like our transcription services department typed it right off the audiotapes.

Second, in real life our patter isn't always this snappy.

Third, there is nowhere in Los Angeles, maybe in America, that I can think of that you can get a cup of coffee for twenty-five cents. It would be easier to find the five-dollar cup of coffee. Clearly, Maggie is being jovial here. In fact, I find out later, both her lines are from a script she'd been working on. There is a certain charm in having a real-life movie star run her lines on you like you're her real-life costar. It's a memory a lot of fellows could lie down with even when they take that final rest, if you know what I mean.

Fourth and finally, there is something that I don't know if she knows, but maybe she suspects, which is that all our conference rooms are wired more thoroughly than the Nixon White House. Everything that happens in a Universal Security conference room is recorded. Audio is routine. Intermittent video and real-time video are both available. So is vocal-stress analysis.

Our personal offices and telephones are monitored, but not always recorded. The principal is "Do unto ourselves what we would have others pay us to do to their employees." We are a shining example of life under total management supervision.

We took her Cadillac and left my old wreck behind. It might surprise you that a star of her magnitude would drive a Caddy, but it was a gift from GM. A promotional thing. They think the new Seville can compete with Mercedes, BMW, Lexus, and Infiniti. I thought it was pretty nice. It was a convertible. She drove. The top was down.

She didn't say much in the car. Just played the radio. Country and western. That was for me. Shows you what kind of class—and memory—the lady had. She once asked what kind of music I liked, back during her divorce action. I told her. It was Hank Williams and Merle Haggard and Johnny Cash and Ernest Tubb and Patsy Cline that got me through the war. That's the truth. All the guys in my platoon that listened to rock and roll, they died. Except for two of them. Mike Galina—he's in a veteran's hospital still—no eyes, no legs. Paul Frederic Hight also came back with pieces missing—of his body and his mind and his heart—died five years after coming home. Acciden-tal OD or suicide. Who's to say? Who's to judge? Three of the blacks lived. They didn't listen to rock and roll either. Two of them came back junkies and I lost track. But Steve Weston, he came back straight and with his body intact. We have a drink now and again. Don't say much. Just have a drink. He listened to C & W like me or soul, like his people. His favorite, though, is gospel.

Also she looked over at me, smiled, and touched my hand.

She put the car in a lot a block off the beach in Venice. We got out and walked. She put her arm through mine. Made me feel six feet tall and good-looking to boot. There was a fancy espresso and cappuccino joint on the corner where you could have your refreshment al fresco and view the human comedy as it passed on the boardwalk. You don't have to be an Angelino to know that Venice Beach is the place for viewing humanity at it's most comedic. That's the place they use in all the movies when they do the L.A. montage with the girls who roller-skate in G-string bikinis and Muscle Beach and everything.

But we walk right by the boardwalk, out onto the beach. She pauses a moment and slips her shoes off. Do movies make us or do we make the movies? What I'm saying is, this gesture she does, leaning on my arm, slipping off her shoes, carrying them in one hand by their straps, it's got grace, and I don't know what else to call it but femininity—when I watch her do it, I'm seeing the scene from a movie. You get what I mean—did she learn it from the same movies I saw, or is this one of those quintessential feminine moves that directors and actresses they're aware of and they set out to capture for the silver screen?

Do a close-up of her hand on my shoulder when she leans on me.

We walk out toward where the surf is breaking. She barefoot, me in my Florsheims. I'm wearing a suit and tie of course, which is company dress code unless you're on an assignment that specifically calls for something else. See, it's like I'm in my own movie with her. I'm daydreaming that it's going to be like a personal thing. But the professional part of me knows that it won't be. A lot of clients take you to strange and out-of-the way places to discuss their business.

Different reasons. privacy, embarrassment, and sometimes its just that they too are in their own movie and they want the cloak and dagger.

Out by the water, where the sand is wet and packed, she says, "Joe, I need help."

"That's what we're here for," I say.

"Not them. Not all of them. Just you," she says.

"Tell me what the problem is," I say. I'm a company man. I have been for quite a while. We have longevity bonuses on top of the automatic annual raises, I have an investment in my pension, I'm part of the company's employee stock-option plan. Sure, I'm going to do something without the company. Sure I am.

"Promise me something," she says.

"What?"

"That you'll listen to what I have to say. If you can't do it without telling the company, you'll forget we ever had this conversation. You'll go back and tell them it's the first anniversary of my divorce and I wanted to find a way to thank you, that we went for coffee because I'm in a twelve-step program. Something like that."

I start to make the promise. That's what you do, then you bring them around to explaining why the company has to know. It's tedious but basic.

"No," she says, "look me in the eye and tell me."

So I look her in the eye. I've looked lots of people square in the eye. Con men, psychos, gamblers, corporation presidents, lawyers. Anyone who tells you the eyes are the window to the soul, they're full of it. Except sometimes. Like when you look in the eyes of a boy who's about to die and he knows it. You can see his soul fly away. You can. That's true. And the windows close. Like someone just reaching out and shutting a pair of old-fashioned shutters. What was transparent becomes opaque. The other time is when you look in the eyes of a woman you want more than is good for you. I'm talking about more than sex wanting. I'm talking about hungry, stupid hungry. She opens those eyes to you and they say "Look right in." Even if she is an actress and the smart part of you figures that they pay her $1.3 mil per picture plus gross points, according to the latest press releases, to do exactly that for the camera, your own eyes might open then and become the window to your soul and she sees what you are and puts her hooks in. I guess that's alright. I guess nature made us to be that way sometimes.

I tell her, "If I can't do it, I'll forget it."

"Joe," she says.

"Just tell me, will you?" I say, irritated.

"A year ago I signed on to do a picture. With John Lincoln Beagle directing. You know his work?"

I nod. Everyone does. Even if you don't go to the movies. Like Spielberg or Lucas or Lynch or Stone.

"We're both at AAC. It's their package. Director, star, writer. I read the script. I loved it. It's not fluff. It's not lightweight. It's not bounce my boobies, wiggle my butt, and act like I think that's cute. It establishes me as a serious actress. That's the picture I'm scheduled to be shooting now. Right now.

"Then the project was canceled."

"But that happens a lot," I say.

"Yes, it does. But this time it shouldn't have. Everything was in place. The package was intact, the studio was on board, a producer had been selected. The money was in place. Suddenly, it gets shut down.

"Officially, the story is that Beagle is sick. I don't believe it. In fact, I'm certain I saw him once or twice up near his place in the Sonoma Valley. He owns a vineyard there. So do I. Also, there was a period between when the deal was made and the cancellation when I saw him mentally go away from the project. One meeting he was all there. This picture was the thing he most wanted in the world. And he was intently interested in me."

"What's the name of it?"

"*Pirandello.*"

"Uh-huh."

"You know who he is? He's a playwright. Italian. But its not about him. That was a working title. Not a finished title. The next meeting, he was off. There was something else he cared about more. There is nothing in Hollywood a director cares about more than his next picture."

"He's supposed to be sick," I say. "Does that mean AIDS? A guy who's going to die, he might care about something besides his next picture." Young guys who are about to die, and know it, care about its not being fair. Or they care about convincing themselves it's not quite going to happen. Maybe that's good, to go not believing that you're going. I don't know so much about what old people think when they're ready to die. I haven't seen that many old people die.

"A director who's about to die cares even more," she says. "Good God, it's not only his next film, it's his last."

"Where is he now?"

"He's missing."

"I read somewhere," I say, "that he's working with the Japanese on HDTV."

"I've heard that story too. But you would think he would take my calls."

"Oh," I say, "it's that way, is it?"

She takes my arm. We walk a couple steps before she says the next thing, which is "When someone's lying to you, you know it."

"Do I?"

"Oh, Joe," she sighs and kind of leans into me. I'm a sucker for this, I admit it. "I'm a woman. Men are supposed to lie to me. I'm a beautiful woman, I'm supposed to enjoy it. I live in Hollywood where truth is a speech defect. You'd think I wouldn't care anymore.

"I wanted that movie. Someone took it away from me. They're lying to me about why. On one level it's about money. If they cancel because Beagle got sick, that comes under the act-of-God clause. It doesn't in all contracts, but in this one it does. If they cancel because Beagle changed his mind, or got another picture, or almost anything except tidal wave, earthquake, typhoon, or war, they have to pay me a serious cancellation fee."

"How much?" I ask her.

"Bottom line, it cost me close to seven hundred fifty thousand dollars."

"OK," I say, "that's worth going after."

"Joe, there's something else going on. I got pissed off. I wanted to know what was going on. What the game was. My own agent, Bennie Hoffrau, he bullshitted me. This means you have to do a little reality check. You have to find out what it is that's more important to him than you are. I went to Hartman—"

"Hartman?"

"David Hartman is the head of RepCo.* Which makes him one of the ten or three or five most powerful people in this business. We had lunch. We talked about everything except what we're there to talk about. Which is, sometimes, how it's done. After the entree and before the coffee he says 'Isn't it a shame about poor Linc—' "

"Linc?"

"If you know Beagle well enough, you call him Linc. It's one of those thing things. I'm about to reply, 'Yes, isn't it. What exactly is wrong with him?' or something to that effect. But what I don't know is that Tom Cruise is coming up behind me. David has to schmooze. For that matter, if I'm smart, I have to do a number too, even if my act is that I'm totally disinterested. David timed his remark so that he could drop it into the conversation and I couldn't pursue it. That's a lot of work to say nothing.

"The day after I had lunch with Hartman, Bennie calls me, he's got a picture for me. It's a World War II home-front picture. Me, Gena Rowlands, Bette Midler. Heavy duty, right. You remember that movie *The Best Years of Our Lives?*"

"Yes," I say. It was supposed to be an ironic title. A story of three guys who went to war and came home to realize that that's what the war had been—the best years of their lives. They'll never make a movie about Nam with a title like that.

---

*The Representation Company, Inc.

"This is a remake. From the women's point of view. How they blossomed, even though they hurt, while the men were away. Good concept, fair script. Women director, Anita Epstein-Barr. She's not bad. It's not the Beagle film, but it's a definite A picture. A big enough prize to distract me from thinking about the movie that disappeared. So I say to Bennie, 'Thank you very much. I am grateful, I am glad, I will do it, and by the way, what did happen to John Lincoln Beagle and the movie I was supposed to do?'

"Bennie says, 'Maggie baby, be a good girl. Go do this picture with Midler and Rowlands, which is the most heavyweight women's cast since *The Witches of Eastwick*. Forget about what's not your business. You're being taken very good care of.'"

"Which you are," I say.

"Which I am," she says. "Very good care. Too good, almost. Knowing Bennie, if there was nothing wrong, what he would have said was . . ." and she does a Bennie Hoffrau routine. I've never met the man and still I know it is a deadly accurate imitation. " 'What the fuck, babe? What the fuck? You lose one picture, you get anudder pic-ture. You got action. Go wid the action. 'Cause that's what it allll about. The action. Go make a pic-ture, collect your check, keep your panties on in publick places. What the fuck, you know what I'm saying.' See, that's what he would've done, his caricature of an agent. It's supposed to be a joke, but it's his real, true self. If it was normal Hollywood bullshit, if they were just trying to sleaze me out of some cancellation money, that's what he would have said.

"Two nights later," she says, "I went to a party and got a little high. Bennie was there. I was talking to Janice Riley. She's an old, old friend. And I say, 'See that, that's my agent over there. He takes good care of me, but he lies to me. That makes me unhappy. Do you think that should make me unhappy?' Janice asks me what I'm talking about. I tell her.

"The next day Bennie calls me to come to his office. A summons. OK, I go. 'I told you to forget about the Beagle film. there is nothing mysterious or strange about the cancellation. He got sick. I can show you a note from his doctor. I'm sure he'll get well sometime in the near future. I don't know the details. You don't have to know the details. You're off this Rowlands-Midler picture. Sorry. Don't argue. Leave it alone. Go home. Go on vacation. Take a break, lie in the sun, somewhere you can breathe real air, you know what I mean. For-get about things. I'll send you a couple of scripts you should consider doing. Come back, we'll have something ready to shoot.'

"There are people," she says, looking me in the eye, "who can actually say 'You'll never work in this town again,' and you're life is over. David Hartman is one of them. So I shut up and I left."

"Sounds sensible. So why are you starting up again? With me."

"Joe, please, let me finish. And Joe, if you agree that I may be right about this, I have to be more than just a client to you."

"What do I have to be, Maggie?"

She looks at me. When she's in heels, she's actually taller than me. But now, in bare feet, on the wet sand, her eyes are level, even a couple of millimeters below mine. I break eye contact first.

"Better finish the story," I say.

"Well, I let it alone. Then, three days ago, my maid, Anita . . . you remember her?"

"Yes."

"She said, 'You remember Mr. Beagle, when he get sick and you don't believe it?' I said 'I believed it,' but a little sarcastic, because we both knew that I didn't. 'Well, my cousin,' she said, 'She work for Mr. Beagle. I am going to see her tomorrow. I will find out for you.' "

"Yeah? Then what happened?"

"She got deported," Maggie says.

"When?"

"The next morning."

"You're lucky they didn't come after you, employing an illegal."

"She's not," Maggie says.

"She's not?" I say, not understanding. Though of course I should. It's a real straightforward statement.

"She's not. She has a green card. A social-security number. All of it.''

"What do you want?" I ask her.

"I want to know what's going on," she says.

"That is foolish," I tell her. "You got sent a message. If you forget about whatever it is, they'll take care of you. If you mess around, they'll break you."

"Tell me something, Joe. You're a guy. A man's man. For real. Not some actor playing a tough guy. What would you do?"

"I don't know, Maggie. The truth is, I don't play in the same league you do."

"If someone owed you seven hundred fifty thousand dollars, would you let them walk away with it."

"I guess I wouldn't. But that's what you got lawyers for."

"Hey, this is Hollywood. It's not supposed to be nice," she says. "But I feel like I signed on to swim with piranhas and suddenly I find out that the great white shark may be cruising in the same waters I'm in. Joe, I have to know what I'm up against. Is it about what they say it's about? Or is my career over? Do I have an enemy out there I don't know about? Is something going on that I don't know about? If I say the wrong thing by mistake, is my career over? Do they make me disappear like they did Anita?"

"What do you want me to do?" I say.

"I want you to find out what's going on. I want you to protect me. I want you to take care of me, Joe."

"Why me?"

"Can they buy you, Joe?" she says, like she knows the answer, like she knows the part I'm supposed to play.

"I don't know," I say. I smile. "No one ever gave it a serious try."

"If they do try, come to me for a counteroffer first, promise me that."

"That should be easy," I say.

"It may not be. But I won't let anyone top what I can give you," she says.

"We'll go back to the agency. I'll have a contract drawn up."

There was going to be some serious spending here. I tried to calculate the commission in my head. But standing that close to Magdalena Lazlo screwed up my powers of computation.

"I don't want you to mention the investigation to anyone."

"How can I do that?"

"Have them assign you to me as my bodyguard and driver. Twenty-four hours a day. I do need protection. I do. This is serious, Joe. Don't tell them about the other. That'll work, won't it?"

"Maggie, you don't understand how an investigation works. The manpower, equipment, contacts, organization, sources. It takes a major company to do it right." This is, of course, part of our standard sales pitch. It's the routine we use to steer a potential client away from some two-man shop that promises to do it cut-rate. It's true too.

"You don't understand how powerful they are. Think of RepCo as the Exxon of the movie business. Big, ruthless, and connected. Everywhere. If your company knows what you're doing, RepCo will know, within hours."

"Our reputation for discretion, absolute discretion, is all we have. That's the bottom line," I say. More sales-pitch stuff.

With that she kisses me. What the hell, she's younger than me, but she's seen more movies and she's maybe had more practice and she does it better than I do. Besides, I'm just a regular guy. When Magdalena Lazlo kisses me, I can't remember that she's Maggie Krebs, divorcee. I'm just an average Joe—my dick is twice the size of my brain. Somehow she makes it seem even more than that, more than just my lust hormone at work. Like it's got meaning is the best I can say it.

Afterward, I reach in my pocket. I told you we expect clients to sometimes want to talk about things in strange places, far from our built-in cameras and microphones. So as standard practice we always carry a minirecorder with us. I take it out. I rewind the tape.

"Why don't we just sit here and let the sound of the surf erase our conversation," I say.

"We can do that, Joe," she says. When the tape is back to the beginning, I push the record button and set the recorder down in the sand, the microphone facing the Pacific. We sit. Side by side. Maggie puts her hand in mine. She's got me in the palm of her hand. It's like she's taking me inside her movie. Which is an A picture, with a top cinematographer and director, the best Hollywood has to offer.

CHAPTER

★ ★ ★

THREE

Melvin Taylor was a vice president of Universal Security. He was moving up slowly but steadily. He was not the type to surge ahead with some stroke of brilliance, nor did he have the knack for selling that would have made him a major rainmaker. But he saw to it that nothing went wrong on his watch. As with many large corporations, the road upward is a long and winding one, from smaller offices to larger ones. Taylor had worked for the company in Columbia, South Carolina; Nashua, New Hampshire; Austin, Texas; Minneapolis, Minnesota; Phoenix, Arizona. There were two offices that were considered the final testing grounds before promotion to headquarters in Chicago: Los Angeles, and Dallas. Three years back Taylor had been posted to L.A. When an important operation was running, he kept an eye on it.

The minute he heard she'd been there, Taylor asked for the tapes of Magdalena Lazlo's visit to U. Sec. He watched her walk down the hall—odd, jerky black and white moves—shot skip-frame to save tape; this was a document, not art. Stop tape. Roll back. Start over. He was holding off seeing her destination.

It was the way he waited after dinner for his cigar. Teasing it. Finding this reason or that—positioning the ashtray; picking exactly the right one, not too dry; deciding whether to use a match or a lighter; pouring out the cup of decaf; watching his wife's lips tighten in silent reproof—to delay the moment just a little longer.

He frequented a Vietnamese mother-daughter massage team. Or so they claimed to be. He'd never asked for IDs and never ran a background check. That was what they said and they never spoke or acted as if they were anything else. He visited them once a week. Tuesdays, 5:30 to 7:00. They gave him a massage and hand job. Once they began, after he was out of his clothes and on the table and had a sip of brandy, about 5:38, it was their job to erect him and keep him that way—more or less—until his ejaculation one hour later. The ultimate exercise, he was proud to tell himself, in delayed gratification.

Let her get closer. Stop. Rewind. Start over.

Delayed gratification, Taylor felt, was the essential precept of civilization in the group or in the individual. It was—obviously—what had made the European races superior. The current decline of America and the rise of Japan was due, obviously, to forgetting that simple and essential lesson. Don't eat your dessert until you deserve it. Don't spend your money until you've earned it. Don't take your pleasure until you're stronger than pleasure and can prove it.

Even closer. Stop. Rewind. Start over.

Closer. Stop. No. Not in time. He'd gone one frame too far. She was turning into the cubicle of Joe Broz. Just like Taylor knew she would. He'd been holding his breath. Now he released it, feeling a bone-deep pleasure.

The visual time code appeared on the lower left-hand corner of each frame. The reference was to the time of recording, not to lapsed tape time. Taylor went to the audiotape. Audio recording of U.Sec. employees was intermittent, not constant. Studies demonstrate that the threat that employees might be taped at any given moment controls behavior virtually as well as constant monitoring, yet is significantly more cost-effective.

Except that in circumstances like this, you just might get caught with your pants down.

Audio recording was monaural. The second track was used for a time code that, like the video, referenced the time of recording. It made search and identification infinitely quicker. Taylor entered the time displayed on the video image into the audiotape machine.

Taylor took a deep breath and closed his eyes. He counted slowly backward. This was a technique he employed in his weekly sexual practice. He'd found it had great effect in quieting excitement. Sometimes he could get so deeply into it that the mother–daughter team had to use their every resource to keep him up.

He opened his eyes. The time code said "14:28.16"—the system utilized a twenty-four-hour clock. The flashing red light said "ready." He pushed the PLAY button on the audio machine with one hand. With the other hand he hit the PAUSE button on the video machine to release the video tape and create some semblance of synchronicity.

He watched Magdalena Lazlo perch on the corner of Joe Broz's desk. Like she was playing a scene from some old Marlene Dietrich film—or was that the impression he got because the video was a grainy black and white? Broz's mouth was practically hanging open, and he looked, in Taylor's opinion, about as bright as a backwoods Croatian bovine.

"Hey, Joe," Magdalena said. "You got two bits?"

"Yeah." Broz said. What repartee, Taylor thought.

"Then why don't you take me out and buy me a cup of Java?"

"Maggie, there isn't much that you could ask me that I wouldn't do."

That was it? That was it? And they went off—where? And did what? And said what? Was there surveillance on her? A round-the-clock watch? He reached for the file with that feeling in the pit of his stomach that he hated. He opened the file. Of course, there wasn't. Of course, he knew it. He had made himself the security officer on this case.

Oh, they had discussed it in conference and the consensus was that this wasn't the time for full surveillance, that it would be counterproductive because Lazlo was known to be egocentric and very reactive. But if they had missed something important and the operation went wrong, he could certainly forget about a promotion to Chicago. He might very well find himself back in Newark in charge of supermarket security personnel.

Still, all was not doom and gloom.

If it turned out that Magdalena Lazlo was still making waves over this John Lincoln Beagle thing and she had just involved Joe Broz in it, it meant that this time Joe was in it really deep. And Mel Taylor had been waiting for that far longer than for some little wait to take a hit of nicotine or to ejaculate. Mel Taylor had been waiting for Joe Broz to step in shit again for twenty years.

CHAPTER

* * *

FOUR

The "don't look" story is one of the primal stories. God let Lot leave Sodom. God said, "Don't look back." Lot's wife looked back and was turned to a pillar of salt. Orpheus went to hell to bring his wife back from the dead. The god of the underworld said, "Don't look back until you're out." Orpheus looked and he lost her. Pandora, the first woman on earth, had a box. She was warned to keep it closed, but she opened it and all the troubles of mankind came out. When a story is that pervasive and that basic, there is a reason. Every culture, in its collective wisdom, has a knowing that there are things that are not meant to be looked at. They appear, in the stories, as magic things or mythological things. But we all know that these stories are parables, teachings by example, which we hear in childhood, or at least in a childlike state of mind—learn at our mother's knee, so that we can take them as general rules to carry with us, to guide us through our lives, so that we may survive.

James Addison Baker III, secretary of state, was Texas-born and Princeton-educated. He knew his Bible and he was familiar with the classic pagan myths. A part of him responded to the atavistic warnings.

But Baker was a Rational Man in a rational mode. To the extent that he acknowledged the supernatural, the paranormal, the mythological, in public or in private—exclusive of Christianity, of course—it was derisively. As in "Poor Lee, the drugs took him over the edge," or "Hey, a brain tumor—you understand. He gives me this envelope like it's Pandora's box and says, 'Don't look!' "

So of course he opened it as soon as he stepped out of the sickroom door. This, at least, was efficient use of time. He still didn't have his cellular phone, a state paper to read, an aide by his side to consult with or give orders to. The walk to the elevators and the ride down was the perfect 420 seconds in which to fit in Lee Atwater's last memo, a dying man's attempt to influence events from beyond the grave.

He read, at first, in silence.

James Baker was, and had been for a long, long time, a public man and automatically maintained a severe censorship over the most casual public utterances. It has been said that "Baker is incapable of expressing passion." That "when you sit across from Baker, it is like looking at a length of black silk . . . stillness . . . occasionally . . . a rather wintry smile. He controls the conversation with perfect sentences, perfect paragraphs, perfect pages."[5]

He pushed the elevator button while still reading. When the elevator arrived and the doors hissed open, he stepped inside without looking up. He was aware that he was not alone. A green-gowned orderly and a patient on a rolling bed were there, as well as whatever surveillance and security systems were operat-

[5]Maureen Dowd and Thomas Friedman, *The Fabulous Bush & Baker Boys*, New York *Times Magazine*, 5-6-90.

ing. And still he said, "Jesus *fucking* Christ." It was sotto voce, but definitely audible. "Atwater's fucking in-fucking-sane," he said.

Then he said, but not aloud, This is one piece of paper that must never, ever see the light of day. This must be destroyed. He was right. All the walls that separated reasonable conduct from freedom to think, meaningful conduct from irrelevant actions, dangerous speaking versus necessary speculation, private versus public, had been breached. The military, for example, spent a lot of time producing "what if" scenarios. What do we do if "there is a Russian counter-counterrevolution and they launch missiles at Moldova, Ukraine, and Berlin"? If "there is violent civil unrest in the United States"? If "China goes to war with Japan"? Anyone with a grain of sense would consider that to be sensible speculation so that when the unthinkable does happen there is some sort of plan. But no! When one of those papers was leaked by some asshole liberal do-goodie, the media reacted as if the president was personally planning to open concentration camps to detain everyone who hadn't voted for Richard Nixon back in 1968. When a man in power told a dirty joke or stuck his dick in the box of some foxy Pandora or expressed his exasperation with some person or group in ethnic terms, that was material that could destroy a career, even an entire regime. Especially if the other side had a Lee Atwater who knew how to use it. This memo, or whatever it should be called, was pure madness. To admit that anyone in this administration had ever even had the thoughts that Atwater had written down would destroy them all.

Nevertheless, James Baker did not burn it, or tear it into tiny pieces and eat them, or head for the nearest shredder. He put the memo in his pocket. And kept it.

CHAPTER

★ ★ ★

FIVE

$\mathbf{M}$aggie lives on the beach. In Trancas, just up from Malibu. I live in Sherman Oaks. They're both in America. That's a joke.

I got a visual for you. Me in my three rooms—bedroom, bathroom, and the room that's everything else—packing. Two large suitcases. Because I'm moving to Maggie's. I don't know what exactly I'm in for, so I overpack. I hesitate over the guns. But for the same reason I pack my good suit and my swimming trunks, I take the Glock 17 with a shoulder holster, a Smith & Wesson snub nose with an ankle holster and the little Baretta that I can fit into a holster at the small of my back. All of them take 9-mm ammunition.

I take my fiber-case kits. The company recommends that we bring them on assignment whenever possible. There are three standard kits. The DS—defense system—includes: the CMS-3, which detects RF bugs, carrier current, transmitters; the DL-1000, that's a handheld, take-anywhere bug detector; a handheld weapons detector; telephone-line tracing set; and a telephone scrambler. Kit 2 contains more active systems, "for those times when it's time to do it to them before they do it to you." An EAR-200—you can listen through walls; a long distance parabolic microphone; a vehicle-tracking device. Computer software to block access to your PC. A remote car starter—

for the truly security-conscious; hey, there are people who need them, believe me. A Minox infrared camera with infrared flash; miniature microphones, transmitters, and recorders. The third kit has a stun gun, a stun bato.1, body armor briefcase inserts, and various mace systems.

All this equipment impresses clients. That's what the company marketing trainers tell us and in my experience it's true. The kind of people who hire us are the kind of people who buy Mercedes and Porsches—they like the bells and whistles. Also, the equipment is a money-maker. Anything you use, you charge for. "You want me to check your phone lines, sir?" You take out a $3,000 CMS-3 and bill $150 an hour or part thereof for the use of it. They understand. You can also sell them the equipment. It's like the Honda commercial—"the car that sells itself." These are toys that people are longing for. Don't you want to listen through walls? Hear what they're saying when you leave the room? Know what your wife does when you're not home? Do you know how macho it makes a guy feel to turn his briefcase, which is normally full of just paper and numbers, into a shield that will stop a .357 magnum. That's a $150 item. Field men like myself get a straight 10 percent on anything we sell.

What I mean about it's being a visual is how small and barren my place is. What's there to look at? I do have one kind of interesting painting on the wall. It's an original, oil, representational. It's a woman holding a baby, standing in a California vineyard. When I came home from Nam, I brought back this kid's stuff. The military has channels and facilities for that—of course they do. But this kid, Kenny Horvath, he was kind of a friend of mine—he died the day before my time was up. I brought his things home. His mother gave me the painting. Kenny painted it. The woman in the picture, she had been his girl. The baby had been his too. But she'd already moved on to another man, even before Kenny died. So that's the one spot of color in the room.

There's a black and white photo of a woman on my desk. Funny that I keep it. The Purple Hearts are in the drawer. Three of them. One of my dad's, two of mine. Different wars, but the medals and jewelry boxes they come in have remained the same.

It's a lonely room. I know that. I can even hear that kind of music they'd run underneath, hear it in my head.

Then there's the contrast. Maybe you show the car ride in between, maybe not. I wouldn't. I'd just cut right to it.

Even make it a sun-shining day. Back inland, toward L.A., there's smog, but out here the sea breeze blows it clear. Pacific breakers are rolling in. A couple of kids out on boards. Playing hooky, they're young enough they should be in school. There's an old man walking a young dog. He tosses a stick. The dog runs. The old man remembers young legs, exuberance, joy. He is grateful that there is someone to perform those things for him. There's a Malibu princess with her perfect personal-trainer body jogging along the water.

There is just one line of houses between the Pacific Coast Highway and the beach. All have fences or walls and a metal gate at the entrance with CCTV and electronic locks. The building just south of Maggie's is a Tudor mansion. The house to the north is a hacienda. Maggie's house is California modern. It has a circular drive. The front yard is filled with thousands of dollars worth of cactus and desert plants. The front door is oversized and its made of some exotic wood. The fixtures are brass and the brass is polished. She's replaced her maid.

The new one opens the door. She's expecting me. This too says something about Maggie.

"Good day, Mr. Broz," she says. She's an older woman. Fifties I would guess. Irish, with a brogue. This one is an illegal, I find out later. But she doesn't worry much about it. The border patrol isn't about to snatch her off the street and deport her, nor is she going to be asked for her green card on a routine traffic stop, and she knows it.

"You can call me Joe," I say, looking around.

"We'll have to see about that," she says.

"OK," I say. "What's your name?"

"Mrs. Mulligan," she says.

"Is there a Mr. Mulligan?"

"There was, but he's dead."

"I'm sorry."

"No need. He isn't missed. Not by me at any rate. You better make up your mind if your coming inside or just gazing at the place."

"I'll come in. Thank you," I say.

"Not at all. Have a seat in the living room. The missus will be right out. Do you want some refreshment? You can have a drink, though to my way of thinking it's a bit early for it. Or you can have some fresh-squeezed orange juice. The missus is big on fresh-squeezed juices. Vegetables as well as fruits. Or you can have water from six different countries, with or without bubbles. In Ireland it falls from the sky and its free."

"The juice sounds fine," I say.

"It's a lot of work, but it's my job," she sighs. She leaves me there. I'm looking around. The living room is two stories high. Halfway up, around two and a half sides, is a railed walkway. There are several doors leading off to bedrooms. A stairway comes down one side. It is out from the wall and behind it the wall is made of stone or simulated stone with a waterfall. There are plants in the niches in the stone. There is a pool at the bottom, live fish in the pool.

The fourth side, facing the beach, is mostly glass.

Underneath the walkway there are other doors leading to still more rooms. A kitchen, a dining room, a screening room.

There are two paintings on the walls. One is very French, made of dots of paint. The other looks like an old 3-D drawing combined with a painting. It looks like the picture of God and Adam from the Sistine Chapel, except Adam is Elvis and God holds a Coke bottle. I look closer and see that there is a pair of old-fashioned cardboard 3-D glasses available to view it in its full splendor. It's an original by James Trivers.

I feel like I've seen all of it, except the painting, before. Nothing mystical or déjà vu, but more like it's been used as a location in a movie or on TV. Perhaps it was designed by a designer who also does sets, or by an architect inspired mostly by films about Hollywood.

None of which is what I'm trying to understand by looking at the house.

Then she comes in. Down from the upstairs room. Barefoot, jeans, cotton shirt. Easy, casual, perfect. The cotton shirt is a man's-style shirt, but not a man's shirt—it's her shirt. Now I realize what it is I'm looking for—man signs. Is she living alone or not?

This is supposed to be a professional relationship. But it's not. What am I going to do when her lover shows up? If she comes back from a party with sleepover company? Or back from lunch for a matinee? Where am I going to put that?

I'm a professional. I have been for a long time. But I stopped being a professional right at the beginning. On the beach. When I erased the tapes. Altered the record. Gave in to a client's paranoia. Served her instead of the company. Made it worse by filing a false report. Why would I do that? Because she kissed me? Maybe it was even earlier, when she walked into my office, looking like a movie star—which is what she is—and delivering her lines like a scene from a film—which is what they were.

"Hi, Joe," she says. "It makes me feel good that you're here."

"Yeah. Beautiful house. Really nice."

"Thanks," she says, looking me square in the eye.

I look away. Things are not irrevocable. I can come to my senses, amend the report to say that after I arrived she asked me to look into all these other things. I can do that. Get back on track. "You'll have to show me around," I say. "Including the utility room and where the electrical is. That is, if you know."

"I know," she says.

"And go over the security system. I saw coming in, the CCTV. We'll walk the perimeter together."

"The perimeter?"

"Old habits," I say. "Also, some clients like it when I talk that way. They like the idea that they're getting security from a former Marine."

"I guess I like that too," she says.

"And is there anyone else"—I say this as casually as I can and can't believe my throat is dry—"living here. At present."

"Joe." She says my name and pauses so I have to look at her and listen. "There's no one."

"That'll make it simpler," I say.

"Except Mrs. Mulligan," she says. Of course, she's right not to have included that when she first answered the question, because that's not the question I was asking and she knows it.

"And now we better find a place for you," she says.

"The traditional place for a chauffeur-bodyguard is an apartment over the garage. I bet this house has one."

"It does," she says.

"It looked like it."

"But I think you should stay in the house. There's a bedroom upstairs."

"Where's your room?"

"Upstairs. Two doors down. Are you comfortable with that?"

Two doors and a couple of yards between us. Was I comfortable with that? I was comfortable when she was out here on the beach with the rest of the rich people and I was in the valley with the smog. Now that I know that there is a spare bedroom two doors down from hers where I'm welcome to park my bags and lay my head, there probably isn't any place in the world far enough away for me to forget about it and sleep in peace. There's only one place in the world that I'm going to be comfortable. "That's fine," I say.

"Joe." She comes close and puts a hand on my arm. "Whatever is going to be will be.

"Easy for you to say," I say.

"Is it?"

"I got you both orange juice," Mrs. Mulligan calls out. She sounds like something you would hear off a rocky coast on a foggy night.

"Thank you, Mary," Maggie says.

The juice is a little cooler than room temperature. Sweet and full of flavors. It cuts through the dryness in my throat.

"Thank you, Mary," I say.

"Have you decided yet where it is you'll be sleeping?"

"Yes."

"Well, I'll unpack your bags for you, but all things considered, I think you should carry them in from the car. You look like a strapping lad, although not so very tall."

I bring my suitcases into the house. Then the fiber cases. They're locked and I tell Mary Mulligan to leave them alone. She's unpacking my clothes, doing a very quick and neat job of it. "Will you look at these," she says when she comes to the guns. "Are we on the beach in California or some back street in Belfast?"

"Is that where you're from?"

"No," she says, "from Roscommon in the middle of the country. It's not as mean, but it's often just as poor."

When we get downstairs, Maggie is on the telephone. She's got her feet curled up beneath her on the sofa. I wait. When she's done, I say, "I want to examine the perimeter." I smile. She smiles back. Our first private joke.

"I have to work," she says. "That is to say I have to make phone calls and appear to be making idle chitchat while I desperately connive to keep up on who's doing what film and who's screwing whom out of what deal. Do you want me to share all the hot Hollywood gossip with you?"

"That's alright," I say.

"Mary can walk you around, or just make yourself free."

"Do you have anything scheduled today? Besides the phone calls."

"Dinner at Morton's—Jesus, don't you wish 'in' spots somehow equated with the quality of the food?"

"I've never eaten at Morton's," I said. "Just so we both know who you're talking to here, my idea of eating out is eating Mexican at a joint so cheap that even Mexicans can afford it."

"I'm sorry, Joe," she says. "I didn't mean to—"

"—to remind me that you're rich and I'm not. That you're"—I look around at the twenty-two-foot-high living room with it's unobstructed view of the ocean and its own indoor waterfall—"a movie star and I'm just a real person. That's alright with me. I mostly know who I am. I don't want you to forget."

"There are . . ." she giggles. It's a girlish, fetching giggle. It's entirely possible that everything about her is perfect. It is more likely that I am in that hormone-haze state of mind that puts the golden glow on my perceptions. Let me possess this woman for twenty years and I'm sure I'll start to see her flaws and her warm and gushing laughter will begin to grate on my nerves. Bound to happen.

"There are . . . ?"

"There are movies about exactly this situation. The rich woman and her chauffeur. If you want the movies to be your guide."

I am not on solid land here. Not by any means. I want to be. "Is that what you want? To play out a scene?"

"You're a serious guy, Joe. A real guy. That's why I wanted you here. I better not forget it," she says.

"OK," I say. Whatever all that meant.

"I have to make these calls," she says apologetically.

"Just keep me informed of your schedule. I'll work around you. That's what I'm supposed to do. That's what you hired me for." And she had hired me. She'd signed a contract with the company for my services and received a set of price guidelines. That's an implied contract in which the client is meant to understand that anything additional that we supply in equipment and manpower will be charged for and it is legal prior notification of the rates thereof. "Today I want to check the premises, work out whatever recommendations I'm going to make. This evening I'll drive you to your dinner and home again. Unless you have requirements to the contrary. In the meantime, there's a couple of hours in there where I'd like to grab some personal time. I run and do a couple of things to keep in shape. Though I know I don't personally look it."

"You're going to sit outside of Morton's for two hours while we eat? Of course you are. Somehow . . . I didn't . . . I've never had a personal chauffeur before. I've been chauffeured lots, of course. The studios are always sending limos. But the drivers, even when I'm polite and talk to them and find out their names and the names of their children and all those things I do to be charming and human, aren't really . . . Of course, they're people. But to me, they're chauffeurs first, people second. This is confusing. To me you're a person first."

"Thanks for saying that," I say. I wonder at it—that's the truth. I've worked with stars before. Stars are people that have their best-ever friends driving them around and polishing their automobiles and don't think anything of having their best-ever friends sitting outside a restaurant for two or four or six hours doing nothing but vegetating. They figure their childhood best-ever friend ought to be grateful for any kind of job at all, let alone one that let's them hang out with the *Lifestyles of the Rich and Famous,* getting to gather the crumbs off the party cake. Don't forget, the sun is a star, and the sun figures the planets exists for one purpose only, to move in circles around it.

Mrs. Mulligan knows little more about the grounds than I do. She's only been there a few days. There's a wall all the way around the house, including the beach side. The living room and the deck are both high enough that when you look out you look over the wall without even being aware of it.

The front gate is an iron grill. The door to the beach is a reasonably solid wooden door. They are both hooked into the alarm system and the CCTV. They were, I automatically note, purchased from and are maintained by a different company from ours. There is no system that protects the wall itself. I could get over it in seconds. So could any other serious intruder. We have forms and checklists that guide us through this kind of survey. That information can be entered into a computer for analysis. This is really a sales tool and the analysis is adjusted to the client's level of fear and ability to spend.

The heaviest installations I've ever done were in Miami when I was on loan to that office for a six-month period in the mid-eighties. It was when it was all happening down there, drugs and guns and money, Marielitos and Colombians and Jamaicans, everyone watching *Miami Vice* and ready to go to war. We turned quite a few homes into electronically defended private fortresses with full system redundancies. Of course, those people had both the need and the will to kill.

But the people in Maggie's life—I got to figure their idea of killing someone is a back-stabbing phone call that murders their next picture deal. Sure, there are those among the rich and famous who get cranked up on their favorite recreational drugs and private brand of madness and hurt each other. But those people don't come over the wall. They're already inside the gate. This is not Miami and this is not Nam. I'm not going to be in a fire fight here. Digging in with the mortars coming in over the wall. Calling in air support. The friendly fire comes in a lot fucking closer than it should.

When I'm done with my inspection I'm fairly grimy and sweaty anyway. I go up to my room and change into shorts and a T-shirt. As I go out through the living room, Maggie is on the phone, preoccupied. She nods, barely, at me. I go out on the deck, down the exterior stairs, and out the back door, onto the beach.

At home I've got to get in my car and drive to one of the parks or up on Mulholland or somewhere. Then drive home in my own sweat and if I get caught in traffic end up spending more time in the car than on my feet. It's either that or run in the streets, breathing exhaust fumes. I run about six miles in the canyons, where it's up and down. I figure to do eight to ten here, where it's flat. I can do more, and sometimes when I have to, I do.

I look back. There's Maggie. She's out on the deck. She's still on the phone, but she's watching me.

I run hard, trying to get her image out from my mind. She keeps walking in and out of my private screen and we play scenes together. Sometimes they're about sex, sometimes about things more complicated than that. Eventually, eventually, I banish her and things go blank. Then the war comes, like it usually does when I run. That's OK. Because it's just pictures. No sound. No smells. You see, it's not like a dream, which can terrify you, give you the cold sweats and wake you up screaming, screams in your ears, and your nostrils full of those peculiar odors of decimation. Burned bodies, the insides of bodies coming out of the sacks of their skin. No, it's just a series of images. Just pictures. A game plan. Sometimes, when I get real deep into it, it turns into a kind of map, like a video game, where I can see the path that I need to take to come out alive. The path I did take. Around this mine, away from that booby trap, behind this tree, into that firefight. I try to show the way to others, but I can't. Survival is a personal thing.

By the time I get back, the sweat is flowing good and the pictures are gone. There's just the beach and the houses of rich people all in a row. Maggie, on the deck of hers, is watching me.

When I get up there, she's gone. Which makes me more comfortable. I do what I was going to do anyway—two hundred sit-ups, a hundred push-ups. I can do more. But to what purpose. I'm not even entirely sure why I settled on this routine. Why I choose to be fit. It's not as if the Marines are going to call me back for another war.

She's there again when I'm done. She smiles at me.

"I need a shower," I say.

The bathroom is as big as a kid's bedroom. And this is the guest bath, not the master bath. I step into the shower and run it hot and full. The room steams up. The water pounds into my back. I wash. I wait for Maggie to open the door and enter through the mist. I wait in vain.

I'm dry and dressed in time for Ray Matusow. He's there to check the house for bugs. I could do it myself, but it's more impressive and more expensive to have Ray come in. Plus, he's better at it. One of the best in the business. I haven't mentioned it to Maggie because if someone is listening—which is possible, but I don't really expect so—why warn them? Some devices can be made passive and, if passive, possibly undetectable. There are essentially two methods of finding listening devices. One is an impedance test. Is there more resistance on a line than there should be? The other is a broadcast test. Make a noise; use a receiver or a set of receivers; at the same time sweep rapidly through all the appropriate frequencies and see if your noise is being transmitted.

Ray is thorough. He checks all the phones. He pays special attention to all the places we normally would plant a listening post: the outlets, stereo, lamps, and any other electronics. He checks the cars. He spends four hours at it.

"Clean," he says.

"Nice job. Thank you, Ray," I say. One less thing for Maggie to worry about. And it means that if what I am so quickly becoming obsessed with comes to pass, we will have the privilege of doing it in privacy.

She dresses for dinner. Does her hair and makeup.

"Did you do all that to impress somebody?" I ask her.

"All of them. We all watch each other."

"It's working," I say.

"Thanks, Joe."

There are three cars in the garage. Her Porsche, the Seville, and my old Ford. We take the Porsche. Again, at Morton's, she starts to apologize for my having to wait.

"It's the way things are," I say.

"You should be coming in with me," she says, getting out of the car.

When she's out of earshot, I say, "Damn right."

She is subdued after dinner. We don't say anything. She does smile at me. She turns on the radio. We get lucky. It's Patsy Cline.

Mary Mulligan does not appear to have waited up for us. That's good. We feel alone in that big empty house. There's even a moon over the water, a broken silver line, white foam.

If I were writing this movie, I would be tall and thin and elegant. I would be Fred Astaire and I would take her in my arms and waltz her out on the deck and we would dance for each other and each other alone.

But I'm short and I'm thick. Thick as a brick wall. She kisses me lightly on the lips. An "excuse me" kiss. An "I'm sorry" kiss. A "you're sweet, but I'm not going to fuck you tonight" kiss. We all learned about that kiss very early. It's not my favorite kiss. But I certainly do recognize it.

She goes upstairs. I watch her go.

Then I follow. For all my running and sit-ups and push-ups, every one of my years weighs like the lead of an old man's life around my ankles and the climb is an effort that leaves me short of breath. I undress, wondering what sort of fool I am.

I can't sleep. I try to review the events of the day in my mind. I go over it all. From the packing and the thoughts that drifted up from my groin and washed over my mind, to the drive over through the bad air of L.A., to the look of the house. The maid. The cars. The fresh-squeezed juice. The conversation, verbatim, with Maggie. The run. Ray, doing the sweep. Maggie Krebs, dressed for dinner, becomes Magdalena Lazlo, movie star. Ray, doing the sweep. There's something about Ray doing the sweep. I don't know what it is. I play it back again.

Now it's at least four in the morning. I've been tangled in my sheets and have kicked my covers off and tried to sleep in positions that I know won't work, and the fact that Maggie is down the hall pounds at my consciousness the way the waves work at the beach. So I say the hell with it. I open up fiber case kit 2 and take out my CMS-3. I'm going to go through the same drill Ray did and see if by recreating it I can figure out what's bothering me. And see if by occupying myself that way I can drive down the dreams of Maggie. I put on jeans and a T-shirt and go downstairs barefoot.

I start with the phones. That's the simplest.

According to my CMS-3, there's a tap on the phone.

CHAPTER

* * *

SIX

There are two beds in the presidential quarters aboard *Air Force One*. When Barbara Bush isn't traveling with her husband, the extra bunk belongs to Jim Baker.[6]

"Bushie,"[7] Jim said, kicking off his shoes and leaning back against the pillows plumped up against the back of the bed, "I was back down in Houston other day . . ." They both liked to talk Texan. It was a macho bonding thing and significant in their synergy. ". . . and this old boy, he come up to me, and he says . . ." It was the start of a ribald story. They both liked ribald stories. But Lord, they had to be careful where they told them. If some hoot owl from the press ever overheard George Herbert Walker Bush say, "Question: Do you know why the good Lord gave women cunts? . . . Answer: So that men will talk to them," before you know it every pussy-whipped liberal commentator would have his dick in a wringer howling about politically incorrect thinking, contempt for women, sexism, Sandra Day O'Con-

[6]*Newsweek,* 1/29/90.

[7]How Baker addresses Bush according to *The Fabulous Bush & Baker Boys, New York Times Magazine,* 5/6/90.

nor, and whatnot.

"You know what," Bush said, "it's the vision thing. Tell me the truth . . . you were . . . you know, with him and now you're . . ." He meant, but did not say, "with me." Baker understood. Bush did that a lot. Incomplete sentences. Half thoughts. Disconnected strands. *Him* was Ronald Reagan.

Baker had started out in politics with George Bush. He managed Bush's campaign when he ran against Ronald Reagan to become the Republican nominee back in 1980. Baker, sensing which way the wind would blow, and aiming at the vice presidential nomination for his boy, discouraged Bush from attacking his rival too energetically and then got him to withdraw sooner than he otherwise might have. The Reagan people were so impressed with Bush's handler that they invited Baker to become Reagan's chief of staff. He accepted. Just as Bush accepted the VP slot. In the Reagan White House, Baker had been a more powerful figure than Vice President Bush.

"Look at the polls," Bush said. Meaning "Look at how I'm slipping in the polls, but Reagan is still incredibly popular and I do exactly what he did, so how come I have a problem?"

"Well, Bushie, ol' pard," Baker said, skinning his cowboy boots off—elegant, eight-hundred-dollar wear-'em-with-a-pin-stripe-banker's-suit cowboy boots but still *Texas,* if you know what I mean—"the man could shoot a line of shit like no shitter before or since. Why, if you could imagine the size of the bull that could create that much bullshit, you would have yourself the bull that shit Texas." He got the second boot off and wiggled his toes. Cowboys boots are toe squeezers, no doubt about it, even custom-cut.

"What's show time?" Bush asked Baker.

"Five hours," Baker said.

Bush sighed. It's tough being president. Frankly, it's a lot tougher than being an actor. Because actors don't work all that often and nobody cares how fucked up they get. As long as their box is good. The president has meetings all day. Then his chopper takes him out to *Air Force One*. Although he has an entire plane as his private hotel room with a fawning staff dedicated to his every whim, he will have to get off that plane in two hours or six hours or eight hours, having traveled some portion or all of that time, and appear to be alert, energetic, healthy, to have had enough sleep, not to be jet-lagged, and glad to be there—wherever there is. Getting sleep whenever he can, regardless of his personal clock and biological rhythms, was even more crucial than having makeup when he was in front of the cameras.

"Time," Bush said, "for the blue bomb."[8] He took out the Halcion. Both of them were using it. By prescriptions and on the recommendation of their doctors, of course. It's a hypnotic, a chemical cousin of Valium and Librium. It's advantage is that it doesn't linger in the body, and so, presumably, the pill taker is less groggy the morning or afternoon or whenever after.

Baker poured them each a tumber of Chivas to wash it down.

Bush was still feeling agitated. It's hard to imagine a president not feeling agitated. Even when there is something to exult over—cutting the budget, beating the Russkies, end-running the Democratic congress, rising in the polls, pushing back the Commies in Central America—someone out there is immediately carping, complaining, whining, and trying to cut that achievement down. Meanwhile, some new goddamn problem is being picked out by the media to be the new crisis that the president, and only the president, must supply leadership for.

---

[8] A phrase attributed in print to Baker (*Time,* 10/14/91). One can imagine that two people so close would pick up on the same slang. In 1990 it was the most prescribed sleeping pill in the world. It was banned in Britain in October 1991.

"Pineapple face," the president said.

"I understand your frustration," Baker said. He knew that Bush was complaining about Noriega's trial. Bush had sent in troops to get the drug-dealing dictator out of Panama. He'd started a whole war to do it. He'd personally approved the name of the project: Operation Just Cause. A great name that said it all. They'd brought the son of a bitch back to Miami. A good venue, you would think, for drug prosecutions. And the damn trial seemed to be stalled forever. Going through motions and appeals and what-not, even before the damn thing started. The longer it went on, the more embarrassing it got. "The prosecutor is a good ol' boy," Baker reassured his boss. "I checked with Justice and we got none better. None better. It's just gonna take as long as it takes, but our boy's gonna bring home the bacon."

Bush got up to change into his sleepwear. Pajamas. Barbara had had them made as a special present for the inauguration. They were white flannel printed with seals balancing little presidents on their noses.

"Y'all want to hear this story I heard down Houston?" Baker asked. There was no answer. Baker poured them each another shot.

Bush picked up his glass. The 747 cut through the night sky, huge and steady, easily able to keep the Head of the Free World safe. But with the Evil Empire crumbling, "Head of the Free World" was rapidly losing it's ring. He was going to have to think of something new to be called. Leader of the . . . ? Put the speech writers on it. They knew about word things.

"Shit," Bush said. "I'm going to miss him."

Atwater had died, just two nights earlier. The doctors had inserted radioactive pellets into his brain. Actually the pellets worked. They succeeded in destroying the tumor as well as an unknown amount of healthy brain with it. But almost immediately another tumor had sprouted elsewhere. The doctors determined that he couldn't take another round of radiation. It was a fast slide down from there.

Baker raised his glass. "To Lee."

"With him here," Bush said, "what I did, that didn't matter. Lee could destroy anyone. That was one *bad* good ol' boy."

By now it was clear that the presidential utterances had a theme, or at least a subtext. He was feeling, as presidents periodically do, insecure. There was nothing too terribly wrong, but there were a great many things not too terribly right. The economy, the S & L mess, his son's involvement in the S & L mess, the country still seeming to slip vis-à-vis Japan and Germany, creeping unemployment, and mostly he just didn't get enough respect. In the hands of the right opponent, who knew what could happen. Not that the Democrats were smart enough to come up with the right opponent, but what if they made a mistake and came up with a winner by accident. Baker realized that what might have brought this vague angst to the front burner was Atwater's death. It was like losing a special weapon. Or like going to war with the rule that you could only have as many guns as the enemy.

"He got religion at the end, and I'm glad that he did," Bush said, like the verse of an old country song.

It might have been the Halcion. It might have been the Chivas. Baker was feeling relaxed, yet powerful and in control. Even his toes didn't hurt anymore and there was none of that tension in his gut. "George," he said, "I have to tell you something."

"What is it, Jimbo," Bush asked, snuggling down under the presidential covers with the big seal in the middle.

"Just before he died," Baker said, "he called me to his side. There was something about a message."

"What did he have to say?"

"Well, he was a bad 'ol boy to the end."

"You mean he wasn't groveling on his knees apologizing for sticking Willie Horton on George Dukakis."

"Bushie, he gave me something. His final campaign ploy. His ultimate campaign ploy."

"Does it apply to anyone the Democrats run?"

"It applies to us. I have to tell you, my immediate reaction when I read it was that it was insane. That it had to be destroyed. But I kept it. It has a certain strange and compelling logic. It just does. But it's a madman's option. Maybe."

"Do you have it?" the president asked.

Baker got off the bed, Barbara's bed, and went to his briefcase. He decoded the lock and took the folded, bent papers out. Wishing for a moment that he'd never mentioned them, he said, "Nobody has seen this but you and me." Then he handed the papers to George Herbert Walker Bush, who turned on the light over the bed, put on his reading glasses, and began to read the last great scam of Lee Atwater.[9]

---

[9]The reader may have noted two different typefaces. They indicate two different time lines. There is a point where the two facets of the story meet up with each other and unite. Then, for the most part, only one typeface is used.

CHAPTER

* * *

SEVEN

You ever have everything turn inside out? Where one minute it's one world, and the next second it's a whole other world.

Tell you what I mean. About what the feeling is. 1967, Vietnam. There's a bunch of us, fresh from Parris Island. Marines are going to I Corps. This is the area at the north end of South Vietnam, it includes five provinces from Quang Tri up to the DMZ. The city of Hue, the old imperial capital, and Khe Sanh are both in I Corps. We're lean and mean, all balls, no brains. We're a John Wayne movie—the Marines have landed and we're here to kick ass. Of course, the first thing that happens is that we sit in Da Nang for a week while they sort us out. Doing nothing. Getting bored, getting drunk, getting in fights, getting the clap, watching the body bags go by, figuring the guys in them were probably careless. Probably not *Marines*.

Finally, we get assigned. We get sent up north, to Khe Sanh, which is an airstrip in the northwest corner of the country. This is not what is later called the siege of Khe Sanh. That occurs in January 1968.

We get sent out on patrol. Usually a day at a time. Sometimes two or three days. It's wet. Rain and fog. The country is rain forest, triple canopy. Steep mountains. Lots of ravines. The only thing that happens is that four guys, they start to drip and they need penicillin shots, and everybody's feet start to rot, but nobody knows what to do about that. Here I am sixteen, most of the guys are eighteen, nineteen, the LT, he's all of twenty-two or -three. All of us are loaded with testosterone, machismo, whatever you want to call it, and this is dumber and duller than being back home and broke on a Tuesday night.

Our third week of patrols. By this time they're letting new guys walk point. Third day, it's my turn. It's tense. But nothing happens. Except it's raining. Everything gets wet. We're climbing up and climbing down. We're slipping and sliding and like every other day discomfort increases, fear and alertness grow dim. But, we get back to the perimeter. Alive. Now I know I'm immortal. Wet and bored, crotch and toes itching, but immortal. Fourth day, I'm second man, oh, maybe a yard or two behind point. All morning, same damn thing. It's just drizzling. If we were out of the foliage, visibility might be twenty, thirty feet. In the forest, it's five, maybe ten, feet.

I'm a yard or two behind point. Suddenly, I see right in front of his foot—trip wire. That moment freezes. I know that the wire is connected to a grenade. Just like I know that the grenade is connected to an North Vietnam Army patrol, killers like us, and they are connected to an army and all of us are in this thing that has it's own existence, like a giant beast, which is called war. From that moment on, everything is forever different.

The wire on the telephone is, somehow, the same thing. It is a small piece of wire, one that I cannot see but can detect with an instrument, and that wire, I know, is connected to a listener, that listener is connected to an organization, maybe Universal Security, which is connected to something else, probably larger, because U.Sec. does nothing for itself, it is always employed, an agent of another organization. There is a power out there, a great beast, watching. I have just glimpsed its existence.

CHAPTER

⋆ ⋆ ⋆

EIGHT

*A*ir *Force One* rose above the turbulence. Down below there were all sorts of storms. Up here was a sort of heaven. A steel cocoon close to the stars. Superb whisky. Excellent food. Dedicated servants. James Baker watched the president read Lee Atwater's memo. When he was done, George Bush said, "Jesus fucking Christ." the same thing that his secretary of state had said. They were very much in tune.

"You bet," his secretary of state said.

"Has anyone seen this?"

"Me and thee," Baker said.

"Talk about nitty-gritty and cutting through to the nuts of the matter. When Lee Atwater is passing, it's hardball.[10] I mean this

---

[10]This is George Bush's speech style: "Fluency in English is something that I'm often not accused of." 6/6/89.

"My running mate took the lead, was the author, of the Job Training partnership act. Now because of a lot of smoke and frenzying of bluefish out there, going after a drop of blood in the water, nobody knows that." 11/3/88.

"I think there were some difference, there's no question, and will still be. We're talking about a major, major situation here. . . . I mean, we've got a major rapport-relationship of economics, major in the security, and all of that, we should not lose sight of." 1/10/92 is either out of the park or get thrown out of the game.''

"That's true," Baker said.

"Does it make sense, or is it from cuckoo-cuckoo land?"

"Bushie, I have to tell you, I don't know. Things would have to be pretty extreme before we considered it."

"Extremism in defense of virtue is no vice."

"I'll tell you one thing, nobody but you and I should see that memo."

"You're right," the president said. "I want to reread it. Then shred it."

It wasn't a long piece. It had been well thought out. It was short and to the point. That's the only way to write a memo if you want to actually influence a president. They have too many things to think about to put up with complex ideas.

Bush read it again. He said three things out loud: "Hollywood?!" "Shred it." "Jesus fucking Christ." Somewhere along the line the halcion caught up with him. He fell asleep with the memo clutched in his hands. Baker was already out.

The crew made a habit of listening in on the presidential cabin. Not for any malicious reason. Solely so they could better serve, so they could appear with a drink or a dinner almost before it was called for. To be ready with a service just as soon as it was thought of. They trained themselves to not really hear words that weren't for them, like stagehands politely ignoring breasts when they must enter women's dressing rooms.

When Stan, the chief steward, heard the double snores, he knew that both of his passengers were out. He entered quietly to remove dirty glasses and dishes, to cover either of them if they'd

---

These, and others, can be found in *Bushisms*, compiled by the editors of *The New Republic*, workman Publishing, 1992.

fallen asleep on top of their blankets.

He found the president with his head on the pillows, reading glasses perched on his nose, and Lee Atwater's memo in his hand.

Stan lifted the glasses from the presidential nose. Bush, co-cooned with the prescription hypnotic and drowsy with Scotch, didn't notice a thing. Then Stan lifted the memo from the presidential hand.

He glanced at it. Only enough to see where it should go.

MEMO FROM: L.A.
TO: J.B.III/YEO

WAR has always been a valid political option, through all societies, through all time. We, who grew up in the south, know about revering our . . .

What registered with Stan was YEO. He'd seen and handled Secret, Top Secret, Top Secret with distribution numbers, Ultra, but this was the first time he'd seen Your Eyes Only. He was so impressed that he didn't notice the J.B.III. Meaning well, with truly the best of intentions, he folded the memo neatly along its fold lines and put it in the president's briefcase.

The next morning when the president and the secretary of state awoke and didn't see the Atwater memo, each assumed that the other had shredded it. The one that they agreed must never be seen.

CHAPTER

★ ★ ★

NINE

Frank Sheehan flew in from Chicago.

Sheehan was one of Universal Security's eight executive VPs. Five of them had clear-cut titles: Accounting and Financial Affairs, Sales, Management and Training, Government Relations, and Overseas. The other three worked for a department called Special Affairs. That was Sheehan's department.

He was a big man who'd played football in high school and one season at Notre Dame. He believed in sports because it built character. He was twenty pounds heavier than his playing weight, but, in his own opinion, his six-foot-two-and-a-half-inch frame could handle it. Frank had once considered the seminary. But he was "too masculine." Everyone told him so. Overall, he was quite glad that he'd listened. He joined the CIA instead. It filled many of the same needs the Church would have done even though there were times when the Agency seemed so flawed and full of failing that his faith was severely tested. But he understood, especially after a brief stint as assistant station chief in Rome, that he would have had to face exactly the same sort of crises in the Roman Catholic Church as in the Central Intelligence Agency. The great advantages of the CIA, aside from sex, had been that the job paid better and that he developed skills that were later transferable to private industry, which paid better still.

He'd been recruited from the Company to the company by the semilegendary Carter Hamilton Bunker,[11] founder and CEO of Universal Security. C.H. himself had sent Sheehan to L.A. to look over Mel Taylor's shoulder and let him know how important this case was. "Show the flag, son, show the flag," was what he'd actually said. There was something about his enunciation and his attitude that always made Sheehan feel like he was talking to God—not the Catholic God, which would have been blasphemous, just God as played by John Huston.

Sheehan had arrived without notice. Mel Taylor had not risen as far as he had by not doing his paperwork. The file on the case was up to date and well organized. Not everything was totally under control, but all the bases seemed covered.

"You know we never second-guess the man in the field," Sheehan said to Taylor. "You're in charge. I just want to keep the boss up to date."

Taylor interpreted that to mean *If anything goes wrong, it's your ass. He and he alone.* "No problem," he said. "Actually, I'm glad you're here. And I welcome some review and oversight on this one." He meant *Now that you've looked, it's the same as signing off on it, and it's your ass too.*

Frank took out the ninety-seven-dollar silver fountain pen his wife had given him on their twenty-fifth anniversary and the embossed leather pocket case that held a small notepad which she had given him on their twenty-third anniversary. He placed them neatly, and with a sense of formality, in front of him. "The only thing that stands out at all is this business with Joseph Broz and Magdalena Lazlo. The way I understand it, she came in, she invited him out for a cup of coffee, she asked him to come to work for her as bodyguard. You decided

---

[11]Not a real name. But the reader can assume, in this case, that the character is modeled on a very real person with a résumé that includes Yale, the OSS, and the CIA prior to starting an investigation and security company.

not to tell him that we have a watch on her?''

''That was my decision,'' Taylor said. There was no point in denying it or waffling. It was that way right there in the file he'd organized himself.

''Why was that?'' Sheehan said mildly. Although large, he looked mild too. Like so many CIA and ex-CIA types did. Thicker in the middle than around the chest, wider at the hips than at the shoulders. Barbershop hair. Given to checked shirts when he barbecued on summer Sundays. Mild and ordinary. Which didn't mean he was incapable of giving the order to fire someone, or in other circumstances, to have them terminated. He'd done both.

It was a decision that could terminate Taylor's career. It violated several major corporate guidelines. Not Mickey Mouse rules either, but stuff that made very good sense. Still, any rule could be violated, if the reasons were good enough and the results were right.

''Let me be straight with you,'' Taylor said. ''We have certain restrictions on this case. The main one is that nobody will tell me what it's about. Anybody inquires too vigorously what John Lincoln Beagle is working on, we're supposed to report it, to your office and to the client. Not to his secretary. Not to his assistant. Just to him, direct. If I knew what it was that has to be kept secret, I could separate the wheat from the chaff. But I don't. If it turns out you want to tell me, it would be appreciated, but we will soldier on in either case.'' Taylor meant *If something goes wrong because we didn't know what to watch out for, it's your fault.* ''The second thing is that the whole job is NTK.'' While not SOP at U.Sec., a certain portion of their work was handled on a need-to-know basis and employees were expected not to talk even to other employees about those cases. Management and Training felt it was good for esprit de corps, Sales said the practice was good for the company image. ''I deduce that the number-one imperative on this job is secrecy.''

''I haven't looked at Joe's file,'' Sheehan said, ''but if memory serves, he's been with us a long time. That says something. Can we get his file up here? If there were a reason to fault or mistrust him, he wouldn't be with us, would he? Seems like you could have used him as a double agent, as it were."

"Frank, I have to tell you, everything about this case just says maximum secrecy." Mel called Ms. Sligo, his secretary, on the intercom. She was a very efficient woman with iron gray structured through her hair and, having cleared her desk of actual work, was deeply engrossed in *Premiere* magazine. "Broz, Joseph, personnel file, ASAP," Mel ordered.

"So the first thing he did was put in a request to have the house swept?"

"Yes," Taylor said. "Fortunately, he asked for the same man who'd put the LDs in. So we were fortunate, he was already in the loop."

"Quite a coincidence that."

"Not at all. I picked Ray to do the installation because he's our best man. Broz knows that too."

"What if Broz somehow picks up on it, that Matusow misled him?"

"What's the downside?" Taylor said. "He can come in and say Ray screwed up. OK. Then we go back and take out a couple of mics."

There was a knock on the door. Taylor opened the door. It was Ms. Sligo, personnel file in hand. Taylor took it, closed the door, handed over the file to Sheehan.

Sheehan said, "You seem to be saying that you expect Joe to step outside the fold? Do you?"

"She's a beautiful woman," Taylor said flatly. "Beautiful women make men do all kinds of things. What about the initial interview? Where's the tape? That story of batteries running down—that's pretty thin, don't you think?"

The first thing Sheehan looked at was Joe's war record. "The old man"—C. H. Bunker, a descendent of the Bunker Hill Bunkers and a distant cousin of Ellsworth Bunker, who'd been the ambassador to Vietnam during the war—"likes war heroes. He likes Marine war heroes even better. He's always making a point of that with Rob Bloch." Bloch was the executive VP of Sales. " 'Tell them we've got more war heroes than Wackenhut or Pinkerton. Tell them we've got more war heroes than anyone except Arlington National Cemetery. Tell them we will put a man on the job who won the Silver Star, fighting for his country. If they don't sign on the dotted line, tell them you'll a assign a Congressional Medal of Honor winner. If they don't sign then, they're un-American and we don't want them.' I think I've heard him say that a hundred times or more.

"That's for starters, Mel. Plus Broz, he's been with the company longer than you have."

"I'm going to go out on a limb here," Taylor said. What he meant was, *I'm out on a limb already, so I might as well admit it.* "I have my doubts about Joe Broz's loyalty." Taylor wondered if, for once, he had let a desire overcome his judgment. Desire did that. Had he let his private purpose, to let Broz have enough rope to hang himself, supersede the objectives of the job? In terms of going by the book, he had.

Sheehan kept reading. He saw what Broz had done after his military service and frowned. He flipped ahead, skimming through Joe's record with U.Sec., and saw what he expected. He stopped and looked up. "When I saw his name, I thought this was the guy we were talking about. He's handled some work for my department." A lot of work fell under the jurisdiction of Special Affairs simply because it was too broad or too narrow or too different to fit neatly in one of the regular service categories. Just because a job was Special Affairs did not necessarily mean that it had a political dimension or legal problems, that it required extreme discretion or had a particular element of danger. But it could. "Even if you're upper management and he's just an operative, you better be right."

"I know his file looks good, but that's my feeling," Taylor said. "Interesting."

"So maybe this is a little test for him. A little trap. Look, Frank, the way I saw it, the way I see it, we win both ways. If she asks him to go after Beagle, then he's supposed to come in and report it. Form JO:C-1,[12] in triplicate—one for the office, one for the client, one for the operative. And if he doesn't, the way that house is wired, we'll know about it, guaranteed. I have a fallback plan to double-check them if for some damn reason I think we're missing something with just the audio material. If he turns out to be loyal, everything is copacetic. If not, well then we kill two birds with one stone."

"Well," said Frank, "it's your show. I just wanted you to know that the job means a lot to C.H. You're to do whatever it takes."

"You want me to put a couple of extra men on him? On them? Watch them?"

"Mel, let me tell you this as a friend. Nothing better go wrong on this job. If you treat it as the most important job of your whole life, you're on the right track. If something fucks up, you're in deep shit. I say that as a friend." Which meant, *I'm not your friend at all. If you screw up, I'll see that you fry, because I hope that will keep my ass out of the fire.*

Taylor understood exactly what Sheehan didn't say. "I'll double up on them. Nothing's going to go wrong." And if Broz turns out to be a traitor, he thought, I'll ruin his ass. At this point Taylor just meant Broz's career. Get him fired. Ace him out of his pension. In spite of the obsessive secrecy surrounding the job, there was no reason for Taylor to think that they were playing at a higher-stakes table. Not yet.

---

[12]All job files at U.Sec. include a job-objective section, so everyone, especially the client, is clear about what they are trying to do. A JO:C-1 is required to be filed if this objective changes. The form asks who requested the change, why, and how this will affect billing. There's boilerplate legal language on the bottom that says that this is a binding financial agreement.

CHAPTER

* * *

TEN

After I find the wiretap on the phone, I find the rest of the microphones. Then I get Maggie out on the beach, down by the water, where I can tell her about them. Her first reaction is to call up U.Sec. and get her money back.

"We can't do that," I say.

"The man's incompetent," she says.

"He's not incompetent. That's the point. If he misses one microphone, even if it's Ray Matusow, then it's a mistake. To miss at least eight LDs, that's not a mistake. That's deliberate. That tells us that he is one of them. Whoever is watching you, for whatever reason, Ray is working for them.

"I know Ray. He and I have worked together off and on, eight years. He's ex-FBI. He's a widower with three children, one still in college, and he's remarried to a woman with two kids in grade school. He has a house that has a lawn out front and a sprinkler. He has a summer house on a lake in the Sierras. He doesn't spend more than he can afford, he counts on his longevity bonuses, and he needs his pension. He's a company man.

"He didn't do this unless he was told to, by the company. By U.Sec."

"So we tell U. Sec. to go to hell," Maggie says. "Fire them and get our money back, and if they don't want to give it back, they can meet my lawyers."

"Take it the next step," I say. "Something very unusual is happening here. This is a conflict of interest, for U.Sec. to agree to work for you while they're maintaining surveillance on you."

"Of course it's a conflict of interest," she says.

"We don't do that," I say.

"Don't be naive. You work for a corporation—they do whatever they're paid for, not what's ethical."

"I don't say we won't do that. I say it's very bad business. If it comes out that we spy on our own clients, then our clients don't trust us. Then we lose business. So there has to be a very strong reason to do it.

"To have Ray Matusow and me working against each other, and him lying to me, that's also bad business. We expect our backup to back us up. We expect our team to be on our side. If it gets out that one of the guys working with you just might be working against you, it destroys something. So we don't do that. Unless there is a real strong reason.

"Also, I've been a company man for a long time. I've done things for them that can't be spoken of, and I never have spoken of them. To cut me out of the loop, there has to be a real strong reason."

"I told you it was serious," she says.

"Yes, you did."

"But you didn't really believe me. You had to wait and see for yourself."

"That's part of my job description."

"Your job description," she says, "is that you work for me. And I think it's time we cleared that up."

That brings me up short. "Yes, Ms. Lazlo, I do work for you. However, I am a professional. And I intend to handle this professionally, if at all. If you went to your attorney and asked him to bring a suit that you were certain to lose and which would damage your career, he would be correct to refuse to do it."

"And I would fire him, forthwith."

"Maybe. Maybe not. If you went to your Porsche dealer and asked his maintenance staff to disconnect your brakes because you wanted to develop a brake-free driving technique, they would be obligated to refuse. If you went to your doctor and asked for morphine because it was the only thing that made you feel happy, he would refuse." This sounds like I am quick on my feet and actually say the things people don't say but afterward wish they had said. The truth is that clients frequently ask us to do things that are dangerous, illegal, or just plain foolish. It is so common that management has developed a variety of responses they teach us in client-relation seminars. These things I am saying I have more or less verbatim from handouts on prepunched pages suitable for inserting in our loose-leaf manuals.

She stops and looks at me. Sincere, but not contrite, she says, "Forgive me, Joe. That was"—she searches for a word—"rude. Speaking to you like a servant."

I have the momentum, so I push it a little further. "What you have to understand, when I'm talking about Ray Matusow and longevity bonuses and pension funds, I'm talking about myself. The reason I figure he won't go against the company is that I know how hard it is for me. I stand to lose a lot. If I go against them and stand by you."

"I guess you do. I should have thought more about that, shouldn't I? But I figured you're a man, an adult, and you could make your own decisions. I didn't beg you or force you."

"Another thing you have to understand," I say. "U.Sec. has a reputation for vindictiveness. They go after traitors."

"Traitors—that's a little heavy-handed."

"Maggie, look at me," and this is my turn. I put my hands on her shoulders and look her square in the eye. "You don't understand who we are. We wear cheap suits, we act humble, and anybody with a couple of grand to spare can hire us. But damn near everybody in the company, they're FBI, CIA, some city cops, some MPs. Almost all of us have been in the service. Those of us of a certain age, we did tours of duty in Nam. We were part of the meat grinder. We carried

M-16s and grenades and set claymore mines. We watched friends die and get maimed. Don't underestimate us. Serious people don't often look like Sylvester Stallone or Chuck Norris."

"Does that mean you're backing out? Is that what you're telling me?"

"No. I'm telling you that if we go ahead, we both have to take it seriously. Look, maybe I'm wrong about it, maybe this is some sort of bullshit, that you didn't sleep with someone who has a lot of weight to throw around, or that someone's wife thinks you did sleep with someone, maybe that's what it's about. But I don't think so. I get the feeling that I'm putting at least my job on the line for you, at the very least. Now you may not think that's much, at a million three a picture, but I have a lot of years in it and it's what I do. So to me, that's a lot. That's what I figure."

"So what do you want, Joe? Go on, tell me what you want." She's breathing hard and so am I. The wind whips past us and the fine salt spray should be cooling, but there's heat coming off both of us.

Maybe I should have the guts to say it, say I want to lay you down, I want to plunge inside you, walk side by side with you with my hands upon you for all the honest world to see. What I say is, "I want you to take it seriously. And me seriously. We're in this together. Or you can go hire someone else and I'll go back to work and investigate some stock fraud or an embezzlement or a cheating husband."

"I can say yes to that," she says. I'm still holding her by the shoulders. The eye contact is electric and seems unbreakable. "Yes, I can take you seriously. I always did." We stare at each other. She nudges the door open a little bit more; "Is that all?" she asks.

"No. Of course it's not," I say.

I pull her close. Slowly. Our eyes are locked. She's saying neither yes nor no. I feel the heat of her body before it touches mine. The wind takes her hair, dashes it around, and that's the next thing I feel, her hair touching my face. There've been women, I've been in their mouth, and not felt half so much as from the touch of Maggie's windblown hair. My hands are still on her shoulders, slowly pulling us together—I got to tell you, when I was a kid and I went to the movies, cowboy movies, war movies, and they had these kissing scenes, I always hated them. Can we get back to the shooting, please? Even when I was grown, I didn't get the romance stuff, even sex stuff, on screen. But I thought, after this, because the thing with Maggie is so romantic, so cinematic, that I'm gonna change and when I see the kissy-face on screen I'm going to finally get it. But after this, when I go to the movies, I still don't get it. The hots, when you got 'em, is the greatest drama in the world next to dying, but it's not a spectator sport. There we are, Trancas, Pacific Ocean, waves, wind, great light, beautiful woman. My hands are on her shoulders, our lips are so close that we can feel the charge coming off each other's body. Subatomic particles, electrons, auric field, whatever that thing is. There's that one paper-thin distance to cross.

And we cross it. Her lips are on mine. This is the second kiss. The first time that I am bold enough to reach out and kiss her. I'm over forty and I'm counting kisses like when I was fourteen. The bodies follow the lips. Touching. I feel her nipples stiffen and her hips go soft. They press against me and I grow hard and I can feel her feeling that. Her mouth opens, just wide enough and perfectly soft.

Then suddenly she just steps back. Not harshly, but definite about it.

"No. I'm sorry. No. I can't now."

"Why not?" It's a growl. I want to behave like a teenage boy and call her the names we used to call girls who do that, offer us a glimpse of what we want, then leave us panting and pathetic.

"I don't know. We have to . . ."

"Have to what?"

"Find out what's going on, Joe. With this thing hanging over me . . . I don't want to decide anything."

"What are you going to do? Put your whole life on hold?"

"You do something to me, Joe. You really do. There's something about you. Something very real. But I don't go to bed with every guy who turns me on or every time I get feeling hot. I just don't do it. And I do take you seriously, Joe. Very seriously, and if we do go to bed together, it's going to get even more serious. You're not the kind of guy who's going to wake up a little before dawn and slip into his pants and walk out the door, with me pretending I'm still asleep and you never coming back anymore."

Sure I am, or have been, exactly that kind of guy. A lot of times I've been the kind of guy who didn't even wait to slip silently away. With a lot of the women I've known in my life, I just put my cash down and walked out, everybody's eyes open and everything in plain sight. But with Maggie, she's right, I won't be that kind of guy. I'll be there as close to forever as I can make it be.

I play the role of chauffeur-bodyguard. It's a role I've played before. When we go somewhere, I talk to the other service personnel and see what I can pick up.

Maggie is unhappy. Knowing that someone is always listening to everything we do—not just talk, but when we eat and shit, piss and snore, grunt or fart or sing in the shower—is a strain. She seems to act out her tension by being busier. She asks for and reads scripts. She has lunches and dinners and drinks. She conferences with her lawyers and accountants, with producers and fiscal schemers. That's fine, because almost every trip is an opportunity for me to meet someone. Most people in L.A. drive themselves, but if there are no other chauffeurs, I make the acquaintance of the maître d' or even one of the kids from valet parking. If we go to someone's home, I talk to the maid or the cook or the gardener. All of them are proud of their stars or power brokers; they all have stories to tell and pretend to inside knowledge.

A waiter at Morton's, outside on a reefer break, tells me how Brian De Palma dumped his girlfriend. I ask him if he knows Beagle. He says, "Sure, Beagle comes in all the time. Used to come in all the time. But he's sick." I ask with what? The waiter takes a deep, sad toke, and says, "What you think, man, what you think?"

Maggie sends me to pick up some clothes for her, that she's already picked out, from Simonettes. A sales girl named Tama tells me that Vanessa Swallow,[13] the pop star, is a lesbian who favors strap-on dildos. Tama swears that she personally saw Vanessa strap one on in the back room so that the seamstress could measure her and alter a whole set of underwear to accommodate the apparatus. I ask Tama if Beagle ever came shopping there. She says no. Then she says, could I do her a favor. I say what? She says she has a boyfriend, more of a best friend really, she loves him more than anyone else in the whole wide world, but it's not like an exclusive thing, sexually, if I know what she means, he's really talented and smart and he's written a screenplay that would be perfect for Magdalena, just perfect, if I could just show it to Ms. Lazlo, just leave it on the seat of her car, you know, it would be so good for both of them, because once Magdalena read it, she would be glad she had discovered it.

In order to speak, Maggie and I either go out on the beach or put on loud music. If it's my choice, it's country. We whisper in front of the speakers. She says Hank Williams is growing on her. Hank junior pisses her off because he switches back and forth between being great and being dumb. She likes Willie, but then, she says, she liked him before me. But mostly she's impatient. She doesn't like the waiting.

I hear about Nick Jackson and the gerbil at least once a day, and every single person who tells me the story tells me that they personally heard it from either the doctor who removed it from his famous rectum or from a doctor who is very close to the doctor who did the gerbilectomy.[14]

[13]A pseudonym.

[14]Fake name. Real rumor. Remarkably widespread. Even referred to in print, at least as a cartoon, in a national magazine. Interesting as a prototypical Hollywood

Aaron Spelling has a little soiree. The driver who brings Kenneth Branagh goes out with a girl who is a maid who, he says, is best friends with Melanie Griffith's maid. He tells me that when Melanie was pregnant, she did special exercises so that she could start having sex with Don Johnson again immediately after she had the baby. She couldn't stand the idea of not doing it, even the very next day.[15] I ask him if he knows Beagle. He says yeah, he drove him once. I ask when. It was only a couple of weeks ago. I ask how he looked, did he look sick? "I heard he was sick," the guy says, "but he didn't look sick. Pale but not sick. He and his wife were having a big fight." About what? "About their son. Beagle gave him some war toys. GI Joe dolls or something, and his wife was livid. Kid wanted 'em, Beagle says. I don't care, his wife says. Real, what you might call strident. I would call her a bitch. Wife talks to a man like that, she needs an attitude adjustment, if you know what I mean. But it's none of my business. I just transport 'em, I don't critique 'em."

When Maggie comes out, it's with Kenneth Branagh. They stop and stand and talk for a minute—out of earshot, but it has a special warmth and intimacy. She touches his arm. She laughs her laugh. He gives her a *ciao*-type kiss on the cheek; her body presses against his and lingers long enough for him to feel it's a body.

---

rumor: big-name star, perverse sexual act, attribution to a personal friend who has a specific relation to the star—maid, doctor, plumber, chauffeur.

[15]Another prototypical rumor. The author heard this one in New York from a very sophisticated literary agent in her mid-thirties who believed it absolutely. It's interesting because it is easy to trace the distortion that created it. Many modern obstetricians and midwives teach their pregnant patients to do an exercise that consists of flexing the vaginal muscles. The exercises are called Kliegals. It is designed to help prepare a set of muscles that are going to be violently stretched to return to their normal function afterward. It is done for reasons of general health as well as a return to sexual function. So what is normal procedure prescribed by your average old ob-gyn for a normal woman, here becomes a tale of sexual voracity and a mythology of secret and perverse sexual practice known only to a few.

I should be cool. I try to be cool. I hold the door open for her and don't say anything. As we drive down Sunset, she puts a CD on the player. Not country. Classical. She puts it up loud. Then she says, "Don't look at me that way."

"What way?"

"Like you're my father or my husband."

"I'm neither," I say.

"That's right, you're not."

"You're an independent, grown-up woman who kisses me on the beach from time to time . . ."

"Twice."

"Yes," I say. "Twice."

"We have to stop this, Joe. We have to. I can't have you trailing behind me like some puppy. Branagh's brilliant. As it happens, he's got a wife he's in love with . . ."

"They all have wives they're in love with. Who the fuck do you think you're talking to? You want to hear tapes of happy husbands? I got tapes of happy husbands saying, 'I love my wife, but she doesn't suck like you do, baby.' I once recorded the wife of the CEO of Douglas Defense Industries, she was talking to her daughter's tennis coach, she said, 'I love my husband, I really do. But his thing, it's just smaller than yours.' Being in love with his wife means shit . . ."

"The point is," Maggie says, "the next time he makes a picture—and he's going to make more pictures—it's important that Magdalena Lazlo is in his mind. Even if he discusses a picture and idly mentions it might be good to work with Magdalena Lazlo. That's the game. And if I have to press a little bit of breast against him to make that impression, that's what I do. Don't be a child."

"Is that what you did to me, Maggie?"

"Go to hell. Just drive me home."

The next morning she drives out alone.

She returns around lunchtime. I'm sitting in the kitchen trying to eat a sandwich that I have no appetite for. She gives me a package. She's bought me a CD player and fourteen Willie Nelson CDs. While

I'm looking through them all, she goes into the living room. I hear the *Stardust* album playing. It's not country, but it is Willie. He's singing old romantic standards. I don't think about programming CDs and such because I'm not used to them. When I walk into the living room, she pushes some buttons and it switches from the first song on the album to the last, which is *Someone to Watch Over Me*.

Like Maggie said, this situation has been the subject of a lot of movies.

But this is real life and it doesn't seem to be either automatic or inevitable that the rich girl is going to fall in love with the chauffeur.

CHAPTER

* * *

ELEVEN

Gary Trudeau in his *Doonesbury* comic strip had been twitting the president about his shattered syntax and making it appear as if the president couldn't organize a sentence on his own. While that was frequently true when speaking extempore, he could do so with preparation. To prove it—not to Trudeau, who wouldn't be there to see, but to himself and those around him—he decided to write his own remarks for a group of Orange County and Los Angeles Republicans.

He had made notes. He wanted to touch several bases. He asked his secretary to get them from his briefcase.

The president's regular secretary was ill. Her regular replacement was on vacation. The regular second backup was already assigned a certain activity. That left Carol Boomsliter, a woman from the White House secretarial pool who had never actually served the president before. She was doing the best she could and going by her personal code: when in doubt, do twice as much.

Bush's notes were little more than a scrawl on the back of an envelope. Ms. Boomsliter, an anal retentive, couldn't believe that no more had been done, even for a minor speaking engagement, even if it was identical in every way to the twenty that had come before it. She searched the briefcase quite thoroughly and, for the first time in four months, the Atwater memo appeared. A single glance was enough to frighten her. Not because of it's content. Like so many people in government, she had gotten to the point, or perhaps had come to Washington in such a state of mind, that content was completely meaningless. Like Stan the Steward, she was cleared for Top Secret–Limited Distribution, for Ultra and even, technically, for YEO, but she certainly did not want to be caught handling one that she had not been handed by a very authorized hand. Now that it was in her hand, with her fingerprints on it, she had to make a decision. And, unlike Stan, she noticed that it was not addressed to Bush but to J.B.III. Of course, she knew who that was. She did not doubt that the president was authorized to see it, but she could visualize a scenario in which J.B.III missed it, went searching for it, and, when it was found, even in the presidential briefcase, demanding an investigation. The FBI would come in, check for fingerprints—she realized she didn't know how to wipe fingerprints off of paper, and even if she did, criminals always made a mistake and left some trace. She decided to come clean.

She handed George Bush the envelope with the scrawls and then the neatly refolded memo from Lee Atwater. She apologized for having seen it and she swore that she had read no further than the letters YEO.

If the president's regular secretary had been in the room, he might have reflexively handed it to her and said to either file it or shred it. If the Baker to whom it was addressed had been in the room, Bush might have turned it over to Baker. But without those options and with so many presidential things to think about, it became that 2,134th detail that the presidential mind could not handle, akin to, Should the black socks be to the right or the left of the blue socks in the sock drawer or should "Mc" follow

"Mac" or come after "Max" in the contributor's-list filing system or where to actually put bills when he vetoed them.[16]

Because there was no one there to take it from his hand immediately and because he couldn't decide if he wanted to shred it or re-reread it and because he had no idea how to file it, George Bush put Lee Atwater's deathbed memo in his pocket. Where it bulked and crinkled and reminded its carrier that it was present.

It was there when the president climbed into his helicopter. Still there when the copter brought him to *Air Force One*.

This was a working flight. Several members of his undistinguished cabinet were on board. Each with urgent matters to attend to. In addition, there were his press secretary; the presidential pollster, Kenny Moran, on loan from the Gallup Organization, ostensibly employed by the Department of Agriculture,[17] and the

---

[16]It is all too easy to make fun of presidents, particularly since they have come to be judged by the standards by which we judge fictional characters who appear on our TV screens. It's ridiculous and it's unfair. TV characters appear in a show that lasts twenty two minutes, once a week, twenty-six or thirty-nine times a year. The TV character gets retakes and his mistakes become outtakes. Jerry Ford bumps his head and he is defined as a bumbler for the rest of his life. Richard Nixon tries, and fails, to pry the cap off the aspirin bottle with his teeth one night and it becomes a character-revealing trait, implying an unimaginable depth of dysfunction. Jimmy Carter had a run-in with a rabbit and was forever after labeled boob and wimp.

Then there's the sex business. For example, there are persistent rumors that Bush has girlfriends. Remember that "power is the ultimate aphrodisiac," look at Barbara, and there are three possibilities: George is a normal male attracted to younger women and he cheats; George chooses to have sex exclusively with a woman who looks like a veritable caricature of a grandmother; George is a eunuch. Think about it—which George would you want running the country?

The only guy who could handle being "on-camera" every public minute and come out of it looking good was the guy who spent his life "on-camera," Ronald Reagan.

If the experiment with Bill Clinton is no more satisfactory than those with Nixon, Ford, Carter, and Bush, then perhaps Reagan will turn out to be the harbinger of things to come and the practice of having someone "act" as president will be institutionalized.

current head of the Republican Party, who had arranged the West Coast fund-raiser to which they were all on their way.

The five hours of flight time passed quickly. There was a lot of business. None of the news was cataclysmic or catastrophic. But none of it was good.

Noriega's lawyers were fighting to unfreeze his assets. This was delaying the trial, and until the trial ended and Noriega was convicted, the invasion of Panama teetered on the edge of an abyss named Farce. The economy was the lead depressant. It was just stagnating. The savings-and-loan scandal stumbled along, growing from billions to tens of billions to hundreds of billions lost, lurch by lurch. Bush's son—why was it that the sons of great men, excepting himself of course, were such disappointments?—was ensnared in one of the messes. Anyone dumb enough to invest in a bank named after a shoot 'em up movie, *Silverado,* should be willing to take their loss and not complain. Fortunately, the sins of the son were not being visited on the father. He didn't expect them to be. After all, Jimmy Carter had survived Billy Carter, Reagan had survived both a "ballet-dancing son" and a Mommy Dearest daughter. But that could change. Just as what a grown man did with his own penis had suddenly become a matter of public policy under the heading of "character"—a man carries the weight of the world on his shoulders and he isn't even entitled to a little discreet release of tension—so could the faults of family. The balance of payments continued to slide the wrong way. The deficit continued to grow.

After about four hours of this damp news, he came to feel like

---

[17]It is common practice to employ campaign people in government posts as a reward for past service, to be kept on call for future service, and as a way of paying them for ongoing service. I have no specific knowledge that there was a pollster employed on a D.O.A. line.

he was standing under an awning, waiting for the rain to pass, with a slow leak above him and a drip that somehow always found the gap between his neck and his collar—plus, he had to urinate.

Which he did.

While he was gone, the fax that they had been waiting for finally arrived over the encrypted communications system. The first thing he saw as he walked out zipping his fly was the new data printing out. Moran had taken the high post beside the machine, watching the data possessively.

"What do we have, Kenny?" the president asked.

"I'm sorry, sir, but it looks to be down another quarter point."

"Me? Me, personally?"

"Yes, sir. But it's just a quarter point."

"But it's the trend. That's what counts. That's what you guys are always telling me. Isn't that what you always tell me? Watch the trend?"

"Yes, sir. I'm just the messenger."

"You're more than that. You're the magician that reads the entrails."

"Huh?"

The president threw himself down in his chair. "Out. Everybody out. I have to figure this out." His aides knew he didn't mean it. They were at eighteen thousand feet.

A few minutes later he retired to the bedroom to change into a fresh shirt and suit for the fund-raiser. Transferring the contents of his pockets, he came across the memo. Partly because he didn't want to go back out and face more news that was neither good nor bad, just dreary, he unfolded it and read it again.

Maybe because it was a little more familiar, it didn't seem quite so insane this time.

And the dead Lee Atwater promised to do what no living

person seemed able to do—he offered a way to slice through all the niggling bullshit, all the tedious nit-picking that was tearing him down in the polls in inexorable half- and quarter-point increments; he offered a way to change it all in one grand stroke.

The memo made reference to a specific person as the key agent to implement the plan. If there had been a conference about the matter, it might have been decided that "someone of that sort" was the point, not one individual and that individual only. It was a man that Atwater knew but that Bush had never met. Yet. Bush was scheduled to meet him, coincidentally, at the fund-raiser, in about—the president looked at his watch as he felt the 747 begin its descent—twenty, twenty-five minutes.

It is also possible to suppose that none of that really mattered. That the power was in the idea. And it was bound to make itself manifest no matter if the physical piece of paper it had been written on was shredded or lost or forgotten. The paper and the print were nothing—the power was in the idea.

CHAPTER

* * *

TWELVE

Maggie wants action. I understand that. I want action too. But it's the one thing we can't do. At least that's what I think. As long as we appear to do nothing, they'll leave us alone. As soon as we appear to move, they'll react.

One of the ways I try to deal with my tension is to up the level of my workouts. In addition to the running and the simple calisthenics, I return to my training at the dojo. I go to a place down in Koreatown. It's in a typical two-story minimall: discount hardware, cards and tobacco, manicures and pedicures, a fish store. The dojo has a name, but all the regulars call it Sergeant Kim's.

I didn't know Kim in Vietnam. There are stories about him, many of which may be true. He can kill with a touch. We all can kill with our hands. I mean a lot of people who study martial arts or who are taught hand-to-hand combat—Green Berets, Seals, the Delta Force—even regular Marine training, they teach killing blows. Kim was involved with a recon team. They'd have some possible VC. Kim would come along and he wouldn't have to throw someone out of a Huey[18] to get the others to talk. Or shoot anyone. He would do it

[18]Huey: Bell's UH-1 Iroquois helicopter, armed with two 7.62-mm machine guns and rockets.

with his hand.

They would line up the prisoners. They'd see this hard little Korean, their own size, but thicker. He would walk up to the first prisoner. Touch him. Kill him. The others would start to talk. Soon there was a legend about him and he didn't always have to kill. Just be the sergeant with death in his fingertips.

I want to explain something here. I don't know how you could ever show it in a movie, because it's got to do with ideas. Also, I don't want you to get the wrong feeling about Kim. That he is a brutal or vicious man. He's not.

Most people were ashamed of Vietnam. So they turned their faces away. I went over *gung ho*. I stayed *gung ho*. I had good times there. I loved Vietnam. In many ways. Including combat. I liked trying to be a hero.

Maybe this is why I haven't turned my face away. I've spent a lot of time looking at what happened and thinking about it. We didn't understand Vietnam in exactly the same way that I'm afraid people won't understand a man like Kim. General Westmoreland used to say things like "The Oriental doesn't put the same high price on life as does the westerner," and "Life is plentiful, life is cheap in the Orient,"

"Now everyone knows about the airborne interrogation—taking three people up in a chopper, taking one guy and saying, 'Talk,' then throwing him out before he even gets the chance to open his mouth. Well, we wrapped det[onator] cord around their necks and wired them to the detonator box. And basically what it did was blow their heads off. The interrogator would tell the translator, usually a South Vietnamese intelligence officer, 'Ask him this.' . . . the guy would start to answer, or maybe he wouldn't—maybe he'd resist—but the general idea was to waste the first two. They planned the snatches that way. . . . By the time you get to your man, he's talking so fast you got to pop the weasel just to shut him up." Elton Manzione, self-described Navy Seal in Douglas Valentine, *The Phoenix Program* (Morrow, 1990). Similar stories abound. See also Mark Baker, *Nam: The Vietnam War in the Words of the Men and Women Who Fought There* (Morrow, 1981), and, finally, Mitchell Siegal in *Vietnam Memories* (New Woodstock Press, 1988) claims to have witnessed a Korean interrogator who killed with his hands to intimidate other suspects.

and "As the philosophy of the Orient expresses it, life is not important."[20]

These were very stupid things to say. They might even be why we lost the war.

For Kim to kill face-to-face, looking into the eyes of the man who is going to die, that does not say that for Kim, life is cheap. That says that Kim is ruthlessly honest. Westmoreland[21] measured the war in body counts. He created free-fire zones, which meant anything that moved—man, woman, child, water buffalo—was presumed to be the enemy and we were supposed to kill it, and he defoliated the forests and used high-altitude bombing. That says life is cheap, life is not important. I'm not saying we shouldn't have done those things. We were soldiers. We were there to kill the enemy. We killed as many as we could. But we shouldn't misunderstand who thinks life is cheap and who respects it.

The ground floor of the dojo is for the public at large. They teach tae kwan do, plus they have become very successful teaching classes in self-defense for women. From the locker room there's a stairway to the second floor. It has a sign on it: ROK—MEMBERS ONLY. There's a joke attached to that which I will explain later. It's sort of a private club that's not restricted to a single discipline and is combat-oriented.

When I find myself there for the third time in a week, I realize that I am thinking of asking Kim for advice.

I change into my gi and go upstairs.

When I find Kim, I bow. I ask to speak to him. I explain to him how I took the job with Maggie and why I think it is so serious that Ray lied about the LDs. Kim has one of those stoic, tough Korean

---

[20]Westmoreland said this on camera. It can be seen in the documentary film *Hearts and Minds*.

[21]General Paul D. Harkins, who preceded Westmoreland, should also be credited with originating some of these concepts and designing the very destructive, and ultimately losing, strategy of a war of attrition. Westmoreland continued and elaborated on it.

faces. I can't read what he is thinking. So to convey to him how I feel I reach back to the shared experience: "You remember, in the jungle, when the birds stopped singing. That's what I hear—the big silence."

"Why do you come to me?"

"Almost everyone I know who might help me, I have to assume that their first loyalty is to the other side. I can't use the telephone. I can't hire help. I can't go wire them. I can't move. I'm stuck."

"Ahhhh," he says, being very Oriental, "you come to me for sensei bullshit. OK, I can do that. You are deer who sees tiger. Deer cannot move, movement will make tiger notice, tiger will strike. Deer cannot stay still, because soon or late, tiger will strike. Oh, Glasshopper Joe, you understand lesson? Lesson is that it is tough to be a deer in jungle. Better to be tiger. How's that for sensei shit. If you want, I whack you on back of head." He laughs. He's having a good time. "Americans see *Kung Fu* and *Karate Kid One, Two, Three.* Think martial-arts teacher guide to life and dojo a twelve-step program. Hey, Joe, you know what I teach people—I teach people how to hit each other, that's all. You're a good guy, Joe. You want to go out for a drink? We go have a beer, eat some fish from my nephew's place. Very fresh, very good."

"No, thanks, that's OK."

"I find that I am drinking earlier in the day now. Just beer, of course."

"I got to tell you something, Kim . . ."

"Come on, we go to the office."

I follow him. I say, "I feel like I walked into an ambush. And it scares the fuck out of me. I should've known. When I was in Nam, I got so I always, always knew. You understand?"

He gestures me to a chair while he goes to a small refrigerator and takes out two bottles of Harp lager. "Irish people. Make good beer. You drink with me, I give you good advice." He opens them and hands me one. He waits and watches till I tilt it back and swallow.

"OK. I tell you Zen-type story." He takes a pull and sighs with pleasure. "Irish people, best beer. One time I go study with Japanese martial-arts master. Very high, very famous. He tell samurai story. Samurai one night go out drinking. Get very happy. On way home bunch of bandits jump him in alley. Eight, ten of them. Samurai very great fighter. He react. Fight back. Kill seven, others run away. Next day he goes and brags to his teacher about it, how many he kill. Teacher say, 'You stupid. Real samurai would have known about ambush and walked home by next alley.'

"I thought about this," Kim says. "I hate Zen stories. Too Japanese. If I were that samurai, I would say, 'Fuck you, sensei. I am samurai. I like to fight. I had a good time. And I am not stupid, because having fights and beating odds of eight to one, baby, that's what it's all about." He takes another swallow of beer. With great enjoyment. He stares at me until I drink some more. Then he says, "You lucky I am not Japanese."

"Why?"

"If I am Japanese, I tell you go back to your company. Confess your error and become loyal again." Kim laughs, very harshly. "I love Japanese. Hai! I am Toyota man. I let Toyota stick gearshift up my ass if it make better car. I am Hitachi man. Test big vibrator and hum company song. Fuck Japanese. Koreans better. Even Americans better. Every man for himself. Very interesting."

I sigh. This is not the encounter I expected. Kim belches. He smiles at me. The top of his desk is stacked with papers. He pushes some aside and uncovers a large paperback. *The Art of Strategy: A New Translation of Sun Tzu's Classic, The Art of War.* He hands it to me. "Gift. I give it to you," he says. "New translation. Very pretty. Ideograms on one side. You like Oriental philosophy advice, Sun Tzu very good. The best. Chinese. Anywhere you look is a beginning. Here . . ." He opens the book, apparently at random and without looking puts his finger down on the page. He's pointing at a line that says, *A strategy of positioning evades Reality and confronts through illusion.*"[22] He says again, "You take."

[22]The book was originally written in ideograms and apparently with the intention

"Thank you," I say, unable to reject the gift even if I have other editions of the same book.

He knocks back the rest of the beer in one long swallow. He stares at me as if I am a disrespectful guest until I too have finished my bottle. He takes it from me and then puts both aside to collect the deposit later. That done, we go back into the dojo.

Kim claps his hands. Everyone turns and looks. He gestures to a tall, skinny black man with a shaven head. I know him slightly. He calls himself Hawk. Just like the TV show. In fact, he claims that the TV character is modeled after him. I don't think that's true.

"Hawk. Give Joe match. Light contact. Only." Kim says.

Hawk gives me a "bad" look. I turn to Kim. I'm not ready for this. I have a belly full of beer.

"Yo, bro," Hawk says, "we gonna get to it, or you want me hit you in the back of the head."

I turn around. We find a place on the mat. The others automatically give way to us. We bow to each other. The beer sloshes internally. We take our positions. We begin.

Hawk strikes first. It is instantly clear that he is my superior. He is quicker and stronger and more skillful. Tae kwan do uses a lot of kicks and special techniques to generate a lot of power. To execute them properly requires great flexibility. By body type alone he is ahead of me. Very soon he is striking almost at will.

I block as best I can, letting him hit my forearms, shoulders, thighs,

---

of creating pithy rules general enough to have universal application. The result is that English-language editions vary quite widely.

In the Thomas Clearly translation this phrase appears as ''the form of military force is to avoid the full and attack the empty.'' B. H. Liddell Hart in *Strategy* quotes the Samuel B. Griffith translation: ''the way to avoid what is strong is to strike what is weak.''

This oracular vagueness, which forces each reader to develop his or her own interpretation, may be the reason these cryptic Oriental philosophs always seem so apt. Readers will always develop readings that suit their own situation—like reading the daily horoscope.

but trying to protect my vulnerable points: eyes, throat, groin, knees. One solid kick gets through and hits me in the stomach. I step back as I taste beer coming back up.

Light contact is not that light.

Martial-arts instructors believe in pain as a teacher. So do Marine drill instructors. And my parents. I have to admit that even as I am taking this measured beating I am becoming more centered and awake. I begin to see Hawk more clearly. I become certain that at some point, when he thinks he has a clear shot, he's going to deliver one of his crippling blows at full power. He is not going to be content with a demonstration. There is a kind of rage in him. And arrogance.

I attempt an attack. He blocks and snaps back with a left hand strike at my neck. I miss my block. His strike has more snap than it should. I back up, hurt. He follows with a kick aimed at my groin.

This is his move. This is full force.

I get my thigh in the way. It's a powerful blow, momentarily numbing. He knows it. I'm even slower now than when we started.

He follows it up. A variation on the same sequence. A hand strike, this time at my eyes, to back me up and position me for the kick that will follow. This time, I feel with certainty, it will be at my knee—these thoughts are not in words. By the time words could form, the actions would be long over. They are instant thoughts, vivid and clear, though I can't say what they are if they're not words.

If he strikes my knee, he will injure it. Either a little or a lot. That will end the match. Afterward, he will offer a formal but insincere apology.

Instead of flinching back to protect my eyes, I step into the hand strike with the intent of taking the blow on the top of my forehead. This is dangerous for both of us. If my timing is not good enough, or his adjustment is too good, I'm going to get hit in the eye. At the same time, the skull is a very hard piece of bone very close to the surface. It is very dangerous to hit people in the head with a fist or fingers. If he strikes full-force and makes no adjustment, he is likely to break something.

He adjusts. But not enough. His stiffened fingers hit the bone just above the eye. The skin beneath my eyebrow splits. Blood starts to flow. It looks dramatic but it means nothing. Kim does not stop the bout. In fact, I think I hear him giggle. Though I'm too concentrated to be sure.

Hawk has hurt his hand. His rhythm is broken. And I am not the one set up.

This turns his ambush into my ambush. But he doesn't understand that yet. Perhaps distracted by the gaudiness of my blood.

Because he doesn't understand that, he continues with what he planned, the kick to my knee. But I'm already too close to him and I keep moving in. Instead of his foot striking my knee, I bring my knee up to meet his knee and join with it. I turn, joining my force to the force he has committed. I drop down, going to the mat, and throw him over me. I follow him down, fast as I can. I thud down on him with my knees. With my hand in a tiger claw I slash at his face and touch my fingers to his eyelids.

Kim claps to end the bout.

We get up. We bow to each other. I'm bleeding. Hawk's hand is starting to hurt him. Kim walks away. He has other business. I am supposed to have learned something from this. Or from the book. Or from his story. Or from all of it. If I have not, the fault is in the student, not the teacher, and the teacher, rightly, has no more to say. Or maybe he was just pissed at me for asking dumb questions and the lesson was to shut up and not bother him. All of these are possible.

"You think you a mean motherfuck, don't you," Hawk says.

"Mean enough." I say.

"You not as mean as me," he says. "If it was my fingers in your eyes, you would have felt the Hawk before he let you rise."

"Probably," I say.

He suddenly grins. He has a wide mouth and large teeth. It makes his smile very big and friendly-looking. "Fuck you, Joe, you all right," he says and starts one of those old-fashioned soul-brother hand-shakes with fist tapping, elbow banging, forearm sliding, and thumb rolls. I was in Nam. All the brothers did it. My version is outdated but so, I guess, is Hawk's. Nowadays they just make finger gestures, gang signs. You know, you've seen it in the movies.

I go back to the house.

Maggie is getting ready to go to an Important Party.

It's hosted by Jon Peters* Who has recently been hired by Sony to become head of Columbia Pictures. His salary is reported to be $2.7 million plus a piece of the profits plus Hollywood perks. There are thousands of people in Hollywood who can say "No." There are several hundred who can say "I'm on board" or "I approve" and it will likely go. But there are only a handful that can actually say "Go" and the twenty or thirty or forty million dollars will be committed and spent and the motion picture made. Maybe there are five or ten or fifteen. Whatever the number, most of them will be there tonight.

Maggie has her hairdresser over. His name is Fredo. I watch him work for a few minutes. Neither of them notice me. He's chattering about the sex lives of stars. He actually mentions the gerbil story again. He swears that his boyfriend cuts the hair of the doctor who removed the beast.

"Fredo, just shut up and make me beautiful," Maggie snaps. As if she's not, and it suddenly frightens her.

I look at her facing her fear in the mirror, then I leave the room.

Later, Maggie comes downstairs. She is devastating. Hair, makeup, clothes, shoes—the whole package. I don't know about clothes, but I can tell this dress is very expensive, the material is something special and it is custom-made for her. Whoever has made it is very clever because it looks simple but it keeps molding itself to her, changing as she moves. One moment I'm aware of her breasts, then the length of her legs, then I'm staring at the shape of her mound.

*Peters left Columbia in May 1991. In order to get him out, Sony gave him a deal so rich that he remains at the time of publication, a Hollywood Power.

Then it disappears.

I, on the other hand, do not look my best. I have a butterfly bandage on my eyebrow, discoloration around the eye, and I'm limping. When she sees me, she looks concerned. Then, afraid to ask about it with the listeners listening, she turns the CD on. She asks if I'm alright. I say yes. I don't even try to explain about the dojo. I still haven't figured out if Kim is going alcoholic or if something happened. *A strategy of positioning evades Reality and confronts through illusion means?*

"I wish you looked more presentable," she says.

"Hey, I'm your bodyguard. This is a good look for a bodyguard."

"It's not funny, Joe."

"Sure it is."

"I could put makeup on that. Cover it up."

"Maggie, you're the most beautiful woman I've ever seen. You look fine."

"Do I look like a goddess?" she says. "That's the real question. Beautiful isn't enough. I remember the first casting director who said that to me. 'Beautiful isn't enough, babe. Beautiful is a dime a dozen. Hey, listen,' he said, 'you got a bod and I can get you some nude work.' I said, 'Thanks, but no thanks.' He said, 'Don't be so high and mighty, babe. It was good enough for Marilyn, it was good enough for Basinger—trust me, it's more than good enough for you.' Then he said, 'You'll be back. Six months, a year or two, and you'll take it off. See you later.' Do you believe that anyone could be that crude, that cliché?"

"Did you go back?"

"No. I never will, I swear it."

"Why should you?"

"Do I look like millions of people will pay for the privilege of peeping at me? To gaze at the shape of my titties? Which have not yet been surgically altered, which means that they can not compete with Melanie Griffith's. Do I look like the person you want to invest millions of dollars in? Do I look that hot?"

"Oh," I say. "That's the question. I should have known."
"Fuck you, Joe," she says, but she smiles.

It's like *Upstairs, Downstairs.*

We, the chauffeurs, are in a section set aside for visiting servants. There's a lot of gossip. That's my job. Since it's his party and he's the new power in town, everyone wants to talk about Peters. It's mostly old gossip. How he was the model for the Warren Beatty character in *Shampoo,* the very heterosexual hairdresser who slept with everyone in L.A., including Nancy Reagan.[23] Several of the chauffeurs are women. One of them says, "Poor Lesley Ann Warren, that's who I'm sorry for. It's one thing that she was married to this pig who's porking everyone in town, but when they make a movie out of it, does she get to play herself? No. Goldie Hawn gets the Lesley Ann Warren part." They go on with the legend of Peters screwing his way to the top, meeting Streisand, who made him her record producer and then her film producer.[24]

I try to steer the conversation to the mysterious Mr. Beagle. I hear several rumors, including two that I haven't heard before. One is that he has a colon disease, odors leak from his body, which is why he doesn't want to go out in public. The other, that he is working on a top-secret project for the Japanese to develop Japanese TV shows that will compete with American shows, that the purchase of Columbia by Sony is an elaborate charade so that we won't notice what the

[23]We assume that this is nonsense and would like to so inform the reader. However, it is so exactly symptomatic of Hollywood gossip that it would be hard to imagine it not being said in this conversation.

[24]It's easy but silly to dismiss Jon Peters as some sort of male bimbo who slept his way to the top. He is the producer—post-Barbra—of *Flashdance, The Color Purple, Witches of Eastwick, Rain Man,* and *Batman.* The something that raises people to the top in Hollywood, as in politics, is incredibly difficult to define. More often than not, the winners are a total surprise and more often than not, those who try to walk exactly the same trail, fail.

Japanese are really doing.

I also hear stories I have heard before: the AIDS rumor and that he is working for the Japanese on production technology for HDTV that will make nonelectronic production obsolete within one or two years.

The party is both indoors and out. We are situated in such a way that we can see part of what goes on in the backyard. From time to time, I glimpse Maggie. She appears, from this distance, to be both very enticing and very flirtatious. I feel that if I were one of the men she is talking to, I would think she was coming on to me. Several times I see men touching her. What we used to call in junior high, copping a feel. Pisses me off. Of course, she can handle it.

One of the chauffeurs sidles over to me.

"You have an interest in Lincoln Beagle," he says out of the corner of his mouth, like an old-time con from a Cagney prison picture or a dastardly spy out of early Hitchcock.

"I'm just a fan," I say. "I love his work."

"Uh-huh," the guy says.

"Do you know what he's up to?"

"I know him." He winks. "What if I were to tell you," he says, "that Lincoln Speigel is working on . . . Are you ready for this? . . . Are you?"

"I think so."

"You won't be. But I'll tell you anyway. Because it's so incredible. He is working on the reincarnation of John Wayne."

"It makes sense to me," I say. "We could use him."

"You have to understand," he says, "the Age of Aquarius is over."

"Yeah, I knew that," I say.

"That was the age of the spiritual. We are now in the age of Neo-Science. New Science which is beyond science. Where art and spirituality and technology and biogenetics are all going to meet in a new synthesis. These people who are talking about HDTV, that's nothing. Talk about virtual reality. That's something. Walk into living dreams and have them talk back to you and touch you. Hollywood has always taken ordinary people and made them into stars, with training and publicity and plastic surgery and hair experts and makeup. But it's so hit or miss. Very wasteful. They're going to go to the source. They're going take the remains of the best of the old stars and, using genetics and microsciences, reincarnate them. And that's what Beagle is really working on. The rest—a smoke screen."

CHAPTER

★ ★ ★

THIRTEEN

President Bush has rarely been described as a racist or as anti-Semitic. But it would be fair to say, at the very least, that he is ethnocentric and by choice prefers a fairly narrow range of people. If one envisions diminishing concentric circles—like illustrations of the rings of hell from Dante's *Inferno*—the outermost ring would be WASPs. Moving inward the rings would be: males, who wear suits and ties, have a lot of money, play golf, are in business, are from old money, are eastern establishment, Ivy Leaguers, jocks, Yalies, from prep schools, members of Skull and Bones,[25] second-generation Yalies.

He therefore looked forward to going to a fund-raiser in Orange County, that area south of Los Angeles County which is

---

[25]Yale's, and America's, most famous publicly secret society. More than a fraternity. What Yalies are to the rest of us, members of Skull and Bones are to Yalies. Until 1992 it was an all-male group. Some of the practices include lying in a coffin, ritual masturbation (will this continue now that sexual integration has come? and if it does, will it change the psychic impact of the practice?), and written confessions. These written confessions are kept in logbooks which are, it is said, intact since the beginning of the practice, with one exception. The year which would have included George Bush's entry is missing.

a bastion of folks who would be just like Bob Hope if he weren't funny and had a straight nose. That is to say they loved the Republican Party almost as much as they loved golf, they lived for martinis, disapproved of sex but could appreciate a pretty girl, still danced to the music of Lawrence Welk, knew that we lost Vietnam because of the media and lost China because of traitors in the State Department. They knew better than to trust the Commies even in 1990, and it was obvious to them that Gorbachov's reforms were a trick to lure us into disarmament. Disneyland is in Orange County.

A relationship between Bush and Hartman—one that ultimately required an incredible amount of faith and trust on the president's part—was not likely to come about as a happy accident, and in fact, it did not. It was sought out and engineered by Hartman with avarice aforethought. Though what he expected from that relationship did not even remotely touch on what actually came of it. That was determined by the genius, or mad despair, of Lee Atwater.

To understand David Hartman it is necessary to reference Lew Wasserman of MCA, Inc.

Lew Wasserman is to agents what Henry Ford is to automobiles, not necessarily the best, but the first one to transform what was essentially a personal-service business, subject to all such an enterprise's inherent limitations, into a major multibillion-dollar corporation.[26]

---

[26]Wasserman's biggest breakthrough is fascinating for a number of reasons. MCA—and Wasserman personally—was Ronald Reagan's agent. They did very well for Reagan even when his career as a film star was quickly fading. In 1952, when Reagan was president of the Screen Actors Guild, he negotiated a deal that permitted MCA and *only* MCA to get a blanket waiver to both represent actors and

For Hartman to feel he had become the greatest agent in the history of the world, he would have to surpass Wasserman.

Like almost anyone who enjoys big-time success in business in America, Wasserman was a major player in politics. He cultivated relationships and gave generously to both sides. A discreet and secretive person, his influence was either far less or far more than it appeared to be. In either case, it enjoyed legendary proportions and it bore fruit. While MCA did not win every battle that was decided by government, it won a lot of the big ones. Its business practices suggested antitrust violations. It enjoyed relationships with unions that were so favorable that it is difficult to believe that they were achieved without illegal forms of collusion. MCA was investigated frequently, but whether the bottom line was that they were basically honest or that they had as much influence as reputed, they were never convicted, and only occasionally submitted to a consent decree.

Hartman had kept a relatively low profile in politics. He had not yet needed heavyweight political clout. But it was time to take that next step, from mere agent to something that owned and controlled vast tangible assets. He was looking at certain possibilities. Some of them involved large investments from Japan. Others

---

produce shows. This gave MCA an incredible advantage over both rival talent agents and rival producers. It gave them power over the studios. For example, they forced Paramount Pictures to produce a Hitchcock film on a lot at Universal—by then owned by MCA—even though Paramount had it's own studio space.

In the late sixties MCA helped arranged real-estate deals for Reagan that made him a millionaire and put him in a position to run for governor. A more detailed exposition can be found in Dan E. Moldea, *Dark Victory: Ronald Reagan, MCA, and the Mob* (Viking, 1986). Moldea paints Wasserman as an *eminence grise* who took care of Reagan and was, in turn, taken care of. Ronald Brownstein, in *The Power and the Glitter: The Hollywood-Washington Connection* (Pantheon, 1990), portrays Reagan and Wasserman as two individuals on separate tracks that sometimes ran congruently and sometimes ran at odds.

involved possible antitrust violations. It would be good to know that if he dialed a number in Washington his calls would be answered. Not that he would ever expect to have a president in his pocket. That would be presumptuous, excessive, and crude. All that anyone wanted, and if they knew what they were doing, all that anyone needed, was access.

Then, in 1988, with Reagan out and Wasserman a key figure in raising funds for Dukakis—for the *loser*—Hartman sensed a major vacuum. Although there were several very visible conservative celebrities, there was no big-time entertainment business power broker hooked in to the national Republican power structure. Hartman was not about to simply throw money at Bush or his party. If he did that, they would treat him the way a prostitute treats a john. Hartman wanted a relationship. He wanted the inner circle to know his name, to be thought of as the person to go to when Washington needed something from Hollywood.

hartman had seen Lee Atwater as a person to bridge the two worlds, and in 1988 he arranged to meet the political consultant. When the criticism of Lee was at its height, David had called him and taken him out to lunch and praised his creativity. He listened to Lee's ideas and told him that he was a genius of politics in the same way that Hitchcock had been a genius of suspense films and Elvis a genius of music: that all three had taken forms that were not even recognized as arts and personally raised them to such high levels of cultural significance that they could no longer be ignored. He knew that Atwater's three favorite books were *The Art of War, On War,* and *The Prince,* so he told Lee that his tactics reminded him of Sun Tzu and that no one since Machiavelli had seen politics with less hypocrisy. After the election Hartman arranged some speaking engagements that gave Lee a lot of ego gratification and about $10,000, plus expenses, for each. Not bad for an hour or two of gab. The relationship was firmly established. Hartman had his

White House entrée. But then came the brain tumor.

With the link through Lee lost, the most obvious line from L.A. to Bush would have been through Ronald Reagan. But even if Hartman had good connections to the Reagan crowd, he wasn't at all sure that the Reagan route was the best way to reach out to the new president. After all, Reagan had beaten Bush quite badly in the 1980 Republican primaries. Then as VP, Bush spent eight years eating Ronald Reagan's shit. Hartman had once been a vice president at Ross-Mogul, at that time the third-largest talent agency in the business. The head of the agency, Allan Ross, recognized David's talent. He helped Hartman to rise very fast and to make a lot of money. That didn't mean that David would ever forgive Allan Ross for once having been his boss. Every star that RepCo stole away from Ross-Mogul brought Hartman deep personal pleasure and the day RepCo finally billed more than Ross-Mogul had been the happiest single day of David Hartman's life.

So Hartman next reached out to Bush through Arnold Schwarzenegger. Schwarzenegger, a clever and ambitious man who had gone further on an astute combination of iron will, pig iron, and steroids[28] than anyone would ever have dreamed, had his own political ambitions and understood very clearly the importance of personal connections.

Arnold dropped David's name at the White House a couple of times. He suggested Bush meet him. That Hartman might be the

---

[28]Like the other gossip and casual character assassinations in this book, we regard this as an unsubstantiated rumor, although *Spy* magazine treats it as established fact: "So let's get this straight: A man who took huge amounts of steroids becomes head of the President's Council on Physical Fitness, but his main worry is that people will think he smokes cigars." (Charlotte Fleming, 3/92) Also, in case anyone doesn't realize it, Hartman is a fictional character and therefore Schwarzenegger, who is represented by a real agent who actually exists, has never done anything with, for, or to David Hartman.

kind of key money fulcrum that Wasserman had been. At some point after Arnold spoke, but before the suggestion was acted on, the president read Lee Atwater's plan. If Hartman, who seemed to be a key part of it, turned out to be one of those loud, pushy, offensive types, that would give the president the opportunity to drop the whole thing. And at least part of him wanted to forget he'd ever read the bizarre but compelling concept. So it was the president who chose Orange County as the meeting ground. The contrast, he hoped, would help him dislike the agent.

Hartman researched and studied people he wanted to deal with. He did not intend to underestimate the president. He was prepared to think the president was shrewd, manipulative, and vindictive, just as he was himself. He had his best reader[29] prepare a synthesized synopsis of several Bush biographies. It hadn't taken much for him to figure out that he should dress like an Eastern banker who had taken a major cut in pay to perform government service. And that he should sound like one. He'd made a list of what to talk about and what not to talk about. He would not, for example, talk about his son's upcoming bar mitzvah and the incredibly lavish plans for it. Although he truly hated golf, he was prepared to talk about greens and bogeys and birdies. He would play down his practice of *kendo* and play up his jogging.

---

[29]Readers are very important lowly people in Hollywood. Anyone with any power or pull has scripts and books and treatments shoved at them all day long. No one has time to read them all. Yet everyone with power or pull is looking for a great property to produce. Hence they employ readers. Readers read and then write the equivalent of a high-school book report, a review that mostly summarizes but also rates. In the rare instance a reader says something is so hot the reader's employer decides to run with it, he or she must then convince others—stars, directors, studio chiefs, name screen writers—to jump on board. None of them will have time to read the property, and they in turn will give it to their readers. Readers are among those thousands in Hollywood with the power to say no. It is also a position from which, legend has it, it is possible to rise.

. . .

Air Force One landed at Orange County's John Wayne Airport at 6:00 P.M. California time, 9:00 P.M. Eastern Standard Time. The limo was waiting along with the various police and Secret Service escorts. The route had been precleared. The president was whisked to the dinner within eighteen minutes. He got out, standing tall and smiling, looking athletic and energetic. He waved at the cameras, said, "Hello, California! Great to be here. I wish I could stay for a round of golf. But if I can't maybe Dan[30] can do it for me." He gave a big thumbs up. Then he went inside.

There were five people for him to say hello to. Four of them were big contributors from previous campaigns. Two were associated with finance and banking, the other two represented defense industries and aerospace. The fifth was David Hartman.

Bush was pleasantly surprised to see that if this had been a police lineup, he wouldn't have picked Hartman out of the group as either the agent or as the Jew. In fact, he looked rather like Brent Scowcroft: balding, serious, but capable of avuncular good humor, with lots of wrinkle lines in his forehead. He was wearing a simple gray suit, a plain white shirt, a muted tie, and, except for a simple gold wedding band and one of the less ostentatious Philipe Patek watches, no jewelry. The image was not shattered when he spoke. He sounded like one of Bush's own kind. No slang, no jive, no Yiddish, none of those funny intonations.

Bush touched the memo tucked in his jacket pocket. He hadn't found Hartman offensive enough to call it off. But with the down-

---

[30]Vice President Quayle. A jocular reference. Quayle was at that time involved in moderate scandal about the use of military jets to take him on golfing trips. A mild irony is that he took most of them with Samuel K. Skinner, later the White House chief of staff, and after that secretary of *transportation*. OK, it's a very mild irony.

side so enormous, he hadn't yet decided to go forward.

So he plunged ahead with what he was there to do. Shake a lot of hands, grin and wink, and make his famous thumbs-up gesture. Everyone in the room had given a minimum of $5,000, most of them $10,000 or more. They were entitled to a little pressing of the flesh and they wanted to go home feeling good. He went through the speech—he eventually went ahead with the speechwriter's version, it was so little different than what he himself wanted to say—with reasonable fervor.

Dinner was over at 8:00 P.M. California time, 11:00 P.M. EST. Air Force One was scheduled for lift off from John Wayne at 9:00 P.M. California time, midnight on the president's biological clock. He was scheduled to meet with the director of the CIA in the White House at 9:00 A.M. EST, with the un-Soviet ambassador at 9:15, then with the ranking minority member of the Senate Judiciary Committee about the selection of nominees for federal judgeships. The only way to survive that sort of schedule was to fall out as soon as he lay down on the presidential bed aboard the 747, sleep all through the flight, no matter how turbulent, even through touchdown, and not wake until the steward came in at 8:00 A.M. EST on the ground back in Washington. The human body won't behave that way on its own. Therefore, with his desert, crème brûlée, the president dropped a Halcion, figuring it would kick in just about the time he got on the plane.

On the way out, as the president was making his final handshaking rounds, the chairman of the California Republican Party fund-raising committee told him that Hartman had just made a $100,000 contribution. Bush was impressed. Not just by the amount, but that Hartman had not waved the money in his face or given it to him directly. The impulse that had been working on him for half the day finally broke through.

He invited Hartman to ride with him back to Air Force One.

Hartman had twelve to eighteen minutes to make a friend. He'd done it far faster than that lots of times. The first thing he said was, "I want to confess something, Mr. President. My conversion to the Republican Party is very recent." This was an old story. Reagan, Heston, Sinatra, and lots of others were all ex-Democrats. Bush was not impressed. "Most of my life I regarded myself as a nonpartisan person whose true loyalty was to business, to the creativity of the economic impulse." More bullshit. "Actually, I was on the fence right up until 1988." Now the president listened. There were lots of so-called Reagan Democrats. No one, he suddenly realized, ever spoke of Bush Democrats. David Hartman had already endeared himself as the first one. "I wasn't that impressed with Mr. Reagan. But you truly impressed me." Music to the president's ears. So many people spoke of Bush as if he were a pale imitation of his predecessor, when it was Reagan who had napped through most of his two terms, never reading or studying, just popping up to perform when the cameras rolled, returning to somnolence as soon as the power was switched off. "I don't want to embarrass you, but I will tell you why. It's not the obvious thing, that you have, probably, the best résumé of anyone who's ever held your office. To me you're the real thing because you were a war hero." The president put on his aw-shucks face.

"To me," Hartman went on, "the great presidents were Ike and Jack Kennedy. I had no use for Johnson, Carter, and Reagan. I didn't think to analyze it until you came along. What was different about you, from Reagan, from Dukakis? I'll tell you. George Herbert Walker Bush, Dwight David Eisenhower, John Fitzgerald Kennedy, they all saw real combat. Let's face it, where was Ron Reagan when the world was at war? He was in Hollywood, with clean sheets and pretty girls, and his uniforms were fresh-pressed every day by the Santa Monica dry cleaners.

"You were out there. Youngest pilot in the Navy. You put

your life on the line. You know what that means.''

''Those were great days,'' the president said, and then asked, as Hartman had wanted him to, ''Were you in the service?''

''Yes, sir,'' Hartman said, making his move.

''Well, you're a little young for the big one, when were you in? What branch of service?''

''I was a Marine, sir. In Korea.''

Bush was pleasantly surprised. ''Well, some Navy men don't think too much of the Army''—this was a good-humored manly remark—''but by God, you can't say anything against the United States Marines. Tell me about your service, Dave. And forget the sir and Mr. President bullshit. Call me George.''

''I have to tell you, sir. It's hard to call the commander in chief George. I'm just too much of a Marine, still, to do that.''

''Well, you can relax, Dave. What'd you do in the service?''

Hartman saw how the table lay, which was exactly how he expected, so he went ahead and played his ace. ''Tell you the truth, sir. I was a pilot. Fighter jock.''

''I'll be a son of a bitch,'' the president said. It had never occurred to him that a Jewish Hollywood agent would have been a Marine fighter pilot in Korea.

''How many missions you fly? How many kills?''

''I only flew five combat missions.''

''How come?'' the president asked.

''I had to ditch in the ocean. I wasn't shot down. I had a fuel-line malfunction, then the engine caught fire. I ejected. Good thing too. On my way down I got to see my plane explode. Thank God for those Air-Sea rescue boys. Actually, I got pulled out by a Navy chopper off of a carrier. You know, sir, better than I do, what it's like to be sitting in a freezing ocean, wondering if it's the first day of the rest of your life. Or the last.[31] Anyway, I hurt my back when I hit the water, and when they couldn't fix it, they gave me my discharge.''

"So I guess you understand how important it is," the president said, "to keep America strong?"

"The most important thing in the world," Hartman said. "Not just for America, for all mankind."

Again, it's possible to ponder the role of coincidence: that Hartman had chosen a way to win the president's confidence which spoke directly to the things the president wanted to discuss with him. But it's more likely that all three of them—the third being Atwater, although he was dead—had simply tuned in to the same thinking about basic themes. Maybe the president would have gone ahead even if Hartman had spoken about banking standards or the need for celebrities to support family values or of his commitment to free trade.

"I have a project," the president said. "You remember Lee Atwater?"

"Very well. I admired him."

"He wrote a memo. He was a good friend," Bush said. "The baddest good ol' boy. I had a lot of fun with Lee. He thought well of you. Did you know he played blues guitar?"

"He was an excellent person."

"This is a concept thing. He said, before he died, that you're the person, what with today's Hollywood. When a friend writes

---

[31]On September 2, 1944, George Bush's plane was hit by antiaircraft fire while making a bombing run over Chichi Jima, about 150 miles north of the better-known Iwo Jima. Pilots made every effort to ditch at sea. Japanese POW camps were reputed to be terrible places. The one on Chichi Jima was run by a Major Matoba. After the war he was reported to have cut up prisoners and fed the pieces to other prisoners. With his plane on fire, Bush managed to get out over water, where he jumped. He landed in the ocean without major injury. He found his life raft—though without water or paddles. He was rescued several hours later by submarine.

a deathbed memo, you have to do what you have to do. I have to swear you to secrecy.''

You have my oath. As an American. As a Marine.''[32]

''The word of a United States Marine. You can't ask for much more than that,'' the president said. It may be that at this point the Halcion was kicking in. According to the president's own schedule, it certainly should have been.[33]

The president sat silent, trying to figure out how to formulate what Atwater had proposed. Then he suddenly wondered if they

---

[32]According to U.S. Army records, Hartman, a draftee, served one year in the Army, not the Marines. He never rose above private. He did receive a medical discharge. However, his previous boss, Steve Ross, had been a Marine pilot in Korea, spoke of it often, and had a collection of military aviation books and memorabilia in the office. The story Hartman tells here, while similar to the president's, is virtually identical to Steve Ross's.

[33]The use of Halcion is controversial. Many, like the president's doctor, consider it totally safe.

Benjamin J. Stein, identified as a lawyer, writer, actor, and ex-speechwriter for President Nixon, said this in an op-ed piece in the *New York Times*, 1/22/92: ''. . . Halcion is the most terrifying drug I have ever used and its effects are incalculably more frightening when they are at work on the President. I have been taking prescription tranquilizers since 1966. I have used almost every kind imaginable . . . but Halcion . . . is in a class by itself for mind-altering side effects. It is not just a classic sedative which basically just slows things down. No, benzodiazepenes are described by Halcion's maker, the Upjohn Company, as 'anxiolytics,' meaning they cut the anxiety in your brain.

"When Halcion hits you, it's as if an angel of the Lord appears in your bedroom and tells you that nothing is important, that what you were worried about is happening on Mars and that Nirvana, Lethe and the warm arms of mother are all waiting for you. People who have used heroin tell me Halcion is better than heroin for making bad thoughts simply disappear. . . . It clouds judgment and forecloses careful analysis. It makes the user alternately supremely confident and then panicky. . . .

"A friend of mine took a small dose of Halcion—less than what the President is reported taking—and then carried a gun through a metal detector at an airport. He had forgotten not only that he had a gun with him but also that guns are illegal at airports.''

were being recorded. Not by some foreign spy but by his own people. Look what had happened to Nixon. Speech was never safe. Although they had decided never to show the memo to anyone, he and Baker, somehow showing it seemed—better. Clearer, easier, and safer. He reached into his pocket.

"I want you to look at this," the president said, and gave Hartman the memo. The limo turned past the gate and entered John Wayne. As it crossed the tarmac to *Air Force One,* Hartman read.

Hartman had admired Atwater's destruction of Dukakis. Lee had happened to see that the America of '88 would vote *for* a waving flag and *against* violent, sexual, black males. He happened to be running a presidential campaign, so that's the choice he offered the public. What else, Hartman thought, should he have done? Most people either lack the capacity for thought or they're too lazy to employ it. They shroud themselves in the fog of conventional morality and substitute knee-jerk sentimentality for thought-out reactions. Lee had refused to be that sort of cripple. Good for him.

But this memo put Atwater in a whole different class. This was beyond intellectual rigor and unsentimental honesty—this required real audacity, this was true clarity. Atwater had proved a most worthy student of Sun Tzu and Clausewitz and Machiavelli. If he had been there, Hartman would have bowed in a formal gesture of respect, as they do in the east, to a teacher, someone to learn from and to emulate.

But Atwater was dead and gone. Hartman didn't believe in ghosts, or at least not in ghosts who listen. His tribute to Atwater was that he was the first to read the memo who didn't say, "Jesus fucking Christ. Atwater's fucking in-fucking-sane." He turned to the president. He thought of a hundred different things he could say. His actual favorite was: George, I don't know if you've ever used an agent before. We get ten percent. Of everything. But it's not what he said. He thought of Oliver North, sat up as straight as the limo seat allowed, his back in a fair imitation of military posture. "Sir," he said, raising his right hand, touching his fingertips to his eyebrow in a salute, "you do me great honor. In giving me this opportunity to serve you and my country. Thank you, sir."

CHAPTER

* * *

FOURTEEN

The event of the season is the bar mitzvah of David Hartman, Jr.,[34] son of David Hartman, head of RepCo, most powerful, most ruthless, most important agent in Hollywood. A select list of 250 are invited. Twenty of them are friends of the thirteen-year-old boy. The rest are people in the industry. It is *the* most sought after invitation, it defines who is who, it is the ultimate A-list.

The cost of the catering, as released to the press, is substantially over $100,000. The cost of the party is hard to calculate. Entertainment is supposed to include performances by Michael Jackson and Bobby and several people I have never hear of. These people will not charge for their services and may, or may not, provide their backup musicians, roadies, mixers, special-effects personnel, light-and-laser shows as part of their homage.

One of the themes of the party—at least for the kids—is Ninjas. There is some talk that this is tastelessly self-serving. Hartman is a student of kendo, the Japanese art of sword fighting. His sensei, or

[34]Jewish Jr.'s are rare, II's and III's even rarer. It is considered ''bad luck'' to name someone after someone living. However, this is merely a custom, not an actual religious prohibition.

teacher, is a Japanese swordsman named Sakura Juzo. It is common gossip that Hartman's devotion to kendo is part of his rivalry with Michael Ovitz. Ovitz is devoted to aikido, a martial art invented in the forties, also in Japan. Hartman whenever he discusses martial arts, points out that kendo, the way of the sword, contains the real teachings of Bushido, the way of the samurai, and that all the movements of aikido are actually based on—that is, derivative of—movements developed for the sword.

Hartman is the prime mover behind a movie called *American Ninja,* which stars Sakura Juzo as a Japanese Ninja master with a group of youthful American disciples who engage in virtually supernatural acts of derring-do in the service of truth, justice, and the American way. Hartman personally pitched it to David Geffen, describing it as *Batman* combined with *The Mod Squad* for the nineties, containing the spiritual and competitive values we should learn from the East.

Again, this is partly ascribed to his rivalry with Mike Ovitz,[35] who

---

[35]I guess it's time to deal with this.

Certain details may lead some readers to think that Hartman is a thinly disguised Ovitz.

When I began to research the "Hollywood" portion of this book, something I know less about than the average viewer of *Entertainment Tonight,* I asked my then West Coast agent, Michael Siegal, to find me a researcher who could pull up some articles about various subjects including major packagers, like Mike Ovitz, since the concept of packaging was central to the events. His assistant called back the next day with a name—someone who did a very adequate job—but he also said, "If your next book concerns Mike Ovitz, Michael [Siegal] doesn't want to represent it."

I repeat that story to give the reader an insight into the power that someone like Ovitz commands. Subsequently the reaction was repeated. Two things are worth noting. One is that these people did not wait for Mr. Ovitz to express disapproval or distaste, they anticipated for him that he might, and that was sufficient. The second is that no one has yet suggested that they feared, or that I should fear, the reactions of the [then] President or the [then] Secretary of State who are not "characters like," but named George Bush and James Baker.

And, of course, I want to confront the issue of whether this is a thinly disguised portrait of Ovitz and if it is and he doesn't like it, or even if *his people* think he is credited with making a movie star out of his sensei, aikido instructor Stephen Siegal.

Japan bashers and paranoids have accused Hartman of having more sinister motives than competition with a rival agent. That he is actually in the service of Japanese masters, who desire to create a new mythology, an illusion of Japanese-American cooperation but with the Japanese as the sensei of the Americans, now become the students. To the Japanese, in whose culture all relationships are hierarchical, this is a powerful statement indeed. Hartman's motives are, of course, described as financial. This film and his sponsorship of Sakura Juzo will establish him as a friend of the Japanese and they will therefore use him as point man, advisor, and deal broker as they buy up America, a position so lucrative it makes mere movie packaging look like spit.

Sakuro and his top students, several of whom have been flown over from Japan, will give a kendo demonstration. All the stuntmen from the film will be present. There will be lessons for children of all ages in how to become invisible, how to infiltrate Oriental castles, how to kill in complete silence, and other things that thrill thirteen-year-old boys.

Food will be both American and Japanese. Sushi chefs have been flown over from Japan. They specialize in serving live sushi, currently the hottest food trend in Tokyo. Included on the menu is puffer fish, also flown over, live, a fish which if not correctly prepared will cause paralysis and death. Serving it in America is illegal.

The party will be filmed in 35 mm, utilizing seven cameras. Marty

---

wouldn't like it, does that mean I will never work in that town again? And am I afraid of that?

You bet I am. A writer can make more bucks off one film flop than a best-selling book.

So, Mike, let me say this to you: this is not a thinly disguised portrait of you. If anything, it is a sort of homage, in general, to how important agents and packagers have become in our society and how truly creative their underrated contributions can be.

Scorcese will direct. Vilmos Zsigmond will be the director of photography. This is both serious and something of an in-joke. David senior's first foray into the film industry, way before he discovered being an agent, was to try to make bar mitzvah movies in his old hometown of Montreal.

It is the first time Maggie is going to meet with Hartman since they had the lunch she told me about. It is also a major see-and-be-seen event, to which Maggie responds competitively. The preparation process takes several days. Selecting her clothes. Getting them tailored and retailored. Changing her mind. Getting extra exercise to firm up and slim down the already perfect form. Getting extra sleep to look radiant and rested.

She gets the guest list and goes through it name by name. Then she starts working the phones. She double-checks who is still married, who is freshly divorced, who she can ask about their children and who's children are best not referred to. There are a few names she doesn't know, mostly Japanese from Sony, Matsushita, and Musashi corporations. She finds out about them. Whether they're from Osaka or Tokyo or the country, if they have wives and children with them or left them behind, if they play golf or tennis. She has a terrific memory, but she jots the information down on file cards nonetheless.

With this much activity I am pushed further into the background. I am not even driving her to the party. Limousine service is being provided by the major studios. The party is to begin in the early evening.

I could take the night off as Mrs. Mulligan has done and go somewhere on my own. Part of me wants to go find some whore that looks vaguely like Maggie, the same color hair, cut the same way might be enough, or a torso about the same shape and size.

But I don't. I stay home. I crack open a bottle of bourbon. I sit down and read the copy of Sun Tzu that Kim gave me.

Actually, I have been reading *The Art of War* since Preston Griffith gave me a copy in Saigon in 1970. Griff was CIA and an opium smoker. He said that he had had many people killed. Reading Sun

Tzu brought him great despair. But he said for someone like me it would bring strength.

It was written sometime between 480 and 221 B.C. It's very Oriental, and the first time you try to read it, it's like trying to get serious about a fortune cookie. "Nature is the dark or light, the cold or hot, and the Systems of time." Or "Those who are certain to capture what is attacked, attack locations that are not defended." On top of that, every translation you read is different. So you wonder what he really said. If he said anything.

But we were in Nam. Where we had the firepower, the logistics, the organization, and the money. On paper we even had the manpower. And we were losing—to General Giap, who read Sun Tzu. And we lost China to Mao Tse-tung, who read Sun Tzu. We got our butt kicked, at least for a while, in Korea, by other generals who read Sun Tzu.

So even if he sounds like Ding Bat Woo, I have to understand that the problem is in my listening, not in his speaking. After I became a sergeant and got my own squad, I began to use what he said as well as I could. It worked. It helped me to save my people and to kill the enemy. When we had a captain who insisted on violating the principles of Sun Tzu, we had great trouble and many of us died.

At first I don't like this translation. In fact, I resent it. Sun Tzu wrote about war. Real war. This book changes *War* to *Strategy* and calls itself the "World's Most Widely Read Manual of Skillful Negotiations and Lasting Influence." It is aimed at those business people who would like to think that business competition is war, that lawyers and accountants and agents are soldiers in the field, that money is blood, that a neurotic tic is the equivalent of life in a chair in a VA hospital, needing someone to wipe your ass and change the urine tube coming out of your dick. But if I refuse to hear what is said because I am prejudiced, then I am as blind as the men who lead us in Vietnam. So I try to listen as one who is ignorant to one who is wise.

The sentence to which Kim pointed is, *The strategy of positioning evades Reality and confronts through Illusion.* It is in chapter 6, which is called, in this translation, "Illusions and Reality (Using Camouflage)." The standard translation is "Weakness and Strength." The translator's commentary says, "The idea of creating illusions to obscure reality is a specific tactical maneuver designed to keep the opponent at a constant disadvantage."

It is a very empty house without Maggie there.

I try to stay sober and come close to succeeding. I go into the screening room and watch Maggie's films. The bottle comes with me. At some point I doze off. I awaken around 3 A.M. I have to piss and my mouth tastes like death. The house is still empty.

Shortly thereafter a car pulls in. Not the limo. It's Maggie come home. With a ride or with someone. It's not my place to be waiting up and watching for her. To appear to do so would be—bad strategy. I go upstairs to my room. I leave the door open so I can hear, go across the room and look out the window to see the car they've arrived in. It's a white Ferrari 348 with the top down.

I hear the door. I hear the footsteps. Then the laughter floats up to my room. She sounds high. I can't help but go to the bedroom door and look down. She is somewhat disheveled. I'm like an aged and jealous husband looking at a young and lively wife. Her nipples are distended. Erect and popping out. Is that from the cool air and the ride in the open car? Or is it the man she's with: Jack Cushing, who plays young pilots and soldiers and gunslingers and spends a lot of screen time with his shirt off. His muscles have lots of definition. In his own way, I suppose, he's as good-looking as she is. His eyes are famously blue and Fredo does his hair too.

They're talking about who said what and who did what and reliving the party. But the subtext is what it always is. He wants her and she's not sure. He wants it as soon as possible. She wants to drag out every measure of admiration and ego fulfillment that she can before she commits. Apparently, the Hollywood gossip has not taken Maggie off the A-list. At the party the famous actress-turned-director came on to her so strong that her current girlfriend stalked out of the party early. Someone, I didn't hear who, told Maggie—in front of

Melanie Griffith—that she had the most beautiful figure in films. Melanie was furious and shook her tits at whoever it was who spoke. Maggie, telling the story, does a deadly imitation of Melanie.

"Are those really real?" Jack says.

"You bet," Maggie says. "A hundred percent homegrown organic, no preservatives added."

"I don't believe you. They're too good. Let me do the touch test," he says. "You know, these are infallible fingers. They can always tell."

Maggie says, "I need the ocean air." She rushed away from him and goes out on the deck.

Now I can't hear them. I step out of the shadows of my room onto the walk that runs around the living room so I can see them better. The wind coming off of the water plays with her hair. I'm in some damn nightmare of a movie. He sidles up beside her. He touches her hair. She responds with pleasure. He puts his other hand on her back, running it down to her hip. She moves away. But not far. Now they're side by side. He turns to face her. She keeps looking out. He puts a hand on her shoulder, gently turns her so that they're looking right at each other. She doesn't make eye contact with him. He lifts her chin with his fingers. They make eye contact. Shit. This is it. You might as well cut away or cut to the hard-core from here.

Yeah, he lowers his mouth to hers and she lets him kiss her.

Didn't I just play this scene with her. Damn her.

Then his arms go around her and she lets him pull her close. Her breasts against his chest. Him feeling her nipples hard. Her belly against his sculpted, every-day-at-the-gym-with-his-personal-trainer torso. The bottom of her belly, the soft rounded part feeling his cock, stiff or not. The mound of her against the thigh that he rubs gently between her legs. His hands find the shape of her ass.

He's gyrating into her. She moves against him. My mouth is dry, my heart beats high in my chest. I should leave. Find a place to be that's far, far away. I can't even take one step back and hide in my room. I watch mesmerized.

He lifts her dress. The skin of her legs is so smooth and fair in the moonlight. His mouth on her neck and shoulders.

She pushes him away. Panting. Her eyes are shining, her lips swollen and wet.

She backs into the house. He follows. They leave the door to the deck open so the night can come in, blowing cool against the fevers. Now they start again. Slower, but just as intense. Totally stoned into sex. I'm watching a porno film of two of Hollywood's top stars and I'm lucky I don't have a gun in my hand.

He unhooks her dress. It slides off her shoulders. Beautiful unblemished skin. His mouth moves down her neck to her collar bone. His hands push the dress lower. She lets him push it down to her waist. She covers her breasts with her hands. Half-naked, half-defensive.

Now he falls to his knees in front of her. He eases the dress the rest of the way down. His hands come back up, caressing from ankle to buttock. His head moves forward and he begins to kiss her belly. She sighs with pleasure. Damn her. His mouth is finding it's way down, toward the fine line of lace that covers her mound. His tongue snakes between the fabric and the flesh. Her hands are on his head. Her head tilts back in anticipation of the pleasures to come. Her eyes are closed.

Then they open and she is looking into my eyes.

Up on the balcony, watching her. God knows what she sees in them.

"Stop," she says to Jack.

He makes a sound in his throat and pushes his mouth downward.

"Stop," she says again.

He doesn't. She pulls away. He holds tight. She puts her hand in his face and pushes back at him.

"What the fuck's the matter with you?" he says.

"Stop," she says.

"Magdalena, baby," he says in his sexiest voice. He looks at her. He sees that she's not looking at him, but upward. So he looks up too. He sees me. "Who the fuck is that?"

"My . . ."

". . . chauffeur and bodyguard." I say.

She's standing there, nipples popping, naked but for her panties, his saliva drying at the bottom her belly.

"Get rid of him," he says.

"Yes, Joe. You should go."

"No," I say. Much to my surprise. This is not what is planned.

"Jesus, fire this asshole," Jack says.

"I can't do that," Maggie says.

"Of course you can," Jack says.

"Joe," she says. "You should go. You really should."

"I wish to God I could."

"Listen, the lady said go. Now go. Or I'll make you go."

I walk slowly down the stairs. I should go. She's not mine. She didn't give me permission, or an invitation. Maggie's body's been warm. Perspiring lightly. Now the breeze is evaporating the moisture. Her skin is alive with goose bumps. I've never seen so much life in a woman.

"Beat it, dude," Jack says.

In spite of myself, I say no.

Everybody in Hollywood does some kind of martial arts. Jack does *taijutsu*. That is the technique they're teaching at Ninja, the trendiest martial arts school in L.A., which is run by Sakura Juzo.

I'm shorter than Jack. Fifteen, twenty years older. My thickness looks like weight. Plus, everybody's brain is in their dick at this point. He thinks he's going to take me out with a Ninja attack that he's been studying for six months. He assumes a stance. Goes for a quick strike. Maggie yells, "No." I block. I step inside. I'm a close-in guy. I hit him hard, a straight punch into the solar plexus.

And it's over.

Jack is on the ground gasping for air. I pick him up. Put him over my shoulder in a fireman's carry. His gasps are desperate. Which is what happens when you take a hard shot in the solar plexus, it just pops the air right out of you, the lungs collapse with an internal vacuum effect and you can't get them to open again. Not right away.

Until you can, it's terrifying. Even if it's happened to you before. Which I don't think it has, to Jack.

"Stop it," Maggie says. "He's hurt, Joe. He's really hurt."

"No," I say. Because he's not. And I know it. I take him outside to the car. Maggie dragging along beside me, naked and, I think, loving the scene. I certainly am—now. I dump the movie star down beside his Ferrari. He's starting to get his breath. His erection is definitely gone.

"You got your car keys?" I ask.

"Fuck you. I'll kill you. Kill you. Sue you. You're dead, dead in this town . . . fucking weirdos . . ." he says from the ground.

"You'll catch cold," I say to Maggie and lead her back inside.

CHAPTER

* * *

FIFTEEN

It was Tuesday, 5 P.M. Mel Taylor drove down to Little Saigon. The two women were waiting for him, chattering and laughing in that lovely, feminine Vietnamese way.

He wondered once again why it was that American women couldn't be that way—exotic, erotic, inventive, always lovely and trim, willing and able to really please a man, in short, subservient and good at it. Most people bitched and moaned about the war. And every time you saw a vet on TV or in the movies or in the news, they were miserable and screwed up. Mel wasn't. He'd had what the British used to call "a good war." The Saigon years had been, in many ways, "the best years of his life." No question. The women, the food, the gracious living. In Vietnam he'd been a rich man. He'd had servants: cook, house cleaner, laundry boy. He'd been a powerful man, with an adoring mistress, whom he merely had to keep, not to answer to or be faithful to. What did he have in America? A microwave, a Hoover, a Westinghouse, and a wife.

The dishes out of the microwave didn't taste anything like the French-influenced Asian cooking in Vietnam; the Hoover didn't bow and put fresh flowers in the bedroom; the Westinghouse didn't fold and iron; and the wife ran to fat, though monogamy was the natural order of things, and failed to worship him at all.

Mel was actually early. Not by more than three or four minutes. But certainly early. And he was erect inside his pants when he walked in. That was unusual. No delicate little butterfly touches to cleverly coax blood down to engorge the spongelike cells of the penis, causing it to enlarge and stiffen, step by tiny step. No warm bath in a pretty mouth, where it could measure it's own increase against tongue, teeth, cheeks, and throat. This last being a measure that proved how large and potent he must be, for even the experienced mama-san had to retreat when Taylor swelled to his full status.

Taylor had been listening to the tape. Over and over, for days. The tape of the night that Magdalena Lazlo came home with Jack Cushing and Joe Broz punched him out. The night that the microphones heard, and the linked slow-play Panasonics recorded, the sounds of Magdalena Lazlo submitting to the lust and passion of Joe Broz. They'd gone at it for hours. Moans of desire, shouts of orgasm, subtle sounds of moisture, a variety of endearments, endless praise for each other's body parts, encouragement and satisfaction.

A new day, a new tape. They sent Mary Mulligan away and they'd gone at it again. The first day they'd started hard and fast and ended sensual and slow, with sleepy endearments. The second, they'd started slow and tender, but it got away from them quickly and they became animals, grunting and—Taylor could swear he could feel it on the tape—sweating.

Somewhere in the middle—Taylor didn't know why he remembered it, fixated on it—maybe because amidst all that moaning and sighing it had been so unexpected. A vividness, like a child's bright plastic toy, cartoon colors, in the middle of a flesh-tone landscape. Somewhere in the middle, giggling, Maggie said, "You know what the best part of being your lover is going to be, Joe? Do you know?"

"No. What's the best part?"

"It's going to be dressing you."

"Aww, come on."

"We're going to start with those gym socks of yours. No more white socks, except for running. Then we're going to get you underwear and ties and shirts and slacks and shoes and I'm going to get Fredo to do something with your hair."

Which is where they were now. Taylor knew. They'd finally left the house, after two days behind closed doors, except for a run on the beach and splash in the sea. He had a two-man team on them. They'd last reported in when Maggie took Joe into an exclusive men's store on Rodeo Drive at 2:00 P.M.

Taylor stripped. He tossed his clothes on the chair in the corner. The mama-san folded them neatly. The daughter-san gaped with respectful awe at his organ. He walked over to the massage table. With each step his erection bounced up and flopped sideways, describing an eccentric oval that leaned toward the right and was wider at the bottom than the top. He hopped up on the massage table.

Mama-san rushed to hand him his brandy. He slurped it down, felt the burn, and lay back with his head on the pillow. The sheet beneath him was clean and crisp and just about body temperature.

"Oh, you are very strong today, Captain Taylor. Very powerful," the daughter said. He'd been in the ROTC, entered the Army as a lieutenant, then rose to the rank of captain in Vietnam.

"Oh my, yes. You are a giant," the mother said.

"I am afraid to touch it," the daughter said. It was obviously fake whore talk. But fake was not the issue, was it? The issue was whether a woman wanted a man to feel good, to feel strong and manly. To feel respected and powerful.

"Do not be afraid," the mother said. "Come, I will show you."

She took her daughter's hands and placed them on the stiff penis.

At the first touch, much to the surprise of all three of them, it began to ejaculate.

Always before, by design, it had taken a full hour. And then, when it did, it spurted hugely, in a high and perfect arc, like the arc of urine of an undiapered infant boy lying on his back, reaching at least as high up as Taylor's own chest, sometimes as high as his head. An ejaculation of power and grandeur.

But this. This just spilled. It spilled out the tip and dripped down and kept on spilling in small, powerless pulses until he was empty. It was a dribble. It didn't even feel like an orgasm. The big ejaculations felt like something. You bet they did. They were timeless, wordless screams of ecstasy. This was nothing. He'd received greater sensation and achieved more release from taking a plain old piss than from this.

Taylor was angry. He felt ripped off. "You fucked up," he snarled to the women. "You fucked up."

They said something in Vietnamese. And giggled. Taylor found the giggles, in this situation, to be entirely without charm. In fact, they were infuriating. They were laughing at him. Laughing at an American. He hopped off the table and loomed over them. "Goddamn you, you bitches, you fucked up." The mama-san started to apologize, but Taylor said, "If you think I'm going to pay you for this, you're out of your fucking mind."

This started an argument as to whether he was paying by the hour or per ejaculation. There was justice to both sides of the case, and an outside arbitrator certainly could have settled it rapidly and even with good feeling all around: "Girls, do 'em again, and Mel, tip 'em an extra fifty." But their giggles and his threat not to pay had pushed each other's fear and anger buttons. Each immediately brought baggage to the conflict. It was no longer Mel against the girls; it had become customer versus whore, male versus female, Caucasian versus Asian, America versus Vietnam.

It got loud fast and promised to become violent almost as fast. But a slim young Vietnamese male stepped through the door. He had a large, dramatic scar on his face and a pair of nun-chucks in his hand. Gangster, pimp, enforcer, husband, or brother, Taylor had no way of knowing. But that was not the point. The point was pay and leave quietly.

Normally, Taylor paid on his Visa card, which showed up on his monthly statement as a reasonably respectable restaurant bill. In his house the man paid the bills so there was no reason for his wife to ask him why he spent two hundred dollars every week at the same

Vietnamese restaurant. But if she ever did, Mel had rehearsed an answer. He would say that he and a bunch of old Army buddies met once a week to reminisce, everybody chipped in cash, and Mel put it on his card. Then he would explain that by doing that he got a free thirty-day ride on the money, pull out his calculator, and befuddle Silvia with dazzling fiscal footwork.

Taylor was not about to stand there with his own ejaculate turning cold and drying around his pubic hair while some scarred-up Vietnamese thug ran his Wells Fargo Visa through a credit-card machine and the automatic telephone dialer to register electronic approval and record the transaction. Nor was he going to pay the full amount, if he could help it. So he stomped into his clothes and grabbed for his cash. He crumbled up a bunch of twenties, flung them on the ground, and made for the door. The younger woman picked them up quicker than a snake, flattened and counted them. The kid gangster barred the door. There was only eighty bucks. They all made noises at him. He dragged out some more money. The mama-san snatched it from his hand before he could crumble it and throw it down. It was another four twenties, all he had except for five singles and some silver. Apparently, it was enough, because they stepped aside and let him go.

CHAPTER

✶ ✶ ✶

SIXTEEN

It just seemed simpler for the
president to give him the memo. If Hartman had taken notes, then
there would have been two documents to worry about. He probably could have committed it to memory, but memory is a trickster
and a traitor. Besides, *Air Force One* was ready to depart.

Frankly, George Bush was glad to be rid of it. It was like an
imp in his pocket, a fairy-tale creature of great potential mischief
who always seemed to be tugging at the presidential awareness,
asking to be let loose. OK, now it was loose and somebody else's
problem. Hartman could either tame it and make it useful or Bush
could simply forget it ever existed. There was just the one piece
of paper. Nobody could even prove that Bush had ever seen it. Or
for that matter, that Lee Atwater had actually written it.

Hartman knew it was the biggest opportunity of his life.

He cleared an entire day. No meetings. No calls. No conferences. No letters. No contracts. No interruptions. No lawyers. No
reading. No nothing.

Perhaps the only way to convey what a profound gesture that
was is to say that he had no intention of clearing an entire day to
die. That if he were a woman, he would not have cleared an entire

day to give birth.

He began the day by going to the dojo at dawn. There he practiced kendo, first in early-morning class and then alone with the sensei, Sakura Juzo, to quiet his body and empty his mind. That much physical concentration and effort created pain. Hartman loved the pain. Only when he had forgotten everything except the pain, gone through the pain, and *transcended* it, did he return to his office, remove the memo from the safe for the first time since the night he had received it, read it, and contemplate what he had to do.

He knew that this was not a done deal. Far from it. He now had to go back to the president and say, "This is how it can be executed." The last thing in the world that Hartman was afraid of was pitch meetings. And really, that's all that it was. Except that most of the time, if Columbia didn't buy it, he'd take it to MCA, and if they didn't like it, he'd go to Paramount or MGM or Disney. This time, there was only one place to go.

Or maybe there were other places to go. He put that thought into a box, closed the lid tight, locked it and stored it back in the cabinet that he visualized as being in the upper-left rear quadrant of his brain.

He ruminated, he sketched out ideas on paper—which he would shred before he left the office—he meditated on the nature of war. Like Atwater and Sakura Juzo, he was a follower of Sun Tzu. The phrase that came into his mind was "War is nothing but lies,"[36] and this made him chuckle to himself.

It seemed to him that there were four areas in which he had

---

[36]Sun Tzu, as translated in A. L. Sadler, *Three Military Classics of China* (University of Sydney, Austalaisian Medical Publishing Company, Ltd., 1944), Also translated as "All Warfare is based on deception"(Samuel B. Griffith,) or "Those who strategize, use the Tao of Paradox," (R.L. Wing), or, most prosaically, "A military operation involves deception." (Thomas Cleary)

to act. They were all overlapping and interlocked: pick a director, maintain secrecy, handle the media, deal with the money.

He had to pick a director. This was the easiest thing. Preferably a director-writer. That would eliminate one person with a need to *know*. The director would have to develop a vision, a scenario, in treatment[37] form initially, with which Hartman would pitch the president.

He would have to come up with a plan to maintain secrecy. Under normal circumstances whenever Hartman was dealing with something major, he assembled a team. They batted things around. Criticized each other's ideas. Brainstormed. Explored potential consequences. But Hartman felt that secrecy was so essential to this affair, the first rule of the whole enterprise was that no one should know anything more than they absolutely needed to know.

As soon as one other person knew, security arrangements would have to go into effect. That person would have to be watched and monitored. His or her associates, friends, lovers, family too. The more people who knew, the more watchers would be needed. Hartman had spied on people in the past, including of course his own staff. All the major agencies, and even the minor ones, were created by agents going independent and taking clients with them. That is, by stealing. Hartman, who had founded RepCo precisely that way, was determined that it would never happen to him. Whenever an agent got hot enough that he was likely to get

---

[37]A treatment is a summary of a screenplay. It frequently functions as a pitch as well. It is also an actual stage in development of a screenplay, meaning that there is payment at that point and the producer will use the summary to decide to stop, go ahead, go back, or change writers. Treatments have become almost universal. There are several reasons. One is that there is less to read. Second is that it reduces the screenplay to subject and structure, which is what a great many people believe are the important parts. A third is that it requires less commitment of time and money—a short treatment, 3 to 10 pages, can be created in a matter of hours (including typing), while a full 120-page screenplay can take longer.

ideas, his calls were monitored and his movements checked. If surveillance indicated that the agent harbored traitorous thoughts, action was taken. Sometimes the action was benign—a raise, a new car, a bonus, some demonstration of the rewards of loyalty. Sometimes it was malignant—abrupt dismissal, with the suggestion to any of his possible clients that the would-be traitor had been dismissed for dipping his beak, in one sense or the other, plus notification that if they went with him, they would never, ever, participate in a project over which RepCo had influence. The point being that Hartman had a very clear understanding of what surveillance and security cost—a lot.

Hartman had a rule: Never put money into a movie. It was an explicit part of the corporate culture at RepCo: if an agent hears himself say the words "I believe in this so much that I'm going to develop it myself," he'd better be lying. Once it's his own money—coming or going—fear and greed, doubt and delusion, all enter the mind, and objectivity and balance are lost.

Yet perhaps it was time for a change. This might be a necessary part of the Next Step. The warrior strove to be calm at the center, but how profound was clarity from the bleachers above the battle? How difficult to achieve if you collected your 10 percent, win, lose, or draw? How did you even know if you were a warrior— that ultimate male creature—unless you were tested in the arena?

Upon more reflection, however, he decided that the true test of himself as a creative person—the proof that he was better than other people—would be to do it all with *Other People's Money*.[38]

He was going to need—a lot. A million here, a couple of million there—Jesus Christ, he could visualize situations in which he would need billions. This was to be the biggest motion picture ever made. If it were made. There would be hundreds of billions

[38] A 1992 film starring Danny De Vito; from a stage play.

spent. Could the federal government handle that? Probably not, he thought, they were so bad at handling money. The next level would be figuring out for them how to do their part. Never trust the client to be competent.

Deep Throat said, "Follow the money."[39]

Hartman was determined that this would not be another Watergate. That no one would be able to track the cash flow. The politicians had learned. They'd proved that in the Iran-contra affair, which demonstrated that a little obfuscation and lots of denial went a long way. People were still asking "What did the President know and when did he know it?" Although the answer was obvious and incontrovertible: he knew as much as he wanted to, whenever he wanted to. Which was probably all of it and as soon as he got up from his nap. Then Vice President Bush didn't nap, so he probably knew it sooner.

They'd gotten away with it, but they hadn't gotten away clean. Bottom line: it reinforced Hartman's basic thinking—that he himself could find better ways to clandestinely move billions out of the federal government and keep the media from ever figuring it out than the government itself could.

Hartman also had a gut feeling that handling the media might not be a major problem.

But he also knew that this would be what the president and his people would be most afraid of. Obviously, they were drawing on different reservoirs of experience. In the Industry the media was totally pussy-whipped. Nobody was afraid of television or the press. If a reporter didn't mind his manners, he was cut out of the loop. If he truly offended, he was fired.[40] Yet politicians saw the

---

[39]*All the President's Men* (1976), with Robert Redford, Dustin Hoffman, and Jason Robards, Jr. Also based on a true story.

[40]Joseph McBride reviewed *Patriot Games* for *Daily Variety*. He accurately described

press as carnivores: jackals and wolverines who, if they hunted in a pack, were capable of bringing down moose and elk and even elephants.

If he could understand why the Industry experienced the media so differently from politicians, then he could develop a plan to handle the media. What if you took a Hollywood press agent and put him in Washington? A kind of *Northern Exposure* thing. Like *Hollywood Doc, The Hard Way,*[41] a fish-in-different-water thing.

And why not? Develop it as a motion picture. The most creative minds in the world were in Hollywood, because that's where the most money was. Hartman had a lunch scheduled the next day with Mike Medavoy, chairman of Tri-Star. If he mentioned that it might be a good picture for—Val Kilmer? No. Michael J. Fox? Yes. Of course, Medavoy would want a Michael Fox picture. They'd kick around the names of a couple of writers, and by the time the salad drizzled with walnut oil and splashed with Oregon blackberry vinegar was cleared from the table, the story would be in development.[42] On Tri-Star's money.

----

the film as a "right wing cartoon of the current British-Irish political situation" that takes "the side of the British occupying forces and their CIA allies." He said the direction was "laughable" and the score was "full of discordant and insulting riffs on Irish folk music." Paramount halted all advertising in the paper. The editor of *Daily Variety*, Peter Bart, sent a letter of apology to Paramount. The reviewer, a respectable and professional writer about films who had worked for *Daily Variety* since the seventies, was subsequently dismissed. Both Paramount and *Daily Variety* have explanations as to why this is not censorship. Bernard Weinraub, *New York Times*, 6-9-92.

[41] A Jewish doctor from New York practices in alaska; a Hollywood plastic surgeon practices in a rural area; a Hollywood movie star works with a real NYPD cop.

[42] "Development" is that period, also the process, between deciding to make a property into a motion picture or television production—a property can be an idea, a treatment, a news story, a book, a script, a previous movie—and the moment when the camera begins to roll. Lots of things go into "development,"

That was the ticket.

Do the same thing with "a Hollywood press agent goes to Vietnam," a period thing. For Oliver Stone? No. Stone wasn't going to do another Nam picture; it wouldn't even sound right. For Val Kilmer—as a drama, not a comedy, place it over at Columbia, promise them someone young, beautiful, and hot as the female lead. Someone Peters hadn't slept with yet. The thing was to get intellectual writers on both. The tedious types who always got involved with *issues* and *serious ideas* and *real meat* in the sugar coating.

Hartman was on a roll.

The roll kept turning and up came the solution to solving the money problem—its name was Ed Pandar. Pandar was an obsessed and brilliant researcher who wrote terrible screenplays. When Hartman had time, which was rare, he loved to read Pandar screenplays. They were always about things that nobody had ever thought of, and they were always thoroughly, absolutely, and explicitly true. Which was what made them so terrible. They were trapped in morasses of reality. No story could rise up and conquer the thick, rank swamp of facts; no dialogue could overcome the necessity of endless exposition.

Hartman decided to come up with a client who would hire Pandar to develop a script based on bilking the Feds out of—name a figure—$10 billion. Under the guise of developing the ultimate caper film, Pandar would research a method, several methods, by

---

not many come out. The major parts of this process are developing a shooting script, assembling a package of actors and a director that will appeal to the money people, and getting the money. The people who do development are producers. Large producers have "development people"; the largest producers have "development departments." Producers pay themselves when they are developing. That is the bulk of the cost of development.

which billions of dollars could move from the U.S. Treasury into private hands. Because it was Pandar—who was clinically insane but compulsively actual—the scam would be doable in the real world.

Pandar would never know the scenario he was really working on. None of these people would need to know—would even suspect—what they were really working on. Hartman loved himself for his own brilliance. He was very happy.

That brought him back to the selection of directors. Was it possible for the director not to know?

He knew directors. All of them. Their strengths and weaknesses, their virtues and vices, their style and their range. He considered, among many others, Lumet, Demme, Coppola, Spielberg, Lucas, Stone, Pollack, Pakula, Scott (Ridley), Scott (Tony), Lean (David, dead), Michael Mann, Stephen Frears, Robert Redford. He needed a director who was an intuitive genius but who governed his choices by strict adherence to his marketing sense. He had to be innovative, capable of handling gigantic numbers of extras and equipment, very organized but ready to improvise. But ultimately the choice would rest less on talent than on temperament and character.

In essence, the director was going to create the largest film the world had ever seen—and never be able to take credit for it. Things would be destroyed, people would die for this production. What was required was an amoral, self-effacing megalomaniac.

Once he put it that way, the choice was obvious. John Lincoln Beagle. The tall, gangling filmmaker who had once, when he was a film student, had a summer job at Disney World, where he'd appeared as Goofy.

John Lincoln Beagle was the next person to see the memo.

CHAPTER

* * *

SEVENTEEN

The Los Angeles offices of Universal Security are located in a forty-six-story glass tower in the central business district, that small section of L.A. that actually looks urban. Most of the space they lease is on the fourth, fifth, and sixth floors. Joe Broz, for example, had his cubicle on the fifth floor near conference room 2 and the training center. Main Reception is on four, the lunchroom is on six.

The executive offices, however, are on forty-four, with windows facing west. That's high enough that it's often above the smog and there's a view of the ocean. After dark it's a view of lights, that geometric pattern that is the hallmark of films set in Los Angeles, just as the tip-of-Manhattan skyline is the signature of New York films. The only curving lines are the freeways and the coast. Inward toward the center of the building there is a room with no view called the Cube.

It is a room suspended within a room built to the same specifications that are used to construct surveillance-proof spaces in United States embassies. In spite of it's nickname, it's really a rectangle, longer than it is wide, wider than it is high. It's walls are fully soundproofed. The gap between the two rooms is large enough to permit visual inspection of all eight sides, most emphatically including top and bottom. These areas, collectively called "the gap," are monitored by video. The walls of the Cube also contain internal wiring that broadcasts a variety of jamming signals and generates white noise into the gap. Alarms will sound if any attempt is made to introduce recording or broadcast equipment into the Cube.

A BZX-7000 is located inside the room. It creates a constantly shifting randomized pattern of electronic and audio signals that interfere with any attempt at recording. As an additional fail-safe, any recording would be degaussed by a powerful magnetic field that surrounds the one and only door. This is the single device that can be turned on and off by request since one of the things that people often use the Cube for is to listen to recordings. For that reason there is a variety of play-only equipment installed inside.

Some of the technology is restricted and cannot be exported without a special license. But the existence of the room and how it functions is no secret. It is, rather, advertised by Universal Security as the ultimate in aural privacy. It rents for $2,000 an hour. That may seem high for a room that is small, hot, and inherently claustrophobic. But all the clients who use it inevitably express a sense of value received and they frequently return to use it again. Rolls-Royces and Lear jets, even high-priced sex, can only make people feel wealthy. The Cube can make people feel something more special and rare—important.

The door to the Cube itself is thirty-six inches above the floor. Cube users are escorted into the gap by a guard who carries a stepladder. After the client has entered the gap and closed the door, the guard removes the ladder, takes it with him, and returns to his post in the outer room.

It was a Saturday. The two men who sat in the Cube were dressed casually but very expensively. David Hartman had been outfitted by a shop in L.A. called DownEast that sold clothes that made the wearers look like they were New Englanders, the sort that had so much money they needn't mention it, and, more importantly, that the last person in their family that had actually earned money had been dead for at least three generations. John Lincoln Beagle was a film director. His style was far more bohemian: jeans, southwestern-style shirt, Navaho belt with a turquoise buckle, and desert boots, about $2,500 for the ensemble. But that included $800 for boots that were hand-sewn from a custom last, which was in no way an indulgence, since Beagle had sensitive feet and off-the-rack shoes, no matter how costly or carefully fit, always hurt. And the belt buckle was $960.

Lee Atwater's memo was in the inside pocket of David Hartman's $1,800 Whittier & Winthrop jacket. He was trying to think of a way to avoid revealing it.

The door of the Cube closed. "Wow, heavy-duty," John Lincoln Beagle said. "I love it. I'd love to use it as a set. But what the fuck could you possibly have to tell me that needs this much secrecy. What are you, taking over Columbia? Taking over Sony?"

David Hartman reached into his pocket. He took out Lee Atwater's memo. He unfolded it. Smoothed it flat on the table.

From the moment they left this room, Beagle would be watched and listened to by operatives of Universal Security. His home and his office would be wired. His friends and family would be monitored.

Hartman slid the memo over to Beagle.

It said:

MEMO FROM: L.A.
TO: J.B. III/YEO

WAR has always been a valid political option, through all

societies, through all time. We, who grew up in the South, know about revering our warriors and war heroes. Even those who have lost! So long as they fought valiantly and gallantly. You and I grew up on the legends of Lee and Jackson and Beauregard. My first president was Eisenhower, *General* Eisenhower. Kennedy was a war hero. George Bush was a war hero. George Washington was *General* Washington. Andrew Jackson was *General* Jackson. The two great names in British history are Nelson and Wellington. The heroes of France are Charlemagne, Napoleon, and DeGaulle.

After Vietnam and in the shadow of atomic weapons, war ceased to be a political option. It was considered to be, and may have been in fact, political suicide to pursue a war option.

Then Maggie Thatcher showed us the way.

It is important to remember that Thatcher's political career appeared to be virtually over. That she was at a low point in the polls. That most forecasters considered that she and the Conservative Party could not win reelection.

Then she had her war in the Falklands. She rallied her country. She won. For her, war was not a liability—it was political salvation. She became a hero of her nation. She won reelection. She became the longest-serving British prime minister in modern history.

Obviously, I am not the only one to take note of the event and the results. It changed all of our attitudes. Especially Mr. Reagan's. He had his adventure in Libya; that rather tentative affair in Lebanon—quickly and correctly aborted; he had his invasion of Grenada.

These military affairs did no harm in terms of domestic political standing.

This proves absolutely that an American president can go to war and survive politically. It is an option. But is it an option worth employing?

We have yet to duplicate anything approaching the Iron Lady's success with her "splendid little war." While Libya, Lebanon, Grenada, and Panama did no harm, they did precious little good.

Why not?

Because we have not fully embraced the fact that modern war is a media event. There is a recognition of a media element in war, especially in the post–Vietnam War American military. It is de rigeur to say that we lost in Vietnam because of the media. If we ignore the possibility that this belief is so universal exactly because it also serves the function of completely removing responsibility from the people who would most logically bear responsibility for the loss, then the implication is obvious, clear, and logical: the new order of battle says we must win on television (and the lesser media) as well as on the battlefield. This is now an article of faith in the military.

> *"You know you never defeated us on the battlefield,"* said the American colonel.
> The North Vietnamese colonel pondered this remark a moment. *"That may be so,"* he replied, *"but it is also irrelevant."* (H. G. Summers, *On Strategy: A Critical Analysis of the Vietnam War*)

The Vietnamese lost every battle. According to our military, the Americans and the ARVN even won the Tet offensive. Yet this battle is without question the battle in which the Communists won the war.

The military has understood only half the idea. Yet the whole of the concept stares us in the face: it is not necessary to win the war on the battlefield as well as is in the media, it is *only* necessary to win in the media. It is possible to lose on the battlefield, win on television—and win. War is not partially a media event. It has become completely a media event.

If the president is to go with the Thatcher option, to establish or reestablish popularity—to win reelection by going to war—he must recognize that it must be handled as a media event. Both he and Mr. Reagan have employed war. They were sensible in leaving the logistics and the fighting to the professional armed forces. Those armed forces did what they do with reasonable success. That is, they got there in good order, they executed with minimal embarrassment, they won the fighting, there were few casualties, and they kept the body bags off camera. Lebanon excepted, of course.

But they did not leave the media war to the professionals. (This is particularly surprising in Mr. Reagan, who should have intuited better. It is possible to fault his intellect and his work habits, but his intuition, never!)

What is war? To you? To me? To the American people?

War is John Wayne. It's Randolph Scott and *Victory at Sea*. It's Rambo, *Star Wars, Apocalypse Now,* it's body bags on CBS. It's *Combat, The Rat Patrol, Patton.* The face of war is not reality. It is television and motion pictures. Even for people who have been to war. Whatever their memories, they have been replaced by what they have seen subsequently on TV. Even if they were "disillusioned" by Vietnam, those illusions came from the movies. As Mr. Reagan proved, people much prefer a good, solid story to an elusive and complex truth.

The war must be run by professionals.

If victory or defeat will be attained on television, then the professionals are not the generals. Or even the politicians. The war should be directed by a film or television director. This may sound, on the face of it, like a frivolous idea. It's not. It's dead serious.

The generals and the politicians—even the media-wise Mr. Reagan—have demonstrated that they can achieve victory on the battlefield without achieving victory where it counts: in the hearts and minds and votes of the American people. To repeat a method that we know is a failure, that is the frivolous idea.

Who, then, is to run this war?

David Hartman, head of RepCo, the most powerful agency in Hollywood today. If anyone can figure out how to package a war and who should direct it, Hartman can. If anyone has a sense of a deal and making it happen, it's him. Remember that it was Mr. Reagan's agent, Lew Wasserman, and MCA that supported and guided, even partially created, that president's career. Hartman and RepCo are the Wasserman and MCA of the nineties.

When all seems like it might be lost, and there are no other options, go to war. It is the classical response to insoluble domestic problems. It is the reverse of the hostage crisis that destroyed Carter so completely—another media event. Don't leave the impact to chance. Find someone who has the gut instincts, the style, the sheer artistry, to create a war that America can love—on television.

Then you will win.

"Wow. Cool," said John Lincoln Beagle. He was capable of writing great dialogue, but he didn't speak it.

CHAPTER

★ ★ ★

EIGHTEEN

Beagle had a box for the base-ball game.

He didn't want to be in it. There were two reasons. The first was that he had yet to come close to solving the problem, which is how Beagle thought of movies, as problems. It was strange—when he first got a project, there was a great and happy excitement. The happy part disappeared instantly. It was followed by another process of trying to figure out how the raw materials could be handled, shaped, discarded, kept, whatever, in order to produce a successful film.

Except for his very first student film, which seemed to spill out of him, he always went through an intensive research phase. He always *knew* that it was totally necessary—it was where all the real work was done. He sometimes *suspected* that it was a way of stalling, procrastinating, avoiding that irrevocable moment when the camera was there and loaded, the actors were there and ready, and a hundred-odd people looked to him to say "Action" while another hundred—or so it seemed—peered over his shoulder fearful of how their millions were being spent, and he had to know what every damn body was supposed to do and that when he was done it would look right, sound right, cut right, and sell right.

He thought of his mind as a sausage maker. A big open funnel at the top. Pour everything in. Turn the handle. Grind it up together. Something happened inside. Out came sausage. The image, of course, suggested something else. A giant mouth, grazing, nibbling, noshing, gorging, devouring, ingesting mass consumables, down the esophagus to a gross and wobbling belly which, because he'd got it wrong, produced nothing but shit—stinking, reeking, fly-catching, sausage-shaped shit.

Someday it was going to happen to him.

It scared him—dared he pun it; yes, but not in public—shitless. He loved his fear, adored his panic, hoped it would keep him shit-free, a pure and stinkless sausage maker. But he knew It wouldn't. There was always failure. Spielberg had *1941*. Coppola had *Finian's Rainbow*. John Huston did *Victory*. John Ford did *This Is Korea*.

He felt it—the certainty that he was failing—every time. Every single time. He wondered if the feeling of failure would feel different the time that he actually did fail.

The first principle, of all fine art, he understood, is plagiarism. The first principle of all commercial art is theft. No artist, craftsman, or thief works in a vacuum. Every artist is a jazz musician, running new riffs on old tunes because old tunes are icons, references, cultural under-standings—they are the language of the people of his world. Since the moment he saw the memo, Beagle had been gorging on war films: documentaries, features, foreign films, short films, training and recruit-ing films, cartoons, raw footage, news film.

The problem was, he wasn't there yet. If he had to turn the handle, he knew that all that would come out the other end was shit, failure, and he was scared. He had to keep gorging until somehow, some catalytic ingredient, an enzyme perhaps, entered the stewing mass inside him, finally, and started the process that made it come out as something that did not stink. Or maybe it was until he was stuffed so full that the internal pressure forced the creative organ, whatever it was, to finally function and make something with form and shape and color and light and meaning.

So his actual preference was to be back at his studio, watching images, organizing images, on his ten HDTV screens with their thirty possible source machines all interfaced with a virtual supercomputer capable of controlling all of it while converting every image that passed through it into digital form and keeping it that way in memory.

The other reason Beagle didn't want to be in the box was that he was hugely indifferent to baseball. He understood it's place as fable and parable in the canons of American mythology and had even included baseball shtick in several of his films, but it's lethargic pace and the arrhythmic structure of what little action it had left him baffled.

His wife, Jacqueline Conroy,[43] and their son, one-year-and-eight-month-old Dylan Kennedy[43] Beagle were with him. It was Jacqueline's idea. She felt Beagle had been neglecting his family—true—and that they should do a wholesome family thing so that Dylan might learn to recognize his father.

Beagle called Hartman, who got the Disney reserved box for them. John and Jackie's cook had packed them an "all-American repast": sliced-turkey sandwiches with goat cheese, sun-dried tomato bits, and homemade may on Sacramento sourdough white bread; munchies of fried pork rinds and beef jerky; potato salad with roasted

---

[43]She started in film, but the role that made her famous was the MOW and subsequent TV series *Woman Undercover*, almost universally referred to as *Dick Chick*. The series was short-lived, probably because it was terrible. But it did produce that famous poster of Jackie, standing, back to camera, filling the foreground the length of the right hand side of the shot, her hip cocked to the side, smoking gun in hand, burning automobile in the background to the left, the flames creating a very dramatic halo effect. There was something about the length of her legs combined with the attitude with which she cocked her hip, and the shape of her butt and waist inside the very tailored police uniform, that made her an instant erotic icon. A feature career ensued. Her credits include *Swimsuit, Never So Dead, L'Affaire Fatale, Very Last Love, Murphy Was Wrong,* and *Cinderella 2000.*

[43]According to an article in *Millimeter* (March 1987), an industry publication, "it's been an informal Beagle family tradition for generations to give male children a president's name as a middle name. There have been Beagles named Joshua Fillmore, Stuart Cleveland, Victor Van Buren, Gerald Polk. John Lincoln's brother's name is Kenneth Buchanan Beagle, and family lore claims that there was once a Taylor Tyler Beagle.''

garlic bits; sparkling water from Idaho; and four bottles of Coca-Cola bottled in St. Louis.[45]

Dylan didn't like baseball either. It wasn't that he had an active distaste for the game in any particular way. The idea that there were people who did not exist to play *with* him but to play *for* him was as yet an incomprehensible abstraction. Worse, it apparently required sitting still while in a waking state.

Beagle had hoped that Fernando Valenzuela would be pitching because he would have recognized the name. But Valenzuela had pitched himself out or gotten old or maybe injured, one of those things that make ball players disappear. The Dodgers were playing Cincinnati. Beagle was glad that Cincinnati still existed.

He sat Dylan down beside him. He was aware of his wife watching the way he handled his son so that she could tell him the *right way* to handle his son. He truly didn't understand whether maternal instincts were powerful and difficult things to live with or whether she was just a compulsive bitch and it didn't matter a good goddamn if she had a child or was a virgin. He began to explain the game to his son. Dylan said something that his father heard as "ah wuss," then reached out and grabbed a pen from his father's pocket. It was a monogrammed platinum fountain pen, the one that's advertised as both decadent and overpriced. It had been a gift from some studio chief. Beagle couldn't remember the name, so he didn't know if the guy had been fired yet. He just remembered that the guy was the kind of guy who checked up on his gifts. A terrible habit and very burdensome for the recipient. He tried to get the pen back.

Beagle got the top. Dylan kept the rest.

Dylan had a very masculine concept of objects. It appeared to be genetic. No one had to show him what a hammer was for or that

---

[45]There actually are Coca-Cola aficionados, and while they don't have vintages, they do claim detect differences based on where the beverage is bottled. St. Louis is considered the best, its bottles treasured in Coke cellars and served on special occasions.

many, many objects could be used for hammering. The first time he got a stick in his hand, he conceived of the sword. When he got a little older and could walk and got hold of a bigger stick, he thought of the spear. He was very cute walking around the yard holding his stick high overhead and flinging it at things. He had sword fights with the bushes. Flailing at them with a twig. The bushes frequently won, catching the stick and forcing their young opponent to overbalance. But he always got back up off his diaper, dragged his stick out of the tangle, and returned to the attack as valiant and beautiful as Errol Flynn had ever been. It made Papa Beagle proud.

So he should not have been surprised, or taken it at all personally, when his son slashed at him with the pen. Got him, too. Not only did the nib almost break his skin—and Beagle was sensitive to physical assault even from very small people—the pen splashed ink across his shirt. It was made of one of the more expensive mystery fabrics, dyed with the soft yet vibrant southwestern desert colors that he had lately come to favor. It wasn't the money. What did $480 matter to John Lincoln Beagle? It was what? The beauty of the object? Having to walk around all day with ink blots where style had so recently been? It was having to shop to replace it? It was that Kids Have to Learn.

The obvious thing to do was whack the kid. Not maliciously, but like the papa bear gives the baby bear a cuff now and again to remind him who's the papa bear and who's the baby bear.

That was a bit from an animated feature that Beagle had been working on shortly after Dylan was born, an adaptation of Goldilocks as told from the ursine side. John Lincoln had been certain that being a parent would add the dimension to his talent that would enable him to do for the children of America what Walt Disney himself had done—while maintaining his touch for adult cinema, of course. He and Belinda Faith, the animator he'd been working with, had story-boarded out several sequences. In one of them the baby bear had annoyed the papa bear when he was having his after-porridge pipe and papa had just knocked him across the room. The baby bear went rolling across the kitchen and up the wall and out the window. It was quite humorous and the baby bear didn't mind at all.

There were a lot of people around. Modern pedagogy, he knew, frowned on whacking kids in public. Even if that's what one did in cartoons. Also, his wife was watching. She'd love to have that on him. And finally, and in truth, Beagle didn't hit his son because he understood with that part of his mind that was firmly rooted in reality that his son was not a Toon and that hitting kids wasn't nice.

There was really only one way he could release the reflexive anger and irritation he felt. He addressed it to his wife. "Jesus, Jackie! Could you goddamn hold him for one minute."

"Could you hold him for one minute is more like it," Jackie said. Her voice extremely calm and ever so much more cutting for it's serenity. "You have a real problem if you can't be with your child for more than one hundred and twenty seconds without help."

Dylan was still on the attack, the pen a tiny saber. Beagle would have looked at his wife, glaring daggers of hate, but he was forced to keep his eye on his son who, at this point, had to be considered armed and dangerous. John Lincoln snatched at the pen. Dylan was too quick for him and managed to mar his father's summer cream trousers with black blotch and splatter.

"Dammit, Jackie, is that washable ink?"

"How would I know? It's your pen."

The fact that she was absolutely and irrefutably correct brought him to the decision that he would divorce her as soon as he had a week free. He'd been divorced before and he knew you couldn't knock it off in a day. Not that he had even a day. What he had was the biggest project of his life. What he had was pressure. And he didn't need this shit.

He captured the pen. Getting splats on his palm and on his cuff in the process. Now he couldn't find the cap. His wife was smiling. Pleasantly. Of course she was. She was happy to see him in a state of incompetence and frustration. It proved something. He didn't know what. But he didn't like it. "Where's the cap, where's the cap of the pen?"

"I'm sure *I* don't know," Jackie said. Even calmer than before. "Why don't you look for it."

"A score," he said to her. "You got a chance to score. Good for you." There was an absentminded-professor aspect to Beagle. He lived a great deal of his life inside the movies in his head, not in the neurotic or psychotic sense but in a creative person's preoccupied way. He frequently did not know where things were, unless, of course he was using them to make a movie. Then he could keep track of thousands of items. In normal life, however, the more common the article, the less he could perceive it. In the initial stages of a romance with him, women often felt like they were with a character in some old film or novel, probably an English one, and his idiosyncrasy lent him a certain musty yet antic charm. Eventually, it drove them insane. In order to get to the ballpark he had asked his wife if she knew where the car keys were, then the tickets, the directions, his favorite shoes (she'd said, "Learn to dress yourself, dear"), the lunch basket, and some office notes he had hoped to read while they watched the game.

"I'm not trying to score," his wife said. A small lie, but so monumentally obvious, it was impossible to believe that she didn't recognize it as a total untruth. But she didn't. "I'm trying to help you." She believed that too. "You need to be more aware."

"I don't need to more aware. I don't need to be here. I don't need to be with *you.*"

Dylan had grabbed hold of the lunch basket and tipped it over. Everything fell out and this made him very happy indeed. Now he could play with the sandwiches and bottles and glasses—their cook had backed crystal glasses; who wants to drink Coca-Cola, especially a bottle bottled in St. Louis, out of a paper cup.

Jackie sat unresponsive to Dylan's small disasters: it was her husband's time to be a Real Human, not a Film Director. It was his time to deal with The Child. His Son. Whom she had borne the Pain of Bearing for Him.

Beagle wanted to respond. But he had a leaking pen in his hand with no cap. It was a gift from some goddamn studio head who would expect him, the next time he did a film with that goddamn studio head, if he still had a job, to sign the contract with the goddamn gift pen and say something inane like, "You gave me this pen. It's my favorite and I want you to know that I've been saving it for a moment like this." Inane, absolutely inane. But important. He knew that from his mother. He also knew, from life as well as from his mother, that wherever he put the pen, it would roll off, it would fall to the floor, keep rolling and disappear into a crack, drop to the bowels of the earth, and some janitor person would end up with an incredibly overpriced and decadent pen. WIthout the cap. He couldn't put it in his pocket because he didn't have the cap and the ink would just pour out of it, a spreading black stain, growing like the Blob. He still didn't know if it was washable ink.

He looked at his wife in silent plea. He saw her face and saw all that she thought. Why had he married a movie star? Even one whose butt meant as much to the world of posters as Farrah Fawcett's hair once had? Why not some placid, undemanding creature who cared about his needs. Who wanted nothing more than to make a home, care for the child, love her husband, have sex with him when *he* wanted the way *he* wanted.

Dylan had one hand on a sandwich, pulling at the wax paper. The cook was adamant about never using plastic wrap. *Jamais.* He had his other paw around one of the prize cokes. It was one of the old-style bottles, with that curvy, womanish shape and the raised letters in the glass, a veritable icon of Americana. What a soft drink!

Beagle had only one hand. He did what he could. He wrapped his free hand, the left, around his son's waist, and lifted him from the mess he was making. Dylan had a firm grip on the wax paper, which began to unfold. When he rose in the air, the paper completed it's unfolding and the sandwich tumbled out. Sometimes the bread falls butter side up, sometimes it doesn't. It didn't. Turkey, goat cheese, sun-dried tomato bits, homemade mayo, all made intimate contact with the greasy, germy, gooey floor of the box reserved for Disney at Dodger Stadium.

Dylan wanted the sandwich. He began to wail.

It was good, Jackie thought, for her husband to once in a while go through what she had to go through all the time. She didn't really have to go through it all the time. Just between the times when she had fired the nanny and before she had hired the new nanny. Not an infrequent occurrence because she only wanted the very best for her child. And sometimes it took as long as a week to find a new one.

Dylan had a distinct sense of proportion. A Coke bottle was not the right shape for a sword or spear. Too thick. Too squat. Definitely not in the stabbing or slashing category. It was, like hammers, clubs, and cups, in the banging class. While he wailed over his fallen food, he flailed the bottle, with a certain enthusiasm, at his Dad's head.

He missed. Much to his disappointment.

Beagle tried to grab the bottle without dropping the pen.

Jackie looked at the food on the floor with disgust and wondered if her husband would have sufficient awareness to pick it up before Dylan ate it. She bet herself a $7,800 dress that he wouldn't. If he picked it up before she mentioned it, she would pay for the dress herself. Or forgo it.

Dylan, really pissed that he'd missed, flung the bottle at his father. Who ducked. Which was difficult since he was still holding Dylan and the pen. He stepped on the sandwich and slid. He loved the kid enough that his deeper instincts finally emerged and he let go of the pen, held Dylan, and did all he could to fall in such a way that he was the only one hurt. And he was hurt. Not permanently. But painfully and embarrassingly.

The bottle flew out of the box, onto the field, narrowly missing a bat boy dashing through foul territory for reasons that might be understood by baseball fans, but not by Beagle. The bat boy looked around to see from whence the dangerous projectile had been launched. Several of Beagle's neighbors pointed at the Disney box, just as Beagle pulled himself to his feet.

"You stupid motherfucking cocksucking asshole drip! You're the type of rich dumb fuck that should be banned from world-fucking existence. I hate your type. Your type should roll over and join the bronto-fucking-sauruses in ex-fucking-tinction. I ought take this fucking bottle, climb up there and shove it up your reamed-out asshole, Drip Face," the bat boy said in the colorful way that we've come to associate with the American pastime. He raised the bottle threateningly. Then he saw it. "Wow!" he said. "St. fucking Louis! Wow. Chill dude. You must be really feely. Give my regards to your babe, dude. I got your Coke and I'm keeping it."

Beagle addressed his wife. "This is your"—Beagle tried very hard not to curse in front of his child; he bit his lip—"fault." he said. Without a single adjective.

"You can't take care of your son without assistance for one minute and it's my fault. I think you better look at yourself." She nodded in that infuriating way. In another age, a more primitive and honest one, he would have killed her.

"This is your idea of a family outing. Thank you very much. It's lots of fun," he said in a little boy's ugly, mocking voice. "Oh, boy. I take a day off to bring my son to something he has no idea of and that I don't like. Another wonderful idea, brought to you by Mommy."

"I was trying to help you," she said. "To do something masculine in which you could bond with your son. Who is a very masculine person. You don't do enough with him. If you don't like what I suggest, why don't you come up with something yourself. You should spend some time with your family."

All this time, Dylan, still held by his father, was squirming to get down. "Ok," Beagle said, and put him down. Jackie watched him go right for the sandwich remnants, which now had not merely fallen on the floor but had been ground into the dirt when her husband stepped on them.

"You set things up," Beagle said. "You set this up to be a disaster."

"I didn't set anything up," Jackie said. Of course she hadn't. She was doing what was best for everyone. Her husband needed a lesson in awareness. If he got one, it was obviously his own doing, and very much for the good.

"You don't even fucking realize it—"

"Watch your mouth in front of the . . ."

"The . . ." he mocked her.

"You have a nasty streak," she said.

Dylan peeled some turkey from the floor. It had attached itself to thick black goo that old soda often becomes. Chunks and flakes of indecipherable substances in various shades of brown and gray also adhered to it. There was a faint aroma of cleaning fluid as well. He put it toward his mouth with great anticipation.

"I knew it," Jackie said, snatching the filth from her son's mouth. "I knew you wouldn't even think to clean that up."

"Clean it up?"

"Yes. The sandwich. Am I your slave? Who is going to clean it up?"

Beagle, who felt he had barely survived his fall and his encounter with the bat boy, had yet to give the mashed sandwich much thought. "I . . . uh . . ." he said.

"Because I'm a woman and you're a man. I make my own money, buster, and I don't have to be a little *Hausfrau* for you."

"What is going on?" he said.

"I'll tell you what's going on. Your son is eating filthy old *shit*, shit from the floor of a public stadium. It could be a public toilet and it wouldn't be dirtier, and you don't have enough awareness, awareness to do anything about it."

"Jackie," he said, "shut the fuck up."

"I will not."

"Of course you won't. You don't know how to shut the fuck up."

"Why don't *you* shut the . . ."

And, having degenerated into a kind of generic husband-wife exchange, it went on for a few more minutes with little to distinguish their celebrity ugliness from the common rancor and spite of people who have neither their glamour nor their riches. Finally, Jackie snatched up her son and the car keys and marched off, leaving Beagle, who had no desire to be there, there.

He was so relieved that she was gone that he decided to stay rather than go anywhere where they might meet by chance. What the hell, a ball game was supposed to be therapeutic. Or something.

It wasn't. It was incomprehensible. He opened a sandwich that Dylan hadn't dumped. It was weird but tasty. He looked around. Thousands of people were watching, with varying degrees of attention, but certainly staying and participating. The guy in the box next to him seemed to be—Beagle searched for a word—happy. That was it.

His neighbor's name was Tubby Bayless. He was an ex-DEA agent who'd made extra money dealing confiscated drugs and pocketing dealer money. He'd invested, rather blindly, but luckily, in some Hawaiian cane fields. A Japanese developer had paid top dollar for the land because it formed the fourteenth, fifteenth, sixteenth, and part of the seventh, holes of a golf course.

Tubby was smoking a large cigar. And showing no shame about enjoying tobacco. Even though he was there at the game, he listened to it on the radio as well.

"Can I ask you something?" Beagle said.

"Shoot, buddy," Tubby said.

What Beagle really wanted to ask him was the secret of happiness. But he didn't Instead, he asked, "How come people like baseball? What is it? I'm a film director. And I work very hard to make sure one of my films goes from action to action to action, always building. You know? With pace, with rhythm. Then this . . ." He pointed at the field. "I don't get it."

Tubby blew a couple of fat smoke rings. He looked philosophic and reflective, a carnal Buddha. Maybe sent here to give Beagle a message. "Ahh, baseball," he said. "Baseball is not a game of action. It is a game of potential and possibility. I was a cop. Of sorts. When you're a cop, you spend lots of time watching and waiting. Maneuvering ever so slightly, hoping your quarry finally gets in position for you to pounce. You ever go hunting?"

"No," Beagle said.

"Well, you don't look like the killing type. But you never know." Tubby shrugged. "Anyway, the moment of the kill, if it's game or busting through some spic's door, guns drawn, there's an adrenaline rush. A definite adrenaline rush. But that's not what it's about. Just like making love's not about coming. I'm a regular philosopher, right? You want a cigar?"

"Uh, sure," Beagle said. Not a smoker, he thought maybe tobacco was the secret of happiness, if the Buddha liked it and the Indians too.

Tubby took one out of his pocket and passed it over the rail to Beagle. "What it's about is the potential. The potential for action. Is she gonna go out with you, is she gonna get a little tiddly or high or whatever her preference is. You're moving, she's moving . . ." He gestured with his hands, they circled each other, two plump predators dancing.

Beagle had the cellophane off the cigar. It was terrifically phallic. He admired it. He didn't have a match.

Tubby popped a big kitchen match with a red and white tip out of his pocket. "Hate butane." He flicked it with a nail. It flared and smelled of sulfur, good old-fashioned demon sulfur. He leaned over and gave Beagle a light. "That's why people stop fucking the people they're married to," he said. "Because coming's not what it's about. It's not about the rush. It's about potential. Anticipation. Baseball is a game about potential and anticipation."

Beagle took a puff. It was rich and slightly sordid at the same time. But it was the gesture—holding, taking the smoke in, exhaling it, watching it float away—rich in cinematic memories, that was really fulfilling. He began to relax and got a sense of male comradeship. *See what the boys in the back room will have.*

"This guy's good," Tubby said and turned up the radio. "Listen." There was a man on second—*in scoring position*—the man at bat was —*the tying run is at the plate!*—the count was two and one—*he better not get behind the batter, if he gets ahead of the batter here, he's got him, he's that kind of pitcher.*

Tubby blew a smoke ring. "You get it?"

Beagle, getting a little buzz from the tobacco now, tried a smoke ring too. It didn't quite do it. "No," he said.

"If the count gets to one and two, he can throw shit and the batter almost has to take a cut. He's changed the potential. If the pitcher throws a ball, he's behind. Now the batter can lay back a little, and choose. And the pitcher has to throw something pretty decent or risk a walk. Changed the potentials, get it?"

"Yeah," Beagle. "I get it." And he did. He nodded and began to see the action in the nonaction. He took another puff, the buzz got a bit buzzier, and suddenly he understood something very basic about directing reality. He remembered being in New York at the time the Mets were in the play-offs against the Houston Astros. There was one very long game that went on forever. It went on so long it totally defeated the schedules and expectations of normal life with the result that New Yorkers, all suddenly turned into fans, found themselves tracking the game in bits and pieces as they passed through their lives—watching a television in a store window or through the window of a limousine with a tiny TV playing in the backseat, asking freight-elevator operators—freight-elevator operators always have radios—or total strangers, *What's the score? What's happening?* It was like wartime. *What's the news? What's the news? Have you heard the latest?*

Reality was a rhythm as slow as baseball. Even stillness was action. Especially stillness was action. Because waiting was a massing of power or a dissipation. Then swift action—like a hit—a man gets to second. That's as far as he gets. No score. But more potential. Waiting again.

"You got another one of those St. Louis Cokes?" Tubby asked.

CHAPTER

* * *

NINETEEN

It's like *Pretty Woman*. Except I'm playing Julia Roberts and Maggie's playing Richard Gere. We start at ten in the morning. By noon I'm ready to quit. She's enjoying herself more than I've ever seen. There's something girlish and carefree happening. She tells every salesperson that I'm her very own GI Joe doll. Except I'm a special issue for girls because I can be dressed up. This, I swear, makes me blush. I protest, but Maggie does this number about I'm so manly I can be secure in my manhood and I should indulge her because she's a little girl at heart. Which may or may not be bullshit. But it's a whole lot sweeter and more digestible than her saying its her money and if I want to be seen with her I better look right. She doesn't say that at all. So it's OK and I let her pick out clothes and I let a series of strange salespersons, virtually all with accents from places that don't quite exist, eye me and measure me and use their very best imagination to discern what would flatter and suit me.

Camouflage and an M-16. A blue suit from Sears that wears for ten years, with a white shirt and cop shoes. A pair of sweats, loose and comfortable for sitting in a Ford all day watching someone do nothing. That's what suits me.

Point of fact, I'm grumbling because I think it's expected of me.

Point of fact, I'm flattered.

We grab a light lunch at one of those places that you have to call two, three months in advance for. Unless you're Magdalena Lazlo or Gena Rowlands or David Hartman. Then you just walk right in, and somehow they just knew you were coming and a table's waiting. I get a sandwich. I recognize it as tuna on white with mayo, lettuce, and tomato, though every one of those items has a different and more expensive name. We have an eight-dollar bottle of water with lunch.

After lunch Maggie takes me to Yamato's for Men on Rodeo. She leaves me with Ito, a tall, slender, stylish Japanese salesperson–artist. He's done several of the pieces hanging on the wall as well as designing many of the jackets. Yamato of Tokyo has a philosophy, "We are art. Each and every person. For me to match a human being with his clothing is an act of creation as deeply moving and sometimes more important than putting paint to canvas." All Yamato salespeople must be trained in the psychology of colors and fabrics and must have produced art work worthy of exhibit. Prices are not marked.

Ito places me in proximity to a variety of jackets. Many of them are made out of things I have never heard of. He has a set of color cards, and he wants me to rank them in order of preference.

I turn around. There's Jack Cushing. He's with Tom Berenger. They're looking at jackets also. They're with two salespersons, Hiro and Nikio. Hiro throws pots. Niko does sculptures in plastic. Ito claims it is a very angry medium.

Jack and I see each other at the same time.

This is about sixty hours after I punched him out and dumped him on the pavement beside his car. We look at each other. One beat. Two. He smiles. Big-time. And marches over to me. Hand out. I take it, I shake it.

"Sorry, old man," he says. "About the other night, I didn't know. About you and Maggie."

"That's OK," I say graciously. "We didn't know either. Not 'til right then."

"It happens that way sometimes, doesn't it. Sometimes that's the best way."

"It hits hard and it hits fast," I say.

"So do you," he says. And we both smile. The amazing thing is, that his seems sincere. "Hey, do you know Tom?"

Of course, I don't. He calls Tom's name and gestures him over. "There's someone I want you to meet," he says to Berenger. "This is Joe Broz—am I saying that right?"

"Yeah."

"Joe and Magdalena Lazlo are . . ." He searches for the right word.

"In love." I say.

"That's what I heard," Jack says. "But I hate to repeat gossip. Joe is in the security business," he says to Berenger.

"Nice to meet you," Berenger says like he could give a shit.

"Good to meet you," I say. And like a hick I add, "Loved you in *Platoon*."[47] This definitely was his best picture. In my opinion. Love him or hate him, Oliver Stone gets performances from his actors.

"Thanks," he says absently. Then he looks at me. Registers my age. And my haircut, probably. "You were there. Right?"

"Yeah," I say. "I was there."

"Decorated too. Weren't you?"

This is amazing. I'm new to this world so I'm not used to it. Two days after the thing with Maggie and I begins, these people know who I am, the business I'm in, that I'm a vet, and that I can pin medals on my chest if I want to. In my world, at the office, a guy gets divorced and maybe nobody notices for a couple of years.

"You know Stone? You gotta meet Stone," Berenger says. "He's

---

[47]*Platoon*, (1986), written and directed by Oliver Stone. This is the film that "made" Stone. There are three main characters: a male ingenue, played by Charlie Sheen, through whose eyes we see the story, and two sergeants. While both sergeants are effective combat soldiers, one, Willen Dafo is a compassionate, fair-minded, pot-smoking killer, and the other, played by Berenger, in great scar makeup, is a vicious, murderous, dangerous-to-his-own, booze-swilling, killer. The Berenger character murders Dafoe.

still into that Nam shit. So you liked me in *Platoon?*"

"I thought you were terrific."

"You were there. So you thought it was accurate? It was right on? Man, I worked at making that right. But of course my knowledge is secondhand, so I had to depend on other people to tell me."

"Yeah, I thought it was pretty right on. Everybody's Vietnam was different."

"I like playing characters with an edge to them," he says. "There's more grit in that. More out there, you know."

"Hey," I say, starting to build my own legend, "I didn't think of your character as out there. Not at all."

"No?"

"No. You were the guy I identified with."

"Ah," Ito says, "I have it. This sixty percent silk, thirty-three percent viscose, seven percent wool blend.

We get home with a carload of boxes. Mostly for me: socks, boxer and bikini underwear, ties, handkerchiefs, six pair of shoes, hats, belts, dress shirts, T-shirts, sweatshirts. More will follow, after alterations. CDs, including K. D. Lang, Ray Charles, and Bob Dylan's *Nashville Skyline*—country music for people who don't like country. Maggie starts tearing through the packages like they're hers, as happy as a four-year-old at a birthday party. In five minutes the living room is littered with bags, boxes, packing material, designer-label tissue paper, and several thousand dollars worth of fabric and leather.

"Let me see this on you, Joe . . . Now that tie, with that shirt . . . This tie with that belt and that shirt. Just hold the tie up and put the belt on without putting it through the loops . . . Oh, you look so—manly and fierce. Come on, smile. This is fun . . . I want to see you in the bikini underwear. The silk ones. Don't blush. Don't make homophobic statements. There are many heterosexual men who wear silk underwear . . . OK, if you won't dress up, then I will." She starts to pull off her shirt. "Cover your eyes. You're peeking." I am. She snakes out of her jeans. "Turn around." I do. She's humming to herself. "OK," she says, "you can turn around." I do. She's like a little girl playing dress-up in Daddy's clothes. A pair of boxer shorts, a dress shirt, a tie, a belt, her hair tucked up under a Borsalino, and a pair of Bally dress shoes on her feet. Of course, she's not a little girl, and while some of it is cute and comic, like the oversize shoes and the baggy shorts, it's also sexy as hell.

She goes to the mirror and draws a mustache on her face. A pencil-thin mustache. "What do you think people are saying, Joe?"

"If you keep buying me stuff, they'll say I'm using you. You can't keep buying me things."

"If you had the money, you'd buy me things all day long. Wouldn't you? Smother me in diamonds, cover me in minks, cover me in diamonds, smother me in minks."[48]

"That's different and you damn well know it."

"Is it, Joe? What is money? A sign of virtue? Of masculinity? Of cleverness?"

"Where I come from . . ."

"Joe, where you come from doesn't exist anymore. Money comes by accident. Like freeway collisions. Why do you think we're all so frantic? Because we know it's all an accident. The face, the body, the way I come across on camera—accidents. Oh, I work at it. Acting classes, acting coaches, exercise, skin care, this hairdresser, that makeup person, trying to make it better, trying to keep it. Fifteen plastic surgeons doing the surgical version of the home show couldn't put one Magdalena Lazlo together. You can go in and get Barbara Hershey's lips, one of Lee Grant's noses, Melanie's tits, Cher's butt, and walk out and you're still nothing. All the desperate wannabes in all the desperate acting classes can't learn how to do whatever the hell it is that the people who pay me a million-plus dollars a picture think I do. It's a goddamn accident. Like winning the lottery or getting

---

[48]A casual quote from Big Daddy, Tennessee Williams's *Cat On a Hot Tin Roof*. Maggie played Maggie the Cat on stage in L.A. before she made it on film.

hit by a bus and suing the city. So if I want to spend my accident money, dressing you up because it's fun, I'll do it."

"There's a name for men who take money from women," I say.

"There's a name for women who take money from men," she says.

"It's different."

"Hey, Joe, you got twenty dollars on you?"

"I got a hundred or so," I say.

"Just give me a twenty," she says.

I reach in my wallet. I give her a twenty. She reaches through the fly of the boxer shorts she's wearing. She's got her own underwear on beneath mine. She folds the bill neatly and sticks it under the elastic. "What's the name for women who take money from men, Joe?"

"I got problems with some of your games, Maggie."

"What's the name, Joe?"

"Whore, Maggie. They call them whores. Is that what you want me to say?"

"That's what I want you to say. I took your money, now I can say I'm your whore."

I don't know how she does it. Whether it's a thing with her face and her posture or some more subtle trick of acting, or a thing with her soul, but in spite of the comical way she's dressed—the man's hat and shoes that are too big, the boxer shorts with hearts on them, the Hopalong Cassidy hand-painted tie from 1952, and the eyebrow-pencil mustache—she changes from cute and girlish into something kinky and sluttish.

SHe struts over to her handbag. She takes out a twenty-dollar bill. "Take it," she says.

I take it.

"Now you're my gigolo," she says. She giggles. "That's such a funny word." So she says, in a husky voice, trying not to laugh, "You're my kept man. I'm your whore and you're my kept man. Guess what, the names for women who take money from men are much worse. Aren't they? So no more bullshit, Joe, about where the money comes from, OK?''

''I'll try. But the first time I hear someone say I's using you . . .''

''You'll punch 'em out and show how tough you are,'' she teases me. ''Joe, I need someone. My instinct says you're smart. And you're loyal. Put *Someone to Watch Over Me* on the stereo and dance with me.''

''Maggie, I'm not doing this to get somewhere.''

''What are you afraid of? That someone will say you're fucking your way to the top? In this town that's a compliment. It should be, because everybody fucks, but damn few do it good enough to get to the top.''

''Are you sure about this?''

''Joe, if you don't want to play *Someone to Watch Over Me*, put on *Lay, Lady, Lay*.''

''Too cute.''

''Yeah,'' she says, ''but it's country.''

I turn the music on. Because that's our way of saying we want to talk, for ourselves, not for the listeners. It's what she asked—Bob Dylan. Maybe it is country. Singing about laying a lady across a big brass bed. ''What the hell,'' I say, my throat dry as sandpaper, ''dance with me.''

CHAPTER

✱ ✱ ✱

TWENTY

"**H**e's right. Too cute," David Hartman said.

The tape on the table in front of him kept rolling. Music started to play. Hartman was not particularly fond of Dylan. Though he'd once pretended to be when he was trying to steal Jack Nicholson away from his agent. And sat through Laker games, watching giant black people sweat profusely while they bumped against other giant black people. It stimulated his latent racism. Which he'd overcome sufficiently to sign several of them. They made fortunes with commercial endorsements and assorted personal appearances. They were employed half of the year and in training the rest; therefore they had less time to demand unnecessary attentions, and in terms of dollars-per-agent-hour they outperformed film stars. So Hartman was still capable of pretending enthusiasm for sporting events but saw no need to do so for Dylan.

"That tape," Sheehan said to impress the client, "is less than an hour old." Sheehan looked far more rumpled than he liked. Too many people believe that security is a low-rent business, little but supplying semiliterate semialcoholics as security guards for supermarkets and intimidating convenience-store employees with polygraph machines to make them admit they'd eaten Hershey's kisses without paying for them. Sheehan made a point of wearing $1,800 suits just for that reason. He called them his CEO and head-of-state suits, because that's how spiffy they were.

Unfortunately, at 10:03 that morning, about when Maggie made her first public appearance with Joe Broz, shopping, half a dozen people had vied with each other to be the first to reach David Hartman with the rumor. Although he was in a meeting and did not take any calls and was not interrupted, he apparently knew about it by the time he emerged at 10:40. At which point he called Mel Taylor and said that he wanted a full update. He turned Taylor over to his secretary, Fiona, who found the first available time slot—8:00 P.M. that evening.

Taylor called Chicago as he had been instructed to do if anything happened in the Beagle matter. The call was directed to C. H. Bunker himself. Bunker called Sheehan into his office and said: "Go to Los Angeles. Be at the meeting. Make sure the client is a very happy person. Thank you." Damn, C.H.'s voice always made him feel like genuflecting. The closest living thing to it was James Earl Jones in a Darth Vader echo chamber.

Sheehan called Taylor. He said, "I want a dog and pony show. I want buttoned up. Neat. Labels. Typed or excellent penmanship. Organized. I want all the materials there. But nothing extraneous." Sheehan had been taught by nuns.

He cleared his other affairs and called his wife personally to say he would not be home for dinner. The first flight he could get was at 5:00—ETA, 7:17. The only available seat was coach. Tight for a big man and hell on clothes. There was no place to hang his jacket. He folded it, neatly, and laid it carefully on top of the other stuff in the overhead rack. But something shifted or fell over, and a box of books pressed it against a paper bag of loose fruit for twelve hundred miles. There were grape stains at the shoulder, and every time he moved his arm, the aroma of banana rose from his sleeve. The flight arrived at LAX on time, but even with only carry-on baggage, he didn't reach the cab stand until 7:38. There was no time to change. It was a hot and smoggy day. The taxi had no air-conditioning. He arrived in time, but wrinkled. The pants of his $1,800 suit had as many lines around the crotch as the face of an AKC champion Shar-Pei.

Besides, Hartman suit cost $3,600.

"It certainly sounds like Maggie and Joe are an item," Hartman said. "How did we get to here?"

Mel Taylor had a written summary, a short narrative, with the appropriate tape numbers marked alongside the actions described. "Ms. Lazlo came home early in the morning after the bar mitzvah. She was driven home by Jack Cushing."

Hartman nodded. Cushing was an RepCo client.

Taylor held up tape 1, slipped it in the cassette player. It had been cued up to the action. "They started to become intimate," Taylor said, and pushed PLAY. The sound was remarkably good, a testament to the quality of the microphones employed. It was possible to hear not just words, but heavy breathing and the slurp of passionate kisses. "Joseph Broz was already in the house. He appeared from wherever he'd been. They saw him." Mel fast-forwarded the tape. Stopped it. "They both ordered Broz out. He refused. There was a fight. Broz won." Mel pushed PLAY. They heard shuffles and grunts.

"There's a gap here," Mel said, pulling tape 1 out and putting tape 2 in. "Actually, two gaps. They went outside, the front. They came back in. And then we assume they went out on the beach. If you listen, you'll hear various . . . noises. The analysts tell me that *thunk* is the front door and the lighter, *thwack* sound is the back door. Beach door." He popped out tape 2 and put in 3. "They came back to the house and they became intimate."

All three men did their best to pretend to be unaffected by the sounds of passion. Taylor grew erect. He was seated so it was hidden, but still it confused him and made him angry. He wondered if he had become a voyeur. A pervert. He sensed that somehow Broz was not only nailing the bitch, he was slipping out of reach, as if immersion in the golden pussy conferred invulnerability, a social kind, as the physical kind bestowed upon Achilles by being dipped in the river

Styx.

Sheehan, who was very fair, blushed. Once the tape had played long enough that everyone was quite sure what was going on, Taylor turned it off so as not to appear to be dwelling on it. He skipped tape 4. "More of the same," he said. He put in 5: "This was recorded in the kitchen. In the morning they sent away the housemaid, Mary Mulligan." The three men listened to Mrs. Mulligan being given time off. "After that they continued to have . . . intimacies." Taylor took out tapes 6 to 11 but did not play them. His gesture indicated what they were.

Hartman took tape 6 and spot-checked. The erotic mixed with the domestic. But there was a great deal more sex than housekeeping. He then played random pieces of #9. It was also very stimulating. Sheehan, who spent a great deal of time on the road, had become a devotee of 900 numbers. This compared quite favorably, and knowing that one of the participants was a real movie star truly enhanced the effect. Although the females that he heard on the far end of the telephones had succulent voices, he always suspected that the husky and lubricious sounds were produced by hags, women who really looked like Margaret Hamilton,[49] Roseanne Barr, or worse, his wife. He determined to get copies of the Magdalena Lazlo tapes for his personal record of the case.

Hartman stopped the tape and gathered the collection to him. "Are these the only copies?" he asked.

"Yes," Taylor said, lying. He'd made copies for himself. So had Ray Matusow, though Taylor didn't know that. Other technicians along the line may have done so too.

"I'd hate to have tapes all over town of Magdalena Lazlo having sex. Make sure they're the only copes," Hartman said. He knew that there were other copies. Just like he know that techs at the motion-picture laboratories made personal copies of the better breast and beaver footage that passed their way, especially if it was brand-name

[49]The Wicked Witch of the West in *The Wizard of Oz* (1939).

breast and beaver. It was unstoppable. He didn't care very much, except that when tapes did show up, it would give him an edge with U.Sec. Hartman collected edges. He looked at the last cassette, as if he expected Joe's face to be on the outside, like an album cover. "This Broz, this happen to him a lot?"

"No."

"Women normally fall all over him?"

"I don't think so," Taylor said. "It's never been an issue. I wouldn't have thought so."

"I want to give you an overview," Frank Sheehan said. "Which is very positive. Our security around Lincoln Beagle is intact and unbroached."

"He's your guy," Hartman said, referring to Broz. "You have a file on him?" Taylor gave him Joe's personnel file. Hartman opened it. "Interesting," he said aloud. "Marine Corps. Four tours in Vietnam. Purple Heart with oak leaf clusters. Recommended Silver Star . . . wonder why he didn't get it? Got two Bronze Stars. Then he went back to Nam as a civilian . . ."

"Can I see that?" Sheehan said. He reached across the conference table and snatched the papers. There were certain things in the file that outsiders shouldn't see. Taylor, he thought, had really fucked up. He should have dumped Taylor the last time they'd met. Sheehan scanned the page quickly. No, Taylor had not screwed the pooch; the files had been sanitized. "Oh, well, I see," Sheehan said, deeply relieved. He pointed at a name on the page. "Apparently, he worked for a construction company over there. That's what this company, Oceania-Americana was, a construction company." To cover his relief he went on. "*Peut-être le mal juene.* That's what the French called it. Yellow fever. The combination of western currency and *les femmes Indochinoises* very enticing. Or it could have been just that he could make a lot more money over there than here."

"Now, as I understand it, you chose not to tell this Joe Broz about Maggie's house being wired," Hartman said. "Looks like a good decision."

Taylor looked over at Sheehan. The client, unconsciously or not, had just signed off on the one decision Taylor had made that was not by the book.

Hartman was reasonably content. He had been able to distract, divert, or discourage everyone else who'd made more than casual inquiries. Now Magdalena had a new dick to keep her body and mind occupied. That's what the tapes said to him. "Actresses," he sighed. Now it was just the usual, simple, bullshit problems. "Every time there's a new husband or boyfriend, they get a new hairdo, change their wardrobe, and start asking for different kinds of parts. They all think they're John Derek.[50] Or worse, the new Jon Peters. Watch. You'll see."

It would be very wrong to assume that because Mel Taylor's sexual life had bathetic episodes that he was a clown. Quite to the contrary. Taylor was astute, and as an agent of his country, or of his company, he was as ruthless and as dangerous as they required him to be. "You're not suggesting we end surveillance just because they hopped in the sack, are you?" Taylor asked. He was as convinced by the tapes as the others. The only difference was that they wanted to be convinced and he didn't. He still had one hole card and he wanted a chance to play it. Nobody could fake that much fucking and sucking with that much detail. Not without going mad in the process. But, dammit, Taylor wanted to check.

"It sounds like they're both pretty distracted," Hartman said. "But no, you might as well continue."

"Is there a question of costs here?" Sheehan asked.

"No," Hartman replied. "Do whatever you have to do to get the job done." That was easy for him to say. He had already arranged to pay for it with other people's money.

Good. Taylor's hole card was the maid. When he'd gotten rid of

[50]Derek, once an actor, has been involved with a succession of beautiful women whom he groomed or help groom to motion picture stardom. They include Ursula Andress and, most recently, Bo Derek.

Maria—not easy, since she'd held a valid green card for six years—he'd had a quiet word with the agency and had them put in an illegal. Ms. Mulligan didn't work for U.Sec. But she would soon. If she wanted to stay in America. "What do we do if Ms. Lazlo starts asking questions again?" Taylor asked. "Or if Broz does that for her?"

Hartman paused a moment. He wanted to be very clear about this. Finally, he said, "I would like you to remember that Magdalena Lazlo is a woman of great value. Aside from her attributes as a human being—sensitive, creative, endearing in many ways—she makes a lot of money for a lot of people. That's worth preserving. So we are talking about a careful and graduated response. Mr. Broz, of course, is entirely your concern. Finally, there is a bottom line: What Mr. Beagle is engaged in is vastly more important than either of them. It is to remain secret and protected at any cost. I don't see how I can be any more precise and explicit than that."

Taylor looked to Sheehan. Sheehan asked, "When you say 'at any cost' . . . that's uh . . . not a financial reference."

"I'm sorry that you don't seem to get it," the client said.

"If we're speaking of . . ." Sheehan was flustered. He'd been more or less told by C. H. Bunker to do whatever the client needed. Also, U.Sec. did do the sort of things that they would deny doing even under the penalty of perjury. But Sheehan, and Taylor too, tended to think of Hartman as a bit of a lightweight since he was in what they thought of as a frivolous business. "If we're speaking of illegal or uh . . . coercive measures, I don't quite know what to say, if your implication . . ."

Which was exactly what Hartman meant to say. Because they were getting closer to the next step, and the level of risk would take a significant step upward. But he damn well didn't want to go on record, not with these clowns, of saying anything that explicit. "There is a bottom line," Hartman repeated himself word for word, but slower. He didn't like to repeat himself. "What Mr. Beagle is engaged in is vastly more important. It is to remain secret and protected at any cost." Then he added, "If you have problems with that, resign the account now. If you don't understand it, talk to C. H. Bunker. If you need to know that you're on the side of truth, justice, and the American way, you can call the man whom you worked for in 1979."

Taylor didn't get it. But Sheehan sat up straighter. He all but saluted. "Yes, sir." he said.

"Is there anything else?" the client asked.

"No, sir," Sheehan said.

Hartman took the tapes and Joe Broz's file with him. Sheehan and Taylor both walked him to the elevator where, just before the doors closed, Hartman said to Sheehan: "By the way, he spoke very highly of you."

"Thank you, sir," Sheehan said. He waited, listening to the cables rustling in the shaft. When he was certain Hartman was several stories away, he said to Taylor, "Those weren't really the only copies of the tapes, were they?"

"I'll make you a set," Taylor said. "What was all that about 1979?"

"In '79 I was still with the Company,"[51] Sheehan said. "In '79, George Bush was our director."

[51]The CIA.

CHAPTER

* * *

TWENTY-ONE

She comes up close, close enough for me to take her in my arms. "I will," she says, "if you want me to. But don't, if you can't handle touching me."

"I can handle it."

She looks—what?—regretful, and steps into my arms. She puts her head gently on my shoulder. We move to the music. "Be patient with me," she says.

"Yeah."

"You think they bought it?"

"Yes," I say. "I'm certain. I can feel it." And I can. Even if we have to remember constantly that we're on mike, the feeling is different. I am no longer the deer who sees the tiger. A *strategy of positioning evades Reality and confronts through illusion.* Now, when the tiger sees me, he sees one of his own kind. Oh, perhaps not another big cat, but at least a jackal.

Maggie starts to giggle. The music is still playing. We whisper underneath.

"What?"

"Mrs. Mulligan will be back tomorrow."

"I know that."

"Remember what we have to do."

"Oh, shit."

"It was your idea. When we sat out there on the beach after you punched out poor, dear Jack Cushing."

"Tell me something, were you really going to go to bed with him or were you doing that to provoke me?"

"I think we better do it in separate rooms," she says.

"OK. Let's go." I head for the stairs. Maggie walks beside me. The music is still loud enough that we can talk. If we whisper.

She grabs me on the stairs. "Joe, it was your idea. Stop tormenting yourself. You said to me that the main thing was to set yourself free to investigate Beagle and Hartman and figure out what was going on, and I asked you if you could handle pretending to be my lover and you said yes."

"I know it was. But I thought we'd just do a couple of *uh-uh-uhs* and *ohs,* and like that. You know, a few minutes long. I didn't think we'd be doing these long, intense—I don't know what to call them— scenarios. Kinky scenarios."

"I told you I refuse to sound like the sound track to a low-rent porn film."

"Nobody in the history of world sex has ever taken as long as you take to fake an orgasm. That's the virtue of fucking fake orgasms, they come quick."

"If I am going to pretend to be your lover for the benefit of a bunch of eavesdropping sleazeballs, probably including David Hartman, I'm going to make them eat their hearts out. I want to make them cry for wishing they were you. All of them. Arrogant pricks, listening in on me. And," she says, "they are loving scenarios. Not kinky ones."

"OK, OK, come on, let's do it."

The reasoning is very clear. What is Mary Mulligan going to think, after being sent away so we can be alone, and with all the noise and to do and all the shopping, if the sheets are clean? The sheets have got to be stained. Even if she isn't working for them, the story will be all over the streets in hours. Maggie's a star. And that's what the maids and chauffeurs and plumbers and electricians and doctors do—gossip about the stars. Maybe the story will be that it's because she's gay and is trying to cover it up, or maybe it will be that it's a desperate ploy to make Jack Cushing jealous, or maybe it'll have something to with gerbils—whatever the alleged reason, the story will be that we're faking it. It'll get back to U.Sec., and David Hartman, quick enough.

She goes into her room. I keep walking down the hall to mine. It's what I learned to do, back in '67, when it was a matter of life and death. I don't mean to jerk off, I mean to take care of the details. Leave nothing showing that shouldn't show. Make sure everything that should be there appears to be there. When you're setting ambushes or walking into them, that's what makes the difference. The VC and NVA regulars, they were masters at it, because they didn't have the firepower, like I don't have the firepower, all they had was their minds—imagination and attention to detail.

Why am I embarrassed? This is not the first time in my life I have masturbated. When we were thirteen, fourteen, we had circle jerks. Competitions to see who could do it quickest, shoot the most distance. It shouldn't bother me, it really shouldn't. Maggie's doing more or less the same down in her room. Though a woman's stains are far less distinctive than a man's, there are still the smells. It may sound like I'm out there, but damn, I remember they could smell us and we could smell them. I could smell day-old rice. I could smell their rolled tobacco and when they smoked reefer. I could smell their body odor and the difference between an American fart and a Vietnamese fart. I don't know that Mary Mulligan is going to look at sheets or close her eyes when she throws them in the wash. I don't know that she's going to sniff at them, but maybe she'll notice the absence of smell. That's the way I think.

Maggie and I are each going to do our own sheet and then we're going to switch.

It's making me crazy. I'm in love with her. I want to be making love to her, fucking her, having intercourse, sexual congress, becoming intimate, however the hell you want to say it, it's what I want. We've been touching each other and gazing at each other in public. We've been talking dirty for two, three days now, creating scenes that I would pay to listen to. I've been living here for weeks. There she is, down the hall. I hear her giggle, like she's embarrassed too, then some other noises, like she's touching herself and—enjoying it. I am as hard and urgent as I'm ever going to get. I feel like a fool, a sap, to be using my fist, when she's right down the hall.

I push away the damn sheet, get off the bed, and head down the hall.

I walk into Maggie's bedroom, fully erect. Determined. I'm going to take her and she's going to like it. How can she not be as caught up in the game, or almost as caught up, as I am? What's wrong with her? Why's she holding back?

I get on the bed and pull her to me. She goes limp. I kiss her. The female-corpse act. "What do you want to do?" she whispers. "Fuck me once while I play dead and never see me again? Or do you want to exercise some self-control and take a chance that it's going to happen for real. And you can fuck me a thousand times with me fucking back. What are you going to do, Joe?"

"Fuck you, Maggie," I say loud enough for all the microphones to hear.

If I was twenty, I probably would have fucked her. And thought it was the right thing to do. As a man. As a Marine. But I'm not twenty. And she's the most woman I've ever met. Outside of Vietnam. There's a thirty-three-inch TV in the wall that operates from a console by the bed. I turn it on. Loud. It's one of the movie channels. John Wayne is a cowboy. I say, "Dammit, Maggie, it's embarrassing."

"No. It's not," she says. "It shows wisdom and self-control. It's probably 'the way of the warrior' not to be ruled by your dick."

CHAPTER

★ ★ ★

TWENTY-TWO

Sheric with the Stars

Our very dear Maggie has got herself a new beau. It's
been a long, long dry spell. Congrats, Mags! No smoothie this time. She's got a real guy's guy and I guess
she likes it that way. *So would I.* He's Joe Broz, a high-
class security consultant. A detective as they used to
say in the old days and I'll refrain from anything that
could be construed as a pun. That's the only one of
this year's New Year's resolutions I've been able to
keep. We hear he's a decorated vet and the sort who
will fight for his lady love. So boys, you better not
hang around too close; we wouldn't want anyone's
nose bent out of shape. This one's for real. You heard
it here first . . .

Taylor wants to make me wait. I look out the window. The smog is
particularly thick. From the forty-third floor you can look down on it.
It's a very strange effect. There are a few office buildings that stick up

above it. They look like some kind of computer-designed island modules sticking up out of a gray-brown sea. Planes fly above the muck, dive into it and disappear.

I turn around. Mel's secretary is gazing at me with stars in her eyes. Her name is Bambi Ann Sligo. She looks a bit like Maggie Thatcher, iron-helmet hair and too tough to fuck. Everybody calls her Mrs. Sligo. Even Mel. She's in her late forties, but so is Cher. This is that other kind of late forties, that entered middle age at twenty-nine, headed straight for the Barbara Bush look, and made it by thirty-six.

I smile at her.

"Oh, Mr. Broz," she sighs.

I nod, what you call condescendingly. Like I'm a star and she's one of the little people that make it all possible. So I say, "Hi, Bambi, how you doing today?"

"Oh, Mr. Broz," she says. Like I'm one of her favorite movie stars. "I told Mr. Taylor you were here and he will be right with you. I promise."

"Thanks, Bambi." Big smile.

She blushes. I sit down and open up one of the trades. Not *Police & Security News, Hollywood Reporter*. Bambi Ann pretends to do things on her desk while she makes covert glances at me. Do I have charisma by association? Mrs. Sligo has seen me pretty regularly for about twelve years now. She has never once acted like I make a blip on her radar screen. Now she needs to know: what does a person look like whose penis has been inside a real movie star?

Mr. Taylor finally gets tired of pretending he has important things to do and buzzes Mrs. Sligo to let her know that he can spare two minutes for Joe. She tells me I can go right in. I get up. She watches me the whole time like she's dying to ask me a question. So I stop as I pass her desk and say, "What is it, Bambi?"

"Is it true?" she gushes. She's got Sherie's column hidden under some business files on her desk.

I look her in the eyes. I take her hand. "It's true. All true." It's as if she wants to faint. But there's something more she wants to know. "Go on," I say indulgently. "Ask."

"Do you"—she hesitates, looks away, gets it together, then gets it out—"do Scientology?"

"No," I tell her. But without disrespect.

"Oh," she says, as if she has learned something important.

I know always that Mel hates me. Which, if you know all the facts, is stupid. I probably *saved* his life; I didn't *ruin* it. And taught him something about reality as it's practiced in wartime. He tries to mask it, or pretends to mask it, but we both know. Now it's gone onto a different level. I can see the tapes of Maggie and me all over his face. He hates me more because he thinks I'm getting something that he's not getting. He has an officer mentality. He actually thinks officers are a superior breed and that they deserve more money, better food, fancier clubs, more expensive liquor, classier pussy, and that the purpose of having lower ranks is to assure the higher ranks that they are better than someone.

"I want a leave of absence."

"Why don't you just quit. I mean, you're a hotshot now."

I don't want to just quit. Maybe I want Maggie and me to be in love. But I have not yet lost my grip on reality. I know that I am playing a game. I remember that the tape recordings are fake. I don't really expect to become her advisor and executive producer, the new wannabe Jon Peters. "I want a leave of absence, Mel."

"It's not company policy. Except in cases of illness or maternity."

"It is company policy to grant leaves as a matter of management discretion." Usually they grant it—actually insist on it—because it's in U.Sec.'s interests. Like when they want you to do a job that they don't want to be associated with. I have done that and I have been on LoAs, so I feel like I'm entitled to one now, when I want it for my own reasons.

"Well, Joe, I'm willing to consider it. Why don't you put it in writing. I'll consult with Chicago and get back to you," he says. He means I'm going to jerk you around, make you ask me about it five or six times, put you off with bullshit excuses, and then, when I feel the time is most appropriate, I'll say no.

"I'd like to settle it now, Mel. I have things to do."

"I'm sure you do," he says. "But that's not how we do things. We have channels. We have procedures."

"Mel, do you want to go for a showdown over this, right now?"

"I just want you to do things the proper way. Through channels. And goddamm it, as long as I'm in charge of this office, that's how it's going to be done."

Now I have acess I can throw on the table and probably top anything he's got in his hand. If we go to war, maybe I win, maybe we both lose. But how would a wannabe Jon Peters, lover-producer, diamond-in-the-rough smoothie handle this? "I'll tell you what, Mel baby. I see where you're coming from and I respect you for it. I really do. A company has to be run in an orderly way. Just like an army. Believe me, the last thing in the world I want to do is cause disruption. I have a thought here. I'd kind of forgotten, in the ecstasy of the moment as it were, that I got a heap of vacation time. A whole heap of it coming. There's at least eight, nine . . . ten weeks. Just from the last three years. Maybe more. Also, I've got at least three months of sick leave due me."

"This is a private-sector company," Mel snaps. "We do not treat sick leave as pseudo vacation time. Sick leave is for the ill and the injured not the lazy and *that is* company policy."

"Mel, what I'm trying to do here, I'm trying to make things easy and nonconfrontational for everyone. What I'm gonna do is put in my request for a leave in writing, just like you asked. And I bet you can get it approved in a week, ten days at the outside. Long before my vacation time is up—"

"Who the fuck said you could take vacation now?"

"I'm entitled to it. I'm taking it," I say very calmly.

"You're on assignment. You stay on assignment."

"I'm done with that assignment. Thank you, Mel."

"I don't care of Magdalena Lazlo is sucking your dick. That doesn't make you something special in my book. Don't forget, I know about you. I know the real you."

"Mel, that was rude." I still stay calm. This is a game, not the street. "You've insulted the woman I love. You've insulted a client of this company. I don't want you to do that. I don't want this to become an exchange of insults or foul remarks about each other or anyone else. I don't want this to become a physical confrontation." Which is not true. I would love it. But the company tape machines may be rolling and I know the recorder in my pocket is certainly on. "So what I suggest is, don't disapprove my vacation request. Meantime, I'll put in my request for a leave. Just like you asked."

"What's the problem, lover," he says. "You afraid she's gonna dump you in a couple of weeks for a better fucker?"

"Excuse me, Mel. Are you trying to provoke me to violence? This crudeness is unacceptable. If I were recording this, I think your job would be in jeopardy." Of course, he realizes that I am recording it.

"You were a problem in Nam. You're a problem here. You think you can do things your own way. Not when I'm in charge. Not anymore."

"Mel, I'm offering you a reasonable way to handle things."

"Just get out of here," he says.

I stand up. I lean on his desk. I look down at him. "Mel. You're out of line."

"You roll in shit and you come up with roses. I got your number, Broz."

"This is personal with you," I say. *Come on, put it on tape, Mel.*

"I can be just as cool as you are."

"Good. Do it."

"Now get out of here. I still have a job."

"Expedite the paperwork, Mel."

When I walk out, Bambi, who before this day has never said a personal word to me, beyond "Good morning—smoggy day, isn't it?" says, "I'm so sorry. He shouldn't be rude like that."

I go back downstairs. I put in for the vacation time. I drive over to sunset Boulevard. That's where my new office is. I grabbed the lease from a producer who finally ran out of development deals and was three months behind on his rent. Times are tough for Indies. Maggie hated the place on sight. But once I promised her she could redecorate it, she said it was alright. I like it because even though it's a small building, there are four possible exits. Hard to watch. I need a place away from Maggie's house. We still have to pretend that we don't suspect the LDs at her place. But with a new place I don't have to call in Matusow. I can sweep the place myself. I'm not setting up as a P.I. I'm setting up as—what should I call it? Maggie's advisor? Lover? Producer? We're going to get her her own development deal. Find properties that are right for her. Match them with the right director, writer, costar. That's what it's all about. Packages. We'll take a lunch with Hartman, have him put it to the studios. Whoever finances her gets first look at what we develop. If nobody offers the right setup, we go it alone. That's the advice I've given her. You can't sit back in this business and wait for them to come to you. Because they'll only come to you with what's good for them. That's so clear, it's glass. None of them care about her or what's right for her. Except herself and—me. That's what I told her and it very much matched with her own thinking.

I now know how fast word gets around in this town. And how hard everyone hustles. So I'm not surprised when the phone rings. Even though there's been no announcement, nothing official, and I'm not yet open for business. Even though there's no furniture and the phone is sitting on the floor. I figure it's someone with a script to push, a deal they want Maggie for, a job as a reader, something like that.

What surprises me is that the first call I get in my new office, in a sense, it's from Vietnam.

CHAPTER
✳ ✳ ✳
TWENTY-THREE

Beagle sat alone in the dark.

In front of him was a touch-sensitive computer screen. With it he could call up images or run entire film on any one or all of ten Musashi G-4 HDTV screens set into the curved front wall of his video room.

The screens were arranged in two rows of five. They were flat screens and mounted flush to the wall. They had an aspect ratio of 2.4 to 1, wide enough to accommodate the full images of those films shot in the glory days of wide-screen formats like Todd-AO, Ultra-Panavision 70, and Cinemascope. When they displayed a picture from a less horizontal source, they automatically generated a flat black matte into the blank areas of the screens. The walls were painted to exactly match that black. The Center Screen of the top row was larger than the rest.

Having viewed thousands of hours of film and tape, Beagle had selected what he thought somehow defined the essence of America's sense of itself at war. From the chosen images he had composed something that was between history and mythology. A high-tech ten-screen version of an American *Iliad*. Now he was going to play that story for an audience of one, himself, in the belief that it would make him understand what sort of war he would have to direct to make his country happy.

Center Screen. *Tearing Down the Spanish Flag.* Just an image. A leitmotif. A trumpet call from a distant silence to start the epoch.

A flagpole against the sky. A pair of hands enter the frame. They take down the Spanish flag. They hoist Old Glory.

That was it in it's entirety, shot in 1898 when America declared war on Spain.[52] It was the first commercial war movie.

Then, on Screen 1, up in the left-hand corner, appeared Leni Riefenstahl's famous 1934 documentary, *Triumph of the Will.* Hundreds of thousands of uniformed members of the Master Race march, turn, salute, stand, sing, *heil!* Hitler rants. It is the declaration of the German people that they have turned themselves into the machine that will rule the world. They will annex, terrorize, invade, conquer, exterminate, incinerate—and this is the self-image in which they will do it. One people, One will. This is the image that they will sell to the world and the world will believe in even long after Hitler is dead and the war is lost.[53]

---

[52]The Spanish-American War. If anyone remembers "Remember the Maine," this is the war it came from. So did Teddy Roosevelt, the Rough Riders, and the Charge up San Juan Hill. The war was waged—America said—for the purpose of liberating Cuba. It's a rather forgotten war, but it's very interesting for a number of reasons:
1. It was a media-created war. Hearst and Pulitzer competed to create war fever because war sold papers. This was before television. Even before radio. So newspapers were not only influential, they were big business and made a lot of money.
2. It marks the beginning of the American Century. The U.S. took on a European power for the first time since being defeated by the British in 1812 and kicked the shit out of them. In the process:
3. The U.S. became a two-ocean imperial power, taking possession, from Spain, of the Philippines, Guam, Puerto Rico, and the Spanish West Indies. Cuba became an independent territory under the protection of the United States.
4. The U.S. fought it's first war against "native" guerrillas. It turned out that many Filipinos were not ecstatic that liberation from Spain meant possession by the United States.

[53]"Although Germany had been defeated, Germany's propaganda remained intact:

On Screen 5, upper right-hand corner, the other beginning: *December 7th*. Quiet, peaceful Hawaii. Formations of Japanese planes appear, buzzing through the silent skies.

The sneak attack. The Japanese catch American boats sitting at anchor in the harbor at Honolulu. Battleship row, pride of the American fleet, turns into the stinking black smoke of ruin. The American planes are all on the ground. Lined up, neat and orderly. Perfect targets. Helpless and defenseless, they are destroyed. Torpedoes. Ships on fire. Planes explode. Flames. Sailors running. Two sailors with a machine gun fight back, firing at the sky. One falls. The other keeps firing.

Backstage, as it were, on the other side of the video screens, a room of industrial shelving, steel racks, bundled cable, a spaghetti land of wiring, an unmasked array of monitors and machines, Teddy Brody was watching too. When Beagle wanted a film that had not yet been loaded into the Fujitsu and digitalized, Teddy was the librarian who roamed through the racks to find it on film, tape, or disc, and put it on a projector, VCR, or player.

He loved the sequence that Beagle had assembled. The implications were so intellectually evocative that Teddy was able to forget his terrible frustrations—stuck here as librarian, not getting anywhere in his desire to be a director, not rising to a station where he could turn back to his parents and say, "Hey, you bastards, look at me, I'm making it, I don't need you to love any me more and I never, ever will." What he loved most was that the base of the pyramid, the foundation, the three cornerstones, were each of them a very special

---

Germans were the best soldiers in the world. American filmmakers accepted the idealized view of the German soldier and perpetuated it. Until the late 1970s, the Germans in American war movies are always clean shaven, with every button of their tunics neatly closed. And they never even flinch during battle." (Jay Hyams, *War Movies* [Gallery Books, 1984])

fraud.

Tearing Down the Spanish Flag was not shot in Manila or Havana. It was shot on a rooftop in downtown Manhattan.[54]

It was a terrific commercial success. The producers, Blackton and Smith, followed it up with the more elaborate *Battle of Santiago Bay*, the triumph of the American fleet over the Spanish in Cuba. That one was shot in a bathtub. The battleships were cutouts and the smoke of the naval guns came from a cigarette puffed across the camera lens by Mrs. Blackton.

The gargantuan rally that *Triumph of the Will* showed to the world really took place. however, the rally was staged for the camera.[53] This may not sound particularly striking today, when all life—personal life, sporting life, political life—is rerouted around prime time. But in the thirties reality was still presumed to be real and photographs didn't lie and no one had ever staged an event involving hundreds of thousands of people just so that the camera could record them.

December 7th won an award as best short documentary.[54] The images that it established became the reference for future films.

---

[54]Clyde Jeavons, *A Pictorial History of War Films* (Citadel Press, 19   ). See also Hyams, *War Movies.*

[53]Paul Virilio, *War and Cinema: The Logistics of Perception,* trans. Patrick Camiller, Verso. ". . . the most startling aspect of the project was *the creation of an artificial universe that looked entirely real* and the resulting production of the first and most important example ever of an 'authentic documentary' of a pseudo event. It is a stupendous revelation to realize that this whole enormous convention was primarily staged for the film." (Amos Vogel)

"Preparations for the congress were fixed in conjunction with preliminary work on the film—that is to say, the event was organized in the manner of a theatrical performance, not only as a popular rally, but also to provide the *material* for a propaganda film . . . *everything was decided by reference to the camera.*" (Leni Riefenstahl)

[54]John Ford directed the version that was released. An earlier and longer version was directed by Gregg Toland, a cameraman who worked with Ford frequently. Toland's cut, critical of America's unpreparedness, was not released (i.e., it was repressed, banned) until 1991. Toland is generally given credit for creating and filming the special effects that make up the actual attack sequence.

Footage was lifted and showed up in other documentaries. When feature films were made that included the attack on Pearl Harbor, filmmakers took great care to model their work on the record created by *December 7th*.

But all the battle footage in *December 7th* was fake. The stricken ships were miniatures. They caught fire and billowed smoke in a tank, a larger, more sophisticated version of the bathtub in *The Battle of Santiago Bay*. The sailors running through the smoke and firing back at the Japs were running across a soundstage. The smoke was from a smoke machine. The tank and the stage were in Hollywood, California, a place that has never been bombed, torpedoed, or strafed.

Teddy Brody loved it. He loved Leni Riefenstahl, John Ford, Blackton and Smith, and Mrs. Blackton too. He loved them for their audacity. There wasn't enough reality around, so they made some up. Teddy had spent a lot of time in academic circles—B.A. from Yale Drama School, M.F.A. from UCLA—where facts were checked, where people were failed for inaccuracy and booted out for plagiarism, so he felt very tied to specific and literal truths and didn't know how to escape them. Besides, his father had been such a liar—so adamant and violent about denying it—that it became very important to Teddy to keep precise score of who said exactly what, when they said it, when they changed it, and how they lied about it.

Center Screen went blank. Cut to black.

Victory in the West came up alongside *Triumph of the Will*. Hitler's armies smashed through Belgium and Holland into France on Screen 2.

Hitler believed in the power of films. He destroyed entire cities for the purpose of creating images.[55] When the *Wehrmacht* went forth to

[55]Most accounts state that Rotterdam was leveled not as military necessity but as a demonstration to anyone who would dare oppose Nazi power, that is, to *terrorize* civilian populations and to paralyze the will of German opponents. They filmed the

conquer the world, every platoon had a cameraman, every regiment had it's own PK, *Propaganda Kompanie.*[58] Hitler conquered continental Europe very quickly and with very little resistance. Part of the reason was that he convinced his enemies that the *Thousand-Year Reich* was invincible. He fought with the power of the mind. By the time the French troops faced the Nazis, they had seen the massed rallies at Nuremberg, they'd seen the result of blitzkrieg in Poland. They'd seen it on the same screen on which they'd seen Charlie Chaplin and Maurice Chevalier and newsreels that brought them the results of bicycle races.[57]

One by one, Beagle filled the screens with images of the enemy triumphant.

---

event.

[58]Virilio, *War and Cinema.* Hitler required the services of filmmakers and entertainers, but his greatest need was for those who could make the German people a mass of *common visionaries* "obeying a law they did not even know but which they could recite in their dreams" (Goebbels, 1931). Thus, while Roosevelt's New Deal America was using radio and film to regulate the "war of the home market" and to restart the industrial-production machine, Hitler was directing the millions of unemployed Germans to relaunch war as an epic. Others would make war to win, but the German nation and its masters already moved in a world "where nothing has any meaning, neither good nor evil, neither time nor space, and where what other men call success can no longer serve as a criterion" (Goebbels).

[57]"Lessons of Hitler's rise to power were not lost on American leaders. The use of propaganda was an integral part of the Nazi strategy and seemed at least partly responsible for Hitler's success." Russell Earl Shain, *An Analysis of Motion Pictures About War Released by the American Film Industry, 1930–1970* [Arno Press, 1976]).

A German general said early in the war that the opponent with the best cameras would be the victor, and the U.S. War Department responded by spending an annual sum of $50 million on factual filmmaking in order to swing the odds America's way. Massive amounts of combat footage were used for military study to show to the troops, and to make into newsreels for public consumption. And while the main emphasis throughout was on factual reporting and technical instruction, leading to a scarcity of documentaries that put forward ideas, shaped opinion, or provoked thought, in the end an incomparably comprehensive chronology of the war had been compiled. Jeavons, *A Pictorial History of War Films.*

On the left the Nazi's marched into Paris, conquered Yugoslavia and Greece, North Africa, the Ukraine, and the Baltic states. The Gestapo rounded up suspects and carted away Jews. They bombed innocent civilians in London.

Wake Island, the fall of Singapore and of the Philippines came up on Screens 4, 5, 9, and 10 as Japan marched forward (cowardly) and the Americans fell back (heroically). John Wayne watched the Bataan death march. The victors put the vanquished in brutal prison camps to languish and die.

Casablanca[59] came up on the Center Screen. To Beagle there was something defining about it. In the rhythm of the history he was creating, weaving, imagizing, it deserved to come out of the dark and be center-screen. It was the moment of choice—that's what it was—when we went from selfish absorption to commitment. Everyone had come to Rick's Café American; the refugees—Czech, German, Jewish, Rumanian, and more—Loyal French, Vichy French, a Russian, and the Nazis. And everyone's fate was dependent on what Rick decided to do.

---

[59]It's entirely possible that there are people who don't know the film *Casablanca.* It's set on the eve of Pearl Harbor, actually released in 1943, the first big year for war films, when Hollywood delivered about 115 of them. The story, though not told in this order, is this: Ilsa (Ingrid Bergman) is married to Victor Lazlo (Paul Henreid), a hero of the underground from Nazi-occupied Czechoslovakia. Lazlo is sent to a concentration camp. Ilsa hears he is dead. She then meets Rick (Humphrey Bogart) in Paris. They fall in love. The Germans arrive. Ilsa and Rick are supposed to leave together. She finds out Victor is alive. She doesn't show up. Rick leaves alone. He goes to Casablanca, where he opens a café and poses as a cynic. The town is run by a deliciously corrupt and genial policeman called Captain Renaud (Claude Rains). Victor and Ilsa and the Nazis all arrive. Rick gets to find out what happened in Paris, Ilsa is torn between love and duty. Rick must chose. He chooses to send Ilsa and Victor to safety together while he goes to off to fight the fascists again. In the final scene he kills the head Nazi, Major Strasser (Conrad Veidt). This is witnessed by Captain Renaud—an official of the collaborationist Vichy government—who decides that it is time for him too to switch sides. He goes off with Rick. This is probably the best closing scene ever written. Woody Allen lovingly recreated it in *Play It Again, Sam.*

Once Rick decided, all the images changed.

Screen 1	Screen 2	Center Screen	Screen 4	Screen 5
The Desert Fox	The Battle of Britain		Empire of the Sun	Bridge on the River Kwai
Screen 6	Screen 7	Screen 8	Screen 9	Screen 10
The Nazis Strike	Divide & Conquer		King Rat	Bataan

became

Screen 1	Screen 2	Center Screen	Screen 4	Screen 5
Battle of El Alamein	Sahara	CASABLANCA	Destination Tokyo	30 Seconds Over Tokyo
Screen 6	Screen 7	Screen 8	Screen 9	Screen 10
The Rat Patrol	Sink the Bismarck	Stage Door Canteen	Stilwell Road	Flying Tigers

By the end of *Sahara,* Bogart and his six guys, including Frenchie, a Brit, and a black Sudanese, had captured an entire company of previously invincible Nazis.

Over on the right the United States begins to strike back in the Pacific.

After that, America was on a roll. There was no stopping it. It was half-real, half-myth, and the two were mixed shamelessly. The military gave Hollywood footage, advisors, equipment, soldiers, transport, cooperation. In return, the filmmakers—gladly told the story that Washington and it's soldiers wanted told, the way they wanted it told.

Center Screen—*The Battle of San Pietro.* The opening statement on the screen: "All the scenes in this picture were shot within range of enemy small arms or artillery fire." Oddly enough, this was true. While all around the Center Screen men ran, leapt, dashed, charged into battle, the American soldiers fighting their way up the spine of Italy *walked* into battle.

Beagle wondered if the film affected him so because it was where his father had fought. Maybe not at San Pietro, but in Italy. Where he had been wounded. Every time he watched the footage and saw the men being carried away or waiting on the stretchers, he looked to see his father's face. He never did, even with freeze-frames and digital enlargements. But he was sure that his father's face must have looked like the faces in the film. So extraordinarily ordinary. Un-shaven. Cigarette smoking. Dying for a cup of joe. Wishing for just one fresh vegetable, a bite of onion, a bath. His father was dead. He couldn't ask him, "Dad, were you at San Pietro? Is that where you won your Purple Heart? Did you feel more for your country than I do? And can I somehow get there too? Was it better then? Was it as good as they make it seem in the movies?"

The men walked into the battle.

The film had been shot without sound. The director, Major John Huston, spoke the narration: "They were met by a wall of automatic-weapon and mortar fire. Volunteer patrols made desperate attempts to reach enemy lines and reduce strong points. Not a single member of any such patrol ever came back alive."

Of all the hundreds of war films Beagle had watched, he considered this the best. It started with shots of barren fields and trees without fruit. It explained the battle, simply and clearly. It showed the fighting. It told what happened. "Sixteen tanks started down that road. Three reached the outskirts of the town. Of these, two were destroyed and one was missing." It spoke of the casualties. "It was a very costly battle. After the battle the 143rd Infantry alone required eleven hundred replacements." But the battle was finally won. The Germans retreated. The Italians, villagers and peasant farmers, came out of the caves where they'd been hiding. Huston showed the faces of the children and the old women. He said: "The new-won earth at San Pietro was plowed and sown and it should yield a good harvest this year. And the people pray to their patron saint to intercede with God on behalf of those who came and delivered them and moved on to the north with the passing battle."

He let all the screens go black so that he could hear this ending.

Bang! They all snapped back on again. The planes were flying over Germany and against the Japanese. Real ones like *Memphis Belle*. Fake ones like *Memphis Belle*, the feature film that had been made fifty years later about the documentary. *Twelve O'Clock High*. *Victory Through Air Power* (Walt Disney's endorsement of bombing civilian targets), *Flying Leathernecks* (John Wayne). *Bombardier*, which showed that we need have no moral qualms about bombing cities—though that was one of the nazi's crimes—because our bombing was precise. How precise? The crewman says: "Put one in the smokestack." There are three of them down there. Bombardier: "Which one?" Crewman: "Center one." Bombardier: "That's easy."

The Center Screen's gone black again. But underneath it, Screen 8, Donald Duck sings, "*Heil, heil*, right in the Führer's face." Bugs Bunny and Daffy Duck fight the war. Bing Crosby sings for war bonds. Fred Astaire dances off to the Army. Gene Kelly dances off to war. Benny Goodman, Peggy Lee, Glenn Miller, Joe E. Brown, Bob Hope, and a lot of girls with breasts and legs whose names have been forgotten, Bette Midler in *For the Boys*, sing and dance and make that war, which was the good war, just a bit more of a fun war.

A wave of naval action sweeps across the screens. Lots of clips from *Victory at Sea*, the television documentary series, made from actual footage shot during the war. But then Charlton Heston and Henry Fonda walk right into the scenes.[62]

Center Screen. Next big plot point[61]—*The Longest Day*—D-Day.

Now the screens explode into action. Lots more color. Less black and white. More fun, less grim. *Dirty Dozen, Kelly's Heroes, Heroes of Telemark, Battle of the Bulge, Bridge at Remagen, Operation Petticoat, Stalag 17, The Great Escape, War and Remembrance, The*

---

[62]*Midway*, filmed 33 years later with *sensurround* sound and wide-screen cinematography, mixes in original 16-mm footage. A lot of the footage shot in the Pacific was in color. Virtually all the footage shot in Europe was black and white.

Guns of Navarone, Is Paris Burning?, Hell in the Pacific, Too Late the Hero, McHale's Navy. Lots of stars, as if one of the secrets of the war was that they were all there, mixed in with the regular Joes.

Once again Beagle blanked the other screens and returned to the center.

Once again Teddy was awestruck at how perfect the choice was.

The liberation of Paris. Real. Not staged. Spontaneous, not planned. An incredible moment, full of flowers and tears of joy, the pride of victory and women to kiss the victorious troops. They were images that made war worthwhile the way a baby's smile suddenly buries the pain a mother has had in giving birth. It was the Paris of our dreams, the America of their hope.

FADE TO BLACK.

Pause. Rest. Korea. Those mean, barren hills. The snow. GIs in heavy overcoats, caps pulled down low under steel helmets. Unshaven. The gooney-bird stare. Americans beaten. Americans in retreat. Not many good films out of that one. Not many films at all, in fact. Mostly they just kept making World War II flicks. *Men in War. Pork Chop Hill. All the Young Men. War Hunt.* Documentary footage. Clips from *MacArthur.* Nothing on the Center Screen. All the images were small.

---

[61]Hollywood is currently very much into story structure. Books, treatments, and scripts are analyzed by readers in terms of plot points—points where the plot turns. Are there enough? Are they in the right place?

Other important buzz words, if you're planning to pitch, are *backstory, inciting incident, progressive complications, setups and payoffs, subtext.* These are courtesy of Robert McKee's screenwriting seminar. Everyone, it seems, in the business who can't write has taken McKee's course to figure out what people who can write should be doing. McKee has never written a screenplay that anyone will actually produce. Back in 1988 he charged $600 for a weekend seminar, $350 for one of his staff to produce a reader's report, $1,000 for a personal consultation on your script. So he makes quite a good living just for sounding off. There are lots of cute and ambitious young women in the audience, so presumably he gets laid a lot. And that, by almost everyone's standards, is a pretty good definition of success. It is an admirable scam.

CUT TO: Vietnam.

News footage. There was tons of it. Not shot by the armed forces. Available and uncensored. Just fill up all the screens with it.

Sound from Screen 2. A picture of a very ordinary-looking guy. "The first time that I knew I killed somebody was another incredible sense of power," he says. "They were gooks, they weren't like you and me. They were things." This was a documentary. *Frank: A Vietnam Veteran.* "When you go out at dusk . . . and you set up and you're quiet and you're waiting, you are the hunter, you are the hunter. There's this incredible, I mean *incredible,* sense of power in killing five people . . . the way I can equate it is to ejaculation. Just incredible sense of release: the *I* did this. I was very powerful. Every where I went, I had a weapon . . . I remember laying in bed, some woman on top of me, shooting holes in the ceiling. I mean really getting off on it. Where else, where else in the world did you have this kind of freedom . . . I was not Frank Barber, I was John Wayne, I was Steve McQueen, I was Clint Eastwood."

Revelation. No one can stand that much reality.

CUT TO: Fiction.

Screen 1	Screen 2	Center Screen	Screen 4	Screen 5
Apocalypse Now	Friendly Fire		Who'll Stop The Rain	The Deer Hunter
Screen 6	Screen 7	Screen 8	Screen 9	Screen 10
Coming Home	Welcome Home, Soldier Boy		The Boys in Company C	The Visitors

Then *Born on the Fourth of July, 84 Charlie MoPic, Gardens of Stone, Go Tell the Spartans, Hamburger Hill, Platoon, A Rumor of War, Full Metal Jacket, Casualties of War.* He left the Center Screen, the big screen, blank. A flat black hole. He let the images run over him. These were some damn good directors. Stone, Kubrick, De Palma, Coppola, Scorcese, Cimino, the best. He let himself feel. It was not good.

Legless cripples. Lies and mendacity. Burning children. He wallowed in it. Drugs. Drug addicts, crazed veterans with guns. The fiction was more garish than the news, but the story was the same. Rapes. Double veterans.[64] Ambushes, booby traps, balls shot off. Burning huts.

had it been that bad? Had all the ideals turned to madness and sadness. Had Americans become the Nazis. Occupying a foreign country. Taking reprisals on civilians. Lidice[65] become My Lai. It must have the Luftwaffe flying B-52, doing to Hanoi what they did to Rotterdam and London.

No progress, just morass. No conquest, just despair. Troops defying their officers, killing their officers. And their officers, mechanical monsters without, apparently, a clue as to how to win this war. Bigger bombs and smaller results.

Beagle abruptly shut it all off.

There was more. But Beagle wasn't ready to see it yet. Because it led inexorably to a conclusion? A call to action? A decision, after which he would have to come out of his room and face the world and find out if this time—at last—he had failed?

---

[64]someone who had sex with or raped a woman and then killed her, common enough among American soldiers in Vietnam that there was a name for it.

[65]Lidice, a village in Czechoslovakia, was totally destroyed on June 10, 1942, by Nazis in retaliation for the assassination by Czech of Reinhard Heydrich, the deputy chief of the Gestapo and the number-two Nazi officer in Czechoslovakia. All men over sixteen were killed; the women and children were deported. Many Nazi atrocities were not known or acknowledged until the end of the war. Lidice, on the other hand, was publicized by the Germans as a lesson to others who might try to resist. It was the use of terror as a weapon. In those days terror was a weapon of the state, and what we call terrorism today was then the heroism of the resistance, of partisans, of the underground, our friends.

So the massacre of Lidice was known. It was regarded with singular horror. yet the Germans spared women and children. The Americans in Vietnam did not.

On the other side of the wall, Teddy Brody sat back, drained. He'd been watching this war shit for months now and he ought to have been immune to it. Certainly, he should have gotten over the shock of the Vietnam footage. He'd grown up post-Vietnam and come to consciousness during the period of revision that came so quickly after. By the time he was twenty, it somehow seemed that *only* the weirdos, the nutted-out, drugged-up, long-haired, rock-and-rolling reefer fuckers had been against the war. In conspiracy with TV guys to betray the noble warriors. A quick trip back in real time was too much reality. How did Americans go from John Wayne to that?

Perhaps the fact that Lidice was a command decision, a policy decision, and My Lai was an action led by a low-ranking officers in violation of official policy, more like a riot than a tactical choice, might make a difference to those who didn't die there.

CHAPTER

★ ★ ★

TWENTY-FOUR

Steve Weston is the voice on the line when I pick up. He says he read about me in the paper. I didn't know that many people read "Sherie." I guess it's one of those things like picking your nose. You only do it in front of other people if they already know you do it. I hear jukebox and barroom noises behind him. It's a week day, so that surprises me.

The first thing that you notice about Steve, if you see him, more than if you hear him, but still if you hear him, is that he's black. But that doesn't mean you expect to hear him calling from a barroom in the middle of the day. Steve came back from Man with the attitude of "I'm glad that over. I got out of that alive, and intact, and I'm going to live the rest of my life straight and peaceful-like." A lot of people didn't come back that way. A lot of people came back thinking the world's a toilet and I'm going to shit in it. Or grab what you can as soon as you can because there's incoming coming. Or I went and I fought for you and now you owe me a hero's life and a hero's living and if I don't get it, I'm going to pout.

I'm lucky. I always knew the world was a hard and dirty place. That nobody cared for heroes. It's always "But what did you do for me lately?" That's what my daddy gave to me. He gave me no illusions to lose.

So when Steve came back, he found himself what he called a good woman. A churchgoing woman. Who wanted to have regular babies, get wide, keep a clean house and food on the table. He got himself a steady job. First it was a car wash or something like that, a lot of people would have felt they were too good for. He went through several others, but he was always trying to get on the line at the GM plant down in Van Nuys. It took him a couple of years. But he finally got in over there. It's UAW and top dollar for unskilled labor, $17 an hour or more by now. That means a base of $35,000 a year, holidays, vacation, sick pay, plus medical and pension and all of that. Anybody who wants to can push that up to $45,000, even $70,000 with overtime.

"I seen that and I ax myself, is there more than one Joe Broz? But I says to myself this got to be the one, 'cause the one I know be the one with more balls than brains. And that's why she love him so, right, Joe?"

Four kids, a fat wife, four cars, all Chevies, what the hell is he doing in a bar on Wednesday before lunch sounding too merry and mournful all at once. "What's going on, Steve?"

"I'm alright. Al-right. I seen this, and I has to call. I calls you at the office and they says you gone. Gone for good. They gives me some number and a real nice lady answer the phone. I ax myself, is this Magdalena Lazlo I'm talking with? So I ax her, is you she? And she is. I tells her I'm a long time friend from, you know, Vietnam. And she says she is sure you will be happy to hear from me because Vietnam was a central experience in your life and she gives me this number. Where is you?"

"My new office. What's wrong, Steve?"

"Nothin' fucking wrong. I's OK. You's OK. Semper fuckin' fi. Marines forever. I just seen you got this fine thing happen and so's I call you."

"How's your wife?"

"She fine, she fine. She not so fine as your is fine, but she fine."

"The kids? How are the kids?"

"Kids fine. They trouble sometime, but that what they're for. Keep your mind occupied with their trouble, keep it off your own. No mo' trouble than the next kid."

"Where you at?"

"This is a fine place. They calls' it Ray's Sweetwater. Down here near where's I live."

"Baldwin Hills? You gonna be there awhile?"

"Yes, I guess I am. I guess I am."

"Why don't I come drink a few with you."

"You come down but you best pass for highyaller," he says. He thinks that's very funny and I hear him chortling away as he hangs up the phone.

I walk into Ray's Sweetwater. It's more what you'd call Watts than Baldwin Hills. It's cool and dark, especially after the high, hard Southern California sun. You've seen this scene in the movies. Mostly Westerns. A stranger walks into the bar. Sudden silence. Deadly stares. Cut away to the toughest hombre in the room. Insert shots as the bartender and various hangers-on look to him for their cue. Is he gonna kill the stranger right this second or toy with him first? Of course, what they don't know is that I'm not a real Chinaman, I'm David Carradine, a Shaolin monk and I can kick faster than an ordinary man can shoot. I'm Alan Ladd, but folks just call me Shane.

Suddenly, there's a voice from way in the back of the room, back at a booth behind the pool table. "Hey, you all, leave him the fuck alone. He's a nigger like us. Tha's just a flesh-colored Band-Aid on his face."

There is reasonably universal laughter. Some of it more amused than the joke deserves, but entirely welcome. The place relaxes. I have been vouched for. I'm passing for black. I walk to the back. The music is not too bad. Old-fashioned, more R&B than rap. It comes out of an extravagent jukebox that plays CDs.

Steve's at a table with four other guys. Three of them are in their late forties, early fifties, the fourth guy is older, sixty or more, hair gone almost white. They all have beer and snacks too. Peanuts and fried pork rinds. I sit down. Conversation stops. It's not hostile, just still. A young waitress wearing Lycra top and bottom, pink against purple, saunters over and sticks out an ample hip. The old guy with the white hair pats it fondly. She tells him he's too old. He's says the problem is not that he's too old, it's that he's too big. I ask for a bottle of Bud and one more of whatever everybody else is drinking. I offer a twenty, she snatches it up.

"Give the man change," Steve says. "Don't you be playing no games."

"He a white man," the old man says to one of the younger ones. "Why don't we ask him?"

"Well, that don't mean he know the truth. He could be iggerant."

"I says we ask him."

"I says you're full of shit."

"This here, with the white hair and the big mouth, is Marlon Mapes," Steve says. "That's Red, and Kenny, and Shavers."

"We got an argument going. And these fools, they can't see the truth," Red says. "Are you ready for the truth, white man?"

"This a friend of mine," Steve says.

"He's a white friend of yours," Kenny says. "And that's the truth."

"There's times and places black and white don't matter," Steve says.

"Always matters," Red says.

"Always," Shavers says.

"Like when don't it matter?" Marlon asks.

"It always matters," Red says. "That's your bottom line."

"Fuckin' A. Black, white. Bottom line. You right, you right."

"OK, Steve, when don't it matter?"

He can't just say, "Nam—didn't matter in Nam." Because it did. It mattered on leave. It mattered back at the base. It mattered when there was music to be played, liquor to be scored, dope to be used, promotions to be handed out, orders to be followed. It mattered all the time and every day. We both knew that.

But sometimes it didn't matter. It didn't matter on patrol. At least for Steve and for me. It didn't matter in a fire fight. It didn't matter when the VC and the NVA announced that they had business that transcended race.

"It didn't matter when I lay dying," Steve says. He's pretty drunk to be saying this, I think. He stands up. He pulls his shirt out of his pants. He's gone to fat. That isn't any fresh-from-Parris-Island lean Marine standing there, bare belly poking out over his pants, scars twenty years old. "Carried me bleeding. Out of an ambush on his back."

"Prob'bly kept your fat body 'tween the bullets and hisself," Red says.

These are fightin' words because that's a sacred memory. Everybody gets that and the others tell him to shut up. Kenny stands between Red and Steve. The Lycra girl shows up with the beers and a gin and tonic.

"I di'n't go no Vietnam," Red says. "Me and Muhammad Ali. Ain't no Viet Cong ever shot at me. White men usin' black men to fight their war. Cannon fodder."

"Fuck you, Red," Kenny says. "You stupid. I been to Nam. You don't shut up I hits you myself."

"What you got to understand," Steve says, "is what it was like."

"They don't need to hear this. This is an old story," I say. I pour my beer into the glass. It doesn't look golden like it does on TV. It looks yellow, like piss. Must be the lighting.

"What the VC liked to do, they liked to get one man, wounded, in a killing zone. Screamin'. It works better if he's screamin'. Then his buddies try to come for him. And they pick them off, one by one. Maybe gets two out there screamin'. You gots two choices. You sit there and you listen to your buddy screamin' and don't do nothing' and feel like you is shit, cause your buddy is screamin' and you're doing nothing'. Or you goes and tries to get him. Then, you know what, not only is you dyin', you feelin' like a fool while you dyin'."

"Don't want to die feelin' like no fool," Marlon says. "That is addin' your insult to your injury. Umm-hm."

"That's what it was like," Steve says. "You got to understand that. I was screamin' and this man . . . this man, he came and he got me and he carried me out."

That shuts everybody up. At least for a moment. The air-conditioning is humming. There's condensation on the bottles. Ray Charles is on the jukebox.

"Listen here, Joe. That's you' name, Joe? Right? Listen here," Red says. "I want you to tell all these peoples here, sittin' at this table, the truth. The white man is afraid of the black man. That is a fact, right?"

"Don't play into his shit."

"Go on, answer the man."

"A lot of white people are afraid of black people," I say.

"Of black *men*," Red says. "The white man is afraid of the black *man*. He don't mind the black woman. He like dark meat from time to time, ain't *that* a fact."

"Ain't nobody afraid of the black woman," Kenny says. "Except you. You 'fraid of your mama and your wife, the blackest womens I ever seen. And they got your ass whipped."

"I am making a serious point here," Red says. "So shut your jive mouth. That's what you do, Marlon. Somebody saying somethin' and you lay your nonsensical jive on it, 'cause you don't have the concentration of mind to deal with the issues. You see what I'm saying. No concentration of mind."

"So is you is or is you ain't gonna make a point?"

"I am. You shut up and you wait. The white man will do anything to cut down the black man. That is an undeniable philosophical truth. Is it not?"

"Amen."

"Uh-huh."

"The truth," Marlon says.

They all look at me. I say, "Anybody want another round?"

"Don't let 'em intimidate you," Steve says.

"I'm not intimidated, I'm a beer drinker."

"I hear you," Marlon says. He signals to the waitress. At the prospect of another free one he slurps down the gin and tonic that's currently in front of him a little faster than he's been doing.

"What I am getting to, is AIDS."

"Oh Lord protect my dick," Marlon says.

"You'all ever try any that safe sex?" Shavers says. "Sheeit, you might as well be doing it yourself. And rubbers, you better off doing it yourself."

"Dogs you been doin' it with, you need a full body condom," Marlon says.

"You so old, you manage to do it, you probably die of happiness and surprise fore you die of the AIDS," Shavers says.

"Problem with you men is you so lost in your dozens and trash talking you forget that there is a political situation going on."

"Nobody forget there's a political situation goin' on," Steve says. "An economic one too. We just want to forget it."

"In the sixties the black man was on the rise," Red says. "And the white man couldn't stand that. America couldn't stand that. So he went to work on ways to stop the black man. It was the CIA in charge. Now this here is a public and documented fact. Even the lying, prevarication' Jew-run white media, they admits to this fact. Which is that the CIA in the name Air America became the number-one heroin runners in the entire planet. They run the opium out of the Golden Triangle, and they made an alliance with the Italian and the Jew Mafias to sell exclusively in the black ghetto. To destroy the black man."

"That's the truth."

"I read that."

"Amen."

"Alright," Red says. "White man, are you going to deny that?"

"Are you with the CIA?" Shavers asks out of nowhere.

Everybody looks at me like maybe I am and Shavers is on to something important. "My man, here, with the CIA?" Steve says. he puts his hand on my shoulder. How drunk is he? What's he going to say? There are things that he knows that these people should not hear. "You don't know, you can't imagine half the things that this here man done. But let me tell you what. You can't tell a book by lookin' at the cover. He may look like a redneck, motherfuck Polack, but he's a lover. That's what he is. My man here, to whom you are being so very rude, is the true love of Magdalena Lazlo."

Everybody has to make a comment about that. None of it offensive, most of it impressed. Except Red. "You know, I am in the middle of makin' my philosophical point and I would like to recommence that when you all get bored admiring on how fine a piece of . . ." He looks at me and decides not to say "pussy." I understand by that hesitation, which is not politeness, but an acceptance of a boundary, that this is not a dangerous place. These are just five old men, though not necessarily with more years than me, but old. Who are not going to rise up in their blackness and provoke an incident to destroy this particular white person. Five men with nothing to do but meet in the back of a bar during the day, passing time, dragging out cheap beers, with talk that doesn't mean action, talk that just passes the time, because they have no place else to go. No mission. No function. No job.

No job. That's what's happened to Steve.

"That wasn't enough. So the CIA, they decides to attack the black man through his greatest strength. So they invented a disease you get with your dick. Acquired Immune Deficiency Syndrome. And they field-tested it out in Africa. Then they brought it to America. See, the black man he's more capable of sexual pleasure than your white man, plus he got a bigger, more powerful dick than the white man and he use it more. Ain't that the truth. Ain't that the truth, white man?"

"I don't know," I say. "I never had a black man's dick. How do you know so much about white men's dicks?"

"Ou-wee. He got you."

"Done got you good."

"Amen."

They're laughing and repeating the punch line. "Steve," I say softly, "can you and me talk. Privately. I need to talk to you about something."

He looks around, sees an empty table, the other side of the pool table. He grabs his beer by the neck and lumbers up. I do the same with mine and follow him. It seems he doesn't have to explain or make excuses.

I hear, as we're walking away, Red still talking. "Alright. He made a funnin' remark. But I'm talkin' 'bout reality here and you are choosin' ignorance. CIA made AIDS. It was the establishment, the honky, uptight, own-all-the-money, establishment counterattack on freedom and good times. Read the statistics, Goddammit. Forget the faggots, tha's just a smoke screen. A smoke screen, to detract from the real target. The real target is you."

Steve and I sit down. He's got a lot of pride, and I can tell that right now he's in a world of hurt. I'm guessing about him losing his job, but I'm pretty sure I'm right. When he tells that story about me carrying him out, he doesn't bother to say he returned the favor. Steve is a person with a kind of pride. He don't cry and he don't beg. Even when he was out there, in the killing zone, he might have cursed out loud, but he didn't cry and he didn't beg. If he doesn't want to tell me that he's a man with a wife and four children, with no way he can think to earn a living, then I'm not going to ask. I understand about that kind of pride.

So I come up with an idea of how to help him while pretending that I'm not. Which, as it turns out, is an idea I should have had anyway. "I'm hoping," I say, "that you can get away from your job for a while. I need some help. There's only two people in the world I trust. And Joey, he's dead." Steve knew Joey. Knows how he died. He was there. Joey died in Nam. "So if you can get away from the fuckin' line, I got a job for you. I can't give you no seventeen something an hour, but I can swing fifteen, if that'll do you."

"Well, my man, you's in luck."

"I'm glad to hear that."

"General fuckin' Motors is going out of fuckin' business. They ain't cutting the chairman and the managers, of course, they cuttin' the niggers and the rednecks on the line. How many years I been building Chevrolets? How many years I been building and buyin' American? How many years, Joe? Fuck 'em."

"I'm sorry to hear that."

"You figured that, didn't you? That I down on my luck. You my frien'. Which it ain't easy to say about no white man, but fuck you, Joe. I don't need no charity. No I don't and I don't want it."

"Fuck you, Steve. Sit down. I need help. Sit down, I'll explain it to you."

CHAPTER

★ ★ ★

TWENTY-FIVE

Beagle went back to the pre-programmed montage. There was an inevitability to what was to come. There had been a second wave of Vietnam films. They had, by now, not just created, but established, a revised memory of what had happened. And where they had gone on-screen, Beagle suspected, was where he was about to take America in reality.

Beagle punched up the Center Screen. *Uncommon Valor* came on.

Gone were *Platoon, The Losers, Gardens of Stone, A Rumor of War, Full Metal Jacket,* all the high-brow, morbid, and septic studies in self-hate.

One by one, Beagle refilled all the screens:

Screen 1	Screen 2	Center Screen	Screen 4	Screen 5
Missing in Action	American Commandos	**UNCOMMON VALOR**	Operation Nam	Jungle Assault
Screen 6	Screen 7	Screen 8	Screen 9	Screen 10
First Blood Part II	Strike Commando	RAMBO	Delta Force	Hanoi Hilton

Gone was the moral confusion. Gone was the defeatism. In the new films the Vietnamese were the bad guys, as cruel as Nazis, as treacherous and lying as Japs. The American invaders had become innocent victims. The answer to Rambo's immortal question, "Do we get to win this time?" was a resounding "Yes!"

That was it. That had to be it.

Black, everything went to black. Silence. All screens off.

"Do I have it?" Beagle asked himself. "Do I have a fucking movie here? Or not?"

There it is. The central myth. America the Invincible. America the Good. Finally falls, and finally fails. On her knees and not looking so good ever since. Well, maybe it was time to go back.

Beagle had read *MIA; or, Mythmaking in America*. He found it quite convincing. He was pretty sure that there were no MIAs or POWs in secret prison camps. He also knew that *Uncommon Valor* was a fiction based on real events although the real events were based on fictions and that they costarred several major Hollywood actors. Retired Special Forces Colonel James "Bo" Gritz actually mounted two rescue missions in 1982. He was funded by William "Captain Kirk" Shatner, who put up $10,000 in return for the movie rights, and Clint Eastwood who put up $30,000. Clint met with ex-actor, then current president, Ronald Reagan, to bring him in on the plot. This telegram was sent to Gritz in Thailand:

CLINT AND I MET WITH PRESIDENT ON 27TH. PRESIDENT SAID: QUOTE, IF YOU BRING OUT ONE U.S. POW, I WILL START WORLD WAR III TO GET THE REST OUT. UNQUOTE.

But in two attempts Gritz failed to find even that one U.S. POW. Nor had the CIA in years of clandestine searching.

It would be easy enough, Beagle figured, to put some POWs in Vietnam, or Laos, or wherever. That shit was done all the time. Hadn't Hitler put some dead Poles in German uniforms and accused the Poles of killing them in order to prove that he'd invaded Poland in self-defense? Filmed them too. Hadn't the Gulf of Tonkin incident, which became the legal basis on which the U.S. committed half a million men to Vietnam, been stage-managed?

If it went fast enough—find them, go to war, win the war, get them out, and get it over with—no one would have time to argue about it.

It seemed to be the answer. Plant some POWs in Nam. Go in not with some half-assed Chuck Norris commando raid or Rambo one-man band, but with the whole of the United States Army, Air Force, Marines, and Navy. Not piecemeal. Not *escalation*. All together—bigger than D-Day, better than the Inchon landing—march straight into Hanoi, grab some Commies, try 'em for war crimes, shoot 'em, announce we won, and have a parade. It would work. Joy. Delirium. Days of triumph, crowns of glory.

Why wasn't Beagle happy with it? What was wrong with it?

Katherine Przyszewski was thirty-eight years old. She was divorced and a single mother. Her daughter was sixteen, her son was ten. Outside of the film business, away from Hollywood, far away, somewhere off in reality like Erie, Pennsylvania, or Fort Smith, Arkansas, or Eau Claire, Wisconsin, she would have been considered a very attractive woman. She had real red hair, fair skin, and blue eyes. But between work and her children she didn't have time to go to the health club daily. While her job at CinéMutt, as Beagle's personal secretary, paid very well by her standards, her standards did not even imagine thrice-weekly sessions in her own home with her own personal trainer. She therefore had neither a washboard tummy nor buns of steel. She had had nothing surgically altered or implanted, therefore she had laugh lines around her eyes and her merely average-sized breasts, made only of flesh, sagged when she stood and flattened when she lay on her back.

Beagle liked her. She was competent, very calm at the office, and had no aspirations to be an actress. Or producer or screenwriter or director or anything whatsoever in the movie end of the movie business. She didn't think making coffee, making restaurant reservations, sending his clothes to the cleaners, getting his car inspected, or buying gifts for his wife, were vile, deviant, and degrading acts of sexism. In short, she helped make the life part of his life simpler. She, in turn, liked her job, liked her boss, and liked the pay.

They had, from time to time, slept together. She didn't know if she was disappointed that it had not blossomed into love and marriage, or for that matter, into a genuinely passionate affair. It may have been because her kids and just trying to live life, clean, neat, healthy and paid for, drained so much of her energy that she didn't have a great appetite for sex and romance, or that may have simply been her nature. Actually, if either of them was bothered by it, it was probably Beagle. He believed that nice, sensible, fair, and caring people came in packages that looked like Kitty and that packaging like Jackie's was almost invariably wrapped around a core self of narcissism, competitiveness, and obsessive self-involvement. He found it annoying and a little perverse that, once the moment of need was past and the pulse of lust satisfied, he just couldn't care for Kitty, that he needed someone more—dammit—Hollywood. Sexier, jazzier, better-looking, someone—and this really was disturbing—like his wife.

Kitty was getting on very well with her son. He seemed to take naturally to studying and school and had a bent for science that delighted his mother. He didn't do drugs and seemed to have bought the whole "Just say no" package, including tobacco and alcohol, that they preached in class nowadays. Only God knew if any of these redeeming qualities would continue through adolescence.

They certainly hadn't in her daughter Agnes, a whining girl who, in spite of all that her mother tried to teach her, thought it was a Barbie Doll world, where Ken would come along and give her, *give her*, a pink Corvette, just for having a plastic perfect body and big hair and wearing high-heel near-white leather booties.

Agnes cut school, went out with the sort of boys that make mothers sick with worry, smoked pot, and wanted to be an actress. Kitty fought it, but managed to live with it, telling herself that each thing was a phase, and that in a world that included AIDS, teen pregnancy, crack, and drive-by shootings, Agnes's behavior was pretty mild.

But then her daughter had come home with bigger breasts.

At first Kitty thought she was imagining it. Then she thought perhaps Agnes had had a growth spurt. Then she had a sickening fear that her daughter was pregnant. She tried to talk to Agnes about it. Agnes did what teenagers know how to do—she denied and denied and denied.

Kitty walked in on her daughter in the shower. Kitty swore it was an accident. She even possibly believed it. She saw the stitches, the ever-so-discrete incision, where Agnes had received a breast implant.

A mother-daughter battle royal ensued.

Agnes revealed that she had it done to further her career as an actress. Her breast size, she was certain, was all that stood between her and a series of major roles in film and television. She rattled off a list of names of actresses who'd had surgery and what parts had been changed.

She refused to tell her mother how she had paid for the surgery and this scared Kitty most of all. Where did a sixteen-year-old girl find the money to pay for breasts? Didn't they cost somewhere from a thousand to three thousand *each*. What insane doctor had done that to a child, without parental consent?

This was the most frightened Kitty had ever been as a mother. Her daughter had spiraled out of her control and she couldn't figure out how to bring her back. Beat her? Threaten to keep her locked in the house? Threaten to throw her out? All of those would just push Agnes to go and do more of whatever it was she had done to pay for the operation.

Where did parental control come from? Once it might have come from a culture that demanded that the child respect the parents. Television or rock and roll or Dr. Spock or something had trashed that one. Now all that was left was force and dependence. How could she make Agnes dependent? The only thing she could think of was by becoming the girl's best avenue to an acting career.

And that was something she was in a position to do. The perfect position. Kitty was, after all, the personal secretary of one of the most successful and powerful directors in the business. More than that, she'd felt his lips on hers, pressed her naked flesh against his, been entered into. She had a *right* to ask. He would have to help her. Have to, to save her child.

On another level she was quite certain that John would be really annoyed—he usually was—when one of the staff pushed an actor or a script or something like that on him for personal reasons. So she hesitated to approach him. Especially as he seemed so busy. So obsessed. She kept waiting for the right moment. Which never seemed to come. And the longer she was silent in her need, the angrier and more resentful she became.

It was a little after eleven in the morning—Kitty glanced at the clock on her desk—when John Lincoln wandered out of his video room.

He had it, but he didn't have it. It was logical. It practically screamed out to be done. Go back to Vietnam and win this time. What was wrong? He wished he had someone to talk to about it. Actually, he'd come out of the video room just to see a human face on a human being and—something. "You ever watch war movies?" he said to Kitty.

Kitty didn't want to talk about war movies. She didn't want to talk about anything that Beagle wanted to talk about. For once, just once, she wanted him to address her needs. She didn't quite know how to mention that.

She was such a regular person, Beagle thought. One of the most middle-American he knew. "What did you think of the war in Vietnam?" he asked.

"John. Mr. Beagle . . ."

He looked at her quizzically, full of inner puzzlement.

All she could do was blurt it out: "I want you to put my daughter in your next movie." It lurched out like an order, a command. The way a mother orders a daughter to clean her room, not the way a secretary speaks to her boss.

"Huh?"

"It doesn't have to be a big part. Just a part."

"Kitty, uh . . ."

Her mouth trembled. She was afraid she was going to cry. Maybe if she'd said "I have a problem and I need your help," he would have said, Sure, let's see what we can do. But she wasn't used to asking favors and didn't know how. Plus, she was ashamed that she couldn't control her daughter and ashamed of what her daughter had done to her own body and she wanted to keep it private, a family secret. So what emerged was angry and demanding. "I want a part for my daughter in your next movie."

"Look, I don't know what's wrong with you—"

"Are you going to do that for me or not?"

"There are no parts in my next movie," he said, which was the simple truth.

"What a . . ." She couldn't bring herself to say the words formed behind her lips—"crock of shit"—but the spirit was present in the silence.

"I didn't even know your daughter was an actress."

"She is. And a very good one," Kitty said, though she had no idea what made a good actress and expected, because she had a very low opinion of her daughter, that she was a terrible actress.

"I thought you said she was going to be a dental technician."

"Well, she's not. She's an actress and I want you to give her a part."

"I'm not using actresses or actors," he said. "Only real people."

"Well, well, then use her as a real person."

Beagle, stuck in the literalism of the moment, couldn't think of anything else to say except, "No."

"You're a . . . a . . . a thoughtless bastard. I hate you."

"What the fuck has come over you?"

"Don't talk to me about fucking. You fucked me, you fucked me alright and I never, never asked a single thing from you until this minute, and you won't give me the time of day. You're a selfish shit. If you won't give my daughter a role—a walk-on, an extra, give her a screen test, just a goddamn screen test . . ."

"Uh . . ."

"If you won't, I quit."

"There's no part to give her, you stupid woman," Beagle said. "Didn't you hear me?"

"Then I quit."

"So quit. Good-bye." A bit stunned, aside from being angry at this assault from nowhere, all Beagle could think was that perhaps he was wrong about the difference between plainly packaged women and the dazzlers, that being ordinary didn't improve a woman one bit. It was a dreary and depressing thought.

CHAPTER

* * *

TWENTY-SIX

Ray Matusow collected the most recent set of tapes that were keeping track of the home life of Katherine Pryzszewski and her small brood.

Ray started at the office in the morning and spiraled outward through Los Angeles. The Pryzszewskis were number four on his list of seven. Like Taylor and Sheehan, he did not yet know what the purpose of his work was, only the names of the people he was responsible for covering. Except for Joe and Maggie, they all worked directly for John Lincoln Beagle. Teddy Brody, day librarian. Luke Pryzszewski, night librarian, no relation to Kitty, though Beagle had thought he must be because of his name, and hired him to please her. Beagle had thought the world of Kitty until this point of confusion. Carmine Cassella, projectionist. Seth Simeon, staff artist and designer. Maxwell Nurmberg and Morris Rosenblum, who were the electrical-engineer, computer-whiz, tech-nerd, tinkering video mavens that had put together the ten-screen view system in Beagle's studio.

Somebody else, Ray didn't know who, handled Beagle himself, including his offices, his home, his child, and his wife, Jacqueline Conroy. Perhaps there was even a third to track the rest of the people employed at CinéMutt, Beagle's studio and research setup.

When he'd collected them all, he went home. That was his

routine. He spot-checked the tapes, logged them, and then copied them on a high-speed duping machine. Ray believed in redundancy. He'd had supervisors misplace material and clients ruin recordings and then turn to him and act like it was his fault. In the morning he'd bring the originals into the office, log them in there, then start again.

He was upset to discover that the last tape from the Pryzszewski set seemed to run out in the middle of a conversation. He knew approximately what their daily dose of talk was and he'd had enough machines and tape to record three times that much. He played them back and listened enough to discover that Kitty had quit her job and had been home all day. Plus, she'd spent a lot of time talking to her daughter. Kitty told Agnes that she was going to find a new job where she could be of real help to Agnes's career, that her mother could help her, and would help her, more than anyone else in the world. There was no way that Ray could have anticipated those events. He would put in a couple more machines the next day. Meanwhile, he'd file a report that explained what had happened.

In the morning, when Ray drove into the office with the tapes from the day before and his report, he didn't notice that he was being followed. Just as he hadn't noticed it all day the day before.

CHAPTER

★ ★ ★

TWENTY-SEVEN

*T*he Return, Beagle's name for
the Vietnam scenario, still didn't sit right.

Apocalypse Red: go in and knock out the remains of the USSR.

It was, in his mind's eye, incredibly cinematic. Real David Lean
wide-screen stuff. *Dr. Zhivago* and *Reds.* The sweeping movement of
massed armies across the flat, stark-white steppes. Tanks, rockets, the
sky filled with combat aircraft, the firing of guns, vivid bursts of color
on a palette of snow. If Coppola was Italian opera as cinema, this
would be Russian opera. Garnder, vaster, and infinitely more profound.

It was also very problematical. However disorganized the Rus-
sians were, they still had nukes. Beagle's wife and all their friends
were incredibly concerned about ecology and nuclear proliferation.
Beagle did not want to turn out to be Dr. Strangelove, a madman
willing to bring on the first nuclear winter or set off the doomsday
machine.

He turned to the screens. Black on black.

Maybe terrorists were the way to go. If the librarians had done
their job, and they were pretty good, he could access material by
subject matter. He began with news footage. Just tossing it up on
whatever screen was open, viewing randomly, getting a sense. The

terrorists were mostly Arabs. Beagle watched CBS graphics of the bombing of the Pan Am jet over Lockerbie. *Achille Lauro* footage. A plane on the ground in Egypt, terrorists and hostages inside. Innocent bystanders dead at an airport.

Movies: Counterattack by Delta Force, by Navy Seals, by Commandos, by the FBI, by Chuck Norris, Interpol, Vietnam vets, by Bruce Willis, by bionic bimbos.[67]

Teddy Brody, in the back room, wondered what the hell Linc was up to. It had been war movies, war movies, and war footage. Now this. Teddy had been making notes and charting the films. And he started reading about them. Of the fifty odd books that he'd read, the one that most intrigued him was *The World War II Combat Film: Anatomy of a Genre*, by Jeanine Basinger, because it had a formula for such films. Maybe, if he followed the formula, he could write a script. Maybe that script would be the one that Beagle was searching for. That was the whole point of this damn job. To find a way up and out.

But now, terrorists?

That could work with the Basinger formula. The combat film was always the story of a small squad of diverse people—reflecting the dictates of political correctness of the period—who manage to overcome their differences to work together to achieve a common— patriotic, obviously—objective.[68] Of course, that could work with a

---

[67]*Programmed to Kill:* a beautiful terrorist is captured by the CIA and transformed into a buxom bionic assassin. *Hell Squad:* Unable to release his son from the Middle Eastern terrorists who kidnapped him, a U.S. ambassador turns to the services of nine Las Vegas showgirls. These gals moonlight as vicious commandos. (Summaries by *Video Hound, Golden Movie Retriever*)

[68]Teddy was essentially right. Details, attitude, and style can reinvigorate a genre endlessly and make for great filmmaking—*Sahara* is reinvented as *The Guns of Navarone* > *The Dirty Dozen* > *Platoon* > *Uncommon Valor*.

At the same time it proves how right Hartman was to select Beagle for the project, because ultimately Beagle did not just run a riff on the formula. When the genre was inadequate, he stepped outside of it and even outside his medium in the way it was normally used. He let the nature of the project define the form.

Commando team against the terrorists. That was obvious. He didn't know why he'd even hesitated over it.

Beagle wrote a note on a yellow pad: *"Scenario: The president is kidnapped by terrorists."*[69]

This had a certain appeal. Beagle had learned not to let his imagination be incarcerated by cost or practicality. Still, it seemed to him that with this reality shit, getting the cooperation of a foreign country prepared to enter into a war with the United States, with the United States scripted to win, might be difficult. But having the president participate in, or fake, his own kidnapping would be a piece of cake. How could he refuse? It was all being done for the benefit of his reelection.

Then the waiting. The drama of not knowing. Whip the country into hysteria. Then the ransom demands. Do we bow to ransom? Do we stand on principal? *Millions for defense, not one cent for tribute!* The negotiations. Deliberately dragged out. While, secretly, the Delta Force (or Navy Seals, or Vegas bimbos or even the FBI) is maneuvering to burst in on them and they rescue Bush in a perfectly timed and executed . . .

What a thought! Have the terrorists execute Bush! Then Dan Quayle becomes president, declares war on terrorism. Not like the war-on-drugs war. But real war where we go in and obliterate entire cities. Search and destroy. If they want to hide in Libya, invade Libya. Syria. Anywhere they tried to hide!

Obviously, the client was not going to go for that. Bush had to stay alive. But that's what he needed—an incident that would kick the

---

[69]Not a truly original thought: "According to Jefferson Morley [in the *Nation*]; several employees of Wackenhut recently worked on an elaborate scheme to help death squad members kidnap the U.S. Ambassador to El Salvador, Edwin Corr. The rightists evidently hoped to place the blame for event on the FMLN." Edward Herman & Gerry O'Sullivan, *The Terrorism Industry: The Experts and Institutions That Shape Our View of Terror.* [Pantheon Books, 1989])

whole affair into higher gear. If the Delta Force rescued the president, then what? Then it became a police matter. Measured force. Investigations, waiting, arrests, and years later—long after Bush won or lost his reelection—a trial. Probably in Italy, where the terrorists would only get ten years anyway and then be traded to Libya after eighteen months for a boatload of oil and support for the lira. Or would the American public be outraged enough—that is to say, could the American public be whipped up to a sufficient frenzy—that they would be willing to go to war?

What if they took Bush and Quayle? Delta Force rescues Bush, but the terrorists kill Quayle.

That was a happening concept.

Bush, in anger and grief, leads the nation—the nations, plural, of the West—in a Holy Crusade against terrorism. So that no wife need grieve like Madilyn? (Marilyn? he made a note to check). So that no child (he was sure Quayle had children) would be left fatherless, ever again. Image: orphan, little, fending for himself, looking for help. No. Try: little girl, curly hair, sweet face, crying herself to sleep at night— waiting for a Daddy who would never return. Nice, nice.

The terrorists would be Muslims. The Rational, Ethical, Forward-looking West, against the Backward forces of Superstition and Repression of the East. It tapped into atavistic hatred. Christians, they are Moslems! There it was—the project title–*The Crusades.*

Excited, he called Kitty on the intercom. He used the speaker-phone. He hated holding regular telephones against his ear. It made him feel like a nerd with half an earmuff.

"Kitty," he cried.

"I'm not Kitty," a female voice answered.

Then he remembered. Kitty had quit. This was a new one. Did she have a name?

"Yes, Mr. Beagle?" she said into the silence.

Did she have a name? Why was he calling her? He remembered. "We got a kid here . . . smart kid. Uhhh, Yalie. Gay kid. What's his name?"

"I could look in the personnel files."

Dimwit. Or were the the personnel files listed by sexual preference? "Are they filed that way?"

"What way?"

Beagle hung up.

And there was something else he'd wanted Kitty to do. He dialed the new person back.

"Would you get my wife a dress," he said.

"Huh?"

"A dress. You know, like women wear. On their bodies."

"I know what a dress is."

"Good."

"But what kind of dress . . ."

"How the hell should I know?"

"What size?"

"Kitty knows all that," Beagle said. He didn't know his wife's sizes. Of course, he realized that buying things was *no substitute for being with your family.* But at least it proved that he was thinking of them. And in spite of what his wife said, she was in fact easier to deal with when he bought her something.

"You have kids?" he asked the faux Kitty.

"No."

"Know anything about them?"

"Some. I have nephews and nieces."

"Good. Get a present for a twenty-month-old."

"What should I get?"

"Never mind," he said as politely as he could.

If he remembered correctly, the Yale kid was a librarian. There was a button on his phone that said LIBRARY. He pushed it.

Teddy heard the phone ring. An actual call. A human voice was going to speak to him. It was a rare event at work and Teddy, savoring the potential—certain, however, that whatever the call was, it would somehow be less than what he hoped—let the phone ring three times before he answered it with a cheery "Hello, library."

"Hey, Beagle here."

"Yes, sir."

"Are you the Yalie?"

Teddy wondered what might be wrong with that, but he said, "Yes." He added, "UCLA film school too."

"You must be very bright. Glad that you're working here. Wish we had more time to spend together . . ."

Oh God, what does he want? He's speaking to me. Opportunity calling.

"Here's what I want. I want one page on propaganda."

"What about propaganda? History of? Ours? Theirs? Definitions? Controversy over? Great examples? Hot war? Cold War?"

"I want one page on the essence of propaganda. The guts of it. The whatever, if I had it, I would be a genius at propaganda. The Zen of Propaganda. Then you can give me more on the rest of the crap. Get it?"

"Got it," Teddy said, though he didn't.

"Good. End of the day tomorrow. No, take your time. Two days, OK?"

"Sure." Of course, it wasn't. What was he doing? Shouldn't he speak up and say a job like that, just to find the references will take two days, then two weeks or a month to do the reading, going round the clock, then if you want something really astute and well written—especially if it's short, short is harder than long—I would like at least a week for that. People hate people who promise more than they can deliver. Bosses like employees who advise them honestly what can and cannot be done and when. That was ridiculous. Bosses hate that. They want people who can do the impossible for them without argument. That's what impresses them. Better not speak up. Just do what you can. And fail. Or not.

"You don't have to do your regular job too, at the same time. Tell Kitty D. to get someone to cover for you."

"Uh, Kitty D.'s gone."

"Right," Beagle said.

"Uh, thanks, Mr. Beagle."

But Beagle was already off the line. He was onto something and he knew it. *The Crusades* was exciting because it at least postulated an answer to the problem of who would be willing to go to war. Supposedly, that was not his problem. His job was to come up with the script, with any enemy he wanted, as long as it did the job. Then it was up to Hartman, the packager, or George Bush, technically the producer, to make an enemy deal. If they couldn't get the enemy he wanted, then he would readjust. Shit like that happened all the time. Hadn't *48 Hours* originally been a buddy picture designed for Stallone? Then it got switched to Eddie Murphy and adjustments were made. A good director shaped his material to his stars. And in a war the number-one enemy has got to be considered a star.

Still, since he would be dealing with so much reality, it would be good to let reality help shape the concept. He would have to, in essence, get into a dialogue with reality because that was the raw material that he would have to manipulate. So dealing with questions like who would fight, who would be willing to die to get George Bush reelected, was important to the process.

The Arabs had a whole tradition of holy war, jihad. If they truly believed that those who died as sacred martyrs would go to some holy hashish, hookah, and houri heaven, then they might be willing—even pleased—to fight a war they were contracted to lose.

The image of Paradise, the Persian garden promised as the Islamic afterlife, intrigued him, and he made a note of it as a possible subject—maybe setting—for a film. It was a lot like what people dreamed L.A. would be. Large, brightly colored intoxicating drinks, hot tubs, exotic foliage, lots of drugs, especially love and sex drugs, a variety of beautiful and subservient women. What if, once you got there, the reality of Paradise turned out to be the reality of L.A.—pollution, hatred, crime, too much time spent in automobiles breathing fumes, eternally irascible, demanding women. In the end, the hero escapes, gets another chance at life, rushes back to the battlefield and says "Don't be a martyr, Paradise is just like home."

Beagle was not in some never-never land. He understood that this was a real war he'd been asked to create. People were going to die. The idea filled him with a sense of power like he'd never felt before. Not even on set with a full crew and thousands of extras and special effects and helicopters all awaiting his command. This was deeper. Richer.

Beagle faced that black wall. He punched up terrorist films. *Black Sunday. Python Wolf. Terror Squad, Commando, Death Before Dishonor, Viper, Omega Syndrome, Invasion Force.* The language of film was clear. Arabs were terrorists. Terrorists were bad. There was no other side of the story.[70] That was useful and important. It made for economy of exposition. Just like with Nazis, give a guy a monocle and a bit of leather, a straight-arm salute and that sneer, and the audience knows that this is an unmitigated villain, and the director can cut right to the chase.

But watching the clips, Beagle was disappointed. In spite of the black and white simplicity, terrorism did not make for good movies. Not like World War II or even Vietnam. It was 98 percent sub–Chuck Norris shit. *Patriot Games* was top-of-the-line. It did not speak well for the genre's potential.

---

[70]Firing Joseph McBride from *Variety* for his review of *Patriot Games* was more than a glaring revelation of the financial incest between the entertainment industry and the entertainment media. It was a recognition of the total victory of our official ideology on the issue of terrorism.

What is now called terrorism is, after all, the method of warfare employed by individuals and small groups against the power of the state. These groups were, not long ago, called the Underground and the Resistance. And they were, not long ago, *automatically the heroes* of our movies. The Secret Police that searched them out and the armies that hunted them down were *automatically the villains.*

It may be argued that our attitude has changed because the Resistance that we loved consisted of civilians who targeted bad military people and the new ones are bad (though unofficial) military people who target civilians. But that would at least be an argument. The point is that there is no argument. It is considered unfit to mention that *another point of view exists.*

CHAPTER
★ ★ ★
TWENTY-EIGHT

The President's job existed beyond logic and sense. It truly belonged in the realm of magic. When The Man was blessed, thrice blessed, all acts were good. Signs and portents ruled the realm. When The Man was cursed, truly cursed, all skies brought unwanted rain, nothing brought gain.

It seemed, looking backward, that the strangeness had come with Camelot. Imagine this, that the nickname was more knowing than knowing knew. That the arrogant affectation—that this was a new age and bright, that these were new knights more special than those that had gone before—revealed a truth so bizarre that no one single person for one single moment considered it literal. The myth of Arthur is that he was the Once and Future King. That he would return. Imagine this, that he did return and that he recreated the kingdom dedicated to dreaming, generosity and virtue. Someone there was Merlin. Who the hell was Merlin? It doesn't matter.

What matters was that once again the King must die, once again be murdered. The corpse—like the body in some fabulous allegory— wove its own shroud into a tapestry of illusion. Everyone who looked upon it saw a different story. Everyone who looked upon it swore that all the other stories—about his death, about his killers—was false.

And he left a curse upon the crown. His death left everything upside down. Or perhaps Merlin, divine necromancer, inter-epochal fixer, in rage and despair, left a wizard's trick upon the throne.

How else to explain the tragic Macbeth—Macbird they called him in delicious satire—who followed him? How to explain the fall of Richard Nixon, master of intrigue and plotting, brilliant and devious—how could the incompetence of a couple of clowns breaking into a hotel, step by somehow unstoppable, undivertable step, bring him down lower than any President before him? Then Gerald Ford, an apparently decent, competent man, with no fault except bumping his head, found unfit to be President because he was clumsy on camera. Then Carter, who worked hard, who studied goodness like a theologian, brought down day by grinding day, by the hostage countdown on television.

Which, of course, is the name of the magic that brought us John F. Kennedy, whatever he was, and the curse that he left behind. The proof is the one and only man who beat the curse—Ronald Reagan, the television man. He didn't work hard, he didn't know much—about all those things that Presidents are supposed to know, economics, foreign policy, law, history, even art. He did the opposite of what he said, seemed unable to tell truth from late night TV, and should have been embarrassed by much of the company he kept. Yet he once again made the White House seem like a palace and the capital a glittering imperium. Luck and blessings seemed to fall on all that he did and there was radiance around him.

A curse? To Bush, whose whole life had been subservient to the goal, whose every choice had been faithful to what the polls said a President should be, do, think, feel, it often seemed as if, having arrived, he had stepped off the edge of the known world. Nothing he did had the result it was supposed to. All the courtiers and advisors and cabinet members and experts scurrying around the White House, very busy, in a great hurry, carrying lots of papers, going up, going down, going sideways, making conference calls, sending memos, screaming to be heard, convinced they were right, requiring limousines and special lunches, were a bunch of rabbits and mad hatters, and not all their energy made one dent in what was really important, his standing with the American people and whether or not he would win re-election.

Bush was on *Air Force One*. Baker was with him. They had been at a meeting in San Francisco with the Pacific Rim Business Association. Most of it's members were Americans, including the majority of the board of directors, but in essence it was a front for Japanese corporate interests. It's pitch was free trade, something that was part of the Republican canon and which the president intrinsically favored. The argument against it was that the Japanese used the rhetoric to mask practices that were, in actuality, both restrictive and predatory.

Bill Magnoli, president of America's Exporters, Inc., had asked for a few minutes to present his case to the president.

A million voices clamor to be heard. The king wishes only to survive. Yet he must make decisions, he must lean left or right, forward or back. On what basis can he choose? The president—who has no time for original research, who doesn't have the energy left to reach outside the loop on every one of thousands of issues—listens to those few voices that get to present their story. Which is what makes access the prize.

America's Exporters had at one time actually been an American-owned company. It was now owned by Musashi Trading Company, the key company in what is called a *keiretsu* in Japan. As every reader of the financial pages or of Japan-bashing thrillers knows, a *keiretsu*[71] is like a conglomerate, but larger, closer-knit, more predatory, infinitely more terrifying.

Musashi had bought American Exporters for it's name and for it's president, Bill Magnoli, the most American guy the Japanese company spotters had ever met. Workdays or weekends, Bill was a

---

[71]It is for the Japanese what the penis is for the black man. The thing that they have that is reputed to be larger than the whites', more potent, more irresistible—the thing about his race of which the white man is most afraid and with which he will sexually enslave the women of the white race.

bouncing ball of cliché. Drove a Mustang, ate grilled steaks and large desserts, watched football, talked football, played golf, boffed his secretary twice a week, his wife once a week, really liked double knits and Willard Scott, played Lotto and thought Vegas was really, really hot. He had two kids, one in college, one in rehab, and carried their pictures in his wallet. He was a go-along, get-along guy, a real booster of whatever put bread on his rather large table and gas in the tanks of the four cars he supported.

When Bill Magnoli got up and spoke on behalf of America's Exporters, it took a real effort to remember that he was really a spokesman for Hiroshi Takagawa, whose title at Musashl was always translated into English as "vice president for the improvement of Japanese-American relations," but written in *kanji*, the ideograph version of Japanese, it could be read as "member of the General Staff, Strategic Planning for Victory in America." It was never translated that way, and it was considered rude to even mention that around *gajin*.

At issue was military procurement, one of the ways that America has traditionally supported private industry. Private industry, in turn, has been very supportive of the military. Some chipmaker with a politician in his pocket—alternatively described as a congressman concerned with his constituents, many of whom made their living in silicon alternatively described as a patriotic American worried about his country's high-tech independence in case of war—had introduced a bill requiring the Pentagon to buy only Made-in-America chips. The congressman was going to get his bill, but it would permit the Pentagon to make exceptions if . . . There was currently a debate over whether the next phrase would be "it was a matter of compelling necessity for the immediate defense, for a period not to exceed one year," or "no reasonable alternative was available." Obviously, the impact of the law, if any, now depended on which clause was selected and how it was enforced.

Magnoli was cogent, colorful, concise. As well he should have been since Hiroshi Takagawa had paid a great deal of money to an

American PR firm to research and prepare the itch, as well as for an acting coach to drill Magnoli.

The question was not whether or not Magnoli was wrong or right, whether he was an agent of influence of a foreign power, or even whether or not the president should have heard those opinions directly. The question was, why did Bill Magnoli have access?

"Bushie, how did you happen to be talkin' with this Magnoli fellow?" James Baker asked the president.

"Neil," the president said, talking about what he was concerned about, his son. "Is there an outcome indicator?" Meaning, *Did Baker know if Neil would be indicted or not.*[72]

"It's taken care of."

"If he weren't my son . . ." Bush waved a finger. Not meaning, *If he weren't my son, I'd see to it he did hard time to set an example;* meaning, *If he weren't my son, no one would care.* "Not some blabbermouth publicity hound." *I hope the attorney at Justice, who is told to quash this thing, doesn't turn around and tell the world he was told to quash it.* "This picking, picking at nits. They better wait and see."

"You know he fronts for the Japs," Baker said. Back to Magnoli.

"Of course, I know—what do you take me for?" Bush said. "Don't answer that," he quickly quipped.[73]

"His company is wholly owned by Musashi."

"I told you I knew that," Bush said. "Read my hips. Do you want to know how I knew that?"

---

[72]If anyone wants to be reminded of the details, they are: 1983, Neil Bush (son of G.B.) goes into the oil business. Neil puts up $100. His two partners put up $160,000. 1985, Neil becomes a paid director of Silverado, which loans his partners $132,000,000. 1987, one of his partners "forgives" a $100,000 loan to Neil. 1988, the developers default, Silverado fails. FDIC bailout cost about $1,000,000,000. (Sources—*Time, Spy*)

[73]I have never in my writing life had a character "quip." I cringe at "he quippeds." However, it seems to me that Bush is a person who does exactly that, so here it is, this one's for the quipper.

"Sure," Baker said.

"Because it was my friends at Musashi, who are helping me out, and who else is? They asked me to give a few minutes of my time to Magnoli. Two plus two, that's not going to escape my notice," Bush said, pleased, as he was from time to time, to do something that Baker didn't even know about.

"Helping you out?"

"With the memo thing. Gosh, I didn't tell you about that, did I?"

"No," Baker said. "You didn't. Not that you have to. I just like being in the loop because it makes me feel important, you know that, Bushie, and who the hell is more behind you than I am."

"Remember the memo?"

"The memo?"

"Atwater's memo," Bush said, smiling his famous lopsided smile.

"Oh. The memo."

"Right."

"How it said, 'Hartman,' show it to him."

"It didn't say show it to Hartman," Baker said. "It sort of said don't show it to anyone, maybe get Hartman to do the job if anyone was going to do the job."

The president cocked a finger like a gun, pointed it at Baker, and said, "It's *in development*."

"In development?"

"That's the way they say it in L.A. 'In development.' And they put their top, top shooter on it. Jonathan Lincoln Beagle. Do you remember *Riders of the West*. That was one great movie. That scene where Clint Eastwood just squints at the bad guys, that squint . . ." The president squinted like Clint.

"I thought you shredded the memo."

"I found it. It was all at the same time, coincidental timing, when Hartman met me in Orange County."

"You had the memo? You didn't shred the memo?"

"It was right there in my pocket."

"How did it get in your pocket?"

"One of the secretaries found it in my briefcase."

"How did it get in your briefcase?"

"I like it, Jimbo. You know what I feel like. Maverick, Burt Maverick. There's a big pot on the table, and I'm opening my cards, real close to my chest, and I look real cool, because it doesn't matter what's in my hand, I got an ace up my sleeve."

Baker didn't tell him the TV characters had been Bret and Bart Maverick. He said, "So you met Hartman and gave him the memo."

"And he put it in development. You know what development is?"

"I know. Who's paying Beagle? Is anyone paying Beagle? Who else knows about this? How many people are in the loop?"

"That's the beauty of it. No one. Except Hartman and me and Beagle and now you. But you always were, sort of."

"Beagle knows?"

"Well, how can he direct a war if he doesn't know he's directing a war? I couldn't. Could you?"

"So they're doing it for nothing?"

"No. Very clever. Hartman he arranged it all. Jews are like that, with arrangements. Musashi is paying for it. But they don't know it."

"That's terrific," Baker said, trying to find a way not to sound too, too interrogatory. "How did he arrange that?"

"You see, there's overhead and salaries. That's what business is about. It creates jobs. Staff and such. And living in L.A. You know the cost of living there is very high. So he just let Musashi know that if they underwrote a development deal with Beagle that the president, that's me, would be very grateful. I'm grateful enough that I'll listen to one guy for seven minutes. I'm reasonably grateful. I am."

"They didn't want to know why you would be grateful that they give a Hollywood picture-show director a couple of million bucks? I'm guessing it's a couple of million—everything out there is a couple of million."

"I don't actually know the actual amounts. It was all that was necessary."

"And this Hollywood agent and this Hollywood picture-show

director, they're not talking this up at parties or with their girlfriends to impress them or whatever?" Baker asked, masking a rising sense of panic.

"You're concerned about security?"

"Well, some," Baker said. He wished he were afraid of flying. That would have meant that the feeling in his stomach was that he was in a tubular aluminum coffin twenty-two thousand feet in the air, not that Bush had started something that was going to be a combination of Watergate and Jimmy Carter being attacked by a rabbit. L.A.! Movie directors planning the next war! This thing had bimbo and bimbo leak written all over it. What the hell was going on? Did Hartman arrange some nubile thing to give George genuine Holly-wood-style blow jobs, leaving him disoriented and deranged? Baker had seen what happened to aging men, especially WASPs, when they discovered oral sex.

"We have total security. Surrounding the clock. Wiretaps, everything."

"CIA?" Baker asked. There was that acid feeling, creeping up his throat. In a moment he was going to taste it at the back of his mouth. He knew it. Some fucking liberal-leftist Democrat congressman or senator would get some scared-shitless, piss-in-his-pants wimp from the Agency under oath and he would blab all the secrets all over the press. It had happened before; it would happen again.

"No," Bush said, pleased with himself. "I had Gates take it private."[74]

---

[74]The various "intelligence" agencies of the United States have always used, owned, created, financed, controlled, associated with, external organizations. In the post-Watergate years a lot of information about the CIA, in particular, came out. Illegal and incompetent and wasteful and silly activities were revealed. The CIA was placed under a variety of new restrictions and "cleaned house." The recent history of Iran-contra demonstrates that alternative formats, a little further removed from congressional scrutiny, were immediately developed. That those efforts were discovered and Ollie North appears to have been so incompetent doesn't mean all such alternatives have been revealed or that all are so bumbling and ineffective. Remember, this is the administration that believes in privatization.

"Oh," Baker said, deeply relieved.

"You forget I was at Langley. I was in charge of Langley. I know all the tricks. Or most of them. I wasn't out in the field. But I sure had some of those field agents in to tell me what was what and how we accomplish some of the tricks of the trade."

"Gates is a good man," Baker said. Robert Gates was. He was a stand-up guy, that is to say a proven liar, unafraid of being charged with perjury or contempt of Congress, unembarrassed if the truth was later revealed. He'd been a Soviet scholar, head of all CIA analysts, executive assistant to Director of the CIA William Casey and then Casey's deputy director. Reagan named Gates to succeed Casey, but his nomination was withdrawn when it came out that he'd failed to notify Congress, as required by law, of Ollie North's diversion to the contras of the profits from arms sales to Iran. He also had an extensive history of doctoring data to reflect political goals rather than reality.[73]

"You bet," Bush said.

"How's the money getting to Bunker?"

"I'm out of the loop on that one," Bush said.

"George, I really think you should have told me. I am secretary of state."

"Well, with things, this opportunity was the occasion."

"I mean if we're going to go to war with someone"—Baker managed a smile—"I should be aware of it." At the time he had read the memo, it had seemed strangely compelling. Now it just seemed strange.

"Don't be a pussy, Jimbo. And you might think you're smarter than me, I know you think that you're smarter than me. But don't underesti-

---

Wackenhut guards U.S. embassies; Universal Security has a variety of government contracts, including urine analysis and drug screening of employees of the Departments of Agriculture and of Transportation. Gates was not at the CIA at this time, he was at the NSC.

[73]After these events, in 1991, Bush would nominate Gates, once again, as director of the CIA.

mate me like so many of them do. I've been a congressman, chairman of the Republican Party, head of the CIA, ambassador to China, and Ambassador to the U.N. Now how many people do you know who've done even one of those things, let alone two of them, without getting their ass in a sling? Huh?"

"I beg your pardon, Mr. President. You have a point. You have an excellent knack for not putting your ass in a sling."

"Or my nuts in a vise. Or my tits in a wringer. Or any other of those things."

"Let me pour you a drink, Mr. President."

"Thank you, Mr. Secretary. And, Mr. Secretary, I want you to know that I have this very much under control. I'm not going to do something stupid here. I am not going to go down in history as the stupid president. But I am going to do whatever it takes to win. Now are you on board or are you gonna jump ship?"

"We're at twenty-two thousand feet, I'm not going to jump ship," Baker said. He passed a Chivas to his president, then took his own. He decided he was going to block this insanity. If for no other reason than that the president had done an end run around him. Not that Bush didn't do that from time to time, just to prove who was in charge. That was OK. Normally. But not about something important.

"I got an ace up my sleeve," the president chuckled. "I love it. Just like Burt Maverick."

Baker raised his glass in salute. He didn't say anything about Bret or Bart. The president touched it with his own.

"To war," Bush said. "To a good war."

"I just want to know one thing," Baker said, waiting to drink. "Who are we going to go to war with?"

"I don't know. It's just in development."

CHAPTER

* * *

TWENTY - NINE

When I open the office, I expect people to look at me with a certain amount of contempt. Sniggering behind my back, that kind of thing. They don't. That's the glory of L.A.: it doesn't matter where you get it; no one cares how you get it; the only thing that counts is if you get it. Or if you don't. I wear my new wardrobe. When I drive, it's as the boyfriend, not as the chauffeur. I start to go places publicly with Maggie, the lunches—which are all business—parties—which are all business—meetings—which are almost all social.

The most important lunch, of course, is with David Hartman. He agrees that Maggie should take that next step and have her own development company. With someone else paying for it, of course. We discuss where the money might come from. There's mention of JVC/Victor and Musashi, possibly MGM, because there's some talk over there of more "women's pictures." He might take it to Paramount too.

Which, of course, is not what the meeting is really about. It's really about him and me looking each other over. Sizing each other up. He makes himself likable. That's fine. He drops in a couple of lines of Marine talk.

Maggie slides her hand over mine. CUTAWAY of her hand as it

slides over mine, takes possession, establishes communication, says *"This is my man."* CU MAGGIE's face as she does so. CU HARTMAN as he takes it in. CU JOE, who feels Maggie's hand cover him like superman's cape. It shows on his face.

"Joe isn't saying anything I haven't thought, or felt, before," Maggie says. "But being with him makes me stronger."

Cut back to Hartman: he appears to believe.

It's a good thing that I'm not sleeping with her. The insanity of celibacy is all that keeps me sane. If I was beside her, inside her, I would have delusions of grandeur, and I would believe that I was her business manager, producer-to-be, general leech and profiteer. Anyway, I look over at her like she looks like a movie star to me, which she is, and like I'm a lovesick fool, which I am. But it's what she's doing—and I don't understand what that magic is—that makes the scene play as reality instead of scam. She glows like she's sated, shot full of the hormones of love. I'm almost fooled, and I know for a fact, from lights and noises, that her nights are as restless and unsatisfied as mine.

The woman can act. There's no doubt about it.

"I just want what's best for Maggie," her agent says.

"So do I."

"I see that."

The waiter arrives with a bottle of wine. It's better than a hundred dollars at the liquor store, over two hundred dollars on the restaurant's wine list.

When I was a teenager, a guy walking toward me down the street, I automatically think, Is he bigger? Toucher? Can I take him? Later, when I get older, when I go to Nam, and after, it changes. I look at guy and the question is, can he kill? Has he killed? Will he do it again? That's my bottom line.

I look at Hartman. I don't think he's killed. Not even in war, not even at a distance. I don't know why I evaluate this, but I do. Later on, when I check his service record, it confirms that he wasn't in combat. Can he kill? Will he kill? My thinking is that he would like to. Not for the dying—there are guys who love the dying—but for his sense of himself.

Agents have a rep for being ruthless, merciless, heartless, for being "killers."[74] But being a killer agent is like being a tough touch football player. Something's missing. Blood. Even in an environment like L.A., with little respect for reality, they know the difference. Hartman would like to look at himself in the mirror and have that secret knowledge that he is a killer. A real one. He would like that.

Hartman raises his glass to us. "To new love," he says.

Maggie's PR person sends out releases about the new office. I am interviewed over the phone by *Variety. Hollywood Reporter* sends a guy over. The *Enquirer* sends a writer and a photographer. someone from *Entertainment Tonight* calls. I agree to make myself available. That never actually happens, though.

Plus, I'm getting calls from hundreds of people, it seems like. Scripts arrive at the office. Letters. Résumés. I see some people. I'm going to need a reader, a secretary, maybe someone else.

There is a reasonably priced restaurant a few blocks from the office. It has two separate back ways out, an easy way through the kitchen door and a more difficult one from the bathroom window. It's where I go if I just want food. I'm sitting there alone when Bambi Ann Sligo, Mel Taylor's secretary, walks in. It's a bit far from U.Sec.'s office. It's possible that she is there by accident. Some people in this business insist there are no accidents. I greet her and she joins me at my booth. She orders a hamburger and a cup of black coffee. I order

[74]Not my (literary) agent. Joy Harris is a sweetheart. And I am sure that there are others like her. Agent jokes are virtually the same as lawyer jokes—the sharks don't eat them out of professional courtesy; their hearts are good for transplants because they've never been used—that sort of thing. There are a few that are powerful enough to actually help and even to actually hurt someone's career. Most of them are just hoping to find—or hold onto, clients who generate more income than they cost in overhead.

a burger for myself. I tell her that Maggie would disapprove. Bambi—spitting image of the Iron Lady—simpers and says, "You should listen to Maggie. She's a star." I smile. "All right, I will." I ask her how her job is going and how it is to work for Mel Taylor. She wants to tell me something, I think, but she doesn't do so. We talk about other people in the office we don't care much about. When she's done with her burger, she lights a cigarette. I order her another coffee and a piece of peach pie. Bambi say she shouldn't have the pie. Too fattening. I tell her that she is slender enough to eat it.

The clock is ticking and Taylor is the type to be strict about his secretary's lunch hour. She gathers up her pocket book, fussing to get herself together. She's out of time and now she must speak.

"Mr. Broz, Ms. Lazlo knows all other big stars doesn't she?"

I have come to understand that celebrity is a small, very small world. "Yes. More or less."

"Does she know—"Bambi looks down at her setting; she cleans up some crumbs; she refolds her napkin, presses it flat—"John Travolta? And Tom Cruise?"

I don't know specifically that she does, but I am reasonably certain that she does. "Yes."

"I heard"—she takes the paper napkin and dabs at the drip of coffee in the center of her saucer; she wipes the tines of her fork clean—"that Scientology cures . . . uhh . . ."—she places the fork down; she tries to look at me and has trouble doing it—"homosexuality. That Scientology can cure it. Can they?"[77]

"I don't know."

"I know you don't know. Does Maggie know? Could you ask her to ask them? Is it alright that I called her Maggie?"

"That's fine," I say. "I'll ask her."

[77]Both Cruise and Travolta are Scientologists and have publicly spoken about how much good it has done for their lives and careers and mental health. Scientology does claim it can alter a homosexual orientation. The last thing in the world that this exchange is intended to do is imply that Mr. Cruise or Travolta went to Scientology for this specific alteration. Both are married men with children.

. . .

I begin to see the appeal of this life. Aside from having money. You spend your time talking to people, exercising so you look good—I'm going to the dojo a lot—dressing so you look good, and, if you don't have someone to do it for you, reading a lot.

A lot of this is smoke and mirrors, part of the mask of me as the lover-producer, but it's also the next step. When U.Sec. does an industrial-espionage investigation, the first thing we look for is a disaffected ex-employee or a disgruntled current employee. What I'm doing is setting up something like a sting operation. If they're out there, someone from Beagle's place, I'm giving them a place to go.

It is a slow and uncertain method and requires great patience.

While U.Sec. watches me, Steve follows Ray Matusow.

Ray is running a pattern. He has eight regular stops. But just knowing the stops doesn't tell us who he's actually recording. One of his stops is an apartment building where his recording post seems to be the basement. Two more are apartment complexes with security which means Steve can't follow him in even to determine which of several buildings subjects live in. One stop is a warehouse building on Flower Street. This appears to have one residential loft, which belongs to Maxwell Nurmberg. I am able to determine that someone by that name is employed at CinéMutt, so I assume that's who is being recorded there. The other three are VDs, vehicle drops.[78] One of

---

[78]Electronic surveillance sounds high-tech, and on a certain level it is. But it is also terribly labor-intensive and full of awkward physical problems—like where do you put the tape recorders where they can receive signals, either hard-wire or broadcast, so that they are secure and can be serviced on a regular basis. Apartment and office buildings offer any number of locations in service areas. Private homes on individual lots in residential neighborhoods, especially those that are security-conscious, are vastly more difficult. One solution is to park a vehicle near the site of the LDs and put the tape recorders in the vehicle, called a VD, vehicle drop.

those, I assume, due to proximity, is for Maggie and me.

What's interesting is that he starts the circuit at U.Sec and ends it at home. And he takes everything in at night.

I make sure that I'm not followed and I drop in on Ray at home, unannounced, on a weekday evening. I note the locks. I knock. There's video surveillance, but he looks out the keyhole.

He opens up. "Joe, what are you doing here?"

"I wanted to talk to you, something private."

"Private?"

"Something profitable." I smile. "For you and for me."

"Oh, yeah, well sure."

He steps aside to let me in. His wife, Myrna, is in the living room. She's cute as a button, even after the two children and all. We've met at company functions. "Nice house," I say to her.

"Thank you," she says, truly pleased.

"Did you do it? All of it?" I ask.

"Well . . ." she says. Almost blushing. She's a quiet one. Always has been. Ray's real happy about that. His first wife wasn't.

"You got a nice eye for color and stuff. I'm no expert, but I can see that," I say.

"Would you like to see more of it?"

"Sure," I say.

"Joe just stopped in on business," Ray says.

"Oh. Of course," Myrna says, shutting down.

"I really would," I say. "It's got a warmth. I have to tell you something, Maggie's house . . ." Myrna's all attention—I am going to tell her secrets of one of the stars! Inside view of her Home Life. A real live outtake from *Lifestyles of the Rich and Famous!* ". . . it's

---

Places like Beverly Hills where there is virtually no street parking, create an even greater dilemma. Technology has some answers: microwave broadcasting permits a narrow-band directional signal; satellite uplinks are also possible.

spectacular, of course. But it's like somebody made it for a TV show. It's not . . . how can I say it, warm and homey, like this."

Myrna blushes. Even Ray is pleased. Proud of her. To have his wife's homemaking compared to a star's. So now he has to let her show off her house. She tells me how she had the paint colors mixed. I note that all the windows are wired to the alarm system and there are motion sensors too. The system is worth more than the goods that it is protecting. I'm certain that there's a silent alarm that rings U.Sec's armed-response number.[79] There may be a sound alarm as well. The two little girls share a bedroom that's very girlish, full of frills and with an overall sense of pink. The bedroom is a bedroom, the kitchen's a kitchen, the dining area has a table. The prize, for me, is the basement, Ray's space. "It was all hodgepodge," she says. "With everything every which way . . ."

"I knew where every single thing was," Ray says.

"It wasn't so much messy, it's true, but it was . . . raw. I found these wall and filing units that you customize into your own system and you can add on at any time and always be consistent."

"It's a wonderful job," I say.

We go back upstairs. Ray locks the basement behind us. "Gotta keep the kids out," he says. We sit down at the table in the dining area. Myrna leaves us. "What's up?"

I tell him that through Maggie I'm in a position to score lots of new business, but since I'm on an LoA I can't get a commission on it. Ray's a great tech man, but not much of a hustler. He's hungry for this. Most tech guys, all they get is salary, none of the gravy.

"How much would I get?" he asks.

---

[79]U.Sec. actually has two armed-response services. The main one, offered commercially, is, like much else in life, semifictional. It is actually a referral service that calls the police to inform them that there is a break-in and to rush right over. Police are armed. It is, therefore, an armed response. U.Sec. will also supply private armed response. This creates a variety of legal problems, which vary from state to state, most of them ones of liability, so it's extremely expensive with a lot of money going to the insurance company.

I let it sit there for a while before I answer. Finally, I say, "Fifty-fifty."

"That's only fair," Ray says, greatly relieved. I could have said, *ninety-ten, take it or leave it,* and he would have taken it. "Only fair."

"It'll take a while to set up, but you'll probably begin to see some action, a couple of weeks, a month at the most."

"Thanks, Joe. Thanks. With the kids and all. There's enough, mind you, but more would sure ease some of the strain. You know."

"I know."

We shake. Ray walks me to the door. The alarm system shut off uses a key, not a number pad. My guess is he put the system in about ten years ago when the high-speed tone-code generators got popular and the number-pad systems became vulnerable.

The next day, when Ray goes into the loft building, Steve and I pull up in a rental truck, a thirty-five-foot van. We park it so that the door can't be seen from the street. Steve, wearing shades and a fake Fu Manchu mustache waits in the cab. When Ray steps out, he sees the truck. It's blocking his way.

I step out from behind and hit him on the back of the head with an old-fashioned blackjack. I steal his watch, wallet, and keys. I drag him over behind a trash bin.

I steal Ray's car, empty the trunk, and take it to a chop shop. I drive to Ray's house in a plumber's van rented from a motion-picture prop-vehicle company. It comes with plumber's tool boxes, by accident or as an extra courtesy. I use them to carry a high-speed tape duplicator and a load of cassettes. The kids are at school. Myrna is at her part-time job. I figure I have two hours. I let myself in with Ray's key. I turn off the alarm system, unlock the basement door, and go down to explore his treasure trove.

A very thorough man. Bless him.

Steve stays behind. I want him to make sure Ray doesn't wake up too soon. But Steve says he won't do that. "I'm grateful and all and I needs the work. I'll do all them other things. Tailing around after people. I got a family to support, I'll do mos' anything, but I got a problem with puttin' a hurt on someone. I done my share, don' wanna do no mo'." So I just tell him to watch Ray and when Ray wakes up, if he heads for home, call Ray's house. Dial, ring once. Hang up. dial, ring twice, hang up.

"Joe," he says, "I want you to understand. I got trouble with my boy. My boy, I make him go to school and work hard and his mama, she's on his case. But he's startin' to run with gangbangers. He says, 'I got to carry a piece, be a man.' I say, 'Bullshit.' I don' wanna be telling him one thing and be doin' another, you unnerstand?"

"Got it," I say. "Just don't forget to call."

The surveillance of Magdalena Lazlo is listed under Operation Dog's Bark. There were seven others cross-referenced to the same file: Katherine Przyszewski, Luke Przyszewski, Maxwell Nurmberg, Morris Rosenblum, Theodore Brody. Carmine Cassella and Seth Simeon. Just these names, with phones and addresses, are a score. If these are the people that have to be watched, that's the reverse of saying that these are the people I should target.

When I find that he has copies of the surveillance tapes—something I hoped for but did not count on—it is like striking gold. Here's the record of who's happy and who cries in the night, who gets laid and who gets high, who's ambitious, dumb, resentful, afraid.

Ray even has a high-speed tape duplicator. I set up mine as well and start running copies on both.

All I have to worry about is whether there is a backup alarm that I've missed. Or a nosy neighbor. Or Myrna comes home early. Doing something to Myrna, who would recognize me, to cover up the break-in would be a very unfortunate thing to do. Or to the kids.

CHAPTER

* * *

THIRTY

Taylor wanted to meet in the Cube. Although his first meeting there had been sort of fun, Hartman considered the Cube an affectation.

They met at RepCo. Mike Ovitz and CAA had gone totally modernist—gray suits on the agents and a building by I. M. Pei—in effect making the statement "We are business persons running a corporation, not fast-talking comic-strip Jews with gold chains like Sib Kibitz in *Doonesbury*." Hartman felt he had topped ovitz with his dramatic re-creation of the Harvard Club, a Georgian Revival cathedral of capitalism, including the historic three-story-high main hall, with it's towering windows and walk-in fireplace. Air-conditioning kept the hall, and the other rooms that had hearths, cool enough for charming and aromatic fires—oak and mesquite—even during Los Angeles summers.

"A week ago, as you know, Katherine Przyszewski, Beagle's personal secretary, quit her job," Taylor said. "The day before yesterday, Ray Matusow, who installed and maintains the listening post at the Przyszewski residence, was mugged while he was making his rounds. Today, Katherine Przyszewski calls Joe Broz to ask for a job."

"Do they connect?" Hartman asked.

"Exactly," Taylor said. "Do they connect?"

"What does that mean?" Hartman asked.

"There are no accidents," Taylor said.

"How much does she know?" Hartman asked.

Sheehan said, "She doesn't seem to know much." Sheehan wanted to reassure the client.

"It's hard to know how much she knows," Taylor said. He wanted to make sure the case stayed alive and that if there were any chance of nailing Joe Broz, he didn't miss it.

"We've reviewed her home tapes and her job tapes," Sheehan said. "And it seems pretty clear that she doesn't know much. About the project."

"She could know more than she thinks she knows," Taylor said.

"Like what?" Hartman asked.

"I didn't hear anything," Sheehan said, "that revealed anything to me."

"That remark about real people," Taylor said, although actually he didn't know if the remark had significance. It could have been just something the director had come up with as an excuse not to give some bimbo a part. "That could mean something to somebody, puts it together with something else."

Hartman kept a poker face and his voice indifferent. "What remark about real people?"

"Beagle said he was only using real people in his next movie," Taylor said.

"That's it?" Hartman asked.

"There are no accidents," Taylor said. "Matusow, he's responsible for watching nine people. Two days after he's mugged, one of them, one of the three or four people closest to Beagle, the classic disaffected ex-employee, suddenly calls the guy I pick as the number-one troublemaker in the deck. That's what I see."

"Where was Broz when the mugging took place?" Hartman asked.

Not a question that Taylor wanted to hear. Because he didn't know. Not for sure. The operative watching Broz had lost him.

However, Mel had decided, if asked, to make the information another piece of evidence rather than an admission of failure. "Broz ducked the surveillance that morning."

"Just keep it simple," Hartman said. "See to it that she doesn't meet with Broz."

PROPAGANDA

★ ★ ★

Propaganda that looks like propaganda is third-rate propaganda.

WE	THEY
are innocent.	are guilty.
tell the truth, inform.	lie, use propaganda.
defend ourselves.	are aggressors,
are law-abiding	are criminals and outlaws.
respect our agreement and treaties and abide by international law.	are liars, cheaters, thieves, and opportunists who break treaties.
are Peace Keepers. Our use of force is a police action to protect law and order	are violent, gangsters, a criminal band.
stand for justice and civil rights.	brutalize, repress, tyrannize both their own and their neighbors.
Our leaders govern with the consent of the people	Their leaders are usurpers with no popular support who will eventually be overthrown.

The enemy commits torture, atrocity, and murder because he is a sadist who enjoys killing.

We use surgical or strategic violence only because we are forced to by the enemy.

Killing is justified so long as one does not take pleasure in it and it is done in a clean manner—preferably from an antiseptic distance—the saturation bombing and the free-fire zones in Vietnam were legitimate, the face-to-face slaughter in My Lai was a war crime.

As a popular passion producer, experience indicates that there is nothing quite like the atrocity story.

This war is a war, as I see it, against barbarism. . . . We are
fighting against a nation which, in the fashion of centuries ago,
drags the inhabitants of conquered lands into slavery; which
carries off women and girls for even worse purposes; which in its
mad desire to conquer mankind and trample them under foot has
stopped at no wrong, has regarded no treaty. . . . What we want
most of all by this victory which we shall help to win is to secure
the world's peace, broad based on freedom and democracy. . . .

Senator Henry Cabot Lodge
to the American Senate, April 4, 1917

Propaganda in America is far more successful than anyone ever thinks it is.

**Its achievement is what is not spoken, not talked about, not even thought.
Even it's invisibility is strength, it's impossible to counter-attack inaction.**

For purposes of making your war look just, the most reliable
device is the self-defense thesis.

**In general, you should seem to prove what people already want
to believe, and to justify what they already want to do.**

CHAPTER

* * *

THIRTY-ONE

Finding the material was not the hardest thing for Teddy Brody to do. Staying up all night, speed reading, marking passages, taking notes, was not all that much of a strain either. Breaking his date with Sam, from Anaheim, who was a fitness instructor at Best Bods in the summer and a ski instructor at Steamboat Springs in the winter, didn't bother Teddy much. While he responded to the body thing—a hot bod is, after all, a hot bod—it was not what he was searching for. After all, in the age of AIDS, genital warts, herpes, condoms, hand jobs, and mutual masturbation, how much better was a bod than a video or a dream?

Teddy had anticipated that cutting the material down to size would be the hardest part of all. One page was astounding brevity for someone who'd graduated college with honors. Let alone a Yalie. It meant more than choosing. It meant shutting up about his choices: simply saying things and letting them hang there, unexplained, unexplicated, neither proving them nor expanding on their implications, trusting the reader to understand them all by himself. That had required a Kierkegaardian leap of faith. But once done, it turned out not to have been difficult at all.

The really hard thing—it froze him for hours, gave him stage fright, touched him as deep as the fear of defecating in his pants in public—was quoting without attribution.[80] My God! in old academia that was plagiarism! University chancellors were fired for having done it once, twenty years earlier. A presidential candidate—that is to say, someone presumed to be a professional liar—had to quit his campaign for doing it. And yet Teddy knew that Beagle didn't want footnotes. He didn't care from whence the thoughts came. In CinéMutt it didn't matter. It was clutter. Intellectual litter. The quote from Lodge, and the date, being the exception, because that was part of the point; that we'd used the same themes for three or four wars now and it seemed to work every time. When he handed in his thesis—naked, every word taken from someone else with no recognition, ruthlessly, with cynical abandon—he felt a sense of graduation. He didn't even have to wait for his grade. Beagle had, by the very asking, taught him something important and deep, and made him a better man. Now Brody had the potential for success in Hollywood. *At last*, he thought, *I can steal.*

The sense of empowerment was so potent that the minute Teddy handed it in the idea for his screenplay entered his mind. He knew exactly where he was going to steal the plot, the structure, and the characters and exactly how he was going to reinvent them to make his version fresh and original.[79] The minute he got home he sat down to write a treatment. The first draft was done in a matter of hours. By

---

[80]Earlier versions—all but the final one, actually—do contain footnotes or other forms of reference. The first line is attributed to Professor Campbell Stuart in Sidney Rogerson, *Propaganda in the Next War*, (Garland Library, 1938). This is a fascinating series, edited by Captain Liddell Hart, of predictions about World War II. Titles in the series included *Sea Power in the Next War, Air Power in . . . , Tanks in . . . , Gas in. . . .* The information in the chart, slightly altered, and the three statements following, came from Sam Keen, *Faces of the Enemy: Reflections of the Hostile Imagination, The Psychology of Enmity*, (Harper & Row, 198   a book about war, war images, war propaganda, which seemed to Teddy to describe the way his family related, especially his relationship to his father and his father's to his mother. The next line, the quote from Mr. Lodge, and the last two lines, all come from Bruce Winton Knight, *How to Run a War*, (Knopf, 1936; reprint, Arno Press & the New York Times, 1972. The underlined passage is a paraphrase of Terence H. Qualter, *Opinion Control in Democracies*, (St. martin's Press, 1985).

morning he had revised it, run it though spell check, reread it, retyped the corrections, and printed it out. He brought it with him to work.

Beagle had the single page—pithy and enigmatic as strategy by Sun Tzu or prophecy by I Ching—overnight. Teddy Brody waited, impatiently, for Beagle's arrival in the morning, for his blessing or his curse. And when—if—Beagle praised it, that would be the moment. The moment to say, *"I have a treatment—would you read it?"*

Beagle had sat bolt upright at 5 A.M. It was dark outside, not even a predawn gray, but still crisp black, and stars too. He was wide awake. He thought it was inspiration when that happened, but it was his liver. That's not to say he didn't have insights and fresh concepts in the early hours, but it was the sluggishness in his liver that woke him.

The new woman—Beagle told himself he'd have to make a point of remembering her name—had made another stupid mistake. The sort of mistake Kitty would never make. In an excess of zeal she'd gone out and bought a present for John Lincoln to give to Dylan, even though she didn't know what she was doing. She'd bought a little football and a little helmet. Beagle thought it was cute. Kitty would

---

[79]Jeanine Basinger, in *The World War II Combat Film* points out that "Hollywood was, contrary to popular opinion, a frugal place. Plots and characters and events were saved like old pieces of string, and taken out of the drawer and re-used. . . . Useful things were—tough sergeants, raw recruits, old veterans, diary-keeping writers, colorful immigrant types; mail calls, Christmas celebrations, barroom brawls; dying men crying out to be brought in, and, when rescued, dying anyway; brave men going up in planes to sacrifice themselves. . . ."

This was exactly what Beagle did. He took bits and pieces "saved like old pieces of string," and we can notice their appearance in the final production. Teddy's brainstorm was to take the classic combat film—the same twelve or fourteen people: Pop, the guy from Brooklyn, the kid with a puppy, the guy who was gonna write novels someday, etc.—and make all the characters gay. In the Pacific War, a homophobic colonel takes all the gays—men and women—in his battalion and puts them on a tiny atoll. He knows that it will be attacked by an overwhelming force of Japanese. He tells them they must hold out at all costs. And so on.

have known better. Jackie climbed the walls when she saw it. She nailed John's hide to the door. All the sins of the male race apparently had something to do with football. It brought on war, killing, wife beating, beer guzzling, belching, and the national overindulgence in junk food.

What he understood, at last, when he awoke in the dark, was that football was his model, not baseball, not movies. In one sense that should have been obvious because one of the standard adages in the drivel of popular wisdom is that *football is the sport most like war.* If you had asked Beagle, before this particular morning when an insufficiency of bile aroused him, he would have said: *"Football is the sport most like roller derby. It can also be compared to professional wrestling with more clothes. Golf is the sport most like war."* But part of Beagle's genius was the ability to overcome his intelligence and arrogance and cater, shamelessly, to a lower common denominator. The lowest, if possible.[82]

If football was what America thought war was, then a Beagle-directed war was going to be the goddamn Super Bowl. Unlike baseball, which used anticipation instead of action in the game, football no longer even needed the game. The players didn't have to do anything. The fans did it all by themselves. Super Bowl was the most hyperbolic version of this effect: two weeks of hype, hysteria,

---

[82]He was fond of a quote from H. L. Mencken, changing *they/their* to *we/our:* "We have built our business on a foundation of morons," and said as much in a interview in *Cinema* magazine. "Who do you think buys movie tickets? Who goes to see the same movie fourteen times—morons and aspiring film directors. Who watches TV? If it's not dumb enough that the morons love it, it will lose money and I haven't done my job. Catering to the morons is Job One! Somebody said that: Lee Iaccoca? Ford? Reagan? Before you go to make a film, spend a couple of days watching a lot of television. Get down with the morons. If you can make a movie that does that and is brilliant too, then you're a genius. You're John Huston, you're John Ford, you're Alfred Hitchcock."

This is actually the last real interview Beagle ever gave. David Hartman saw to it that Beagle never again spoke for publication without a handler present and without previewing the questions.

wagering, turmoil, media blitz, and ado—without a single block, tackle, or penalty, without one ball thrown or kicked or carried.

The game itself—that final, end-of-the-season, ultimate, championship confrontation—was normally a dud. A blowout, decided early, barely worth watching for those few weirdos who watched for the sake of seeing what happened in the actual game segment of the event. Yet it was never a disappointment. No game was bad enough to diminish the hysteria of the subsequent Super Bowl.

That, Beagle now knew, was the pace and the shape of a war that America was going to love.

Heroes and villains. The hero was a given: George Herbert Walker Bush. He would have his costars. They would be . . . hold that for later.

The first thing Beagle did when he got to CinéMutt was run villain footage. Hitler, Joe Stalin, Ho Chi Minh, the kaiser, Jack Palance. Eric Von Stroheim. There was just one word, one definition of "villain"— Hitler. Change the face, change the language, change the rant, but call the character Hitler.

But the really interesting thing was that the importance of a villain was illusory. Bush had done a Hitler bit with Noriega and it didn't play.

Maggie Thatcher had done the Falklands *without* a bad guy.

What did she have? She had Pearl Harbor!

The perfect villainy. The absolute centerpiece of American mythology as well: Mr. Nice Guy gets sucker punched. Mr. Nice Guy gets up off the floor, squares up mano a mano with Mr. Sneak Attack. Mr. Nice Guy turns out to have been John Wayne, Clark Kent, a Superpower—Mr. Sneak Attack wishes he'd never been born.

What America needed—or Bush needed—or Beagle needed— was someone to invade America.

That was a problem. Big-time. Who was going to invade the U.S.? Mexico? Canada? Laughable. The remnants of the USSR?

They'd use nukes, we'd use nukes, that would be the end of Hollywood as we know it. Japan? Would Japan be willing to invade us again? Could the economic thing be made to look like an invasion? No. The job didn't call for economic war. Too sophisticated for TV and, frankly, the images were nonexistent.

He went back to the Vietnam scenario. He needed to know what that was to understand what was wrong with *The Return* in order to figure out what would be right. He started running Nam clips. It was clear in less than a minute: *jungle*. That was a big one. Americans don't like jungle wars. Too wet. Too hot. Hot and wet was disease and sex. Americans liked fighting the Nazis. They didn't like fighting the Japs. Americans liked Germanic warfare. Mechanized. Civilized. Clean and dry.

Yet, America had fought the Japs in the jungle. And that had been good. A lot of good films had come out of it. John Wayne had been mostly in the Pacific. There he was again, on Screen 8, in the only pro–Vietnam War movie ever made, *The Green Berets*, an old, fat John Wayne strutting around like it was still World War II.

And that was the final insight.

The real fundamental problem, the structural problem, was that vietnam wasn't Vietnam. It was never intended to be it's own thing. To go back to Vietnam was to miss the point. The point was to be what Vietnam was supposed to be in the first place—a remake—not for theaters, for television—of 1942–45: *World War II Two–The Video*.

He heard the words underlined in his head. That was it. That was the essence.

He remembered an anthology film—*Going Hollywood: "The War Years*. It said something pertinent. He searched it out and punched it up: "A war where there was no doubt about who started it or what we were fighting for or who were the good guys or who were the bad guys. In other words, it was a war that could've been written by Hollywood." That was good, right on target, but still not the statement that he was looking for—there: "Gone were the movies of the thirties with their screwball rich people, their fast-talking heroines, their wisecracks about banks, government, unemployment. The war canceled all criticism. A new and total wholesomeness pervaded Hollywood's America. It was decided that the true character of the nation was just—nice. There were no demonstrations, no complaints, in nice America." That's what it was really about. That's what the client wanted. The war was just a means to an end. World War II was the war that delivered the proper end. That was the America Bush wanted—where rich people were respected, banks were good guys, nobody criticized, even the darkies turned out to be nice, and women kept their goddamn mouths shut.

John Lincoln Beagle had chosen the film that America would make next: *WWII-2-V.*

CHAPTER

* * *

THIRTY-TWO

In 1967 the CIA instituted a program in Vietnam called Phoenix. The name is a rough translation of *Phunng Hoang,* also a mythological bird. The program was run by William Colby, who later became head of the CIA.

One of the phrases that Teddy Brody pulled out of Sam Keen's *Faces of the Enemy* for his one page of adages on propaganda, but which did not make the final cut, was, "Notice, the undertone beneath the self-justification in all propaganda is the whining voice of the child: 'He did it to me first—I only hit him back.'" They did it first is the foundation of Phoenix. It happens to be true. They did do it first. The Vietcong had an extensive and very effective terrorist program. It targeted everybody and anybody whose work supported the routine functions of government—mayors, tax collectors, police, postmen, teachers. Guerrilla warfare isn't nice, and opposing the power of the state is always difficult. Yet, however politically correct the VC may have been, it's fair to say that only motive separates what they did from the most ruthless forms of gangsterism. They established their underground rule in much the same way as the Mafia in Sicily or the drug gangs in Colombia.[81] There are lots of good atrocity stories—

[81]Of course, the VC can say *"He did it to me first—I only hit him back."* And that's

good in the sense of "As a popular passion producer, experience indicates that there is nothing quite like the atrocity story[85]—about VC terror. These include young boys and elders impaled on stakes where the rest of the village is sure to see them and pregnant women disemboweled, the fetus cut out and left on the ground as a public display.

The South Vietnamese government, the CIA, and the other American organizations had all made attempts to imitate these tactics before Phoenix. The CIA had various CT—counterterrorist—teams that consisted of Vietnamese, and sometimes Chinese, who are frequently referred to as mercenaries because they were not regular Army and they were paid. Some of these teams consisted of convicted murderers, rapists, and other criminals, recruited from Vietnamese prisons, real-life versions of *The Dirty Dozen*. The Special Operations Group (SOG), which ran Project Delta and Project 24, Navy Seals, hunter-killer teams, and most especially the Provincial Reconnaissance Units (PRU),[83] all engaged in counterterror operations.

What Phoenix did was centralize all the South Vietnamese intelligence services under American supervision and target what was

---

true too. State terror—a concept discussed at length in *The Terrorism Industry* by Herman & Sullivan and in the works of Noam Chomsky—can be, and frequently is, more murderous and less discriminating than any guerrilla group. Certainly, Diem and the imperialist French before him ruled by force, not consent, which is to say *through terror*.

[85]Oddly enough, the U.S. failed to make very good use of enemy atrocity stories in the Vietnam war. This was partly deliberate. Johnson did not want to whip the American people into a war frenzy. Later the Nixon administration did push the atrocity line, at least a little, but only about the treatment of our own POWs.

[83]". . . one form of psychological pressure on the guerrillas which the Americans do not advertise is the PRU. The PRU work on the theory of giving back what the Viet Cong deals out—assassination and butchery. Accordingly, a Viet Cong unit on occasion will find the disemboweled remains of its fellows along a well trod canal bank path, an effective message to guerrillas and to non-committed Vietnamese that two can play the same bloody game." (Chalmers Roberts, *Washington Post*, 2-18-67)

called the VCI—Vietcong Infrastructure—in a systematic way. The Americans and the South Vietnamese actually had a lot of information about who the VC and their sympathizers were. Phoenix put it all together. They put up wanted posters, they offered rewards. They set up interrogation centers. They sent in teams to arrest and to assassinate.

To the degree that Phoenix was known, it was instantly controversial.[84] And it remains so. Vietnamese named to Phoenix as VC or VC sympathizers were not innocent until proven guilty. Assassinations did not wait upon due process. Suspects were detained without trial, on the basis of anonymous accusations. In prison they were often beaten and tortured. The opportunities for profit were boundless. South Vietnamese district intelligence officers got rich through extortion—threatening to put people on the list unless they paid—and by letting real VC buy their way off of the list.

For some people Phoenix was a lot of fun. This was tropical Lawrence of Arabia stuff. Dressing up in native garb, eating indigenous foods, setting up ambushes, sneaking into villages at night to kill silently, committing bizarre yet colorful acts like hammering custommade calling cards into the third eye of their victims and cutting out their livers because you can't get into Buddhist heaven without one. Actually, it was better than the Lawrence scenario, especially for heterosexuals—instead of veiled females covered in layers of robes, there were the accommodating girls of Indochina in their *bao dais;* instead of eating goat bits and rice with their fingers, they had steak and ice cream from the States or Vietnamese cuisine which, combining the traditions of France and Southeast Asia, is among the most

[84]"By analogy," said Odgen Reid, a member of a congressional committee investigating Phoenix in 1971, "if the Union had a Phoenix program during the Civil War, it's targets would have been civilians like Jefferson Davis or the Mayor of Macon, Georgia." The Phoenix Program "The Phoenix operation aroused an outcry from American anti-war activists, who labeled it 'mass murder.' But several Americans involved described it instead as a program riddled with inefficiency, corruption and abuse." (Stanley Karnow, *Vietnam: A History* [Viking, 1983])

enticing in the world; there was no prohibition of alcohol; the drugs were of superb quality; and to be an American was to be very rich.[85]

With all this—the cowboys, the profiteering, the moral corruption of participating in torture and assassination—the truly strange thing was that Phoenix worked. It hurt the Vietcong very badly. Combined with their losses in the Tet offensive, it crippled them to a degree from which they never recovered.[89]

Taylor brought in two men to intercept Kitty. They were waiting outside her house. They knew what time she was supposed to meet Joe Broz and how long the drive took, so they knew approximately when she was expected to leave. They had photos of her for identification purposes. She was very attractive in the photos, smiling, bright-eyed, voluptuous. Both of the watchers were graduates of Phoenix. Their names were Charles "Chaz" Otis and Christian "Bo" Perkins. There are a lot of ways to describe both of them, but bottom-line and the simplest is to say that Bo was a sadist and Chaz was a rapist.

---

[85]"The CIA people were the worst. I was appalled at the kind of people the CIA had out in the provinces . . . these guys loved to ride through the streets and down the country roads in their Jeeps with all manner of weapons strapped to them, gun belts and helmets and all of it. They had lots of booze, lots of women, the best furniture, and the nicest places to live. They had their own private airline, Air America, to take them anywhere they wanted to go on a moment's notice. They played the Terry and the Pirates game, swashbuckling, lots of bravado. Some killing, too. They were after the VCI, the Viet Cong infrastructure. This is where you get your assassination squads." (Robert Boettcher quoted in *Strange Ground: Americans In Vietnam 1945–1975: An Oral History* Harry Maurer, [Henry Holt, 19])

[89]"In 1969 according to the wonderfully precise statistics released by the American mission in Saigon, 19,534 Vietcong organizers, propagandists, tax collectors, and the like were listed as having been neutralized—6,187 of them killed." *(Vietnam; A History)* Karnow was at first very skeptical of these numbers and "the claim, advanced by William Colby . . . that the program . . . eliminated 60,000 authentic Viet Cong agents." After the war, however, Viet Cong and NVA sources confirmed to Karnow that Phoenix had hurt them very severely.

Obviously, they won anyway. But they did so with North Vietnamese forces, mostly regulars, and without the local guerrilla forces.

CHAPTER

* * *

THIRTY-THREE

Wᵂ*II-2-V*, Beagle wrote it
down.

He could read it, but to anyone else it looked like *scribble-II-*√.
That was not a marquee title—it was a working title, a project name.
Other titles starting running through his head:

> *Morning in America*
> *American Century*
> *American Storm*
> *Pax Americana*
> *Hope of the World*
> *American Hero*
> *The Reincarnation of John Wayne*
> *The 7 Incarnations of John Wayne*

He wrote them down under *scribble-II-*√, but even as he did so, he
realized that he wouldn't find a final title until he actually picked who
we were going to have a war with.

Where? What war?

There was no shortage of wars around the world. They were

going on all over the place all the time. Should he tap into something ongoing? Or start his own. He knew there was a list somewhere. He swung over to the workstation in the corner. It was an alternate way to tap into the Fujitsu and easier for print-based information. He typed in *"War, Current."* An alphabetical list began to scroll up the screen.

Afghanistan Resistance War
Guerrilla-Civil War in Angola
Bangladesh Guerrilla War
Bolivian Drug War
Burma Guerrilla War
Central America
War in Chad
Conflict in Chile
Colombian Guerrilla War
East Timor Resistance War
Ecquador
El Salvador Civil War
Ethiopia - Eritrea War
Guatemala, Guerrilla War in
Holy War - Jihad
India- Pakistan War
India: Sikh-Hindu War
Iran-Iraq War
Kampuchea—Vietnam's War Against Guerrillas
Kurdish War of Independence
Lebanon
Liberian Civil War
Morocco-Polisario War
Mozambique Guerrilla War
Nicaragua-Contra War
Northern Ireland Terrorist War
Peru's "Shining Path"
Philippines "Communist War"

Sudan—Civil War
Sri Lanka Civil War
Togo
Zulu–ANC War[90]

He hadn't stopped the videos. When he looked up, by fate or coincidence, there, obviously misfiled, was Rommel. America's favorite Nazi. Why did we like him so? Desert warfare? Tanks? Clean and dry—it was hot, but hot and dry is OK. The wet is necessary for sex and disease. Machines do the killing and the goal is to kill machines.

It was time to check with that parallel universe: reality. Reality said yes. The desert was the best place for armored warfare, and it was the one place where air power was really decisive. *The World at War* had been very clear about that.

That was it then. *WWII-2-V* would be a desert war—air power and tanks.

We use surgical or strategic violence only because we are forced to by the enemy.

Killing is justified so long as one does not take pleasure in it and it is done in a clean manner—preferably from an antiseptic distance . . .

Oh! He had it! What a thought! What an image. He started pushing buttons on the console—he was sure of the title—*Bombardier*. It's 1943. Pat O'Brien is trying to show why Americans should bomb people from way high up. As opposed to dive bombing. To prove his thesis he stages a demonstration and literally drops a bomb into a

[90]A similar list can be found in John Laffey, *The World in Conflict 1991: War Annual 5*, Brassey's. Obviously, there's one every year. The number of wars seems to be relatively constant.

barrel from twenty thousand feet. Later one of the bombardier candidates at bombardier school is freezing up over the target. "When I look at the target, I see people. Women and children. Those letters . . ." They're from his mom. "She says I'm making myself into a murderer." But the chaplain (not Pat O'Brien—he's the head bombardier this time) explains: "The enemy's targets are everywhere. But yours are clear and confined. Not women and children. . . . That's why the American bombardiers are trained to hit the target." The boy believes. His conscience is clear. He can go on to drop bombs. Which he does. In the climactic scene they fly over a Jap munitions factory.

> CREWMAN: *Put one in the smokestack.*
> BOMBARDIER: *Which one?*
> CREWMAN: *The center one.*
> BOMBARDIER: *That's easy.*

Beagle knew he was going to use that. He didn't know where he was going to find a smokestack in the desert, but he was going to use that scene. Our war was going to be so surgical, we would drop our bombs right down the enemy smokestack. Never touch woman nor child nor noncombatant of any kind.

It brought him back to the big problem. Who would attack America? Even an American outpost. Didn't we have Falkland Island—type places? Puerto Rico? The Virgin Islands? Guam? One of the Pacific Islands? It was pitiful. Nobody was going to attack America.

Maybe that wasn't necessary. It's a remake of World War II. He knew that. What if—what if, instead of appeasing Hitler, we'd stood up to him early. Hitler invades Poland. Maybe we've learned from the Second World War and *we do it better this time*. We stand up to him when he invades Poland. That was great. Nobody has to attack the United States. We just have to find a Hitler and have him invade Poland.

Was that doable? Yes. He thought so. There were lots of Hitlers around and lots of Polands.

Was that enough? Was that it? Yes.

Beagle rose and stretched. He walked out of the control room, feeling immensely satisfied with himself. Without being conscious of it, he swaggered, with a walk familiar to anyone who watched classic Westerns—he swaggered just like big John Wayne.

Agnes Przyszewski hugged her mom. Even though Agnes had been raised on television, where if someone lost a job or quit their job they always had a new and better job by the time the thirty sitcom minutes were over, it had gradually penetrated that what her mother had done, and was doing, was a remarkable gesture of support. It had brought mother and daughter closer than they had been for years.

They picked out clothes together for Kitty's upcoming interview with Joe Broz. "I'm not going to take the job," Kitty said, "unless it means I can do something for you." When Kitty stood in front of the bathroom mirror and started to do her hair, Agnes offered to brush it for her, something she had loved to do as a little girl but hadn't done since she was seven. It was all Kitty could do not to cry.

Chaz and Bo were about half a block away. The car they sat in was stolen, as were the plates, acquired separately at long-term parking at LAX. They had decided to take the Przyszewski woman right when she reached her car, where it was parked out on the street. That was the quickest, cleanest way. Once someone is in a car, stopping them can be very complicated, and, once stopped, it can be difficult to get them out.

They'd done this sort of thing before. But they still talked it through. They would start moving, with Chaz at the wheel, as soon as Kitty opened the front door, cruising toward her. Then Bo, who had a sweet voice and a kind of wimpy look, would say, "Excuse me, miss, can you help me. I think we're lost." She'd stop. He'd get out of the car with a map in his hand. By the time she saw the gun, he'd be right up close to her. Chaz, who already had a boner thinking of her, would have the back door flung open. Bo would hustle her in.

She'd be alive when they were done. There would be no permanent visible damage to her body. But she probably wouldn't talk to anyone for a long, long time.

When the commands stopped coming from the control room, Teddy Brody got restless. He really, truly expected Beagle to say something, anything, about his one-page propaganda piece. Actually, he didn't expect Beagle to say "something, anything," he expected Beagle to praise him, give him recognition, and give him the opening to say, "Please sir, won't you read my treatment."

Teddy squeezed between a pair of monitors and peered through a gap where one of them was mounted. The control room was empty. Video monitors playing, no one watching. There, in a corner of the console, looking neglected, was a single sheet of paper that might or might not have been his essay on propaganda. His heart sank.

He decided to enter the control room. He'd never done that, except the first day of his employment when he was taken on a tour of CinéMutt so that he would see how his humble efforts in the back room came to fruition in the director's room. For that matter, he hadn't entered any room, uninvited, since he was six. Or was it seven. Or eight. Or five. He'd blocked it out. What was it that he'd blocked out? Something came over him when he put his hand on the knob of the connecting door. A terrible fear that he felt in his bowels. More specific than that, in his sphincter. He knew that what he'd seen was his parents having sex. Not an unusual thing for a child to stumble on. Why so traumatic? What was it about those tears that so troubled him. Tears. There had been tears and rage. He turned the knob. The door swung open on perfect silent hinges. There was no one—no vision—no tyrant—no rage—no tears—waiting for him inside. Just an empty room with a lot of video screens running silent, flickering colors out in the air where they quickly dimmed for failure to find reflective surfaces.

He was in. And he knew, in his heart, that he was right to enter. He was a good boy. Too good. This was not a world where propriety and politeness, punctilious honesty and genuine respect, were the tools to achieve success—if there ever was such a world. Anywhere. Ever. It was a place where knowledge was power, even stolen knowledge, especially stolen knowledge. Where you told people what they wanted to hear—not the truth—because who wanted truth? That was for private moments with yourself, if you liked mirrors that were mean and ugly. Where a stolen screen credit was better than no credit and the only rule for plagiarism was to be certain that you had better lawyers and trickier accountants than whomever you stole from. Goddammit, it was time for him to grow up or get out. Go—not home, never home—but some halfway house for losers, like a university.

He walked, silent feet on silent carpet, to the console. He saw his paper there. No grade on it. He'd expected one. Dumb reflex. He saw Beagle's meager notes—the titles.

There was a bottle of sparkling wine in the kitchen. Beagle thought he deserved a champagne toast to himself. He called home, for his wife. But she wasn't in. He went out in the reception area and . . . well, she was a stranger. Kitty was so great. Used to be so great, before she went bonkers. At least he could have celebrated with her and she would have acted happy about it even if he couldn't tell her what exactly they were drinking to.

The obvious person to call was David Hartman. After all, David was the one other person in the world who knew.

Hartman took the call.

"I am standing here, sparkling wine in hand. And you should be too. Because I have figured it out," Beagle said.

On the other end of the line Hartman leaned back and closed his eyes and sighed with relief. That was the hell of the job. Waiting for the damn talent to do whatever it was they did. It always took as long as it took. "I'll open a bottle over here," Hartman said, "and I'll drink to you over the phone." Beagle waited while Hartman went away. When he came back, they clinked their glasses against their respective telephones. While Hartman looked through his appointment calender to see who he would have to dump to see Beagle that day, or tomorrow morning at the latest, he remembered that this business about the secretary was bothering him.

"Linc, this Przyszewski woman, your secretary, was she any good?" Hartman had an idea about placing her somewhere safe, where he could keep tabs on her and not have U.Sec. do whatever it did.

"She was great."

"Really."

"Kitty, yeah. Until she went nuts."

"What happened?"

"She asked me to give her daughter a part in my next movie. That got my back up, or it would've, it usually does, but there aren't any parts anyway. So I said that and she lost it."

"Would you have her back?"

"Sure. I'd love her back. If she were sane, of course."

"Why don't you do this," Hartman said. "Call her up. Tell her you called me and I said RepCo would represent Agnes. We'll give the kid an agent. Kitty'll be happy, you'll be happy, and we can all go on about our business."

"Done," Beagle said.

Then they figured out when they could meet.

Chaz saw Kitty's door open. He smiled and put one hand on his crotch. He was thick and pulsing in anticipation. Bo, who noticed the gesture, laughed. Chaz's game was not strictly what Bo would have done if he were alone, but he got a kick out of the fear and pain parts.

Kitty came out. Chaz put the car in motion.

Inside, the phone rang. Agnes picked it up.

"Hi, is Kitty there?"

"Who's this?"

"This is Linc."

"I don't think she wants to talk to you," Agnes said, rude and virtuous, playing it the way she'd seen it done on prime-time soaps.

"Well, I was hoping I could talk her into coming back to work."

"Too bad," Agnes said. "I don't think she wants to come back."

Outside, as Kitty moved toward her car, Chaz and Bo pulled up to just about where they thought the snatch should take place.

"Is this Agnes?" Beagle asked.

"Yes."

"Do you know RepCo?"

Of course she did. She was an L.A. kid. "Of course I do," Agnes said.

Bo held his map in front of his face and put on his baffled and helpless expression.

"Well, I'm good friends with Dave Hartman, head of RepCo, and, um, well I talked to him about you and he said RepCo would be happy to represent you, if you want to give it a try."

Bo rolled down the window. "Uh, excuse me, miss," he called out to Kitty. "We sure are lost here."

Kitty looked at her watch. She had a minute to spare to help out a lost stranger and still make the job interview in plenty of time. "What were you looking for?" she asked.

Let her take one step closer, then Bo would get out of the car, holding a map and a piece of paper. "Let me show you the address," he said. The map would cover the gun. The trick of it was to get 'em close to the car. They'd see the gun, be shocked, be in the car before they had a chance to scream or run or fight. And it'd be done.

"Mom, Mom, come quick," Agnes yelled from the doorway.

Kitty hesitated.

"Hurry, Mom, hurry."

"Excuse me," Kitty said to the stranger and, thinking her daughter was in some sort of trouble, by the urgency in her voice, she dashed back to her house, leaving Chaz and Bo behind.

After Beagle spoke to Kitty, she called Mr. Broz and canceled. If Mr. Broz was disappointed, he concealed it well. She didn't know, of course, how deeply disappointed Chaz and Bo were. They thought they'd have another shot at her. But after Beagle spoke to Hartman and Hartman called Taylor, they were pulled off the job. Chaz, now that he'd seen here, was downright brokenhearted.

"My father was a son of a bitch," I say to Maggie. "What difference does it make?"

"Just making conversation," she says.

"Just making conversation—that's talking about what's gonna happen to the Lakers without Magic, without Pat Riley, without Kareem. That's making conversation. What was *your* father like? When was the first time you got laid?"

"You're angry," she says. "You're an angry man underneath that . . . pose you have."

"I'm a regular guy, is all," I say. "There are lots of fathers out there. . . . or used to be—steel town, mill town, work hard, drink hard, teach their sons: life's hard."

"Alright, Joe," she says. "Don't tell me about your father. What was your mother like?"

I have my shoes and my shirt off. "I got to change," I say, "if I'm gonna run before we go to the party." I walk away from her and upstairs. I get into my room—I still have a separate room where I keep my clothes and actually sleep. I pretend about the sleeping but not about the clothes. It's one thing for a woman to make room for a man in her bed, another to give up space in her closets. I get into my room, I unbuckle this damn three hundred dollar belt—I can't figure out what makes it worth three hundred dollars, I just can't, never will—unbutton, unzip, drop my pants. When I turn around, she's there. She's looking at me.

"So many scars," she says.

"What do you want from me?"

"Are you going to run?"

"I'm gonna run," I say. I reach into my bureau and grab a pair of running shorts, quick. Why should she watch the hardening of my cock? She already knows how much power she has over me. But she is staring at me. Looking me over. Seeing the arousal. I know she is. "You don't get out of here," I say, "I'm gonna . . ." I don't say *Fuck you. I'm going to fuck you. And once it starts, it'll never stop or it'll be all over.* The microphones are listening.

"Maybe I'll run with you," she says, turns, and walks into her room.

I get a shirt on, then head out. I have no intention of waiting for her. I just want to get the hell out of there. The investigation is going nowhere. I thought we had something with Kitty Pryzszewski, but she slipped away. It's a stupid case anyway. Who cares what John Lincoln Beagle is up to. It's just another goddamn movie. His wife and kid hate him. That's common gossip by now. Husband and wife are each only waiting for a point of advantage to file for divorce. If I blow off this idiocy with Maggie today, and go back to U.Sec., where I belong, by tomorrow I'll probably be right back on Beagle, but this time for his wife. Or the other way around, on her for him. The line running around town on Jacqueline Conroy is, "The bitch knows the golden rule of Hollywood—always fuck up." Certainly, every name she is linked to—Patrick Swayze, Kevin Costner, and Madonna—indicates a strong upwardly mobile orientation. Maggie and I and Mrs. Mulligan, each of us, seperately, has heard that John Lincoln had been doing it with his receptionist and that he wanted to do it with her daughter too. The mother was so upset that she quit. But Beagle called and promised her daughter a part in his next picture so she came back.

The rumors about their sex lives, accurate or not, are that specific and quick to circulate. Yet there's not one word about what that picture might be.

Maggie's left the door open. I take care not to look. As I get past, her voice caresses my back. "Wait for me. Please." I don't want to. Really, I don't. But I stop. I don't want to turn and look. Let me turn into a statue of salt if I look. Let one of us remain in hell forever if I look.

I don't have to describe her in detail. You've seen her on screen. If you haven't, go rent a cassette. The vibrancy, they say, comes across on film—the curve of her back, how long her legs are—remember that long pan up her legs, seemed to take forever, when she played a call girl in that Burt Reynolds film—the shape of her breasts, even the texture of her nipples when they're erect—the full-screen CU of one of them, and it really is her, she didn't use a tit double, in *White Lady*—that is what it is I'm looking at. She's got her shorts on. But she's topless. She stands still long enough for me to look at her, then she turns her back, slips into her running bra and puts a shirt over it.

When we go out, I'm sullen and silent. We start. I have no intention of cutting her any slack. She's quick. I can't outsprint her. She's light and lithe and I'm a truck. But I figure, over distance, I can grind her down some and keep going when she tires. I break a sweat after a mile. After two it starts to feel real good. I even zone Maggie out. The pictures begin to come. You have to remember that Vietnam wasn't just war. It was Asia. Like in the movies I saw when I was a kid. Exotic. Especially for a kid from the Ohio Valley, didn't know much but Slavs and Hunkies and Polacks, working the coal mines, working the mill, sooty and black and drinking a lot of cheap beer. Coming home drunk, whacking their families around. Waking up hurting. Them and their families both. Hungover. Joints all achin'—from lifting, loading, turning, shoveling, shoving, humping, grinding, holding, carrying, pouring, chipping, digging—from being a man. Wood-frame houses, tar-paper shingles, built on the hill.

There were some pretty girls. But not like the girls we saw in the movies. If we had the money to take them somewhere, where the hell would we take them? For a beer at the VFW hall or the corner bar. No. Backseat of a car, trying to get past girdles and the fear of getting pregnant. Belches tasting of beer and cheap whisky. My father takes me to a whore when I'm thirteen. Maybe twelve. Old enough to do it. Young enough I thought she was ugly. She's upstairs from a bar called Swat Sullivan's. My father's downstairs drinking while I'm up there. He's in a good mood. Buys a round for his buddies, to drink to his son, fucking his first whore upstairs. But he can't afford both the whore and the round. So when she comes down with me to collect her pay, it's gone to the bartender. They have a big fight.

Marines were a relief. The Marines were optimists compared to home. At least in Vietnam, we figured, you could go to glory.

Running with a full pack. Fifty-six pounds. With combat boots. With an M-16. Run past the hurt. Run till you're numb. The blisters break. Heat rash in your pits. Pack scrapes your shoulders and your back. Rifle makes your arms ache, like to fall off. And it all felt so goddamn good. We were studs. Young studs. Harder than hard. Tougher than leather. Running, running, running.

Vietnam was beautiful. Exotic. Beautiful women. As beautiful as the women we saw on screen back in the Ohio Valley. We called them slopes, zippers, gooks, and slants, bought 'em, whore 'em, raped 'em, killed 'em. They killed us. But if you stopped, stopped being part of that thing and just looked—there were beautiful women. Preston Griffith, he helped me stop being as dumb as a dumb jarhead is dumb. Through the smoke and lessons in war and night killing, he said, "They're people, Joe. You think some blond round-eye is going to be better than the woman you got now? You're a stupid fuck, Joe. Wake up and see what you got." He loved the food, Griff did. Lemon grass. That's the flavor of Vietnam. He smoked reefer to eat. Opium to sleep and to live. Street filled with soldiers and cripples and whores. "Can you imagine," Preston says, sitting in the Café Gascon, a mural of D'Artagnan on the wall inside, painted by a Vietnamese, probably from a picture in a storybook, drinking *café filtre*, "can you imagine this without a war to fuck it up. Let's go to Bangkok, or Rangoon. They'll never find us." Of course they would.

"War don't fuck things up, Griff," I say like the stud Marine I'm trained to be. "War is what makes it fun. Dying puts living in perspective."

"Have you ever been in love?" Maggie asks, her voice cutting from somewhere else. From the present. The beach.

I don't answer. I pick it up a notch. She stays with me.

"Have you?" About as much of a sentence as she can get out, breathing hard.

" 'Sides you?"

"Do you love me?"

I run. What am I going to say to that? Of course. It's obvious. No question. She owns me. "Fuck you, bitch."

"I'm sorry," she says. She falters a little. Slows down. I don't. I keep on pushing. If she can't keep up, she can't keep up. I go back. Me and Griff, sitting in the café, like a couple of Frenchmen, watching *la vie de la ville*. Armed, of course. *Café filtre, baguettes.*

"What about Joey?" he says.

Joe and Joey. We joined the Marines together. I was sixteen. Joey was seventeen. Almost eighteen. We lied. They didn't check. He died. I lived. "Fuck you, Griff."

"What's the problem, war lover?"

"You're out of line."

"No, I'm not. I didn't kill him."

"I'm outta here," I say.

"Don't go, Joe."

"Don't talk about Joey."

"Why not?"

"He's family."

"Bullshit. I've seen your record. You have no family, Joseph Broz. That's part of why we like you. So very much."

"You're becoming a dope fiend, Griff. A dope fiend."

"Let's go to Madame Thieu's. She has some new girls. Sweet and happy girls all the way from Cambodia."

"Why the hell would anyone run from Cambodia to Vietnam?"

"Why the hell would anyone sell Cambodian girls when there's so many Vietnamese girls for sale? It's not like they're noticeably different. It's not like she's got some blond round-eyes. But there is a difference, Joe. Takes a connoisseur to tell, of course."

"I thought you had a girlfriend. That reporter woman."

"You know, I don't think I can ever, ever go back to western women. They're all take. All fight. Eastern women, it's Confucian, places a man above them. Now a western woman would say that's wrong. But a man, if he's got a choice, between a woman who looks up to him as her lord and master or a woman who's always trying to climb up just so she can look down on him, he's crazy if he takes the woman always trying to look down on him. Mind you, I'm glad my sister was born in Boston and went to Radcliffe instead of being born in Da Nang and going to Madame Thieu's. And if her husband doesn't mind that she leaps up to take a shower immediately after having sex, like it should be washed away, that's his affair, none of mine. May God bless and keep them."

"We're losing, aren't we?"

"Shit, yeah. We're motherfucking losing. You motherfucking know that, don't you. You motherfucking knew that when you were an FNG.* So what you wanna do about it, you wanna go out and kill some more people anyway?"

"That's my job," I say. "You got another job, maybe I'll take that instead."

"War a good job, Joe?"

"Yeah, the best, Griff."

He throws some scrip on the table. The waiter's been hoping for real money. Any kind, except scrip and Vietnamese. But he doesn't say anything. "Come on, Madame Thieu's. New Cambodian girls.

*Fucking new guy.

Got no place to live anymore. Their home's a bomb crater. They're happy for the work. We'll take two at a time. We'll take four on the floor and swap 'em around. Come on, buddy."

I think about it. But I say, "No."

"Gonna go see Dao?"

"Yeah," I say.

"You're missing your opportunities, Joe. You go back to the states, and you're gonna go back to the states if you live, 'cause we're losing and they're gonna kick our asses out of here, our motherfucking sorry white asses, you go out see some whore, your lady wife will take out a knife or call her attorney. Not Vietnamese women. They understand, a man's a man and a' that."

"I don't know, Griff. I think Dao would hurt if I went to Madame Thieu's instead of home."

"Home, Joe, home? You're starting to call something in Name home? You're going native, Joe? White man has to watch out for that, going native."

For me, after about three miles, the machine kicks in. Now I'm below the bluff that marks six miles. I turn around to head back. About a half mile later I see Maggie, still running. Good for her. When we meet, I gesture for her to turn around, stay with me. She thinks about being stubborn, but it's still going to be about five miles longer than she's used to. She turns. I slow down a little bit, enough that she can run beside me. I'm not angry anymore. Sweated it out. We run in silence. No more questions. The place where we exist—where the lust and desire and whatever else is happening—is contained, rebuilds inside the steady rhythm.

Maggie begins to hurt. I don't speak, I just try to hold her up with my running. Like we're in the same platoon. It works. She goes away from the pain into the zone. Maybe she's learning something. Maybe she already knows.

Let me tell you something: Maggie is a mystery to me. I don't ask her many questions because there are no facts. I know nothing about her except her existence.

The house comes into view. With the goal in sight she comes out of the zone. Ideas about stopping, rest, tiredness, pain all enter her and it affects her running. "There is no end," I tell her. "We won't stop at the house."

"OK," she says and steadies.

As we get closer and closer, she begins to hope that I'm lying. That we will stop. She goes back and forth. When she thinks it's the end, her running is ragged, when she thinks there is no end, it's steady. When we do stop, right at the house, she's exhilarated. She takes me by the arm and leans on me like she can't walk. And by tomorrow she probably won't be able to.

"Tell me," she says. "I want you to tell me."

"Yes."

"Who was she?"

"Dao Thi Thai was her name."

"Was?"

"Was."

"I'm sorry, Joe."

I shrug.

"What happened, Joe? What happened to her?"

"Friendly fire."

"Friendly fire?"

"Enemy fire."

"Enemy? What enemy?"

"Exactly. What enemy?"

"Don't be cryptic."

"Cryptic?"

"Don't . . . just tell me so I can understand. Tell me once. I won't ask again."

"She got shot. In Hue. In our apartment. Where we lived together."

"Who? Who shot her?"

"Friend or foe, I don't know. It didn't matter, did it? Friendly fire, enemy fire. It got to be all the same. Her people were my enemy. My people were her enemy. Is the enemy of my friend my enemy? Maybe it wasn't even meant for her. We were there to kill. They were there to kill."

"Did you love her very much, Joe?"

I go through the gate and head up the stairs into the house. To a shower. We have to get ready for this party. "Oh, Maggie," I say, I guess because it has to be said to complete the story, "oh, Maggie—she was pregnant."

The party is a Hollywood party. A lot of money Is spent on the booze and the catering. There's valet parking outside, five bartenders, and five circulating waitpersons inside. The valets, bartenders, and waitpersons are all better-looking than me, better-looking than 99.9 percent of the people that exist in real life. They all have perfect teeth. They look better than most of the guests, but are not in the same league as the best-looking of the guests. Like Maggie, Julia Roberts, and Michelle Pfeiffer.

Jean-Claude Van Damme is there. He ripples and poses for Maggie—I think it's for Maggie, not for me—when we're introduced. She treats Van Damme like he looks like Tip O'Neill. Like I said, there is something very thoughtful and courteous about Maggie, even with the feeling that all life is a movie.

John Travolta is there in what I am told is a rare public appearance. His wife is home with their child. He greets Maggie with real warmth. I ask him if he minds talking about Scientology. He says he is glad to. "I got to ask you something," I say. "Can Scientology cure homosexuality?"

It is a conversation stopper, apparently. John just looks at me. Maggie looks at me like I have committed a faux pas. "I don't mean it's a disease," I say, "or like that. I mean, if someone who is homosexual doesn't want to be, could it help them not be. Hey, guys, I'm asking because Bambi Ann Sligo wants to know." What the hell, if I'm out of this life and back to the old life, I might as well score a few points with Mel Taylor's secretary, because Mel is not going to be happy to see me.

Travolta says Scientology helps you become *clear*. Once you're *clear*, a lot of important psychological and emotional things happen, almost anything you want, and you take control of your life because you're *clear*. I figure I can tell Bambi Ann what she wants.

David Hartman arrives with Sakuro Juzo and two other Japanese martial-arts types with him. Someone tells me they are his bodyguards, that he no longer travels anywhere without them. Another person tells me how they are trained to kill with a touch. I get to see Van Damme introduced to Juzo. There's a fight that I would pay to see.

Hartman greets me effusively. But then, even if he was planning to have Sakuro decapitate me, I don't think he would be any different. I smile. He asks me how it's going, if I've found anything for Maggie yet.

"A couple of things that are interesting," I say.

"What?"

"I don't know if I'm enough of a hustler for this business," I say. "Now that you ask me, I find myself doubting myself. This is my first pitch meeting, isn't it?"

Hartman laughs. Maggie hears him and comes over.

"What are you laughing at?"

"You know, he's not as bad as I thought he was going to be. He's got a nice approach," he says to Maggie. "Go ahead. It's a free practice session for you. If I like the material, I'll help you with the pitch, I promise."

"OK. Here goes. First one. Big picture. Historical. I know nobody likes costume epics anymore. But—Catherine the Great. Hear me out. There's a new biography of her. I'm told it's very twentieth-Century in feeling. Also, think Russian-American coproduction. They're desperate for hard currency. How much do you think it'll cost to rent the Russian Army for a couple of days? They have crews and equipment and they're pretty good. So I see high-production value for reasonable cost. Second, I just got a book about an out-of-work actress who gets a job as a detective. Part-time. Instead of parking cars or being a waitress. A New York film. It's available. Nicely written."

"Action film?"

"No," I say. "It's a character thing. It's more about being an actress than a detective, plus it's got this clash of cultures thing, kind of like *Tootsie* meets *Someone to Watch Over Me*."

"What about the war story? Give that up?"

"I have yet to see anything good in a war story for a woman."

Hartman looks around the room, waves at someone, and leads us over near the bar. "Barry, you already know Maggie, but you haven't met Joe, Joe Broz. We're teaching Joe how to pitch. Practice on Barry. Maggie and I will watch and critique."

Now Maggie seems happy with me, but it's pointless. It's an act that can't play much longer. I go on automatic pilot. Maybe that's why Barry likes the pitch——I don't sound like I care. I promise to send over a copy of the book and the coverage in the morning.[92] I'm drinking bourbon. Slow and steady. It doesn't seem to matter one way or the other. Our host has an eleven-year-old boy. He's in black tie. It's very cute. The bartenders won't serve him. So when other people put their drinks down, he snatches them and dumps them in his glass of Coca-Cola. The drunker he gets, the more he stares at women's breasts. Around midnight, distinctly glassy-eyed, he goes over to Michelle Pfeiffer and in a voice that has yet to change says, "Lemme touch 'em. Just lemme touch 'em one time."

Clint Eastwood comes to her rescue and takes the kid away. He says, "Come on, son. Boys your age should be playing with guns."

Maggie looks at Clint. "I hate him," she says.

"Why?"

[92]Barry Levinson, director of *Diner; The Natural; Young Sherlock Holmes; Tin Men; Rain Man; Good Morning, Vietnam; Avalon*. The book was *Alibi for an Actress*, Gillian Farrell; (Pocket Books, 1992). This is the way material is pitched—as exactly like something else successful, with a twist. The twist is that you're combining it with something else successful.

AMERICAN HERO

"You think anyone will want me to work when I'm his age?"

CHAPTER

* * *

THIRTY - FIVE

When the party was over, Hartman went back to his office. Sakuro Juzo and the other two Japanese took up stations outside his door. It was 3 A.M. Nonetheless, he picked up the phone and called Mel Taylor at home. Taylor was asleep.

"Is it an emergency?" Taylor asked.

"What I want to know is the truth about Joe Broz."

"You have the file. Don't you have the file?"

"Do you really take me for that much of an asshole? These missing years, and the civilian work in Vietnam, what's the real story?"

"I'll get it for you," Taylor said. "Is first thing in the morning alright? Is that OK?"

"Sure," said Hartman. He hung up. He liked Joe. Liked him and Maggie together. On the other hand, he liked silk ties, Hunan cooking a couple of times a year, the Pacific coast of Costa Rica, and London tailors. He liked RepCo agents to wear black socks, but he'd yet to fire anyone for wearing navy blue. "Like" was not one of the heavies.

C H A P T E R

★ ★ ★

T H I R T Y - S I X

"I don't want to go home,"
Maggie says when the party winds down.

"Well, take the car, I'll call me a cab," I say.

"Hey, Joe, you got two bits, Joe?"

"Maggie, don't start . . ."

"Buy me a cup of Java, Joe. Come on, Joe."

It's a cool night, by L.A. standards. Maggie's dress is on the skimpy side. I give her my jacket. I drive. Maggie turns on the radio. Pirates of the Mississippi, K.D. Lang, Patsy Cline. "Who is Bambi Ann Sligo?" she asks. I tell her. Maggie slides close, puts her head on my shoulder. "Won't you tell me about yourself, some," she says. The top is down. One time I went home. On leave after my first hitch. Joey's dad said Joey'd done his duty, it was time to go home. Joey said he was going to re-up. Like me. With me. His dad, Pasquale, owns a grocery, has four kids, three girls and Joey, so, you know how it is, his son is what matters to him. Anyway, he has some money. Tells Joey if he come homes, stays home, he'll buy him a convertible. We went down to the Chevy dealer, test-drove one, top down, me and him and his sister, Annette. Pasquale, he comes to me, says, "Tell Joey, stay home. He listen to you, Joe." I owed him, owed him a lot. So I should've done it. But I didn't.

"What you see is what you get," I say. "Where we going?"

"Venice," she says. "There's an all-night place on Pico. I'm hungry."

"You're hungry?" There had been plenty of food at the party, nouvelle southwestern cuisine. That's Mexican food redesigned for Hollywood with less fat and fart-free beans because there's nothing worse than a room full of movie stars all stressed and contorted trying not to pass gas.

"I can't eat at those things. I get afraid someone is going to see me eat. Once they see you eat, they look for signs of fat. Then they decide not to even call you because they don't want to have to tell you to your face that you have to lose four pounds before the start of shooting or they can't get a completion bond."

"That's crazy."

"Of course it is. But it happens. So sometimes I don't eat at those things. Let 'em think I live on air."

When we get to the restaurant, Maggie goes into the bathroom, right away. I get us a booth. It's one of those places that could only be L.A., imitating a place that's just like America was supposed to be, back about between Buddy Holly and going to Vietnam. Maggie washes her face, takes off all the makeup, and pulls her hair back into a ponytail. Our waitress recognizes her anyway. But she doesn't fuss about it. Maybe she's good about that sort of thing, the celebrity thing, or just tired.

Maggie orders a stack of pancakes, some sausage—which most of the time she wouldn't approve of—and coffee. I get a couple of eggs and toast. There's a bunch of musicians in back. Everything black and lots of leather.

"He was a drunk," I tell her. Why shouldn't she know about my father. "When he got drunk, he used to whale on me some. Not like on the movie of the week, where he's breaking my ribs and sending me to the hospital and such. Just beating on me."

"I'm sorry, Joe," she says, full of sympathy.

"Don't be. You say shit like that, I won't tell you nothin'."

"I'm sorry. That I was sorry."

"I'll tell you a story. How I come out on top. First off, you gotta understand, you got an old man like that, it teaches you you can take it, makes you tough." She still looks at me with sympathy. Which makes me angry. "You don't get it." She doesn't.

"OK, tell me."

"Kids used to brag about how hard their old man hit them."

"Men are such assholes," she says.

"Yeah, men are assholes. No question about it. Why don't you get yourself a girl. Maybe that's what you should do. Maybe that's what you really want."

"How tough was your old man?"

"He worked a foundry most of his life. Ever been in a foundry?"

"No."

"They make molds. They pour molten metal in the molds. Most of the molds are made out of sand. Plain old wet sand. Like at the beach. So the man spent his life carrying around boxes of wet sand, buckets of molten metal. Hundred pounds, two hundreds pounds, five hundred, whatever. All day long. And it's hot. The metal splatters. It finds any bare skin you got. You can't drop what you're doing, because what you're doing is carrying one side of a hundred-pound bucket of liquid aluminum, so hot it flows like your morning coffee. So that's how tough my old man was."

"Pretty tough."

"Pretty tough. Man's work. Good work for a man. Anyway, problem was, problem was, he drank. So we weren't living too good, between him missing work and spending his money down in the bar. It was mostly when he got drunk that he'd get angry and beat the shit out of me, or take a couple of swipes at me, anyway. It was just a matter of surviving until he thought he'd done enough or he went to sleep. I'm not bitching about it. That's the way it is, until a boy grows big enough to go out and make his own place or big enough to stand up for himself and say 'No more.' That's the way it is in nature, you know that."

"If you had a son, is that the way you would raise him?"

"What do you mean?"

"I mean, would you beat him until he was big enough to beat you back?"

I have to stop and think about that. Funny, you would think that I would've thought about it before, lots of times. But I never put it to myself and nobody else did, that simple and straightforward. I didn't grow up thinking, the way kids do, If I ever grow up, I won't treat my children that way, I'll always let them stay up late and eat candy or whatever it is that kids think that parents do wrong. Oh yeah, and I'll always be fair and never punish them unjustly. Stuff like that. "I always said I would never be a drunk like my old man. And I never have been. I guess, I guess I sort of intended to have a woman around. A mother. A man alone, raising a kid, it's hard. Especially with no others, no grandmothers or aunts or nothing, around. It was the luck of the draw, bad luck of the draw, that my mother didn't leave anybody around to take her place, raising me. So, no, I guess not. Not with a woman around. It wouldn't have to be that way. There are other ways a boy can turn into a man besides getting beat up all the time. Maybe not as effective," I say, as a joke, "but there are other ways. Of course there are other ways."

"You were going to tell me, about the last time, how you made him stop."

"I was about fifteen. Almost fifteen, anyway. He comes home, drunk again. Which means no money. We start to arguing. I should know better, but I don't. 'Cause even stumblin' drunk, he's a damn sight bigger and stronger than me. A damn sight. He starts up to beat on me. I tell him, 'No more. Not this time.' He swings at me. I duck. That makes him madder. Then he comes at me for real, big right hand, in a fist. I don't run. I don't hide. I step in and take it, right here," I point to my forehead. "He busts his hand. Drunk as he is, he feels it. He just sits right down and stares at it. At his hand. He holds it and cradles it and he hurts too much to hit me anymore.

"I didn't beat him, but I beat him. I walked out. I never went back."

The waitress is behind the counter, having a smoke. She sees Maggie finish her coffee and comes over with a pot, gives us refills.

"Pardon me, do you have an extra cigarette?" Maggie asks her.

"Sure, hon," she says. She gives Maggie one. Hands me a pack of matches. There's a silhouette of a girl with a ponytail on the cover. Underneath, it says, "Can you draw this?" I light Maggie's cigarette. I give the matches back to the waitress and she walks away. Maggie looks at me through the smoke. She's playing some kind of scene, I guess. That's OK. A woman thing or an actress thing.

"Do you love me, Joe?"

"Yes, I guess I do," I say.

"Then you better take me home," she says, "and make love to me, Joe."

CHAPTER

* * *

THIRTY-SEVEN

I was right about one thing: once
it starts, there is no stopping.

Mrs. Mulligan arrives at seven, just a few hours after we get
home. We still haven't been to sleep. She goes about her business.
I cancel myself out of the office. Maggie and I come downstairs,
hungry and thirsty, I don't know, eleven, twelve o'clock. Mrs. Mulligan
makes us orange juice and tea and scones. Can she tell the difference
in us? Yeah. Who couldn't. I didn't know it could be like this. We
manage to drink the juice, but we can't finish the tea and scones. We
need each other. Again.

We're ready to go back upstairs. Or on the couch. Or the deck.
We really should be alone.

"Mary," Maggie says.

"Yes, Maggie, what I can be doing for you?"

"Why don't you take a couple of days off."

"You two," she says. "Like kids. American kids, not Irish kids. No
Irish person, even a teenager, would behave like this. There's something in the Irish water that maintains the human glands at sensible
levels. It's altogether missing in California. Maybe it gets washed
away with the shipping of your water all the way from the North. In
Ireland we get our water direct from the sky, whole, as God in-

tended."

"With pay," Maggie says.

"Of course with pay. Should I make you a bit of dinner before I go? A salad you can pull out of the fridge, or something to pop into the oven?"

"That's OK."

"You know," Mrs. Mulligan says, "he's not such a young one. He's going to need some good solid food, keep his strength up."

"I love him, Mary."

"Oh. Oh, yes. I see. I'll be going then."

"Don't gossip about us too much, alright?"

"Oh, no, miss. I wouldn't ever gossip about you. Well, yes. I better get my things and be gone." She goes and gathers her handbag and her coat, which she doesn't wear since it's too warm, but always has with her. She goes to the front door. Then she turns and comes back. "Ms. Lazlo, there's something I've got to be telling you. They've come after me. They say they're Immigration, but I don't know if that's true. I'm thinking it's not. I'm not legal, you see. I don't know if you know that—I'm not legal. They said they would turn me in and ship me out. Now how much money do you think I'd be earning scrubbing floors in County Cork? To hell with the Irish water, all rain and damp it is, hell on rheumatism. Not enough to keep body and soul together and under a dry roof. They want me to tell them things about you. You and him in there. If you were truly involved with each other or if you were up to something. I'm frightened o' them. Immigration, they treat you with total contempt and you've got no place to turn, now have you? But I'm not an informer. None of my people have ever been informers. Never will be."

"If they come again, tell me," Maggie says. "If you need a lawyer, I'll get you one. Meantime, tell them . . . what you see."

"That you're in love with that lug of a man?"

"Right."

"I'll do that. With your permission, ma'm."

"Yes, Mary. Do that."

She goes and it doesn't matter that Mel Taylor and U.Sec. are still checking up on us. It doesn't fucking matter. We're in a different world now. We make love. We talk. We go out on the beach a couple of times, but we need to touch each other in ways that we don't want to do in public. We stay home—not taking calls—not going out—for about three days. We talk about maybe making movies together. For real. I say that my bullshit is bullshit. Maggie says everybody's is. The book I found is good, she says, we have to see if a good script can be developed from it. When and if I get out of bed and into the office, I'll track down the agent and option it. The Catherine thing is more difficult. It's bigger and against the common wisdom. So it needs a name writer. Who will be, therefore, expensive. And therefore should be paid for with Other People's Money, through the development deal that we do not yet have. I tell her a little more. About how when I left home, on my own, almost fifteen, Pasquale, father of Joey, took me in. Gave me a home, for a year, year and a half, until me and his son joined the Marines. Joey was older than me. Maggie, of course, keeps asking me about Annette—did I make it with Joey's sister? Well, we fooled around a lot. Those days, she is still supposed to be a virgin when she marries. This is before the pill practically. Everybody who does it, it seems like, gets knocked up. Every wedding, it seems like, the bride is glowing and on the plump side, the groom embarrassed, wishing he was somewheres else. And she's Joey's sister, so if I fuck her, Joey's got to get angry at me, we have to have a fight. I don't want to do that. I love Joey like a brother. And Pasquale like a father. Because he is more father to me than the asshole who broke his hand on my head. "So what *did* you do?" Maggie wants to know. I get embarrassed, because of course she is right. I just say, "We fooled around." She insists that I get specific. By hand? Yes. Her mouth? Well, once. How was it? Why only once? "It didn't work that well, that's why." What about me? Did I use my mouth on her? "I was fifteen, I never heard of that," I tell Maggie. She thinks that's really funny. She holds me and kisses me and says, "I love you, Joe Broz." It puts me in another dimension to hear that.

But Maggie's back at it again. "Come on, didn't you get it into her once? Didn't you even try?" "Nah, nah, I told you, she was Joey's sister, she was afraid of getting pregnant, Pasquale would've thrown me out and where hell was I going to go?" "I don't believe you," she says. "She was a good Catholic girl and wanted to be a virgin," I tell her. "Oh–oh," Maggie says, "you put it in the back way." She giggles. "No," I say. "Don't lie to me, Joe Broz, I love you, you can't lie to me." "OK, yeah, I admit it." Why am I embarrassed. Because I never told that to anyone in my life?

I love her.

Maybe there is a future here. Maybe the masquerade has become the reality. The illusion, an actuality. Maybe Magdalena Lazlo's next role is Catherine the Great and mine is Potëmkin.[93] When I finally arise from her bed, I let my empress dress me as her producer. Are we going to forget John Lincoln Beagle and our quest for his secret? I think we don't know. I think we're too involved in each other and in our possibilities to know.

I will tell you one thing about our lovemaking. When we get to bed the first time, I reach into the drawer beside the bed where I know there are condoms. I've been all over this house. I know everything in this house. She puts her hand over mine, to stop me. Neither of us has mentioned HIV or AIDS or blood tests. Also, I'm virtually certain

[93]Potëmkin, Grigori Aleksandrovich (1739–91), a Russian statesman who became the lover and favorite of Catherine II in 1771 and remained until his death the most powerful man in Russia. He was the governor general of "New Russia" (Ukraine). The famous story about him is that he claimed to have established entire cities and villages that in fact had not been built. Catherine insisted on sailing down the Volga to view them. Potemkin had crews set up false fronts—like the façades of a town in a Western movie. As soon as the empress's barge passed, they would tear down the set and race ahead to the next location to set up a new one there. Then the next and the next. The expression "Potemkin villages," which means to have the appearance of a thing but to really be empty, virtually nonexistent, comes from this.

Potemkin engineered the colonization of the Ukrainian steppes and the conquest of the Crimea. He became a field marshal in 1784 and was commander in chief during the second Turkish War (1787–91).

that she doesn't use any other form of birth control, at least not pills or a diaphragm. So without the condoms, if we have sex, maybe there's a birth, maybe someone dies.

"Do you love me, Joe?" she says.

I say, "Yes."

"Maybe there's a birth," she says, "maybe someone dies."

That's what I'll tell you about making love with Maggie.

When I finally go to the office, there's a load of messages and mail is stacked up and I'm going to need people to help me for real. I haven't even picked the mail off the floor, the phone rings. This kid, not a kid, he's twenty-five, twenty-seven, he says, "Hi. My name is Teddy Brody. I heard from a friend of mine that you're looking for someone. From the description, someone just like me. I've been to Yale Drama School and UCLA Film School. And I currently do development and research for John Lincoln Beagle."

"Yeah, Teddy," I say, "I'd love to see you."

CHAPTER

* * *

THIRTY-EIGHT

The peculiarity of Atwater's proposition was how compelling it seemed at one moment and how preposterous it seemed at the next. It had the sort of duality of a sluttish lover that you just can't see yourself with, but to whom you succumb whenever he or she, as the case may be, comes around. While he was away from it, the president rather expected it to disappear. He was surprised that it survived his first meeting with Hartman. Now what he truly expected from a full-blown presentation of a motion-picture director's idea of what a war should be was that dressing the whore for the ball would just be putting a red dress on impropriety, it would only serve to make what she was—gaudy and meretricious—unbearably obvious.

James Addison Baker III was opposed. Even though he'd brought it to the president. That should have been warning enough for Bush. Baker had a knack, a true genius actually, for distancing himself from disaster. Bush's attitude toward "little brother" Baker was, "Why is Jimmy always right?"[94] Baker was more than his pajama-party companion on *Air Force One*. The president's regard for Baker was so high that he thought that the whole world would think that a problem

---

[94] *Time*, 2-13-89.

was solved if he simply announced that he was assigning Baker to it.[95]

Although Baker had made it clear, in an understated way, that he

[95]Later on, when Bush's reelection campaign was in trouble, he announced that "Baker is coming," as if, like *the Mighty Quinn,* his mere presence would immediately turn things around. With the economy, over which he had presided for four years, as the main issue against him, Bush announced, in the second presidential debate, that, if reelected, his solution would be to put James Baker in charge of the economy, and he apparently expected all America to say, "Well, that'll be alright then."

Is Bush right about Baker? A scan of the press on James Addison Baker III will convince you that he is either the only person in Washington actually capable of true accomplishment or that he is the best spin doctor in Spin City.

Baker began his political career working on Bush's Senate campaign, which he lost. In 1975 Bush persuaded Ford to make Baker under secretary of Commerce. He took over president Ford's reelection campaign and got the credit for bringing the incumbent "within an eyelash of beating Jimmy Carter." (*Time,* 2-13-89) He ran Bush's first campaign for the Republican presidential nomination in 1980. He convinced Bush to withdraw—although Bush still had at least a statistical chance to win. Reagan rewarded Bush with the vice presidency and Baker with the post of chief of staff. Baker later traded places with Don Regan to become secretary of the treasury.

His major accomplishment at Treasury was the devaluation of the dollar. It was his initiative and his insider political savvy that is credited with making it actually happen. It was supposed to make America more competitive and reduce the trade deficit. Obviously, it did not. Baker's defense is that things would be even worse without devaluation. For a critique of this policy see, among others, Daniel Burstein, *Yen!: Japan's New Financial Empire and Its Threat to America* (Simon Schuster 198   ) It argues that this abrupt devaluation, in isolation, doing nothing else to prepare American business to take advantage of the change and to become export-oriented, had the result of handing the Japanese an incredible gift. Their money literally doubled in value. It made them twice as rich as they had been the day before. It did not lead the Japanese to buy more American goods; it lead them to buy more of America—real estate, businesses, financial institutions, and Hawaii.

In sum: Bush lost, Ford lost, Bush lost, the economy of the United States lost. Bottom line: Baker went 0 for 4. The result: Baker's reputation as the man who's always right and who gets things done continued to grow.

Baker ran Bush's 1988 presidential campaign. Except, of course, for the selection of Dan Quayle, which has become widely cited as *the decision that Bush made without Baker,* and for the negative advertising, which is attributed to Atwater and Ailes.

At last, Baker won one. If there were justice in the world, that would have diminished his reputation. There isn't. It didn't. He became secretary of state, a was against the project he had not yet mounted an attack. He believed, even more than the president, that this strumpet of an idea was no Galatea, and that neither Hartman nor Beagle was a Pygmalion, able to bring it to life. Baker was born into wealth, raised to know that you don't squander capital, financial or personal, fighting unnecessary battles. And even Baker had to be careful about opposing Bushie, who, once he'd made up his mind, was apt to devastate his opponents with the ultimate withering retort: "If you're so smart, how come I'm the president and you're not."

Hartman and Beagle felt no ambiguity. They wanted the idea to fly. Beagle's motivation was that of the artist, who wants to see his work realized, regardless of cost in cash or life. For Hartman there would be the joy of consummating the biggest film deal ever done. Maybe that ever would be done. Yet it was more than that, more than glory or ego—he was also motivated by a compelling lust for power and for riches.

Beagle knew he could direct a brilliant war. Part of what makes a great director is the ability to spend ten or twenty or sixty million dollars of someone else's money just to tell a story—about a man who cheats on his wife, who dresses like a bat, who teaches pronunciation, who chauffeurs an old lady. The problem was the pitch. He was the veteran of many, many pitch meetings, from both sides of the desk. He knew that success and failure did not rest in the details. Details could always be changed, fixed, lied about. It didn't rest in "the deal." It wasn't even the Concept. Though it was a very common illusion that concept was the key. Even people hooked on a pitch

---

position he held while Eastern Europe broke free of the Soviet bloc, Gorbachev rose and fell, Communist rule ended in Russia itself, there was a coup and countercoup, and even in China there was a movement toward democracy, though it was brutally crushed by the government. The United States appeared to have no particular policy toward these various events. If one believes that almost any action makes things worse and no position is the best position—a philosophy that is sometimes demonstrably correct—Baker should have only gained in stature. He did.

thought, more often than not, that concept was what they were buying into. But being a great pitch person was more like being Luke Skywalker bombing the Death Star, finding that sole route, whatever twists and turns were required, that led to the undefended opening, so you could drop a bomb right in their brain.

Hartman agreed.

He was comfortable that Beagle had done a good job. Granted that it was still just at the treatment stage, still, he'd designed a great war, a perfect war, really tuned in to up-to-the moment audience tastes and expectations. It would even stand up under so-called real-life combat analysis by real-life colonels. And Hartman thought they had most of the other bases covered: security, money, the press. But people don't do things because the arguments for it are good; they think the arguments for it are good because those arguments support something they want to do.

When Beagle had his war to the pitch point, Hartman communicated with the president. It is remarkably hard for the president of the United States to do anything in private, let alone in secret. The scheduling, the protocol, the wave of attendants and courtiers, the palace guard that protects his every move, their equipment and his equipment, are as elaborate and inescapable as the excesses of the Sun King and the rigid ostentations of the court of the Ming emperor. Where once court watchers gossiped by word of mouth, now they do it by microwave transmission and satellite and tune the whole world into what His Presidential Majesty had for breakfast, to whom he spoke, upon what subject and at what length; they make news not only of his bowel movements but of his bowels themselves.

Of course, the official transcripts and the daily bulletins may not reflect what was actually said. That is the door to presidential deception: like the purloined letter, his actions must be hidden in plain sight. There was no way to pretend that the president was not meeting with David Hartman and John Lincoln Beagle. The trick was to make it appear casual and unimportant, yet leave time and space enough to talk and to consider. The place they came up with was Bob Hope's house in Palm Springs. The trip itself was passed off as a golfing vacation. But Hartman had not yet found that space-pilot route into George Bush's brain, that surefire path to closing the sale. He turned to Sun Tzu. Sometimes his aphorisms were spotlights that illuminated the battlefield, sometimes they were cryptograms in a scavenger hunt. Still uncertain, Hartman went into the meeting with a miniature edition of *The Art of War*, two-by-three inches, in his pocket, a talisman whose magic words would have to reach him osmotically or etherically.

Bush came in from his golf game happy. Bush liked games and being outdoors. That was a positive for Hartman and Beagle. But it was still early in the day. Much too early for the president to be on Halcion. That would make it tougher. There was Baker, cold as ice. One look told Hartman that Baker was not neutral, prepared to decide on the merits. That was what Hartman needed—someone to compete with, someone to beat. The formless enemy cannot be defeated.[94] But once the enemy takes a position, we can devise a strategy.

What would Baker's attack be? The obvious one? That he and Beagle were Hollywood. Frivolous movie people. Not to be entrusted with matters of state? With reality? Hartman smiled. He had thought of his favorite line from Sun Tzu—*War is nothing but lies.* Could he meet Baker's objections head-on? Only a stupid man confronts. The intelligent man maneuvers so that there is no need for battle. Imagine jumping up and down trying to say, "*But we are serious people—take us seriously.*" To defend against that charge would be to validate it. No defense. Let Baker attack that space and find it empty.

At last the line from Sun Tzu that spoke to this situation came to him. Once he understood, it was obvious, it was comic, he deserved a slap in the face from a Zen master, it was the very first sentence:

---

[94]*The Art of War* expresses this in the inverse: *The ultimate Positioned Strategy is to be without apparent position. Without position even the deepest intelligence is unable to spy; and those who are clever are unable to plan.*

Military affairs are of the greatest importance to a county, for life or death, survival or destruction, depend on them.

"Mr. President," David Hartman said, "the great leaders of America—Dwight Eisenhower, Harry Truman, Jack Kennedy, and yourself, sir—were forged in war. Victorious war. But now we have a problem. Where are tomorrow's leaders going to come from?" Watch this, Mr. Baker, Hartman said to himself. I'm taking the high ground. "From the Vietnam generation? I don't want to take a thing away from the boys who fought there. Died there. Were wounded there. Believe me, I honor them. But what did they experience? Defeat. They experienced defeat. That does a terrible thing to your mind. When a confrontation comes, what are they going to say? They're going to say; 'Remember Vietnam. We can't go to war. We'll lose. We better back down.' They do say it. The sons of bitches in Congress did it to you over Grenada, Panama, Libya, Lebanon. It's a chorus, a chorus of losers. 'We don't want it to turn into another Vietnam.' I would never say that those people are cowards, inherently. They are responding to what their experience has taught them . . ."

"Well, I don't know," Baker said, "about America running out of leaders.s"

Oh, Mr. Baker, Hartman thought, I have just invested the hills around your flanks and you didn't even know they were there. He said, addressing both of them, "You're from Texas. Now if a son of yours got thrown by a horse, what would you tell him to do? You'd tell him to get back up there. What if he said, 'No, dad, no horseback riding for me. I think I'm going to learn how to do ballet dancing instead.' You'd make damn sure that boy got up on that horse again. I know you would.

"America needs you, Mr. President. America needs you to help it get back on the horse. To be tall in the saddle again and to ride." Reality check. Too thick? No. Too thick is impossible.

Mr. Baker, Hartman thought, here it comes. I reveal to you where I've mounted my artillery. "I read Lee's memo, we all read it. I want to tell you something—if all that this was about was an election, I would not do it. Period. I would not risk one American boy fighting on a foreign shore for anybody's reelection. And my bet is, Mr. President, neither would you. I know your record, you've been there, you know better and you are an honorable man."

Son of a bitch, the Jew bastard is taking the high road, Baker said to himself.[99]

"But that's not what it's about," Hartman said. If he read Baker's thoughts, he didn't seem to mind. "America needs a war to remember what it's like to win. The next generation of leaders needs to be tested in battle, to win, and go on from there, with confidence and pride. If you sit down at the poker table and every two-bit, tin-pot gambler in the world knows you're scared to go all the way, they'll bluff you out of pot after pot and strip you down to your underdrawers. The men who stood up to the Soviet Union, the most dangerous military power the world has ever known, a nuclear power, were men who had been victorious in war. What happens, if, after you, we get another Jimmy Carter? An America that backs down to anybody and everybody—to an ayatollah, to South American drug dealers and gangsters, to a Qaddafi.

"What scares me, Mr. President, is that in the generation after you we will see the return of appeasement. You have to save us, Mr. President."

"Slicker than deer guts on a doorknob," Baker said. He liked to talk Texan from time to time, it made him feel colloquial. But actually, he sounded respectful. He knew—unless Hartman and Beagle hopelessly fucked up the rest of the presentation—that this was no longer a self-defeating proposition. Once again Lee Atwater's strumpet memo was asserting it's right to life. Was it a brilliant stroke of realpolitik, actually more historically profound than it appeared, or

[99]Would Baker think this way? Did Baker say, "Fuck the Jews. They didn't vote for us"? The *New Republic* reports that he did, although his spokeswoman, Margaret Tutwiler, denies it.

was this loony-bin Napoleonics?

CHAPTER

★ ★ ★

THIRTY-NINE

Story time. Hartman turned the pitch over to Beagle, who made the story very simple, just as he would pitching across the table at Spago for some producer who was wobbling between the four corners of a producer's life: Valium, cocaine, the unremitting certainty that he was about to lose his job if he didn't make a decision soon, and that nagging sense that any decision he made would cost him his job.

The story was this:

"We start with an INVASION. Sudden. Unexpected. Unprovoked. Tanks rolling across an undefended border. It has no justification in morality or international law. The invaders are brutes. They commit ATROCITIES against women, children, and property. Their leader is another HITLER. A new Hitler.

"In recent years there've been several people labeled Hitlers. But they've only operated in their own countries. This guy is different, he's bent on CONQUEST. This invasion is only the beginning.

"Once upon a time, we would have been slow to understand that, we would have said, 'None of our business.' We would have sat back and waited—until they bombed Pearl Harbor. But not now. Because we have a LEADER who has *learned from history*. If we'd stopped Hitler in Czechoslovakia and Japan in Manchuria, there

would have been no World War II. So not this time, buddy. This time:
NO APPEASEMENT

"We round up the ALLIES. There's England and France and us
and Russia—all together again. In defense of Democracy and the
Rule of Law and the Integrity of National Borders. We have the
Government in Exile of the invaded country. This time even the
Germans and the Japanese are on our side. And all those little
countries. The United Nations. It makes your heart swell to see all
those different flags waving, proudly, defying the Tyrant.

"You see, the world understands that the conquered country Is the
Underdog. That no matter how much bigger we are than the New
Hitler, there's an Underdog we are fighting for. We're *fighting for the
underdog.*

"The next phase is the PREGAME HYPE.

"We mass our forces. And those of the allies. Bear with me here,
but it's my opinion that, given certain guidelines, there are damn few
countries in the world that are going to stand up to us much longer
than Panama or Grenada did. I want you to know that safety is very
high on our list here. We want so few casualties that more people
would have died if they stayed home and drove on a holiday
weekend. The last thing we want—and we are not going to let it
happen—is week after week of body bags on America's home
screens. In spite of that, while we are massing our forces, we are
doing a MEDIA BLITZ on how powerful and dangerous the other guys
are. How difficult our task is. How much dedication and heroics it will
take to beat this fanatic, hardened, well-armed, experienced, killer
enemy.

"Our model for this war is the SUPER BOWL. The Super Bowl has
a long, long period of buildup. Not counting the play-offs, the buildup
is at least two weeks. That's 336 hours of buildup—for a sixty-minute
game. And it works.

"Comes the Big Game. WE GO IN. We BEAT THEM. Just like
a three-hour football game. We GO HOME. It's over. We have a
VICTORY PARADE."[96]

Hartman, to make the segue to the next step, asked Beagle, as if it were a real question: "Now let's step back and talk real world. Can we assemble the elements: Hitler, Poland, Allies, Certainty of Victory?"

Beagle looked the president square in the eye. He didn't rush to answer "Yes!" It was important to convey that this was no ill-considered, dimwit, hung-ho, can-do, cowboy, Ollie North version of heroics. "There are certain things that are matters of fact. The United States can go to war without negative political fallout. That's a fact. We can fight a war with virtually no American casualties. That's a fact. So really, the issue is only one of framing. We're talking about nothing new, only of framing something more effectively. Once we realize that, we understand that my role is not nearly so radical as it appears. In that light, I'm willing to say the answer is yes. A definitive yes."

The battlefield should be in the Middle East or North Africa, Beagle said, and he explained why.[97] Given that, there was a decent

---

[96]Hartman was pleased that the plan, though Beagle had arrived at it by driving up the opposite side of the mountain, agreed entirely with one of the most important of Sun Tzu's precepts: *While I have heard that a quick though clumsy campaign may pay, I have never seen any merit in a long one. There has never been any country that has benefited from a long war.*

[97]What Beagle thought that the United States needed, cinematically, militarily, and politically, was a football field: a flat, clear space with lines.

In the jungle or the mountains you go fight some guys, you win, you turn around and half of them are still there, hiding behind trees, in tunnels, and in caves.

In the desert, on the steppes, on the plains, you drive them out, and they're out.

Based on terrain alone, the U.S. didn't want to have a war in South America, Southeast Asia, much of Africa, Indonesia, the Philippines, Korea.

In addition, there were political considerations: No European war. Too expensive. The money people would never stand for it. No nuclear war. That eliminated Russia and China. While parts of black Africa may have been suitable militarily, Beagle's gut reaction was to stay out: whatever you do you're a racist, even in a black-black war. The Russo-Mongolian steppes were attractive but inacessible in a ring made half of mountains, half of nuclear powers.

choice of Hitlers: Muammar al-Qaddafi, Hafez al-Assad, Saddam Hussein, Rafsanjani, or—something to be considered—a new ayatollah.

There were lots of potential Polands. Libya invades Chad again, or the Sudan, or Algeria, or even Egypt. Algeria could invade Morocco. Iraq could attack Saudi Arabia, Kuwait, or Syria. Iran could cross the Gulf and go after the United Arab Emirates, Oman, Kuwait, even Saudi Arabia. Syria invades Jordan.

"We are going to enter," Hartman said, addressing himself to the president, "into an arena that requires a master of diplomacy. Someone who knows the heads of state personally."

"Maggie Thatcher will stand by us," the president said, thinking out loud. "Mitterrand, I can deal with him. Gorby, tell you the truth, I think he needs us more than we need him. We have a real advantage here, in my having been with the U.N."

"I'm about to ask you," Baker said, "How you expect to convince one of these heads of state to play Hitler for your movie. What if they remember that Germany lost and Hitler died in a bunker. It sounds to me like your offering them a no-win situation and they are, by God, going to know it."

"We see Hitler as a villain," Beagle said. "In the Middle East, a lot of people see him as a hero. They admire strength. They believe in martyrs. And there's the Jewish thing. Second: It's a chance at the big time, to play a major role on the world stage. Third: Taking on the United States, even taking on the U.S. and losing, makes someone a hero in the Arab world. So, although it looks like a no-winner from here, from over there it looks like a no-lose proposition. Or it certainly can be made to look that way."

"Here's where you're lucky to have me as your president," the

---

The Indian subcontinent is both politically tricky and nuclear. It would certainly be a religious war, but Hindu versus Moslem, not the appealing Christian versus Moslem confrontation. Of course, as it turned out, Moslem versus Moslem must be considered a stroke of genius, real genius.

president said. "I kid you not—how many presidents would have the experience and contacts and judgment to run with this thing? This is a complicated thing you have planned here. I guess a war always is. But this one includes allies and an enemy and you probably have to get the CIA in there somewhere and even the U.N. There's not another president in America, not one, who could say they've been in the U.N., that they know the U.N. Or China for that matter. You see what I mean." The more he heard, the more Bush liked what these Hollywood fellas had come up with. It gave him something to do. And George was a doer. He liked doing. It was strange that as president, although he did an incredible amount of running around, he didn't do so much doing. It was in part because he was committed, sort of, politically, to not doing very much. Actually to carrying out the Reagan mandate, which was undoing. But it just wasn't the same for him as for his predecessor, for several reasons: the undoing had been done, in many cases, overdone, and the consequences were coming due, demonstrating that they probably shouldn't be any more un-done—in fact, probably should be redone, but he couldn't do that; he didn't actually believe in undoing; and finally, he didn't nap nearly as much as Reagan had, so that the absence of constructive, or even destructive, activity weighed pretty heavily on his hands.

"I always make friends. I have good friends everywhere, because people are just people, even foreigners. I truly like people. I want you to know something because people don't understand this about me—I like Ron. He's a great guy. And you never met a better storyteller in your life. A lot of people thought he was hard to relate to, but he wasn't, you just had to tell him jokes. He likes jokes. And Barb likes Nancy. Truly likes her. Still does. We'd have them over for dinner if we had a chance and I'm sure we will. But the point was—friends. We're talking about a war in the Middle East and I have friends there, and that will make it easier to get them cooper-ated. I could get on the phone right now and Hosni Mubarak—he's having some tough times over there, over in Egypt—he would answer even though it's God knows what time it is in Cairo right now. Does anyone have on one of those watches that tells time in six different zones? What I'm saying, David, is it's not because I'm president of the United States, but because he knows that George Bush is his friend. Barb has him on our Christmas card list. I know he's not a Christian, but that's not what Christmas is about. Christmas is something to consider—it would be a good idea if we could do the war over Christmas. There are always a million good stories around the holidays. Servicemen—and women, let's not forget our women in the service, they do a fine job—far away from home, getting letters. Kids sitting around the table, an empty chair where Dad—or Mom, for that matter—normally sits. Somebody explains why Dad has to do what Dad has to do, so the world can be safe, so our children won't have to go."

"There's something glorious could happen here," Hartman said. "You're going to put your mark on a point in history. Jesus, they're all out there saying the American Century is over. I think we just might be putting the naysayers, the whole world, on notice that the American Century has a long, long way to run. By God, I feel like we've just begun."

James Baker watched Bush deciding to make video war. If the president went with it, his secretary of state would need to make a decision, whether to be found out front on the war to come, or to be far, far away, in which case his number one priority would be to make sure that the world knew he had as little to do with it as with the selection of Dan Quayle. "What if the media does to us what they did in Vietnam?" he asked.

"The key is a short war," Hartman said. "I have several theories about the power of the press and handling the press, but the bottom line is that all the press writes is what they're told, so if the bulk of what they're told is what you want them to hear, then that's what they'll report. This is not a question of censoring them or keeping them from sources. If you move reasonably quickly, you are the only source.

"The painful truth," Hartman went on, "is that if the war in Vietnam had lasted a month, the administration would have had total media support.

"I don't want to be absurd about it, but visualize the Super Bowl. Now imagine that there's no fourth quarter. In fact, no particular end. Nobody knows when, or if, the game is going to end. They play all day. Then through the night. The next day, next night, all week. More and more players, on both sides, are injured. One side gets ahead. Then the other. There's no time limit. No maximum score. They just keep slogging through the mud. All of the original guys are out, crippled. Now the substitutes are being crippled. Their substitutes are being crippled. The coaches are grabbing guys off the street, guys who don't want to play, and forcing them out there. And they're getting crippled. There's a lot of mud. Pretty soon America is going to get tired of the Super Bowl.

"Even sports reporters, who are paid cheerleaders, watching that long, are going to get bored, and out of boredom they'll make up questions: Should so many people get hurt? Should the game be ended? Why are we playing? Maybe the game should be banned? They don't mean anything malicious by it. They just have nothing else to do with their time.

"The critics didn't kill Vietnam. It was a lousy movie. It went on too long. People walked out. World War II was a great movie, a perfect story, well played, well paced, and everyone wanted to stay right to the end."

Now the president was onto something. He stood; he began to pace and gesture as he spoke. "I'm going to let you guys in on a secret. Normally, I wouldn't do this. I would carry this secret to the grave with me. But I think we've gone far enough here, the four of us, that I don't think they'd hang us separately, they'd hang us together. Not that they'd hang us at all, if they really understood our motivation here. A leadership opportunity. A chance to finally lift America out of the malaise of Vietnam. And to show the world that we are not a crippled giant or tied-up giant, whatever they like call it, we're no paper tiger.

"Bear with me on this, the guy to play Hitler—Saddam Hussein.

He's a friend of mine. I know this is a casting decision," the president said in a waggish mode, "and I hope you don't feel like I'm stepping on your toes, John. Your friends do call you John? Do they? Or Linc?"

"John'll be fine, Mr. President."

"You can call me George, that's OK. If we ever go hunting poon together, you can call me Bushie. Right Jimmy?" When the president enjoyed himself, his jocularity emerged. But then he got back to business. "What I'm trying to tell you here is that I have dealt with all of these people. I think I have the experience to judge who you can do business with and who you can't. There's secret stuff that I can't tell you about, but Saddam Hussein, over there in Iraq, he could well be the guy to go with, for this Hitler thing.[103]

"The thing that I like about Saddam is that he plays the game the way the game should be played. He made a deal and by golly he held up his end of it. And you didn't find him leaking all over the press. Not like those bastards in Iran. They leak and it was our pants that looked wet all up and down the front.[104] And when he found out that we were aiding Iran against him, did he storm off in a snoot? No. He

---

[103]"In the Loop: Bush's Secret Mission," by Murray Waas and Craig Unger, (*New Yorker*, 11-2-92), reports that when Bush was vice president, CIA Director Bill Casey sent him on a secret mission to make contact with Saddam Hussein through Mubarak of Egypt or King Hussein of Jordan, both of whom Bush was scheduled to speak with during a Mid-East trip. Casey wanted to encourage Saddam to use his Air Force to bomb deep inside Iran. Iran would then need American arms equipment to defend itself, and this would give the U.S. leverage to get better terms in the arms-for-hostages deal that later became the Iran-contra scandal. Iraq did so. In return, Saddam got economic and military assistance, including access to satellite intelligence, western arms and technology. Iran responded to the air attacks with a desperate and bloody ground offensive outside of Basra.

In other words, Bush and Saddam had a relationship that long preexisted Desert Storm. And Saddam committed certain specific acts of war at the request of the United States government even though those acts were costly for Iraq in terms of the lives of its people.

[104]What came to be known as Iran-contra began with a story on November 3, 1986, in a Beirut newsmagazine, *Al Shiraa*, which reported that the Reagan administration was shipping arms to Iran. Presumably, the information came from Iran.

came right back and you know what he said? He said, 'Hey, fellas, you do that, you better cut me in for more. Balance things out, you owe me.' You see what I'm saying here—this is someone we can deal with. We can say to Saddam Hussein, 'How about invading Kuwait—you'll look like a hero to the Arab world, as big as Hitler even.' Then we'll have a war, and may the best man win. He likes a good fight.''

"A lot of the images I see here," Beagle said, growing enthusiastic, and now loose enough with the president to start sharing his feeling and his craft, "is this real low-tech video of high-tech operations. Like infrared night bombing. There's this one thing that's absolutely central, imagistically speaking, to the whole production, is—I'm sure you know I've had access to Pentagon film and video, even top-secret stuff, and I want to say thanks, it helped, helped a lot—they have these smart bombs, laser-guided, computer-guided, can drop them on a dime, they say—I want a shot of one of these smart bombs going right down Saddam's chimney. It goes right down the chimney, then the whole building sort of expands outward and *boom!* Explodes. Right down his chimney.

"And what that's going to tell America is that this is surgery, not slaughter. That these are targets we're hitting, military targets, not women and children. This is not Vietnam. Surgical strikes. And we're going to show them on every TV set in the country and by satellite, on every TV set in the world, that, goddammit, this is surgery."

"What I see here," Bush said, "I want to see a heroic fighter pilot, you know I can relate to that because I had my moments, I don't have to tell you about that, it's pretty well known. A fighter-bomber, coming in low, beneath the enemy radar. Do you know they have cameras mounted in the noses of fighter planes? Of course, if it's a bomber, the camera's in the belly, that's how they know you're not cheating when you claim your score, not that you would expect that the kind of young man that would have the guts and all that, the Right Stuff, to fly one of our megaspeed, top-of-the-line, state-of-the-art jet aircraft, you wouldn't expect a fine youngster like that to be dishonest.

No, you wouldn't. And he wouldn't be. In the heat of combat, though, you can't always be looking back to see where the fallen have fallen, when you're looking forward to what you have to do next, it's good to have a record."

"Of course we can do that, George. I love fighter and fighter-bomber footage. The stuff is so great. The trick to making it seem real—gut-level real—is low-tech. You know when you watch the old WWII movies, whenever they cut in that scratched-up, dirty film, with the spots—everyone knows, everyone gets it—real combat footage."

Baker still had one thing that bothered him. Big-time. It was the thing that he had been intending to use to blow the whole project out of the water. "How the hell are we going to pay for it? An issue is going to be made of that. Of paying for the war."

"Mr. Secretary, Mr. President." David Hartman spoke. This was a question that he was ready for. "In this event, the United States is The Studio. When A Major Studio makes a movie for, say, forty million dollars, they don't reach into their pocket and take out forty million dollars. That would be insane. Let's say we're making *Cat-woman*, the third Batman sequel. To start with, fifteen percent goes back to the studio for studio overhead. Then there's interest on the full amount from day one. See, I really only have to worry about thirty million dollars.

"If I want to, I can cover that with foreign, cable, and cassette sales. Before I start shooting. England, two million, Germany, six million, France, three million, Italy, two million, Scandinavia, another million, Spain, a million. That's fifteen. I need another thirteen. I pick up three in South America, eight in Japan, and I still have Africa, Asia, Australia, HBO, Showtime, Network TV.

"Do you see what I'm driving at? Only the United States can truly produce this picture. Who's going to pay? That depends on the war. The president says Saddam Hussein. Let's say he invades Saudi Arabia.

"Let's say this war is going to cost fifty billion dollars. A lot of that is overhead. We have a standing army and reserves, equipment, the generals and their staffs, and the munitions and tanks, billions of dollars worth of stuff that we pay for whether we use it or not. OK, let's say, conservatively, that fifty percent of the cost of the war is true overhead. But for billing purposes let's say our overhead is twenty percent, ten billion dollars. Now we have to find forty billion. How much do you think the Saudis will pay to get their country back? Fifty percent of their oil revenues for the next ten years? We would never even ask them for that much. How about fifteen billion. Plus gas. For the planes and tanks and all ships at sea. Let me just jump ahead for a moment. Think about how much armament they are going to buy after this war. *Wow! We don't want to be invaded again. We better double our Air Force!* Planes. Spare parts. Training.

"Now, let's get five billion dollars each from Kuwait, the Emirates, Qatar. Now we're at thirty billion.

"Meanwhile, the day Saddam marches into Riyadh, the price of oil goes from three and a half dollars a barrel to twenty-five dollars a barrel? Thirty-five dollars a barrel. Fifty dollars. The Nikkei index drops two thousand points in a day.[105] Mr. Secretary Baker picks up the telephone. He says, 'Mr. Prime Minister, what is it going to cost your country if the price of oil stays over thirty dollars a barrel? My army is willing to go in there, straighten things out, get the price down somewhere reasonable, under ten anyway. What's that worth to Japan? Is it worth five billion dollars?'

" 'Mr. Kohl, how many people are going to drive Mercedes and BMWs, with gas at the pump, in America, at four dollars a gallon? In Europe at fifteen dollars a gallon? What's that going to do to the German economic miracle?'

"I say," Hartman continued, "that before a shot is fired y'all are

---

[105]Actually, oil went from $3.56 to $28.05 a barrel. The Nikei index dropped 1,264.25 points, about 5 percent. Of course, Iraq only invaded Kuwait, not Saudi Arabia. While Hartman may or may not have been pulling numbers out of his hat here, the cost of the war was later estimated at $60-to-$70 billion. Cash contributions were expected to cover $42 billion, plus "in kind" contributions of fuel, food, and other goods.

gonna have this hyuh war paid for.''

"Now correct me if I'm wrong here, but I think I'm very tuned in on this," the president said. "According to John Lincoln's scenario—is that the right jargon there? scenario?—according to his idea, this is the invasion of Poland and in this context, Saudi Arabia would be the equivalent of France. Maybe France and England combined. I wouldn't want things to get out of control, if you see what I mean. So what I think our Hitler should do is conquer some place a little smaller and threaten France. Which would be Saudi Arabia. That would be next, if we didn't stand up to them. See, that works even if Saddam turns out not to be the one, but say it's Iran that's the aggressor nation. Against any one of the little countries there—Qatar, Kuwait, the Emirates. Any one would do, don't you think?''

"That's brilliant, Mr. President. That's what I'm talking about. Exactly it. Let's say it's Iraq. They take Kuwait. It looks like the next move will be Saudi Arabia. Just like the Germans took Poland and everyone just knew, just knew, that France was next. In the space, in the waiting, that's where you build the thing. Perfect, sir, perfect.''

Baker had kept his mouth shut while the president spoke. But the idea of making war on Other People's Money demonstrated not just brass balls, but a pair that was downright stylish and freshly spit-shined. Now he spoke. "You are one smart Hollywood Jew," he said to David Hartman, "Y'all can call me Bubba.''

CHAPTER

* * *

FORTY

Surveillance is rarely flawless. Especially when it's passive and spread thin. So it's not surprising, nor is it a mark of great shame, that U.Sec. totally missed Teddy Brody's first call to Joe Broz.

It was one of those gaps. Joe's office wasn't wired, for reasonable reasons that had been reported right up to the top of the chain of command. Everyone assumed that surveillance would pick up contact from the other end, as they had with the Przyszewski woman. After all, Teddy's apartment was wired, as were the offices at CinéMutt. Out of a sense of etiquette, he called during business hours. Combined with discretion, he used a pay phone outside of CinéMutt. They missed him.

Teddy was pleasantly surprised at how willing Mr. Broz was to see him.

Of course, he didn't know, didn't dream, that he had just taken bait that Joe Broz had thoughtfully crafted just for him, Teddy Brody. Unfortunate, really, because he would have been flattered by that. Teddy was at a stage in his life when he could have used some flattery. Or something. That's what prompted him to make the call. He needed a change. Any change.

He wanted only two things in life. To make a movie and to find a lover. By a lover he didn't mean someone to get hot over, hold hands with, go to the movies with, kiss, have sex with, even live with, sharing the cooking and cleaning and bills. Though that was getting pretty close. What he wanted was someone who loved him enough that they would swear to be true to each other, go down to the clinic or the doctor's office, get tested together, and then, when they could show each other they were both HIV negative, uninfected—clean, pure—they would give themselves to each other, in total physical and emotional surrender, sharing bodily fluids, the way sex was supposed to be, unrubberized, unshielded, for real and natural and tasty and wet and fun. Fun! And in love! Thoughts of the lack of it ripped through his nights. Tremulous dreams and crying voices, sending him bolt upright, near to tears, the lips of his mouth turned down like a toddler boy crying "Mama, Mama."

He was born too late. Too early. Too something. Centuries of human existence had had sex without death. He had one constant nightmare. A face, a lovely, sweet, kindly face, pretty eyes, long blond hair, a sweet and pouty mouth making love to him. And as he came, ejaculated into that mouth, it's teeth raked him, opening up the skin of his penis just enough so that saliva, blood, and semen all mingled. The face grinned, released him, looked up, and it was as garish and ugly and deadly as a ghoul from a cheap horror film. It was such a tawdry and obvious image. Yet he could not banish it.

All he wanted was one true love. Not forever. Just for a time.

He didn't seem to be getting any closer to making his own film either. The job with Beagle was not happening in terms of contacts or climbing higher or getting access or getting his treatment read. He was just back there in that damn room running from machine to machine, from storage rack to storage rack.

Then a buddy, Don Burkholtz, not much of a friend really, barely an acquaintance, but one of the Yale gang and therefore a connection, called him. Burkholtz, who was an agent now at ICM and drove a leased Lexus convertible and already owned a condo almost in Malibu and one in Aspen, not far from Don and Melanie's house, said, "This guy, Joe Broz, who has just started schtupping Maggie Lazlo, big-time—some guys have all the luck—seems to have schtupped himself into the job of president of development of Maggie Lazlo films. I heard he's looking for an all-around assistant, reader, developer, whatever. Wants a Yalie. A smoothie. 'Cause apparently he's barely a high-school graduate. So he's impressed with our kind of bullshit. Doesn't even know film. So he's looking for someone with an encyclopedic knowledge of film. It sounded a lot like you. So I thought if you were bored with the barking at CinéMutt, you might want to buzz this guy."

Of course it sounded a lot like Teddy—it was a description of Teddy by Teddy. It came from a conversation he'd had complaining of his lot to a friend on the phone that had been taped by Ray Matusow and copied by Joe Broz, who then, each time he met a Yalie in the circles in which he was now traveling, went out of his way to express an admiration that he did not feel for their education and to describe the characteristics of Teddy as the ideal characteristics for the job of his assistant. A job which, of course, did not exist, because the whole boyfriend thing, the whole development business was a ploy designed to lure out someone, like Teddy Brody, who could explain the mystery of John Lincoln Beagle. Or at least when it was conceived that's what it was. Now the tale's creators—like the man in the Mark Twain story who started a rumor that there was gold in hell and then followed everyone else there to find it—were beginning, in the state of awe and wonderment that so often accompanies a fresh erotic arrangement, to believe in their own fiction.

Anita Hesper Barrow, USAF Intelligence Analyst, Lt. Col. Ret., now at U.Sec. in the Transcripts and Analysis Section, came across a subsequent conversation between Teddy and his friend Sam, the fitness instructor from Best Bods who was a ski instructor at Steamboat in the winter, discussing the possibilities presented by Teddy's upcoming interview with Magdalena Lazlo's lover. She promptly sent the transcript to the head of the section, who passed it on to Mel Taylor. Taylor succeeding in notifying Chicago, but he couldn't reach David

Hartman. David Hartman was meeting with the president of the United States.

Taylor was impressed by that. If he'd been a less military man, he might have been frustrated by it. But he knew what to do when he couldn't reach the commanding officer: go by the book and use every page that would cover his ass. Which he proceeded to do. He increased surveillance on Brody, although he knew exactly when the meeting was scheduled to take place, the next day at noon.

The office was stretched thin because there were rumors of a Writer's Guild strike and the producers wanted U.Sec. to thoroughly research the officers of the union and their positions. If possible to find out what the union's real bottom line was, as opposed to their negotiating position; if there were any internal disagreements on the union's negotiating team; and, of course, who among that group might be having personal or financial problems. That meant phones to be tapped and homes wired, friends and neighbors interviewed, credit ratings to be checked.

Almost the only two guys he had available were Chaz Otis and Bo Perkins. That was alright. If there was an intercept ordered, and, based on what had happened with the Przyszewski woman, there probably would be, Otis and Perkins were indeed who Taylor would assign anyway. But if something more subtle was required, they wouldn't be his first choice. Plus he had no backup for them, a situation he didn't like as a matter of policy. He put in a request for more men so that if anything did go wrong he could lay blame on the system for not acting on his prescient recommendation.

The project was definitely at a new stage. It even had a working title —American Hero—and a code name—IVP, Interservice Video Project.

Beagle insisted on casting the generals. If this was going to be WWII-2—The Video, he needed talent that would come across like George Marshall and Dwight David Eisenhower.

The president was excited at the idea of bringing the allies together. He knew he could get the Japanese in line. And the Chinese too. That was exciting. And the U.N. This was going to be real only-George-Bush-can-do-it stuff.

The president really wanted to have this war. It would serve the country well. Prove that America is back! Both to the world outside and to Americans inside America. It would prove to history that George Bush had served the presidency with honor. There was only one "if." It was a very Hollywood if: without the right star—in this case a real Hitler type, with his own army to back him up—they couldn't green-light the picture.

Of course, there was brief discussion of security. So far, only the four of them knew the real story. Code name *Hitler* would make five. Was there anyone else? Hopefully not. Because if this came out, with the wrong spin on it, it would make Watergate look benign.

When Hartman and Beagle left, the president picked up the phone. He had a secure landline and a scrambler. He called the National Security Council. He spoke to Robert Gates. "Would you do me a favor, Bob? Would ya call old C. H. Bunker and let him know that the job he's working on with that Hollywood fella, tell him to treat it like it was top-secret national-security stuff. Matter of life and death even. It's not, of course, but tell him it is. Guy raises a lot of funds for the party. And Bob, ask C.H. how his granddaughter Martha's doing.[106] She has the mumps, you know. Tell him Barb says not to worry, mumps build character as well as bumps. Thanks, Bob."

A limo whisked Hartman and Beagle from Hope's house. Hartman was elated and his director should have been too. But Beagle stared out the window, into the desert night, and when the agent looked at

---

[106]Bush was famous for knowing everyone in politics—every county chairman, all the contributors. It was considered one of his greatest strengths. Until he blew it—then it was considered a weakness as compared to, for example, Reagan's vision and principles.

him, he saw a tear rolling down John Lincoln's cheek. "What's wrong, John?"

Beagle looked over at him. Eyes as brown and sad as his name would make you think. They were full of salt water and he would have looked comic—he was on the verge of it—this guy who'd been Goofy at Disney World and would never have been cast as anything but—except that the sadness was so real and so vast.

"What's wrong, John?"

"Jackie's filing for divorce." He held up his hand to say, *Wait, that's the intro, not the point.* "That's OK, I guess. But . . . I mean, what the hell, I mean it wasn't a marriage-marriage was it? It was she's the beautiful, I'm the brilliant, trophy, trophy, trophy. She wanted a picture out of me. But . . . beautiful, she's beautiful, but act? She's a bitch. Nothing to do with her acting or not acting, there's bitches can act. Notorious, right. Do you know what I'm saying—getting to—here? Do you know, David?" He wiped the tears away with his hand. When he did, he inadvertently dragged some snot from his nose and wiped it across his cheek. He wasn't aware of it. Or if he was, he didn't really care. Hartman gave him a handkerchief. Beagle took it, redried his eyes, and held on to it. "She's gonna take the boy, David, she's gonna take my boy. It's gonna be shit. My lawyers bigger than her lawyers or vice versa, we shit on each other all over the courts and the television and the fuckin' papers. Shit all over each other. How good is that for the boy? Jesus fuckin' Christ. Does she love him? Is she good for him? Do I love him more? Am I better for him? I wish to God, I wish to motherfuckin' God I could motherfuckin' say, 'Yes! She's shit. She's an unfit mother. I'm a fit father.' Fight to the death to save him from her. Bullshit. I'm gonna miss him. I'm gonna miss him.

"Is it all bullshit, David? This marriage-marriage thing? Family thing. Where the hell is the time gonna come from to do it? Here I am with this goddamn megagiant reality movie, that's totally top-secret, that is the peak of achievement and eats up all my hours, all my days, because it should. That's the catch, the weirdness, the trick. It should. That's what I was born, have worked, for. That's the all—to be the greatest whatever I am that I am. It's costing me my son."

"You know, you've done the biggest part of your job. There's a hiatus now. For you, anyway, I would guess. Until we find out which way we're going. *IVP, Interservice Video Project,* I like that. *American Hero.* You're great with titles, John. Really great. You could take some time off. At least a week. Maybe you could fix things up. If you want to."

"I don't know if I want to. I hate her, David. It's like, do I hate her more or love him more?"

"That's what divorce with kids always is. Every time. It's like an equation. Kids minus spouse divided by property plus income equals pain times a constant."

"Wow, that's a pretty good metaphor coming from you, David."

"What's that supposed to mean, agents can't do anything arty like metaphors?"

"I'll take the week. Get away from the office. I'll try."

"Good idea."

"At least then I can tell myself I tried."

"Good idea."

"But if I'm with my wife for a week . . ."

"Yeah?"

"What the hell am I gonna do for sex?"

The next morning, Hartman arose early. He went to the dojo. He worked out for almost two hours. At nine he went for a steam and a message. He felt clean and empty. He felt like a mythic warrior, like he walked in the Way, in the Tao of Packaging.

Then he got into the office and saw a message from Mel Taylor that Theodore Brody, a film librarian at CinéMutt was going to see Joe Broz about a job, at noon. In two hours. He picked up the phone.

"What's going on?"

Tayler knew what the question was about. "We just picked up on it yesterday. I reported to you——"

"Do you know where I was?"

"Yes, sir, that's why I didn't interrupt."

"Cretin."

Taylor's officer training and experience paid off. He could be called all sorts of rotten names and keep his cool. He simply continued with his report. "I have two men watching Brody's apartment. We will take whatever action is appropriate."

"You have two men watching Brody's apartment. Is Brody in the apartment? By the way, how much does Brody know? How long has this been going on? Is this their first meeting? Come on, man, get with it."

"Yes, sir. We saw Brody enter the apartment building. He has not come out. I spoke with my surveillance people not long ago. Twenty or thirty minutes. I don't know how much he knows. It's hard to say because I don't know enough to judge. That's not a complaint. That's a fact. It seems pretty clear that they have had one contact. Brody called Broz, asked for a job interview. Broz said sure, come on over. If you don't mind my saying so, if Broz is fishing for something, why not let him get it, catch him with it, and then deal with both of them."

"And suppose Broz communicates with someone else in the meantime. Like Maggie. And she calls her girlfriends. Or her press agent. The risk grows geometrically. The disturbance grows in widening ripples. Keep it smooth. Keep it from happening. Anticipate and find the position that prevents. Those are your orders."

"Excuse me, sir," Taylor said. "Excuse me, I have to ask you to hold for a moment—"

"You what!" Hartman cried. Nobody put Hartman on hold. Hartman put others on hold. Who was this twit?

This twit had a big problem. It was C. H. Bunker on the other line, the one person in the world whose calls he had to take, even over the most powerful man in Hollywood. But he wasn't happy about it.

Bunker's call had come through on the scrambled line. "Tay-lor," Bunker said, in those rolling, enunciated, interminably slow tones. "Tay-lor, my boy, this dogwatch of yours, has lay-ers u-pon lay-ers.

Di-men-sions of which you dream not . . . Umm . . . Umm . . . You may . . . You may, if ne-cess-i-ty pro-vokes, let slip the dogs of war. Do I make my-self clear, Tay-lor.''

''Yes, sir, you do.''

''Cry ha-voc-k.''

Bunker hung up. Taylor said, ''Jesus, fucking Christ.'' He wasn't quite sure if he believed what he'd heard, or believed what it meant, 007 shit—he'd just been given a License to Kill. Inside the United States. Not in Nicaragua or Chile, using natives to do the actual hits, most of the time. Not in Asia. But here, among—what else to call them—white people. Over Hollywood shit? Not that he minded. But what the fuck was going on?

As soon as he hung up, another phone line was ringing and the intercom was flashing. ''What the fuck is it, Bambi?''

A bit put off by the obscenity, she said, ''Mr. Hartman is calling back.''

''Did you cut him off?''

''No, sir. I think he hung up on you.''

Taylor grabbed the line. ''Yes, sir. Sorry, sir. Where were we, sir?''

''Are you sure he's in that apartment?''

''I'll check, sir. Right away.''

''Do you know how to do that?''

''Yes. We know how to do that.''

''You fuck this up and you're fired. You'll never work in this town again. I can see to it that you never work in this world again. Do you know who I am?''

''Yes, sir, I think so,'' Taylor said. When the phone slammed down in his ears, he couldn't help himself, the words just hopped off his tongue, like popcorn exploding in the heat, ''You're another Holly-wood asshole, sir.'' Nonetheless, he did the obvious thing. He picked up the phone and called Teddy Brody. It was a pretty fair assumption that if he was home, he would answer.

The phone rang and rang and rang. Taylor prayed that Brody was grabbing a shower and a shave, taking a shit, cleaning out the old bowels. Things to do before a job interview, yes, sir! It rang and rang and rang, Taylor's heart sinking.

Then, an answer: "Hi, there. Teddy Brody here."

Taylor sighed with deep, deep relief and started to hang up the phone. But reflex inside the reflex made him stop. He lifted it back to his ear and heard ". . . leave a message at the sound of the tone. Thanks. I'll get right back to you."

Teddy's printer had acted up. It was not as if he had left things for the last minute. He hadn't. He had printed up his material the evening before. Everything appeared to be going along just perfectly.

Then, in the morning, right after a shower and shave, he went to sort the material and put it in binders. He was bringing damn near everything with him to Joe Broz: his résumé, his essay and notes on war films—he figured he was one of the world's leading experts on war films and war footage by now—his propaganda one-pager, his letters of recommendation, his film treatment, and a special rewrite of the treatment so that it had a starring role for Magdalena Lazlo: He'd spent the last week tweaking and polishing that, getting it down to three neat pages. In fact, he'd only finished it the day before and that was the reason he got to the printing so late. It should have been time enough, but when he sorted the pages, he saw that everything after the third page had a meandering blank spot, a wandering failure to print, that made its way from the top of each page to the bottom.

He didn't panic. Yet. He replaced the ink cartridge. He fired up the computer. Opened up a file, gave the print command—just one page. A test. He watched the paper roll silently out of the $1,289.95 laser printer. Whatever each of those many, many dollars represented, in hardware, software, manufacturing care, and engineering effort, the bottom line was that they failed him now, when he need them most. The problem remained, a crooked white sneer, right through his thoughtful, effort-laden Yale- and UCLA-trained words. He was, as the poet cries, in deep shit.

He reached for the Yellow Pages and tried not to weep at his watch. It was just possible that he could find a commercial printer that could print from his discs. If they were close and could take him immediately and their printer didn't break down. Then he remembered that Sam, of the hot body and broken date, who lived a few blocks away, had said that he had some kind of computer and a printer. Maybe, if Sam was home and he had a Mac—Teddy prayed for compatibility—and a printer . . . Teddy called. Yes. Sam was home. Sam would be delighted if Teddy wanted to use his computer. Now. Anytime. It was an LC II with an HP Laser Jet, not a new one, but still, what more could a boy want?

He grabbed his box of backup discs and the binders and everything and put them into his backpack. By going out the back way, the service entrance where the trash was taken out, past the dumpsters, Teddy was a block closer to Sam. So, completely unaware that two heavies were watching his front door, he slipped out the back.

Surveillance is rarely flawless and Newton's First Law of Motion, also called the Law of Inertia, which states an object in motion tends to stay in motion, would seem to imply that an operation that starts fucked-up tends to stay fucked-up.

CHAPTER

* * *

FORTY-ONE

Sam found himself falling in love with Teddy. He just didn't know how to tell him that. Well, he thought, maybe he had a way. But it wasn't ready quite yet. It would be ready soon. But even if he did tell him, how would Teddy respond? Sam thought of himself as a bit of a bimbo, a dumb blond, dim but pretty. It was lack of self-esteem, he knew that, a real problem in California. There had even been a state commission to study it. It was one of those weird things that seemed to run a thread through all of life. He knew dumb, ugly people with big esteems, and they had just success upon success. Lovers that they weren't good-looking enough to get, great jobs that made lots of money even when they couldn't read their way through the morning paper. He wished he could self-esteem more. But esteem didn't seem to be that easy to control. Maybe it wasn't what it appeared to be. Maybe lack of self-esteem was like a vitamin deficiency. Or a disease, like they'd discovered alcoholism is. It could be a disease—hell, everyone knew that you felt more self-esteem when you took drugs. If drugs could fix it, it was a disease, that was practically a definition.

The thing about Teddy was that Teddy was smart. With all that education. All those books. At the health club, on the exercise bike, in the sauna, he was always reading stuff. Sam knew he should read more, but what? What should he read? *Premiere? Blueboy? Cosmo-politan? The New Yorker?* He tried to read all of the *Los Angeles Sunday Times.* It came out once a week and it took him a week to read it. Really two weeks. So he always got behind and really, it was from a *different planet.* He meant it, the people who wrote it were from a *totally different planet.* The question was, where was that planet and how come he, Sam, had never been there? He liked *Spin* and *E. C. Rocker,* which were hard to find here in LaLaLa.

Here was Teddy with that box of discs, just turning on the computer, figuring out what was what without asking any questions even. Just looking at it and knowing. Which was a good thing because if he'd asked, Sam couldn't have answered. The computer, printer, the whole setup had been, like, you know, a gift of friendschtup. He didn't want to explain *that,* not to Teddy. And truly, bimbo or dim or not, Sam was not that way. That was not a *thing* with him. Sometimes, in his life, it happened. What does one do? Say "No Gifts Please, it will ruin me for marriage?" Anyway, he wasn't a slut and he wasn't a queen, he wasn't a fag and he wasn't a pansy, he was just a regular guy who liked guys, and what was wrong with that? It sure wasn't easy.

He asked Teddy if he drank coffee. Teddy said yes, so he ground some beans—nothing fancy or prissy—just 100 percent Colombian, medium roast. They both took it with milk, no sugar. Something in common.

By then the printer was running. Teddy was checking it page by page and collating it into those great little binders he had.

Sam wanted to say, "Call me and tell me how the interview went and come on over after work, no matter how late it is."

Teddy was relieved and grateful. Sam had been willing to go out with him but hadn't seemed wild about it. Or disappointed when he canceled. Actually, Sam was so good-looking, such a great body, that it was—not intimidating. It just made Teddy sure that Sam was not his type. Too good-looking. With guys always after him. Rich, powerful, in-the-biz-type guys. Sure to be making the scene—

scenes—and that was too much stress for Teddy to deal with. Not what he wanted. Not at all. Maybe there was some way that he and Sam could be—friends. Just a friend. Was anybody in this fucking town, in this business, just a friend? In this life? Maybe, if he got things going with this Broz guy, or somewhere else, where he got a shot at making his film, and made films and became a person of stature and substance, then maybe a thing with a guy like Sam would work out.

The Law of Inertia, which is different from Murphy's Law—it's more specific and directional—continued in effect. Otis and Perkins's car phone was out of order.

The only saving grace was that they knew it. So they had instructions to call in as soon as possible if the subject started to move, or on the hour, so as not to be totally out of touch. According to their last call, thirty, now almost forty minutes ago, Brody was in the apartment. So now he wasn't. There were two possibilities: the kid had left and Otis and Perkins were following him, or the kid had left and Otis and Perkins had missed him. And there was no way for Taylor to know which it was for at least—he looked at his watch and it hadn't moved, how could it not move, his anxiety was moving forward full throttle, why was time on a freeze?—twenty minutes. While the client sat and waited for Taylor to get back to him *right* away. Even if nothing was wrong, every minute that Hartman had to wait—with his anxiety engaged to the gears that churned his stomach acids— would be held against Taylor. Hartman was that kind of guy. He not only wanted the right answer, he wanted the right answer right away.

In the minutes that ticked so tediously away, Taylor became more and more certain that Brody had slipped away from his minders. The dumb fucks had let the subject get past them. What were they doing? The crossword puzzle? Taking lunch at Le Dome? Slurping each other's schlongs? What the hell had they been doing? And Taylor couldn't pick up the phone and scream at them. He couldn't find out what had gone wrong to wait for them to call in to find out how they'd screwed up.

OK, Taylor said to himself, I'm an officer. I have faced enemy fire. I do not panic. I plan. I adapt. I adjust. He straightened his back. He took out a scratch pad. He made notes. Where was Brody? Uncertain. Check. How? What was known? That Body had an appointment with Joe Broz at noon. A known time and location. If we don't know where he is coming from to get there, there is only one choke point, just before the destination.

Now Taylor had a plan. Three things. First, check the apartment. Go up. Knock on the door. No answer—Taylor was certain that there wouldn't be. Break in. Be sure. If he was there, make it look like a robbery and mugging. Either way, call in. Never mind trying to figure out where he was, because they didn't have a clue, a hint, an idea. So forget that. Simultaneously, send someone to intercept Brody at the choke point. He was going to try to get some additional personnel on it. But he knew it wasn't going to happen. There was no one around. Certainly not anyone he could use for a break-in or for strong-arm work, except for Otis, Perkins, and if need be, himself. And he couldn't even get that started until those two called in from the field. Sitting there with his career ticking away as loud and as insistent as a clock with audio dementia while the phone kept failing to ring. And the third thing. The hard thing. Call the client. Tell him what was going down.

Maggie, fresh from her workout, with nothing that she totally, utterly, completely, inescapably *had* to do, found that she *had* to drop in on Joe. There was a kid on the street with a plastic bucket selling lousy single roses for no more than they were worth and bunches of fresh-cut carnations. She bought her lover both and brought them with her.

She loved Joe's office. There had been happy moments in her childhood—not everyone's youth is unremitting hell—and one of the great joys was playing house. This was exactly like that, a child's game, but call it playing Hollywood. She loved her home. Now that

Joe was in it. Loved sex. Loved country-and-western music. Hell, she loved Joe.

He looked just like a for-real producer in the Fierouggi suit she'd picked out for him—with the Unger & Unger shirt and Partigiano loafers, with those damn white sweat socks, a touch that worked, she had to admit it, to love it—feet up on the desk, script in his hand, scripts already filling the bookshelves. When she came in, he put the script down and looked at her the way a woman wants to be looked at, daydreams about being looked at, a gaze that smolders and adores on the covers of silly and childish romance novels. She gave him the flowers. He took her in his arms. Life is a movie. They ended up, it just worked out that way, making love on the desk. Someone should've been keeping one mind on the time so they'd be done by noon so they wouldn't be caught with all their pants down when this Brody kid arrived. But they just didn't seem to care.

The printing was done and there was an awkward moment, after Teddy had thanked Sam again, but before he actually left. It was one of those weird things, where synchronicity just wouldn't happen. The spark was there, but when it showed in one's eyes, the other person wasn't looking. Wanting, and because they wanted so much, not just a reaming and a pipe cleaning, they had grown awkward with the fear of failure. Then Teddy left. He had everything printed up clean and neat and in spiffy binders.

When Chaz and Bo finally called, Taylor sent Perkins, who was the brighter of the two, to Joe Broz's office. His instructions were: "*Make sure that Brody doesn't get in to see Broz. If he has papers with him, get them.*" He had Otis do the break-in. He gave Otis the number of his car phone. After he called the client—he knew he was going to be reamed out; he could only hope that it was a ream of limited duration—he was going to head for Broz's office himself. He was actually closer than Perkins. If Brody arrived before Perkins, Taylor was going to do the intercept himself.

Hartman heard Taylor out. Hartman was not happy. He pointed out that nobody knew what the kid knew or didn't know. Or what his intentions were. If U.Sec. had notified Hartman a day earlier, even two hours earlier—no excuse that he was incommunicado; U.Sec. should have picked up on the situation sooner—then it would have been the simplest thing in the world to offer this kid some other job, somewhere that parked him away safe and sound. Probably all that he wanted was a position from which he could climb a little higher a little faster. He wasn't out there peddling John Lincoln Beagle's secrets, was he? At least that wasn't what it looked like. Now what were they going to do? A strong-arm thing?

Hartman didn't bother to mention what he thought, at that point, was the real bottom line, which was something like, *Well, as long as it solved the problem and didn't cause more problems, what the hell,* because that would have let the idiot off the hook. And he didn't want to do that.

So he told Taylor what an idiot he was. Which Taylor knew he was going to do. And he made it very clear that Taylor was not to fuck this up any more than it already was. Also pretty standard. On the other hand, the Hollywood asshole apparently had presidential clout. So Taylor jumped in his car and raced toward Joe Broz's office.

If the timing had been a little different, perhaps the subsequent events would have changed. Or maybe not. Maybe, when the forces are set in motion, they find a way. It doesn't matter which channel is open. If one is blocked, they flow to the next. If all are blocked, they flood over the dam. Maybe there is kismet.

Otis and Perkins had parked so that they had both the front door of Brody's building and Brody's car in sight. That's why they were so sure he was still inside. Taylor, feeling pressured by the client's anxiety and his own, didn't want to hear explanations, stories, excuses. So he just said, "Do it. Do it now. One to the apartment, one to Broz's office. Stop him."

It's hard to say that this was a mistake. But if Otis or Perkins had waited, they would have seen, from the vantage point of where they had been parked and watching, Teddy Brody walk down the sidewalk to his own Subaru Justy. Where he stopped and thought about whether or not there was anything upstairs that he needed—if there had been, he would have run smack into Chaz Otis. But then he decided that there wasn't. He got into his car and drove, in a leisurely way, toward Joe's office.

Joe's office had the sweet smell of satisfaction. And it was filled with languorous giggles as well. "I have to look out the window," Joe said.

"Why?"

"I just have to know how many people could possibly have just watched that."

"Do you care?"

"That's that many fewer people to buy the video."

"What video?"

"Jane Fonda has her workout tapes. I thought we could do this."

"You thought that?"

"I thought that."

"You did, did you?"

"Yeah."

"Should I be insulted by that?"

"Oh, no, no, no. It's 'cause you do it so well. Better than anyone."

"Than anyone in the world?"

"Outside of Southeast Asia."

"Southeast Asia?"

"Yeah, you should see some of the things I saw in Bangkok."

"Why, so I can do them for the video?"

"I'll be a son of a bitch," Joe said, looking out the window.

"What?"

"Come here."

Maggie came to the window. Joe pointed. Down at the Buick, parked across the street, to Joe's right, with one tinted window, the driver's, rolled down. Mel Taylor's face visible. "Who's that?"

"That's Mel Taylor. Head of the L.A. office of Universal Security. He's watching our front door, personally."

"Is that bad?"

"Is it bad? OK, so they see Teddy Brody come here? What does that tell them? Anything? I don't see why it should? I don't know."

"So it's not bad?"

"It's not good, but it's hardly fatal."

"You know what I did today?" Maggie said, looking out over his shoulder. "I got John to call Bambi Ann Sligo."

"Who?"

"Travolta."

"To tell her that Scientology cures being queer?"

"Um-hm."

"That's very nice of you."

"It's because I love her name. I really do. And because I could just imagine her face when she got a call from John Travolta."

"And John was willing to do that?" He scanned the street. There weren't too many people on foot.

"Why do you think she wanted to know?"

"Son or husband," Joe said, "in the closet. And she just peaked in the closet. She wants to clean the closet. Make it all neat, the way it's supposed to be, way she thought it was. Very neat and orderly woman, Bambi Ann." There was a parking lot, across the street and down the block to Joe's left. Then he saw a guy, rather lanky, short hair, serious attitude, coming from there. The knapsack—which he had over one shoulder, like a shoulder bag, not over two like a hiker—seemed in character for the person he imagined Teddy Brody to be. Then he looked across the street and saw how Taylor looked at the kid. That confirmed it.

Taylor wasn't doing anything. Just watching. It was too late to alter anything.

Maggie leaned against Joe. The wetness beginning to drip out of her. It felt good, a reiteration of eroticism. That was because they were new lovers. In a mature relationship, it feels slightly repulsive—adult humans don't like being wet and sticky—and then, as it dries, crinkly, tightening, and staining, it becomes one of those mildly irritating cleaning problems. Something to be dealt with, though not as bad as red-wine stains.

"That's the kid," Joe said. Once Brody crossed the street, Joe opened the window to get more angle so he could keep watching. Maggie adjusted her clothing, covering her breasts. Then, just as Brody got ready to enter his building, Joe saw movement out of the corner of his eye. A car door opening.

Sight goes to movement. He saw Bo Perkins step out onto the sidewalk. Stepping quick, right behind Teddy Brody, following him into the building.

"Stay here," he said to Maggie. "Don't open up for anyone but me." He ran out.

Bo was right behind Teddy. He had him pegged for a faggot right away. That made him happy. He liked to hurt faggots. More than regular people. There was something about it that was just—there was no other word—satisfying.

Great, the lobby was empty. Stairs to the left, elevator to the right. A door at the back. Where to do the number on him? Fucking rush job. This was risky. Best shot—do it now, do it fast, get it over with. Why not? He who hesitates is lost. Lots of truth in the old maxims. As Teddy reached for the elevator button, Bo punched him in the kidney. Teddy never touched the button. He turned in agony. He saw Perkins. Partly because he'd pegged Teddy as queer, partly because it gave him a sense of power, Bo yanked Teddy toward him and drove a knee up into the kid's groin, smashing his testicles and his pansy dick.

The freak would be walking funny for a long, long time, if he lived. Which—what the hell, he had looked at Perkins, right at him, seen his reasonably memorable face, sometimes shock makes people forget, sometimes agony fixes a memory in place, why take a chance—he was not going to do. Perkins stepped back and very efficiently broke Teddy Brody's neck with a single blow.

It had been real fast. Even running, by the time Joe got there, Perkins was gone. In his car, driving away. He hadn't forgotten the knapsack. Joe checked the body lying on the ground. Dead. He went outside.

Taylor was still there. Across the street. He and Joe looked at each other.

CHAPTER
* * *
FORTY-TWO

No one else is in the lobby. I kneel down and search the body. I take out Teddy's wallet and find his address. I put it back.

I go back upstairs. I tell Maggie the kid is dead.

"You knew something was going to happen."

"Is that a question?"

"Yes."

"Yes." I did know.

"Why? How did you know?"

How did I know when I see Perkins that it is not coincidence, him there to see the dentist downstairs? And that his job is not just to follow Brody, find out where he goes. "I knew. They way you know how to act."

I call Steve.

Maggie's full of questions. "Who was that? Did they shoot him? Who did you see? I don't understand."

Steve answers. I say, "I need you to meet me, at Maggie's house."

"Sure thing, Sarge," Steve says.

"I want you to protect her," I say.

"Why? From what?" Maggie asks me.

"What do you mean?" Steve wants to know.

"It's a real remote possibility, you know. I don't think anyone is going to move against her—"

"Joe, tell me what's going on?"

"Joe, bro, what's goin' down?"

"Steve, you got a gun of some kind?"

"I done tol' you, I'm gonna do what I got to do, but I don' wanna put a hurt on nobody no mo'. Guns don' solve shit."

By now I hear sirens. Someone's found Teddy Brody and called in a corpse. "Steve—"

"Don' worry, I be there. Tell you what, you min' I bring my son?"

"No. I don't mind. I got a couple of guns in the house."

"He like that shit. You gonna be surprised when you see him."

"How's that?"

"It's like back to the future or somethin': Put him in camies and you be lookin' 1968 square in the eye."

Maggie's got questions. Too many questions. I promise to answer them later. Right now I want to get both of us out of there before the police show up and we have to stay and make statements.

Jesus Christ, I am sick and fucking tired of having to turn on the radio every time I want to have a conversation. I pull over. We both have to get out so I can lay on my back and squeeze under the dash. I know where the thing is. I get in there, on my back, and tear the little sucker out. I put it on the sidewalk and stomp it, like an ugly bug. Then we whip up on the freeway and I take Maggie home.

How can I explain to her who Bo Perkins is and how I know him.

There's still so much she and I don't know about each other. I ask her nothing about her history. I don't care. She asks, some, about me. I think it's just enough to prove that I will do the trendy thing, open up to her, if she wants me to. Communicate. I don't live in the past much. I don't feel that need to tell people I've done this and that and some goddamn thing made me cry when I was nine, and I was traumatized at the high-school prom because just when the home-coming queen said she'd dance with me I broke wind. It's possible to be a soldier and be an honorable man. There is no doubt about that. All of history, all cultures say that. Most religions say that. The notion of a just war is a fundamental Christian doctrine. There are chaplains of every denomination in the Army. You know why Islam stretches from Morocco to Jakarta? Jihad. The Upanishads, the holy books of the Hindus, are battle epics. Ninja are followers of Buddha. To kill is not to be evil. There is a distinction in killing. To kill without morality or honor is to be a degenerate.

Which is what Bo Perkins is. A degenerate.

"The guy across the street, watching," I say to her, "I told you who he is. He wasn't watching to see if the kid showed up. He was watching to be sure he was stopped."

"How do you know? How do you know they killed him to keep him from . . . That can't be true. If it's true, then I'm responsible."

"No. The guy that killed him is responsible."

"Who is that? Who is that, Joe?"

"His name is Bo Perkins. The guy who walked in behind Brody and who was gone by the time I got there and found Teddy dead. He usually works with a partner."

"Where do you know him from?"

"He works for U.Sec. We've done . . . jobs together."

"What kind of jobs, Joe, that you knew he was going to do . . . what he did?"

"I'm going to leave you at the house. Steve and his son, they'll take care of you. He's a good man. I don't know about the son. You make sure the alarm is on and everything is locked up. I'm going over to Teddy Brody's apartment. I'll see what I can find. He had a knapsack on when he walked into the building. It was gone when I found him. He still had his keys and his wallet. So they were after something specific, I guess."

It makes me feel good to see that Steve is there, waiting, when we arrve. He introduces me to his son. He's right. It's just like seeing him all over again the way he was way back then. Back in '68. Eighteen-year-old lean, mean Marine. It also makes me see all the years that Steve's got on him and I'm not that vain that I think they're not on me too.

As I turn to go, Maggie grabs me. "Joe, did they really kill him to stop him from talking to us?"

"You'll be alright, Maggie."

"I don't understand, I don't understand," she says. "It's just movies."

When I get to Teddy Brody's, I don't need the key. The locks have been punched out. Not very subtly either.

The computer is gone. The monitor, keyboard, and printer are all there. What I'm figuring is that Teddy Brody knows what John Lincoln Beagle is doing. He writes it down. He's bringing it to me. Or they think he is. And they kill him for it. Then they clean out the apartment. I have to admit, Mel Taylor seems to be running a step ahead of me. Cutting me off at the pass each way I turn. Also, at this point it makes no sense. I'm saying to myself, What the fuck is it? It's just a movie, isn't it?

I check anyway, hoping that they missed something. Sooner or later, the police are going to show up here. I don't have gloves with me, so I go to the kitchen and get some paper towels. I handle everything with them. I'm looking for notes, printouts, drafts that he trashed. I go through the desk first, then the wastebasket. Taylor's boys have been through both.

In the garbage, in the kitchen, I find a stack of papers. There's a résumé and a treatment and some other stuff. I can see why he threw them out, a printer problem.

Then I go to the phone. First I try redial. That'll tell me the last person he called. It rings twice. "Good afternoon, Mr. Taylor's office," Bambi Ann Sligo says. Of course. Not Teddy's last call— Taylor's black-bag boys checking in. Clumsy, they should've dialed something else afterward.

I have an impulse to say "Hi, Bambi Ann. Did you speak to John Travolta? By the way is Bo Perkins around. Don't get in the elevator with him. Looking middle-aged is no protection. He once raped a mama-san with no teeth and one eye. And how about his buddy, Chaz Otis. If I hadn't been living in a wiretapped world for the last couple of months, I probably would have said something. But I'm aware, all day long, it seems like, which phone is tapped, which phone is clean—*turn on the music, whisper in the wind*—I realize that Brody's apartment is a hot zone and anything I say on the telephone will cross Taylor's desk in the morning.

There's a noise behind me.

I'm in a dead man's apartment with the locks broken. Who's behind me? Taylor's boys? The cops? Some goddamn civilian, going to memorize my face and give a description.

I turn around. The door is swinging open. There's this real good-looking guy standing there. Young. Blond. If he was his sister, my heart would go *thumpty-thump*. He's got flowers in one hand, wrapped in paper, and a box, about four-by-four-by-seven inch, in the other.

"What's going on? Who are you? Where's Teddy? What happened to the door?"

Fucking microphones. What am I going to say? "LAPD." I reach into my pocket, pull out my wallet. Flip it open. If the kid can read anything at that distance, he should be a bald eagle, five hundred feet up, able to spot a mouse running through the grass. "We got a report of a break-in." I walk toward him as I put the wallet away. "Don't come in here, mess up the crime scene." I get out in the hall, pull the door shut. "Who are you?" I say.

"I'm a friend," he says.

"Of who?"

"Teddy, Teddy Brody," he says. "He lives here."

"Who the flowers for? Him?"

"What if they are? What of it?"

"Son, we better go somewhere we can talk."

"Why?"

"I just want to talk to you. You're not in trouble. I'm not going to make trouble for you. Is there a coffee shop, something around here."

"There's one a few blocks west."

"Come on. We'll take my car."

He follows me out to the Cadillac. "Fancy car for a cop," he says.

"I have a rich friend," I say. Of course, he reads that as "male friend." He looks at me differently, trying to figure it out. "Get in," I say. When he's in, doors shut and locked, I ask him his name.

"Sam Carmody," he says.

"Teddy was something special to you?"

There are the flowers in his hand. And a card. "I wanted him to be."

"Uh-huh. Listen, I got bad news for you. Real bad."

"What?"

"He's dead."

"Oh. Oh, oh shit."

"I'm sorry."

"How?"

"A mugging. Someone hit him too hard."

"Fucking L.A. Fucking L.A. I fucking hate fucking LaLaLa. La-de-da, LaLaLa." He throws the flowers on the floor and the card with it. He looks at the box. "What am I gonna do with this?"

"What is it?" I ask him.

"Teddy's discs. I was bringing them back. I was using them as an excuse to come over. He came over to my place. This morning. His printer was fucked up. He wanted to use mine. I looked at him . . . I had . . . I started thinking . . . you know, you look at someone . . . you think . . . fucking *maybe*, fucking *maybe*, right? Maybe you got a fucking shot at . . . at . . ."

Teddy Brody's discs. OK. Thank you, Lord, I'm saying to myself. Out loud I say, "I'm sorry, Sam. Look, can I do anything for you? Drive you home, to your car, something?"

"No. No. I wanted to . . . What do you care? You don't care.

You're just . . .''

"I'm sorry."

"Fuck it," he says, starts to get out. "What am I gonna do with these?" The discs.

"I'll take care of it for you. If there's next of kin or something, they want it, as part of his stuff, I'll make sure . . . you know."

"OK, sure," he says, and gets out. Good-looking kid. If it were his sister or you were of that persuasion, make your heart go *thumpty-thump*. I'm zeroed in on the discs. I never ever think to pick up the card that's on the floor. Maggie picks it up later. And in fact it's got nothing to do with nothing, in terms of what John Lincoln Beagle and David Hartman are up to. It's a little poem, that either Sam put some thought into, or maybe it's just one of those gay things, part of their subculture, not all that original, but what it says is:

> I'm HIV negative, just got the news.
> Isn't that grand, how about you?
> I'd like to celebrate with someone like you,
> If someone like you would like to be true.

CHAPTER

* * *

FORTY-THREE

Perkins wasn't entirely sure about having killed the kid. "I figure he bought the farm. But I wouldn't guaran–damn–tee it. Maybe he's down but not out. Might wake up as a dickless wonder with a crick in his neck." So Taylor figured he better check, on the off chance that Brody had lived and then he wouldn't have to tell Hartman that Brody had been—no one liked the word "murdered" in these instances—killed? Eliminated? Terminated? Taken out of the game? Made redundant? Ciphered? Bumped? Crashed? Initialized? Consummated? Deconstructed?[107] Taylor had to make his inquiries discreetly and circumspectly so that the questions didn't blow back on U.Sec. As a result, it was nearly 1:00 P.M., before he confirmed the consummation.

[107]William Safire, conservative pundit, onetime Nixon speechwriter, op-ed contributor, writes a column on language for the *New York Times Magazine* section. He is particular fond of exploring the etymology of slang and new usages. In an article on euphemisms for murder he propounds, as a matter of ontological reasoning, that the derivation of current slang strongly suggests a generation of more literate hit persons. "Intialize" and "crash" are computer references, "made redundant" is a Britishism, "deconstruction" is a term of literary criticism, and "consummation" comes from Hamlet (III,1): "To die: . . . 'tis a consummation devoutly to be wish'd." Or, more simply, express a certain literary pleasure in the playfulness of a sex-and-death pun.

Then he reported in to the client. That was at 1:00. Hartman listened and hung up. At 1:01 he called C. H. Bunker in Chicago.

Once Bunker had aspired to being peripatetic. He loved going on missions at a moment's notice, leaping from a sleek companion in a rumpled bed in the dark of night to speed to wherever the game was afoot. He had dreamed for decades of the private jet that he did eventually acquire and he had looked forward to a life of being whisked from action station to action station. He had created a worldwide empire of security services, in part so that he would have to do just that. But he had grown old. So old that his age made noises—joints that creaked and popped, breath that wheezed, little groans and grunts that accompanied actions as simple as putting on his shoes or even a shirt. Now he liked the big old mansion by Lake Michigan with it's formal dining room and real library and nursery room full of toys for when the grandchildren came to visit, he liked the servants who knew his comforts and whims and rhythms. He didn't like to travel. Not anymore and certainly not in a rush.

Even if you discount the speed by pointing out that he did not travel on a commercial airline but on a company jet that was kept on standby and took off at his convenience and that he picked up two hours by traveling west, the fact that the old man got to Los Angeles by 3:00 P.M. signaled two things loud and clear: David Hartman and Operation Dog's Bark were of the utmost importance—red flag, ultra, total alert—and someone's job was on the line for having created a situation for which Old Man Bunker had to leave his hearth.

Sheehan traveled with him. Taylor met them at the airport with a stretch limo. It had a bar and a television. The television stayed off. Bunker had a Scotch and soda, a single malt very weak, as if just the whiff of the barley was enough to make his cells sigh and ease themselves of the pain of life. He sat in back. Taylor sat facing him. There was a telephone on the jet, but Bunker did not like discussing sensitive matters over broadcast technologies, even with scamblers at both ends and his own experts telling him that his communications were secure. So Taylor briefed him while they rode in the big car. It had bulletproof windows.

Taylor had recommended that they meet in the Cube. Clients loved the uncomfortable glamour and high cost of it. It bewildered Taylor that Hartman didn't want to meet there. And it made him unhappy. The Cube was a profit center and having the meeting there would have been a point, even a point and a half, in Taylor's favor—the client may be unhappy but we're making money off him even as we try to turn him around—and he certainly felt that he was going to need every point he could get.

"Just give me the facts, Taylor. No explanations. No excuses."

Taylor told it without obvious editorials, but from his point of view, which was that stopping Brody—once he got the intercept order—was his total priority. Nobody said, "Intercept, but only if you can do it in a certain way with certain people." He used the resources available and achieved what he understood to be his mission.

Bunker asked if Joe Broz had seen Perkins. Taylor said he didn't think so. Bunker asked if Broz had seen Taylor. Taylor said yes.

"I enjoyed the recordings of Joseph and of Magdalena Lazlo very much," the old man said. He spoke slowly, as always, with a certain formality and a definite baritone richness. "Very much. Are there more?"

"Yes," Taylor said.

"Hmm. You might consider . . . video." He changed topics without changing inflection. "There was a knapsack with documents?"

Taylor, prepared, offered the papers to Bunker. Bunker ignored the outstretched hand. However, Sheehan, sitting beside Bunker, took them. "Can you tell from the material what John Lincoln Beagle is working on?"

"No. I couldn't," Taylor said.

Sheehan scanned the material as if he could find something there that Taylor hadn't. Bunker didn't speak until Sheehan finished reading and shook his head.

"There's more," Taylor said. He had another stack of papers, over four hundred pages. "Everything that was in Brody's computer."

Once again Bunker acted like he had no need to touch material objects and Sheehan took the pages.

"Have you deduced the nature of the project?" Bunker asked.

"No, sir," Taylor said. "But I haven't had a chance to read all of that yet."

"Hmm."

Sheehan had taken a speed-reading course. It had brought a significant boost in his paperwork productivity. Taylor hadn't weeded the product. Nor should he have. Something significant might appear disguised as a short story, in a love letter, or hidden inside a game.

Taylor said. "Not knowing its nature makes the job difficult, sir."

Sheehan, reading one of Teddy's personal letters, gave a grimace of distaste. "Faggot," he said aloud.

"Umm," Bunker said, in his legendary baritone, to Taylor, or Sheehan, or to his own musing thoughts. It was too bad that John Huston had died before Carter Hamilton Bunker. No one else could ever play the old man with the right combination of assurance, roguery, guile, self-satisfied cunning, and authority. Maybe Nicholson, when he got older, if he got old and lean inside of old and fat, which seemed unlikely.

Bunker had promised to be there by three-thirty. Hartman wanted to establish who was who—even beyond having made the old man fly two thousand miles—and to express displeasure. He felt thirty minutes of waiting would be about right.

Hartman had a thirty-minute practice session with Sakuro Juzo scheduled for three o'clock in the exercise room attached to the office. This suited Hartman very nicely. He could have Sakuro stay and stand guard over the inner office, where he would be facing Bunker and his team while they waited, giving them that unblinking way-of-the-warrior stare the whole time. The stare expressed great ki[108] and many

---

[108] Japanese, synonymous with the Chinese word *chi*, as in *t'ai chi*, the inner strength

strong fighters withered simply by looking upon it.

When the group from U.Sec arrived, Sakuro was in place, looking deadly and inscrutable. Frank Sheehan approached Fiona, David Hartman's secretary. Fiona, who claimed to have been raised in the same crowd of Sloan Rangers[109] as Fergie and Di, and had the accent to prove it, which made her one of the highest-paid secretarial twits on the West Coast, said, "Please take a seat. Mr. Hartman will be with you shortly."

"How shortly," Frank said.

---

or existence or power. Martial arts are designed to develop chi. "In this broadest sense chi means energy . . . the fundamental component of the universe, and also manifests itself within the bound of the Earth. Mist, wind, and air contain much chi and so do human beings. Breath is chi . . . it is the vital force that keeps us alive. The Chinese believe that chi pulses through the body in a similar (but distinct) way as blood. . . . Acupuncture is [a] system for manipulating the flow of chi." The Fighting Arts, Reid and Croucher, Simon & Schuster '83. Originally published in GB as The Way of the Warrior.

[109]British slang. The reference is to the Sloan Square area of London—very expensive, very posh.

[110]Are there companies in America, whose business is generally noncriminal, tied to the government or not, that kill people and then go on about their business?

Certain high-profile prosecutions—Boesky, Milken, Watergate, Iran-contra—tend to convince us that crime never pays, and that even the high and mighty are dragged down when they stray, that the system works.

It is very important to the system that we believe in it.

When movies were subject to censorship, which they were in a very formal way from 1934 to 1968, by the Hays Office, one of the strictest rules—as strictly enforced as not letting ten-year-olds view close-ups of oral copulation—was that crime must not profit. If someone committed a crime on-screen, they had to be punished. Later, when TV came around, network codes of standards and practices had much the same requirement. For dramatic reasons we are always seeing stories about independent-minded cops who defy all institutional resistance to bring down the biggest of corrupt bigwigs.

However, for as long as criminology has been a field of study, it has always been haunted by the theory of "the competent criminal." For obvious reasons criminologists (and psychologists and sociologists, etc.) only study failed criminals—that is, those persons whose criminal acts led to their conviction and to punishment. If there is a group of people out there who commit crimes and are

"I rilly cahn't say," Fiona said.

---

not caught and live happily ever after, then criminology is not a study of criminals but of incompetents, bumblers, fuckups and, should instead be called fuckupology.

In a sense the very definition of "criminal," at least in America—"innocent until *proven guilty*"—says that a criminal is a person who commits an illegal act in such a bumbling or unlucky way that even a prosecution system as cumbersome and full of restrictions as ours can prove it beyond a reasonable doubt.

It is clear that both casual and organized illegal activity constantly goes on in a successful way. There are obviously practioners of illegal acts who manage to go about their business quietly and regularly, who encounter the criminal-justice system little more than do straighter members of society.

Anyone who lived in New York in the sixties was a witness to the drama of the Knapp Commission and Serpico. The point is not that corruption was exposed. The point is that it proves that the entire department was corrupt *systemwide* and had been so for at least *several generations* of police. They were involved in gambling, extortion, loan sharking, prostitution, narcotics, racketeering, murder. *Thousands* of people knew about it and *participated* in it without exposure.

Although New York City embarked on an extensive and possibly successful reform, the vast majority of those officers who had been "on the pad" virtually all their police lives retired in their own time, as if nothing had happened, to enjoy both the fruits of their corruption and their pensions.

It requires an act of willful blindness to imagine that it only happened in New York or that it only happens in big cities, never in small towns or at the state level, or nationally or internationally.

Back to Universal Security.

Can there be a business that acts as a surrogate for national-security agencies? The answer to that happens to be a documented yes. These may be owned—CIA proprietary companies—or financed or contracted.

The next step is more difficult. Would such an agency engage in murder, to use the harshest term? It is documented that the CIA has engaged in systematic and extensive assassination, as in Vietnam. There, much of the killing was done by surrogates. However, the surrogates were, for the most part, political entities. U.S. government agencies as well as private American companies have run a variety of police, intelligence, and army "training" programs in South and Central America. There is an incredible correlation of these programs, what you might call a through line, with the practice of police torture and assassination and the emergence of "death squads" and "disappearances." That too is reasonably well documented and has even been the subject of, or implicit in, several feature films (*Missing, State of Siege, Under Fire, Salvador*). We are not interested in left-wing America-bashing here. These may be necessary and useful steps in the protection of society. Liberals can wince and whimper all they want, but the Vietcong have

"My dear gal," C. H. Bunker said, "would you be so kind as to inform me if there is a fire in the hearth?"

"In the main hall? Do you mean?"

"Yes, in the main hall."

"Of course there is. There is always a fire in the main hall."

"Then tell the estimable Mr. Hartman that I shall await him there. At his . . . um . . . leisure." Creaking and wheezing, he shuffled out.

It was a very satisfying room, a spiritual cousin of his own library. Obviously, it was vastly larger and semipublic, nonetheless it had the same we-own-the-world-and-we're-quite-comfortable-with-it attitude. After all, the original had been built for Harvard men in the plutocratic twenties.

Sheehan knew that C.H. liked to sit close to the fire. He pulled one of the high-backed leather chairs close enough that the old man would feel the warmth. Bunker sat down with pleasure and Sheehan give him a cigar and a leather-bound copy of *Bleak House*. Bunker seemed to carry nothing, Sheehan had brought both in his brief case. A steward, at the sight of the cigar, rushed over to inform C.H. that he was in California, a no-smoking zone. But there was something so—so like God as played by John Huston about him that instead the steward took a book of matches from his jacket pocket, struck one, and held it to the tip of the Havana.

"Just a little soda, please," Bunker said. "Thank you."

Upstairs, Hartman knew what he thought about the situation but wasn't sure what he *felt*. Initially, his reaction was that this was a

---

told us—they did not like Phoenix.

Then there is the final step. Can there be a private security agency that, from time to time, kills people for commercial and/or political reasons? And which is competent—unlike, say, Ollie North—competent enough that we never, ever hear of them?

Paranoid fantasy or simple, logical realism?

fuckup. On the other hand—and this feeling crept up on him during the hours that passed while he waited for Bunker to arrive—there was something very potent in what had happened. A man had been killed to keep *his*—David Hartman's—secrets. This was power. Even if it had been a bit unnecessary, still, nothing else that he had ever done or been involved with had the sheer *absoluteness* of this. It was almost intoxicating. No—intoxication implied disorientation, befuddlement, loss of acuity. On the contrary, when he had practiced kendo with his sensei, he had experienced clarity and centeredness. He had truly felt his ki for the first time. There had been other times when he *thought* he had felt it, but in retrospect, now that he'd felt it for real, the other times had been wishful thinking. It was the feeling of having been raised higher on the mountain, where few go.

This event opened a door for him and through that door he had a glimpse of what he was becoming: a maker of war, a shaper of human destinies. The paths to power wend through strange forests— his the Hollywood scrub of deals, ancillary rights and 10 percent off the top—before they emerge past the tree line in the jagged peaks above the clouds where the air is thin and pure, where only the strongest arrive, and when they do, they can see across the world. A mythic feeling. Say it in a whisper: they who make the ascension, literally have the power of the gods.

The peculiar result of this panoramic exaltation was that he no longer knew what he wanted from the meeting. That was really strange. Hartman always knew what he wanted. That was one of the keys to his success. Oh, someone's head was going to roll, just so it was understood that he made heads roll. But what did he want? The assurance that no mistake would ever happen again? Or, having tasted blood . . . ?

Bunker, on the other hand, knew exactly what he wanted. He wanted to find out what this project was about. Gates, over at the NSC, hadn't given him a clue. He'd just given this peculiar person— this Hollywood agent—carte blanche. Bunker would, he was certain, win in the end. He almost always did. In the meantime, he loved the infinite detail and endless narrative pace of Charles Dickens. Reading Dickens made Bunker feel like he had all the time in the world. Which he did not.

Frank Sheehan knew what he wanted. He was pretty sure someone was going to get the ax. His goal was damage control—limit the the damage to one person and make sure that the one person was not himself. He didn't think that would be too difficult to do. He had the steward bring him a martini with an olive. He examined the papers that had been printed from Teddy Brody's computer. Mel would get points for getting hold of it right away, and printing it out so expeditiously, but not enough to get him off the hot seat. Happily for Sheehan, who knew that someone had to sit there.

Taylor knew what he wanted. He wanted to save his job. Once again it came back to Joe Broz. If he could show that Broz was a danger—difficult for Taylor to do because Taylor didn't know this damn secret—then any measure, however extreme, as killing Teddy Brody was extreme, was justified. If Broz was assumed to be an innocent party, then Taylor had made an expensive mistake. It wasn't a moral question—hey, it wasn't nice that the kid was dead, but people die in the course of things: war, traffic, playing cops and robbers, having sex and overeating too—but one of efficency and of costs. Covering up a killing was expensive. Though oddly enough, if you thought about it, consummations almost never had blowbacks. It was the diddly-squat that led to blowbacks, from Watergate to Iran-contra: break-ins, money transfers, cash receipts, lying under oath, keeping memos of things that should never have been written anywhere, people taping their own confidential conversations and forgetting that they'd done so.

Taylor sat, Taylor sweated, Taylor plotted.

Sheehan came across several letters that made reference to what Brody thought John Lincoln Beagle was up to. He handed them to C. H. Bunker, who reacted as if they were an intrusion, but who took them and perused them nonetheless.

Done, the old man tossed them at the fire. The draught blew them back toward the room. Taylor picked them up. He read them. They just talked about making films and miniseries. It didn't make sense that he'd been told to stop someone, at all costs, on the off chance that they were going to reveal this chatter about movies.

Fiona Alice Victoria Richmond, once of Knightsbridge, before Daddy lost it all and Mummy disgraced herself, knew, from birth, that keeping people waiting had nothing to do with how long business took, but with rank and position and attitude. So she let Hartman know how Bunker had finessed the gesture.

As a result, the steward told C. H. Bunker that "Mr. Hartman will see you now," in fifteen minutes rather than the intended thirty. Bunker rose and handed the boy his cigar as if it were a fine tip, which, if half a ten-dollar cigar is worth five dollars, it was.[110]

CHAPTER

* * *

FORTY-FOUR

When I get back to the house, all I want to do is get those discs on the computer and read them. Steve is unhappy to be on guard duty. His son is elated to be holding a gun. I send them to the kitchen, for Mrs. Mulligan to get them something to eat. Maggie wants to talk. Fucking microphones. She doesn't want to hear country music either. Or Bartok or Bach or Dylan or Guns 'n' Roses or Miles Davis. She wants to talk about her *feelings*. I want to load the computer and find out what the hell we've got. Find out, maybe, at last, what's going on.

Maggie is not used to people getting killed.

We go into her office.

I put in the disc marked 1. It is a backup system called Smart Set. There are twenty-six discs. I start loading them. She wants to talk.

I stand up. I hold her. "Don't worry, baby," I say. "I'm going to protect you. I'm going to take care of you." You know, the usual shit a guy is supposed to say when a weak woman is shaking and weeping in his arms. But I have to get back to these discs. They killed the boy for what's on there. Now I'm going to know what it is. When I know it, then I've done what I set out to do. With that—I hope— we've got Hartman and Beagle and we can control the game.

It takes about fifteen minutes to get them all loaded in. There is an extra disc. When I put it in, I get a message on the screen that it is not an Apple disc. I figure it is a DOS disc. So I open up the translation program. But even with that up and running the computer doesn't recognize the disc. I put it aside. Though naturally I am certain that it is *the* disc that contains the magic bit of information, the clue, the truth, the thing that everybody is chasing. Maggie tells me later that Hitchcock would have called it the MacGuffin.

In the meantime, until I can figure it out, I look at what we do have.

I pull a chair over so Maggie can sit beside me. That way I can hold her hand and *be with her.*

"What are we doing, Joe?"

Brody had some games—which don't interest me. A series of computer programs that do computer things—speed up, manage, protect. He's got Prodigy and Compuserve. His phone book and date book are—as I suspected—in there. He's got check-balancing and tax-preparation programs. Then there are documents: film treatments, short stories, several screenplays, letters. It's going to take days to read.

"What about that boy? Shouldn't we be doing something? Going to the police?"

I decide that the best bet is the letters.

"Be patient. Stick with me, baby. I'm going to find our way out of this." I punch up letter after letter. I am not a fast reader. I try to scan, find key words, sure enough, eventually "secret" with three exclamation points pops out at me.

Dearest Mother

. . . our work of course is secret!!! *Da-dum!* We have all taken oaths. Never to speak a word of what we do to Outsiders. A strange Xenophobia, I think, CinéMutteteers against the world. Though I must tell you, Mother, that here in Hollywood—the new *au courant* is LaLaLa—it is not unusual. CAA is mad for secrecy. More CIA than CAA.

RepCo is demonic about it. Anyone who speaks of—or
leaks—agency business is summarily fired! Ipso-presto, no
appeal! Stripped of his leased Porsche and car phone at high
noon on Sunset Boulevard. So what does everyone do all
day? They traffic in secrets. Gossip is the coin of the realm.
It brings out the Queen, or at least the Lady in Waiting in
everyone, chatter, chatter, chatter.

Yet our little crew must be loyaler than most, for I hear
nothing, nothing, nothing of what our Beagle doth shoot. Or
plan to shoot, actually. For since I've come, he shoots
nothing, nada, rien, zip, zilch, not foot of film nor field of
video. I wouldst weep for the frustration of it. Had not *he*
beat all the weeps out of me, long, long ago.

He plans—what does he plan? What does he plan? What
does that endless review of footage, of war, devastation,
destruction, fire, flames, pyrotechnic of death, portend?

I think, from the shape of *le montage des montages* which
he creates and re-creates and re-creates—I, humble slave in
the bowels of the techie *bibliothèque,* racing from VCR to
laser disc and back to the stacks to make it all happen—he is
planning the epic to end all epics, or—as so oft happens in
this sadly diminished day of ours—a miniseries to end all
miniseries. I am guessing here—totally, wildly guessing—but
I think what he's planning is the video equivalent of one of
those awful John Jakes saga series books, except that this
will not cover a mere single war, but all [American] wars.
Or all 20th-century American wars. Maybe with a
multigeneration connection, the son of the son of the son of
the son of the bitch. I use the word bitch in only its canine
form, this bitch being the dog of war. Sorry about that.
Ought I to have erased it? Too vulgar? Too punnish? To
punish the punnish.

I came across a piece of paper. This is my other
evidence. Across the top it said—I have to get better at the

grafix program to re-create it, it was handwritten, but it sort of said: *scribble-II-2-√*. which part I don't understand. But under that was a series of what I take to be possible titles:

> *Morning in America.*
> *American Century*
> *American Storm*
> *Pax Americana*
> *Hope of the World*
> *American Hero*
> *The Reincarnation of John Wayne*
> *The 7 Incarnations of John Wayne*

As to my prospects—they are still still.

Don't tell *him* that. Lie for me. Make *him* think I'm happy and prosperous. 'Twill give *him* nightmares. Am I joking?

"Poor boy," Maggie says. "Poor, poor boy."

"Damn," I say. Is that it?

"Hold me, Joe. Put it away. Hold me."

I don't want to. I want to do my job. I want to go through everything that Teddy Brody wrote down. I want to find someone who can figure out what the unidentifiable disc is. But I take her in my arms and I hold her. She buries her head against my chest and she's crying. Maggie's not used to people being killed. People don't get killed over movies.

"I think I'm going to be hysterical," she says.

"It's OK."

"No, really. It's awful. There's a joke in my mind. I'm trying to make a joke out of it."

"What joke?"

"Stupid joke."

"What?"

"It's one thing to be killed for a movie. But for a miniseries?

. . . It's not funny.''

''No.''

''Now that I said it, it's not. It's so sad.''

Suddenly, it's real simple. People don't get killed for movies. Or miniseries. So it's not a movie. I'm playing this wrong. Way wrong.

''Maggie, listen to me. This is out of hand. We have to get some things straight. I want you to call David Hartman.''

''Why? What?''

''Trust me. Do it. We're going to end this. Now. Call him and get in to see him as soon as we can.'' Microphones are listening. We're being watched. In the morning Ray Matusow will pick up the tape of what we did today. Then it will go to transcription services. Mel Taylor will have it in the afternoon. Hartman sometime thereafter, if it's interesting. Or titillating.

Maggie dials. I listen on the extension. ''Fi, it's Maggie. I need to see David.''

''Oh, dear, you do know the sort of shed-ule he keeps.''

''It's urgent. Fi, figure out some way I can see him today.''

''I simply cahn't do it.''

''What about tomorrow.''

''He's leaving the country for a week. It's not going to be possible.''

''Who's he in with?'' Maggie asks, figuring there are some people she simply outranks on the Hollywood scale. ''Come on, Fi, who's he seeing today? Help me, Fi, and I will tell you what Fergie really did at that party in New York last month.''

''I assure you, Maggie, that while you may have been at the party, I have already heard reports that include the color of her underdrawers, not to be vulgar. However, since you are a dear and do give me a bit of good gossip from time to time, I will tell you. Right now he is in with Sakuro, and you know how he is about his kendo. After that he has a meeting with C. H. Bunker.''

''Who,'' Maggie asks, ''is C. H. Bunker?''

''I don't know, but he is terribly important.''

I gesture Maggie to cut off the conversation.

"Thanks, Fi," she says.

"Nothing of it. I really am sorry I couldn't do more for you. He'll be back in a week."

CHAPTER
* * *
FORTY-FIVE

Taylor began to explain, step by step, what had happened.

"I was hoping I wouldn't have to hear this," Hartman said. "I was expecting you to say that the man in charge had already been dismissed and you had seen fit to replace him."

"I want to assure you," Sheehan said, "that I have reviewed the event already. So I can reassure you there were no witness to the actual event. There is nothing to tie the person involved"—it was considered a courtesy not to burden the client with the name of the person who had actually brought about the consummation—"to the incident. There will be no repercussion. Nothing that will come back up the line, as it were. We can guarantee that."

"Excuse me," Hartman said. "You force me to explain this like ABCs for children. Do you expect Joe Broz and, by extension, Maggie Lazlo to ignore a body on their doorstep? You people underestimate Hollywood totally. You think a woman like Maggie is lucky. A pretty face that photographs well. Or maybe a bimbo, fucked her way to the top. Trust me on this, the ones that make it to the top are smart, shrewd, and totally focused. Even when they're young, pretty, and female.

"That brings me to Mr. Broz. I read his file. The real one. Thank you very much. This is one real son of a bitch, isn't he, gentlemen? So you did not solve a problem. You created at least double the problem."

"Given the mandate," Taylor said, "the resources, the situation—"

Hartman didn't let him finish. "I'm in a business," he said, "where resources, situations, none of that matters. A movie either performs or it doesn't. After a flop, everyone sits around, they talk., they analyze it, they write books about how it flopped. Does it matter? No. Does it make them a success the next time out of the box? If there is one? No. Did you ever see *Home Alone? Wayne's World?* Have you seen the last three Eddie Murphy movies? It is *impossible* that these were successful. Yet they were. Do you get it? Give me a guy who steps in shit and smells like roses. I don't want a guy who tends the roses perfectly, but comes in stinking like shit."

Everyone looked toward Taylor. Everyone always looks at the condemned man.

"Point well taken," C.H. said. "It seems to me, if I am to select the right person, and if we are to prevent problems from reoccurring, then there are some matters that must be discussed. Must be." Looking at Taylor and speaking gently, Bunker said, "Mel"—he gestured toward the door—"this won't concern you."

Taylor got up. End of career. He walked to the door.

"Wait a minute," he said.

"Mel . . ." Bunker said, meaning Go quietly. *Your time has come.*

"I want to, I want to say something here."

"Taylor," Sheehan snapped, meaning *Shut up and get your ass out of here.*

Mel was a good soldier. So this was hard for him to do. But he went for it. "Sir, I have a statement to make. Let's start with this. John Lincoln Beagle is not making a movie. We do not let slip the dogs of war over a motion picture. Universal Security frequently acts for the benefit of the United States of America. I hope that what happened earlier today happened in order to protect the vital interests of our country. If it was for anything less, then whoever gave me my orders is in error.

"Then there's this. An incorrect assumption. If you think that this event is creating a problem with Broz and Lazlo, that is, pardon me, an incorrect assumption. It is backwards, sir, ass backwards. We have surveillance on over twenty people. We have been watching them for months. Because we have streamlined things and we use a lot of electronics and because people do develop patterns, we have about thirty personnel, full-time, on this one operation. With all of that, there have been only four blips on the radar. Four. One with Maggie Lazlo before she hooked up with Broz. The thing with her maid. Two that connect directly to Broz—Kitty Przyszewski, and Teddy Brody. One unknown—the mugging of Ray Matusow.

"Since I don't know the details of this operation, which is not a movie, I can't tell who the opposition is. I don't know if it's the Soviets, or the Japs, or the Islamic Jihad. But I can tell you that Broz is not some innocent bystander who has his curiosity aroused by what we did. To the contrary, he is a player. You can fire me today, you can bring in some other guy, but even if you bring Brody back to life, Joe Broz will still be a player. Excuse my vernacular, sir, he's fucking with us.

"Rather than firing me, you should be considering when and how to shut him down. It's not a question of whether you have to. It's a question of whether you do it in time."

Hartman was intrigued. Partly because there was a possibility that Taylor was right. Partly because, having had one person killed—through many intermediaries and not by bringing his will directly to bear—having had one person killed, he was intrigued by the idea of doing it again. Maggie Lazlo and Joe Broz were so much more luminescent and powerful people too.

Bunker was content to let Taylor run with it. "What would you suggest, Mel?"

Taylor sighed with relief. He'd saved himself. Now it was his turn to deal the hand. Should he sit or should he stand? Be commanding or humble? Consult or direct?

"You know what's at stake and you know what's at risk," he said to Hartman. "You're the only one in this room who really knows. There are all kinds of options. One is to step up surveillance and interdiction. Actually, we've done pretty well with that. Broz knows nothing. We're on him like ticks on a hound. And you might want to say, just keep it up.

"But I have to admit, surveillance is an art. Not a science. There are always cracks in the door. The KGB makes mistakes, the CIA makes mistakes. So you might want to get more active. I don't know what resources these two have beyond their own, but if you cut off the money, you do a lot of damage. Then there's a variety of tricks that will absorb their time and attention.

"Finally, if the downside risk of leak is large enough, it justifies any defensive measure . . ."

Sakuro Juzo, outside the door of David Hartman's office, glared at Maggie Lazlo and Joe Broz.

Fiona said to Maggie, "I absolutely cahn't."

"Just please tell him I'm here, and it's urgent."

"Maggie—"

"Would you please tell C. H. Bunker," Joe said, "that Joseph Broz is here."

That was different. While she couldn't interrupt her boss, she could get a message to a visitor. "Alright," Fiona said. She picked up the phone and pushed the intercom button. "It's for Mr. Bunker. Joe Broz is here."

"Show him in," C.H. said.

Hartman tried to characterize the look on the old man's face. He looked—what was it—entertained? "Alright. Fiona, let him in."

Joe Broz came in with Maggie beside him. She looked distraught. Like she'd been crying. "C.H., thanks," Joe said.

"Well, well, Joe. Good to see you." Bunker rose from his chair, for Maggie. He half-bowed in a courtly manner. It forced the other men to stand as well, and because it hadn't occurred to them until he was already standing, it made them seem gauche and Bunker even more courteous by contrast. "And the delicious Ms. Lazlo. I have but few years left, but I would give all of my days for just one day in Joe's place." He said it in a way that brought no offense. "A chair for Ms. Lazlo."

Maggie clung closer to Joe. "I'll stand," she said.

"Pardon an old man, then," Bunker said, and sank back into his seat. Sheehan and Hartman sat. Taylor still stood.

"C.H., you know me, you know I've keep the secrets," Joe said.

"Yes, you have."

Joe nodded as if something was settled. He turned to the agent. "Ok, Mr. Hartman, let's not fuck around. It's pretty goddamn obvious John Lincoln Beagle is doing something secret. I know it. Maggie knows it. You know that we know it. You knew it a long time ago when Bennie told her to shut up and she didn't and then her maid disappeared and all of that.

"The thing is, we don't care. We're in love. She's got a great career. I might have one too. Why the fuck should we care about John Lincoln Beagle? I don't have enough time to kiss Maggie as much as I want to. Let alone read the stack of scripts in my office.

"Some kid is coming to see me. For a job. I want to see him because he's got all this education—Yale, UCLA—and me, I left school at fourteen. Ninth grade. It was the Marines put me straight. Then I look out the window . . ." Joe pointed at Taylor. "This son of a bitch is staring at me. Then Bo Perkins shows up . . ." He turned to Bunker. "C.H., it's none of my business, but what the hell are you using Bo Perkins for? Who is this Brody kid? Some Nicaraguan guerrilla? Shining Path? Fanatic Moslem assassin?

"Bo kills the kid, right in my lobby.

"Guys, I've been in the game. One plus one equals big trouble. You gotta be thinking that I'm after John Lincoln Beagle's secret. I'm here to say, I'm not. Whatever you want me to walk away from, I'm already gone. Anything you think of tomorrow, you want me to walk away from, consider me gone."

"Bullshit," Taylor said.

"What about it, C.H.?"

"Umm," Bunker said.

"One more thing," Joe said. "A week ago, I was moving some of my gear, from my house to Maggie's—excuse me, Maggie, I didn't tell you this because I didn't want to upset you and I hadn't figure out what the hell was going on yet—but you have her house wired."

"They what?" Maggie cried. Full of shock and shame and anger. Strange men listening to her sounds of love. To her pissing and shitting and chastising herself when she looked in the mirror and saw age or excess. To the sounds that she made in her sleep, that she herself didn't even know about. "Our house is what? Who did this? Who did this?"

"Taylor over there," Joe said. "Hartman. Ray Matusow probably did the installation."

"You've been listening to tapes of me?" Her face was a window that let them see every painful and shameful thought. She glared at all of them but focused in on Taylor. "You like that? You pervert. You scum." Enraged, she advanced on him. "Does it excite you? Do you jerk off listening to me make love?"

Maggie swung to slap Taylor across the face. He had to know it was coming. Reflexively, he grabbed her arm. She started to swing with her other hand. Taylor began to twist the arm he held to force her back.

Joe pulled the 9-mm automatic from his belt holster, chambered a round, took half a step, and had the gun in Taylor's face.

Through the door, and all the tumult and yelling, Sakuro Juzo heard the sound of the gun being cocked. He stepped into the room, a *shuriken* in his hand. Joe was aware of him but ignored him. "Go on, Taylor," Joe said. "Hurt her."

"Better not, Mel," Bunker said, unperturbed, calm and slow. "After all, you deserve it, violating the privacy of such a lady. This is not some slut or cheating tramp."

Taylor let go of Maggie.

Maggie slapped him. The room rang with the sound. The blow knocked Taylor's head back. It took an act of will, and the staring eye of a 9-mm in his face, to keep him from striking back.

"Broz, you're a dead man," Taylor said.

"On behalf of"—Bunker made a vague gesture that included everyone but made no explitict admissions—"I apologize to you."

"Who else listened?" Maggie cried, full of hurt and wounded pride. "David?" She looked at Hartman. Then at Sheehan, who was red and sweating. "You did, you blushing Catholic schoolboy. I hope you learned something." Sheehan got redder, as if he had.

"I'm taking the wiretaps out," Joe said. "You violated Ms. Lazlo's privacy. Think of her, now that we're being personal, as my wife. If the electronic shit comes back, I'm going to make it personal, Taylor. And you too," he said to Hartman. He turned to the old man. "Any problem with that, C.H.? Come on, C.H., you owe me. I got Griff out. Got him home, didn't I?"

"That you did. Though he didn't last long. Not your fault. You did the best you could," Bunker said, wisps of sadness around him. Then courtly: "You have a wonderful woman there and great expectations. Go with it, son, make the most of it. Brass ring . . . not there every time."

"David?" Joe said.

"I don't really have any secrets. John Lincoln wants his privacy but—"

"However you want it, David," Broz said emphatically, "that's how I'll play it. Deal?"

The agent came out from behind his desk. He had a file in his hand. He looked thoughtful, serious, friendly. "Here's the file they gave me on you." He said it to Joe but handed it to Maggie. Then he looked back at Broz.

"Deal," the agent said.

Joe nodded. He put the gun back in the holster. He put his arm around Maggie and they backed out.

The next morning Hartman flew to Tokyo. He had two days of meetings there. He continued eastward. He stopped in New Delhi. Several Indian film producers wanted to speak to him about representing them and their product in America. He continued eastward. To Baghdad.

CHAPTER
★ ★ ★
FORTY-SIX

Linc was having a better time of it than he expected.

Jackie was being sweet. As if they weren't married. And she helped him with Dylan. She didn't play setup games, or manuver for catastrophe. She seemed to understand, and more importantly, accept, that a man's attention span and tolerance for genuine infantalism, is more limited than a woman's. In other words, she let him play with Dylan until he was bored or stressed, than she pitched in to relieve him.

The second day Linc decided to cook. He tried to pick a couple of good recipes. Their country kitchen, just remodeled for $42,950, not counting the hanging copper pots and the hand-painted tiles around the fireplace, had an entire set of bookshelves just for cookbooks. Actually, there were 148 of them. At first glance, they were very exciting. A sort of *pornographie gourmandaise*. Image after image piled upon each other, each with its special demands and slightly incomprehensible instructions. Then there was the certainty that Jackie would hate whatever he made. Not just hate it, find a way to use it against him. He began to itch. His scalp and then his thighs. Then the itch moved around. It was a symptom—he was certain—of SASS, short attention span syndrome, a condition he'd read about only last month that he was now certain had ruled his childhood and affected his adulthood. It was SASS, possibly electrical, maybe chemical, could be glandular—but not psychological in the Freudian or Jungian neurotic sense—that made it difficult for him to deal with recalcitrant physical objects, with teachers who had wanted to teach him stuff he already knew, teachers who had wanted to teach him stuff they thought they knew but didn't, with organizing closet space, filing, writing down his expenses every day, dumb fucks who wanted to talk about football as if it mattered.

He hastily put the cookbooks away.

Most men have two to six things they know how to make[111] and, except during the chemically altered state of fresh courtship when they can read and execute recipes right out of the cookbook on the very first go-round, that's what they fall back on. Beagle could mix mayo with curry and canned tuna, he could make omelets and French toast, he had recently figured out rice, he knew how to grill meats and, by extension, fish. Oh, yeah, he could make a salad with packaged dressing and pasta with packaged sauce. He added his own stuff to the sauce so it didn't have that totally store-bought quality and was proud of it.

He asked Jackie what she thought of grilled fish, rice, and a salad. There were so many things that Jackie could have said: "I told you last week I'm on a diet of no rice, how could you forget? I bet you forgot that your son is allergic to that awful buttermilk dressing you always buy? I told you we're eating dinner with Francis and his wife

---

[111]There is no question that this is a sexual stereotype. There is no question that there are many men who routinely cook, cook well, cook from cookbooks without flinching. Similarly, there are many women who can't or don't or won't do those things. This particular stereotype has been studied "scientifically" (*Food Industry Monthly* 11-'89, *Psychology Today* 9-'88, *Green Grocer, The Journal of the Retail Food Purveyor,* 5-'91), and in each case the hard marketing data states that a very large segment of the adult male population fit this profile.

tonight, you never pay any attention to anything I say, do you? I hope you don't burn the food, the way you always do. Don't let the fish man see how little you know about shopping or he'll sell you the stuff that's old and smelly." But she didn't say a single one of those things. Or anything like them.

She responded as if he said something reasonable and that cooking dinner was a sensible thing to do. She didn't correct him at all. "Can we shop together?" she said. "That'll be fun."

Beagle agreed. So they got in their Saab Turbo—their country car—packed up the baby backpack and the stroller, put Dylan in the baby seat, and went off to market together. They bought fresh produce, fresh herbs and spices, mahimahi—which used to be called dolphin, but everyone got tired of explaining that it wasn't porpoise and it sounded more exotic and expensive anyway—some local chardonnay, a bit flinty, but coming into its own, and if one was truly objective about it, superior to the French. Nobody fought. Dylan was cute as the dickens. A bit like Dennis the Menace, but when it's your kid, and you like each other, if only for the afternoon, that makes it adorable. So what if he pulled some wine bottles off the shelf—they didn't break. He grabbed a peach at the fruit stand and flung it—it only bruised, it didn't splatter, and no one was hurt. Good arm. And he banged on the lobster tank. It didn't break, and if the lobsters minded, they weren't going to live long enough to write a letter to their congressman. When he got cranky, which he did, they gave him a bottle and put him in the backpack on Beagle's back, where he fell asleep. And wasn't that adorable. Jackie made Beagle stop in front of a mirror and look at his son, head flopped sideways at an angle impossible for adults, totally casual, completely trusting, a snot bubble expanding from his nose, drool dripping on Da-da's shoulder. It was heart-melting.

When they got home, Maria, the country cook and housekeeper, made them a light lunch and put the groceries away so that Beagle could cook with them later. She would have fed Dylan in the kitchen—it was easier to clean—but his parents wanted their one and only son with them in the breakfast nook. When John Lincoln got frustrated trying to explain to Dylan why he shouldn't fling food at grown-ups, Jackie took over and handled the situation.

In the afternoon they strolled through the vineyards admiring all that they owned.

John Lincoln cooked dinner. He made separate portions for Dylan and his nanny. They ate in the kitchen. Linc wasn't up to another experience like lunch quite so soon. Tomorrow he could try it again. Eating with the kid twice a day was pushing the outside of the envelope.

Dinner was successful. Jackie seemed to actually like it and ate most of her portion and didn't complain about anything, even his choice of wine. There was a fat moon when the sun went down, and a cool breeze. They strolled together, not talking. Not talking was the safest thing they could say to each other.

Jackie had some Maui-Wowie, *sensimilla,* really fine and exotic stuff with blue tendrils—some incredibly potent herbal mutation, $500 an ounce, a real one-toker smoke. So they each took a hit or two and . . . yeah . . . they turned out the lights . . . lit a candle . . . some soft music and he . . . he reached out . . . he touched her . . . she didn't flinch . . . or explain why she didn't want him to touch her . . . and by golly, John Lincoln Beagle had sexual intercourse with his wife. It wasn't any of your fancy fucking or inventive hinky-pinky Joy of Sex, Dr. Ruth strawberry gel and edible undies, but still! She even let him kiss her.

CHAPTER

* * *

FORTY-SEVEN

I can't tell you what a treat it is to make love without goddamn country music blasting. The window open and nothing but the sounds of the surf and of each other.

After the Hartman confrontation I start tracing LDs and tearing them out. The next day I have a guy from Fleischer's Audio Security in to double-check my work, and he does in fact find two microphones that I missed. I also invest in a Micron 28-40 which broadcasts microwave and radio-wave interference patterns. It will prevent transmission from a wide variety of LDs to off-site listening posts, but don't get one if you have a short-tempered neighbor with a satellite dish.

That night we are alone for the first time since we met. The feeling of—relief I guess it is, relaxation or something—it's like getting out of Vietnam, to Tokyo, Bangkok, Sydney, or Oahu for R&R. 'Cause the thing about Nam was there were no battle lines, so it never stopped. You'd be in a bar, a whorehouse, somebody throws a bomb or a grenade. In camp, if there were Vietnamese in the camp, mama-sans who did the laundry or mess boys or any of that, even ARVN troops, some of them were always some of Them.

Of course, Maggie reads the file that Hartman gave her. She asks me if it's true.

Well, how true is a piece of paper, ever. Is it going to make her stop loving me. Does the record mean we're over?

She just wants to know if it's true.

Sure, it's true. I went to Vietnam to kill people. Enemies of the United States of America, my country. An opposing army, that fights in a particular way. At first I'm there in uniform.

It's hard. War is supposed to be hard. It's frightening and the commandments are broken and you find out if you're a man and what kind. It's the insects and the snakes and wet, the skin fungus and the smell of unwashed bodies. The smell of shit and urine and sweat and fear. I become a sergeant and I liked it. More than liked. It was what I was born for. The truth is, it didn't really matter that it was the United States of America. If I'd been born for some other war, that probably would have been alright. Winning would have been good too. The whole war, I mean. I won most of my battles and I killed more of them than they killed of us and I kept my guys, my squad, and when I had a lieutenant would listen, the whole platoon, safer than most, most of the time, and I made the enemy fear and respect us.

Then there comes a time, things get out of hand. I get into a dispute with an officer and the easiest way to solve it is for me to leave the Marines. I'm thinking that the Marines are a career, that that's my home. So that's hard, but under the circumstances it's a better deal than I have a right to expect. It's Griff, Preston Griffith, who helps me find an out. If they'll let me go, he's got work for me. I can stay in Vietnam. I can fight.

It's a different kind of fighting. More like the VC's way. It's called *Phunng Hoang*, Phoenix. Dress like VC, eat like VC. They say we own the day, the VC owns the night. We take back the night from the VC. We are assassins.

So I tell Maggie, yes, the file is true.

She doesn't leave me. She doesn't grow frightened or angry and pull away. She presses her body next to mine. Moonlight comes in the window and she goes to sleep.

. . .

I begin to look for someone who can tell me what the mystery disc
is.

We split up the material that we can read. Everything that Brody
writes in his letters and his notes says that Beagle is working on a war
movie or television series of some kind. This is more or less in accord
with what everyone in town knows. In two days of reading we
discover nothing that tells us significantly more than did the letter to
his mother than I found on the first go-round, except that Teddy wrote
a piece for Beagle about propaganda. There are several versions of
it, each getting shorter and shorter.

Of course, what Teddy couldn't know was that someone would
kill him rather than let him talk to me, or perhaps to any outsider.
We—Universal Security—have done employee-departure cases
before and we assume that an employee will talk to his new empoyer
about what he did at his last place of employment, even—or especially—if those things are trade secrets or some other form of proprietary information.

Had Teddy seen his assailant, that would not have told him what
it told me. Bo Perkins was Phoenix. There were people who became
affected by the power that they had. I won't say that I didn't. That I
was pure or something. But there is a difference between loving
war—the contest, the danger, the risk, the adrenaline rush, the feeling
of power, the high feeling—and loving pain and death. In Phoenix
it was possible to hurt, to torture, to kill for pleasure. It was possible.
For some, that is a great temptation.

The Dark Side—*da-dum*—like Darth Vader, once in a Galaxie,
long, long ago . . .

But that's a movie and a kid's story. It doesn't tell you how dark
the dark side is.

Bo went over—maybe was always over—and he didn't come
back.

The other thing, of course, that Teddy couldn't know, very few people know, is that U. Sec. does work for the government. I mean secret work. Stuff that if you worked for the CIA you are supposed to inform somebody, like in Congress. And you're supposed to see a special memo or order before you do it. Plus, there are certain things, like assassinations, that by law the CIA and the other security agencies of the United States, and there are quite a few, cannot do. It's possible, though I don't know, because it's not the level where I operate, that U.Sec. may be, or maybe once was, a CIA proprietary.[112]

Bottom line, Maggie said it—you don't kill someone over a movie.

You especially don't send Bo Perkins unless it has been authorized at the highest level of invisible government.

The thing is, if we write down the few simple things we know, it's like an equation. Simpler than that even. Arithmetic.

John Lincoln Beagle is working on a war movie.
—   Nobody gets murdered for   a   movie.
=   John Lincoln Beagle is working on a war.

At this time I don't think the answer is as simple and stark as that. That appears to be, on the face of it, insane. Beagle makes excellent films but—that's insane. Yet the equation remains.

---

[112]It may not be news to anyone any more what CIA proprietaries are and that they exist. If it is, they are ostensibly private businesses secretly owned or funded by the CIA. They are more than fronts in that they really function as businesses. Some of them make a profit and need no subsidy. Some of them have been known to make money for the Agency, which makes for very secret spendable funds. The most famous proprietary was Air America, an airline in Southeast Asia that flew agents and commandos and opium and cash and virtually anything else. When Ollie North wanted to send arms to Iran, he approached an airline that he knew to be a proprietary. Their response was a very businesslike one. In essence, they said their relationship to the CIA was irrelevant—if Ollie could pay the normal airfreight charges, deal with customs, and supply the required documents, they would be happy to fly anything for him anywhere.

Add to that the whole operation. The amount of surveillance—personnel, electronics, transcripts—someone is spending a tremendous amount of money.

What I figure, at this point, is that Beagle is working on war propaganda. From the memo the kid wrote. Why would that be such a serious secret? No big deal. In Vietnam we built television stations to broadcast propaganda. Then when someone realized the Vietnamese didn't have televisions, we gave them televisions. People do propaganda in war. In all sorts of forms. Unless he's doing propaganda for a war that he knows will exist that nobody else knows about. I mean that somebody has already decided that we're going to have a war and they've hired Beagle to tell them how to present it. So they don't fuck it up like they did Vietnam.

I have read *On Strategy: An Analysis of the Vietnam War*, by Colonel Harry Summers, and he believes, as do many others, that America failed to mobilize the population with propaganda and that is the real reason we lost the war.

That's something to keep secret, that they've already picked a war and they're going to make it happen.

Having just enough information to deduce this does us more harm than good. Hartman and Bunker, who are smarter than me, can figure out that I can figure it out. And sooner or later, that will be unacceptable. David Hartman tried to tell Maggie not to get involved, way back at the beginning. I don't know that there is a way, anyway at all, to get uninvolved.

"Tell me, Maggie, why? What do you want?"

"A little power," she says. "David could stop my career dead. Or more likely, when I get a little older and it's easier to sell a younger piece of merchandise, he just won't bother. Nobody cares. Bottom line. There isn't a person in the world that cares for me and my career. Except you. Now. But you're not David Hartman or Ray Stark or Mike Ovitz or Michael Eisner or David Geffen. That's not self-pity, that's a financial statement.

"I'm lucky to be where I am. I understand that. But I also understand it could all go away. If I have something on David that gives me an edge, that gives *me* power over him for a change—I want it. That's my truth. Now, are you going to fall out of love with me for that?"

"No."

The last hope that there is some easy way is the disc. Three-and-a-half-inch floppy. Black plastic. Indistinguishable from any other Mac or DOS disc. No label.

CHAPTER

★ ★ ★

FORTY-EIGHT

C. H. Bunker came to much the same conclusion that Joseph Broz did.

His arithmetic was slightly different. But the sum was the same.

John Lincoln Beagle is working 14 hours a day, 7 days a week on a war movie.

—		Gates does not employ U.Sec. w/out "limits" for					
a	movie.						
=	John	Lincoln	Beagle	is	working	on	
a war							

or, since that's insane,
something very like it.

He thought a long time about firing Mel Taylor. He liked David Hartman's logic. In the world as Bunker saw it, there were qualities far more mysterious than IQ and measurable education and whether actions were logically correct. Some people won, some lost. Some day the people measurers—the psychologists, sociologists, test writers—would realize they were measuring the wrong thing. They would make up fancy new words for winners and losers. Then they would think up fancy new standards to measure them. And they wouldn't get that the measuring sticks were already in place and that everybody but them knew what they were—money and power.

But even trickier than recognizing today's winners and losers was figuring out how they would perform tomorrow. Or rather, what shape tomorrow would have, because the world changed, constantly, and the exact same things that won for you today would make you a loser in the new world you woke up to tomorrow morning.

That, in the end, was what he decided to bet on.

Bunker happened to know why Taylor hated Broz. Griff had told him all about it. It was one of Griff's favorites stories. Joe had won a lot of credit with C.H. by getting Griff home. Who would have thought that Preston Griffith would have been that weak. Turned into a goddamn sniveling junkie. That wasn't quite true either. Griff had turned into a cynical, charming, smart junkie. With a lot of baggage, too few illusions, and in a conspiracy with his pain to utilize opium and its derivatives.

Goddamn Vietnam. Next time they have a war, they better run it right. Nobody that came back from that goddamn place had a good war. Except maybe Joe Broz. Not even him. Joe would never admit to it, but it took him some years after he came back to handle it.

They came back heroes from C.H.'s war. American heroes, saviors of the world, ready to run the world, for it's own good, and they'd done a damn good job of it. If Griff had come back the way they all expected him back, he would have made a goddamn good son-in-law. The best. Been the heir apparent. Given C.H. grandsons. Goddamn, he knew the boy had good seed in him. Seed enough to plant grandsons, C.H. knew that for a fact. There was a little bastard boy running around somewhere, he'd heard about it before Griff left for Vietnam. Everyone hushed it up. C.H.'s daughter had cried for a month over that. College-kid stuff. A little wild oats. They'd made it up, the girl and Griff, before he left. But the way he'd come back . . .

Next time they have a war, they better run it right.

But he kept Taylor.

He knew that Taylor wasn't going to change. He would be neither better nor worse. But Bunker figured that this little universe, the one that orbited around this particular secret, was going to change, and when it did, those things that Taylor was would turn out to be the right things, just as they appeared to have been the wrong things yesterday. Taylor was dogged and persistent and he hated Joe Broz enough that Joe couldn't fool him.

C.H. liked Joe. Owed him for that matter. But he had a suspicion that Joe was throwing sand in their eyes. Ballsy move walking in. It was exactly what an innocent man would do. If he wasn't throwing sand, then more power to him, hope he had a good ride on that randy woman with her good breasts and long flanks. Certainly as prime as prime could get.

What C.H. did was put Sheehan in charge of the L.A. office, temporarily, with Taylor under him, a serious loss of face, so that Taylor would feel the pain and the goad.

He told Taylor, "Let Broz run if he's running. He's a damn fine ferret. If there's something there, let him find it. Then snatch it from him. *Then shut him down.*"

According to David Hartman's passport, he was Episcopalian. It was a small deception and made everyone more comfortable when he entered Iraq. Apparently, no one at Passport Control or among the intimates of the country's ruler was a regular reader of *Premiere* magazine or of "Sherie" or "Suzi" in any of the many places that they're syndicated, because nobody said to him, "Hey, I read about the mega–bar mitzvah you had for your son. How come he had a bar mitzvah if you're Episcopalian? Huh?"

If James Baker had met with Hussein, or George Bush had made contact, someone would have taken note. But the world's "serious" media paid no attention when David Hartman arrived in Bahgdad. Hartman had a letter of introduction from the president that said, in appropriately flowery Arabic, that the bearer brought greetings and was acting on the president's behalf. Hartman destroyed this letter as soon as possible after meeting Hussein. Unlike the Atwater memo, which still rested in his safe.

Although Saddam is a naturally cautious and deeply suspicious person, the offer did not appear to shock him or disturb him at all. He had certain conditions, of course. Also, because some of his needs were very pressing, there were things he wanted from the United States *immediately*—as a gesture, gifts of goodwill, even, Allah willing, a first exchange in the bargain that they would soon strike.

Hartman said that sounded reasonable.

It would have been ungracious to refuse the tour of Baghdad that his host offered him. As a result, he stayed the night. The next morning he flew to Rome, where he met with several old acquaintances involved in finance and film. They were part of that labyrinth of personal connections that runs Italy. Hartman was looking, he said, for a bank that could handle large sums with great discretion. Preferably, one with an American subsidiary or branch because, if the funds came out of the states, at least on paper, they could be guaranteed by the United States. His friends knew of several.

Hartman wished he could stay. There was something wonderful about Rome. It was the mother of cities and had defined so much of civilization. Empire. Wealth. Corruption. Opportunity. When he was there, as in few other places, the stones of the centuries, layered in ruin and glory, spoke to him that Hollywood was nothing new. It reassured him that that much insanity had existed, in exuberant splendor, somewhere else, and that it had not fallen apart in minutes, as it ought, but lasted, growing ever more grandiloquent, for generations.

From there he went to Geneva. Another banking conference. The banker shook his hand when they were done. "Just don't hire Fawn Hall[113] as your secretary," he said, "and all will be well." He

---

[113]Ollie North set up a secret Swiss bank account—he'd seen them in the movies or read about them in thrillers—to transfer funds to the contras. He received ten million dollars from the Sultan of Brunei. He directed Fawn to have it sent to the

chuckled mightily. Swiss bankers are aware of their image and take great care to live up to it. So by Swiss banking standards, chortling was high hilarity.

----

numbered account. She transposed two digits and had the money sent to someone else's account. It was missing from August to December, 1986. (*Los Angeles Times* 6/3/87)

CHAPTER

✶ ✶ ✶

FORTY - NINE

"The object in war is a better state of peace. Hence it is essential to conduct war with constant regard to the peace you desire.

Victory in the true sense implies that the state of peace, and of one's people, is better after the war than before. Victory in this sense is only possible if a quick result can be gained or if a long effort can be economically proportioned to the national resources. The end must be adjusted to the means."

—Sir Basel Henry Liddel Hart, Strategy (2nd rev. ed., 1967).

The disc turns out to be written in UNIX. It is, I am told, an incredibly complex and ingenious program for editing on multiple screens at once. Probably ten screens. It is similar to EditDroid, which is the Lucasfilm editing system, but a lot more powerful. The disc is not the actual command program; it is the plain text printout of the commands. It's interesting to film people because it actually gives the names of the sources, where in the film, by time code, the clips are, and how long they last. There doesn't seem to be any particular reason for Teddy to have it. Or not have it. All it shows is that someone with a sophisticated editing system is making a montage of war movies. If you get all those movies together, you could figure out what the montage might have looked like. At least a few minutes worth, anyway.

So that does nothing for us. Which brings me back to the joke about Sergeant Kim's dojo and ROK.

When Kim first opens up, it's right after Vietnam and there are a lot of crazies around who are into martial arts. On the edge, over the edge, out of control. Because Kim is who he is—he has this military reputation—these types gravitate toward his dojo. Koreans are hard-working, business-oriented people. They figure out what customers want and give it to them.

Most civilians, most normal people, who want to learn martial arts, they don't want to be practicing with some gonzo vet who might snap into a combat flashback. At the same time, Kim does not want to lose any part of the market. You can see that—he's got that section where he sells all the martial-arts equipment, and he's always telling his students they'll do better if they eat Korean food, and he sends them next door to his nephew's fish store and Korean grocery, and whenever he hears about some way that another dojo is getting more customers, Kim does it to. Like the self-defense-for-women thing. So what Kim does, to keep the crazies who see martial arts more as unarmed combat than as a future Olympic sport, but to get them out of the way, he opens a special room upstairs.

Let me explain it this way. ROK is sort of a pun. You don't expect Sergeant Kim to have much of a sense of humor, but he does. ROK is Republic of Killers. That's what you have to be to be a member. You have to have killed somebody. Preferably hand-to-hand.

It's not as intense as it sounds. Though it's intense enough. Killing someone in the war, that counts. That's where most of us did it. In combat. It's a club of killers, not of murderers.

This, of course, is what Kim is telling me when he puts me on the mat with Hawk. Here are people outside the loop of U.Sec. and RepCo who will do anything. It is from ROK that I can recruit backup. I have been expecting this time to come and I have, in fact, picked out some guys who I think will be good and will help. There is Hawk, who I have told you about. Hank Dressler is an accountant and ex-Green Beret, working on a divorce, so he is full of rage and a need to commit justice and if he can't, injustice will do. Dennis O'Leary, a one-eyed gaffer who gets less work than he should because he once argued about a pair of seats at a screening that had been held for guests of David Geffen. Bruno, the plumber, and Jorge, the grocer. Depending on what happens, maybe more. Plus, there is Steve and his son. Also, if we end up going up against Sakuro Juzo and his Ninja, I think Kim will come out. Behind the money making and the drinking and the grousing is the best soldier that I have ever known. Including the best of the VC and the NVA.

Steve and his son travel with us. Hawk and O'Leary, who just got off a nonunion picture, travel separately and meet us at Maggie's house in Napa. Not far from John Lincoln Beagle's vineyard, where, as all Hollywood knows, he is attempting a reconciliation with Jacqueline Conroy in the hopes of being able to live a family life and keep his son.

Maggie has acres and acres. The vines, staked out in rows, travel in lines over the hills and follow the contours. It makes me realize a whole other level of her wealth and the wealth of the world that I have entered into. The master bedroom, which is on the second floor, has a large window. There's a fat white moon that shines into our room. In the middle of the night I say to her, "Do you have a father or a brother around somewhere?"

"Why's that?"

"Doing what we're doing, the way we're doing it, you're going to get fat and round one day soon. Then someone, like a father or brother, they're supposed to come around with a shotgun, make me marry you."

"That's the only way you'd marry me?"

"It wouldn't look like I was marrying you for your money."

"Umm, that's nice," she says. She holds me tight.

Later I unwrap her arms from around me and slip out of bed. I go downstairs to the other end of the house, where the guest rooms are. Hawk and O'Leary are waiting for me. They're dressed in camouflage khaki and brown. We darken our faces and go out.

CHAPTER

* * *

FIFTY

Two men sat in a van on the side of the road. One poured a cup of coffee from a thermos, then unwrapped a ham sandwich covered in Saran Wrap. It had Grey Poupon mustard on it because his wife believed the things she saw on television. The other man got out of the car to take a leak in the bushes.

They were out of the Sacramento office of Universal Security. It was too bad that someone had found every single LD in Magdalena Lazlo's house, ripped them out or neutralized them. They hadn't a clue what was going on inside. They made rude speculations what with her being in there with white and black men, but they didn't believe what they suggested, they were just passing the time. They were on the midnight-to-eight shift; time moved slow.

They could see the driveway and both directions along the road that led to it. Nobody was going to go in or out that way without being seen. They had night viewing devices. But they didn't need them. The moon was fat and bright.

A man and a woman sat in a car on the side of the road. Both of their spouses were certain they were having an affair. Whenever she went on surveillance with a guy, any guy, the wife was always certain they were doing it. They weren't.

They had John Lincoln Beagle's house in view. They had night viewing devices but didn't need them. It was the kind of moon that was so bright that it threw shadows and even let you see what color things were.

A third vehicle cruised restlessly the nine miles between the two. Partly to check on the others. Partly because Mel Taylor was sure that Broz was going to make a move and he wanted to be there. He knew about Hawk and Steve Weston and Steve's son, and there was a white guy too. He didn't know the white guy's name yet. But he would. Soon. He didn't know what, exactly, they were up to, but he figured he would know that soon too. If Broz somehow did pull something, Taylor had some countermoves.

CHAPTER
⋆ ⋆ ⋆
FIFTY - ONE

The cornerstone of the White House was laid on October 13, 1792. It was completed in 1800, the first public building in the new capital of the new country. It was built to reflect the spirit of the great experiment upon which the country was embarking. The leaders of this new creation were adamant about avoiding even the trappings of monarchy and so it was definitely not to be a palace. Yet they wanted something fine and noble and expressive of their ideals.

In spite of time and weather, fire and smoke, additions and reconstructions, the moral nature and human frailties of it's occupants, the White House remans an elegant expression of the aspirations that motivated the age of revolution and rationalism.

The cab that inconspicuously carried David Hartman in from Dulles International Airport offered the passenger a series of views of the White House before it brought him to the entrance gate. He'd seen them all, as we all have, countless times, in movies and on television, on the news, in newspapers, in magazines, in cartoons and comics. Still, it had an impact. Hartman didn't know if that was a result of some aesthetic that infused the setting or it was because he was about to enter the seat of the Imperium as a player.

It was one of those days when the president had a lot of meetings.

Nothing earth-shattering or especially newsworthy. They slipped David in a little before 9 A.M. The president's appointment calendar would show *Sec. of Com. & D. Hartman.* There would be memos that the subject discussed was the importance of entertainment software as the number-two export of the nation, just after aviation. There was nothing in the memos to indicate that the commerce secretary left almost immediately and that Hartman stayed.

When he was alone with the president, Hartman explained what Saddam Hussein wanted. He wanted access to western arms and arms technology. He wanted money. Up front, even before they had a deal. Neither of those, Hartman suggested, should be a deal breaker. It wasn't a lot of money. At least not yet. A few billion dollars. And didn't have to appear in the budget.

Bush was relieved by that. The whole budget fantasy was out of hand. It was a fictoid or factoid ten times the size of a balloon in Macy's Thanksgiving Day Parade. There was nothing that anyone said about it that seemed to actually connect with reality, yet every time it went up, everyone made a lot of noise.

The money would go to Saddam as a loan. "We don't even have to make the loan," Hartman said. He'd already line up several Swiss and Italian bankers happy to do that. "We just have to guarantee it." David was going to get a couple of points from both sides. Banking was an exciting new vista. "I would suggest the Department of Agriculture," Hartman said. He was virtually quoting Pandar's screenplay. "Guarantee the loans for agricultural credits. That looks like the money goes to our farmers—which it very well might—they do have to buy butter as well as guns. It's obscure and wholesome at the same time."

Then he got to the main items. Win, lose, or draw, Saddam wanted a guarantee of his personal survival; his country intact, at least to its current borders; sufficient military force to maintain those borders as well as to suppress any attempt at a coup or any attempt at rebellion by dissident minorities. Actually, Saddam had compared his need for armed forces to keep the Kurds in line to the way America used it's armed forces to keep blacks in line. He had said it in a buddies kind of way, a remark designed to engender camaraderie, one put-upon head of state to another. It was an unfortunate correlation, but understandable, since an Iraqi would see the police, the Army, the national police, and the National Guard as single facets of one force, not as distinct entities in the way that Americans do. Nonetheless, Hartman didn't think the insight would help and didn't pass it on.

There were, finally, some smaller points. One—the worldwide price of oil should rise. It didn't have to be abrupt, but it had to be certain. Two—Saddam wanted direct access to the media—world media means American media—right through the whole war. He wanted to be able to get on TV at prime time and deliver his message to the American people, to the Arab people, to the world.

Hartman had already consulted with Beagle about the second item on a scrambled line from the U.Sec. office in Rome.

Beagle had fallen in love with the idea. "It's totally Capraesque," Beagle said. Frank Capra had been in charge of creating America's propaganda films during World War II. His sources for the footage with which he created images of the Japanese and the Germans as monsters were their own films. Both peoples had been proud of their blitzkriegs and swift conquests, their sense of racial pride and purity. They worked brilliantly, especially the Germans, to get those feelings on film. Capra was delighted by it.[115]

"Give it to him," Hartman said to the president. "The man's understanding of television is worse than Michael Dukakis's. He's from another century. Trust me. The more he uses TV, the more he'll harm himself. Beagle loves it. He visualizes seeing Saddam strut, with his stormtroopers, through the burning ruins of a conquered country."

---

[115]Capra's most significant project was the seven-part *Why We Fight* series. He discusses obtaining Axis footage in an interview in the "Propaganda" segment of Bill Moyer's *Walk Through the 20th Century*.

. . .

In the California hills Magdalena Lazlo awoke, before dawn, sky just turning light, with an empty space beside her. She reached out, knowing he wasn't there, and put her hand on the pillow where his head had rested. A sentimental gesture. It felt so good to have a man to miss.

Holding that mood close, arms held so as to literally cradle it to her breasts, she slipped into a robe and went down toward the kitchen. On the way downstairs she heard noises. She felt chilled and the feeling—holding dreams of a protector-lover against her body— left her quick as a ghost in the daylight. But then a beat, a moment, after that, she smelled the aroma of coffee brewing. And other smells. Bacon in the pan, bread in the toaster. Then the sound of a black man speaking softly and laughing.

She moved silently so that she could look and listen without being seen. She didn't know, at first, what prompted that. Then she realized she wanted to see a father with his son. She wondered about herself and touched her belly. She had used birth control, on and off, since she'd been sexually active. But not always. She did not get pregnant easily. If she did, there would have been more than one accident by now. There hadn't been. Even with her husband. Was that why it had been so easy for her to say "Yes, come inside," that she wasn't really afraid, at least not of pregnancy and it's consequences—interrupted career, stretch marks, sagging breasts and belly, widening of the hips, squaring off of the buttocks, and responsibility. And of course that companion that then clings to you for twenty or thirty years. She should have been afraid—she pushed her hair back with her fingers—it was madness not to be afraid, of the other thing. The disease. Was that a matter of sheer denial? Or was it that other streak in her, the one that meant it when she said "Let it be birth or death with us," liked it that way, because otherwise it didn't seem worth doing.

She had a name for that part of herself. The way some men have pet names for their penises and for the same reasons, because the part often led the whole and the person took pride in where the piece took them, stupid and dangerous places included. Mary Magdalene was her obvious but secret name for that side of herself, and Maggie liked to let Mary out in front of the camera, the sainted whore, saucy, wicked, vulnerable, dangerous. Dangerous to herself most of all. It was that quality, that sense of working without a net, that gave her performances magic. Not the craft, not the cheekbones, not the tits. Daring to be ugly, rude, pathetic, stupid, scared, domineering, vicious, a bitch, a cunt, an ice maiden, a saint, daring to find the line in the air that could not be sustained and sustaining it.

Martin Joseph Weston, eighteen, looked over toward the door and saw her standing there, her robe pulled tight at the waist, her hair tousled with sleep, just finger combed, and nothing on her feet, and it was all he could do not to whistle and say things that went down just fine in the street in L.A. but which he knew would just sound all wrong here in this ultrafresh other world. Then she smiled at him. It was a shy smile, like she was intruding on their house and was worried what they would think of her. And he fell in love with her, his heart truly stricken.

His father wanted to laugh out loud just looking at the look on his son's face. But he knew how dumb and tender a boy's pride is in puberty, especially in front of his father and a goddess. So Steve just said, "Morning, Miss Lazlo, how do you like your eggs?"

She said good morning to Steve and to Martin, told them to call her Maggie. She didn't want the eggs or the bacon, but if there was enough coffee, she'd take some of that and a piece of toast off of the unsliced loaf of sourdough rye. Steve poured her the coffee. She took it black, as most women whose shape is their fortune do. He put a slab of bread, beside his, in the toaster oven. Maggie sat down at the table by Martin. He already had soft-scrambled eggs, a thick hunk of Canadian bacon, and toast in front of him. But with her that close he had the unsavory feeling that he didn't quite know how to eat right and that chewing would make him look like a dog. "So this is what you looked like when you went into the Marines," Maggie said to

Steve.

"Spittin' image."

"You were a good-looking boy."

"You bet. Had all the young girls just chasing me all over Macon. It was different in them days. A girl got pregnant, you was expected to marry her. Made you cautious. A little bit. And they didn't have this AIDS thing."

"Come on, *Dad.*"

Steve slid his eggs out of the pan onto the plate next to the ham. He took the toast, Maggie's and his own, from the oven, found a plate for hers, and buttered them both. There was a fancy jar of ginger marmalade in the refrigerator that'd caught his eye. He got that, plus the two plates, utensils, and his own cup of coffee, and sat down at the table.

"You were with Joe, in Vietnam."

"Um-hmm."

"Will you tell me about it?"

"What do you want to know?"

"There's this man, Taylor. He hates Joe. Do you know why?"

"Joe didn't tell you?"

"I didn't ask him."

"Well, if he didn't tell you . . ."

"I just didn't ask. Steve"—She gave him a look that asked for help in a special kind of way—"I love Joe. Please."

In the early dawn two men from the Sacramento office of Universal Security sat in a van. One poured himself a cup of coffee from a thermos. The other climbed out to take a leak off in the brush. Nothing had happened all night long. It's hard to watch nothing. But it's easier than digging ditches.

In the early dawn Joe, Dennis, and Hawk watched the house from three different positions. Joe to the east and Dennis to the north were hidden among the rows of grapes. Hawk, to the south, was in the shadow of some apricot trees.

Dylan, who normally woke with the dawn, stood up in his crib and cried for attention. The nanny came and picked him up. From where he was, Joe could see when she turned on the light and then saw her pass, in silhouette, holding the boy, in front of the window.

They were the first ones up. Nanny got Dylan his bottle. Then she let out the dogs.

"Once Joe got to be sergeant, he could run things," Steve said. "With him running things, everythin' starts to get better. People stops dying. We stop losing guys to booby traps and all of that. And ambushes. Nobody ambushes Sergeant Joe Broz. It's like he's got one of them sixth senses or mystical powers. But he don't. He used to explain it to me. How he done it. And to Joey. Joey was his bes' friend, from where he come from. They's like this, Joe and Joey. He had a whole set of rules for ambushes: terrain, expectations of the enemy and such like. And they worked.

"What you had to do was work hard. Go the long way around, cut your way through brush and stay off'n the trail. Wear your helmet and flak jacket no matter how hot it get. Dig deep when you digs in. Camouflage. Stick some damn leaves in your helmet, and paint your face, especially white guys.[116]

---

[116]This does *not* suggest that Joe Broz is some sort of superhero. Others report exactly the same experience, including H. Norman Schwarzkopf.

In his autobiography, *It Doesn't Take a Hero*, Schwarzkopf discusses what happened when he finally got "his" battalion in Vietnam. They were in terrible shape, incapable of inflicting damage on the enemy and constantly taking casualties from vastly inferior forces. Schwarzkopf got them "in shape" by making them do what the book said they should do: patrol properly, wear helmets, dig holes, etc. He turned things around and the VC began to avoid his sector. He writes: "Our intelligence people sent us a captured enemy report that warned Vietcong units to stay away from LZ Bayonet. The report said a strong new American battalion [it

"You ever seen that movie *The Dogs of War?* Chris Walken, he's got this motto: 'Everyone goes home.' Well, we wasn't that good. But we was good. And after a while, Joe Broz, he gets to be like, like a star. Almos'. He was proud. Real proud. Takin' care of his boys, you know how it is. Make you take care of your feet, gets you clothes, make you do everything you gots to do but write home to your mama.

---

was the same force retrained by Schwarzkopf] had moved in. The enemy had paid me the greatest compliment I ever received as commander of the 1/6.''

At the time he was interviewed for the oral history *Strange Ground: Americans in Vietnam,* Walter Mack was the head of the organized-crime division of the U.S. Attorney's Office, Southern District, New York. He had been in the ROTC at Harvard, then became the commander of a rifle company in I Corps near the DMZ: "Little by little you learned how to fight the war. The test is small-unit leaders— the sergeants, corporals, lieuteneants, captains. Can they learn the lessons and train their troops so they'll survive? Because it's not the popular thing to do. Americans are lazy, unless they have somebody kicking their ass. . . . They don't like to put greasy paint all over themselves in the hot sweaty daytime. They don't like to wear flak jackets. They don't like to wear helmets. They don't like to take care of their rifles . . . , The don't like to use fire discipline, which is essential. They don't like to take care of their feet.

". . . a large percentage of the people who were wounded and killed in Vietnam were hurt because of mistakes made by small-unit leaders. . . .

"I'm talking about professionalism, the willingness to stay up that extra hour the night before the patrol to do your homework. Like taking the time when you're extremely tired to do your map study and plot out where you're likely to be ambushed. To have the discipline not to walk along a treeline, or a trail, or a road, at a time when you're likely to get ambushed. To check with your intelligence officer. . . . To check with the person responsible the next day for air operations. . . .

"After a while, the company got a reputation, and we stopped getting hit. The other companies would get hit, but we were very seldom attacked by a North Vietnamese unit. They couldn't find us in a situation where it was to their advantage, so they stayed away: And the radio traffic intelligence was that our company was singled out as one you just didn't mess with. We had so much firepower and we'd get it in so fast . . . that we seemed more efficient. . . . Morale was good, and casualties were low.

. . . *You should never be ambushed. . . . being ambushed is always the result of not thinking or being rushed.* And the experienced person recognizes that the North Vietnamese ambushed everybody that way.''

"We gets this new lieutenant. Gelb. Jew boy from Atlanta. I remembers that because I'se from Georgia myself. Anyways, he was alright. He seen that Joe's got it all in hand and the bes' thing he can do, for hisself and for all concerned, is to leave well enough alone.

"We're up in I Corps, tha's up north, near the DMZ, mountain country a lot of it, you know. These officers, they come. To this day, I don't know who these people is or why's they there. One of them, he's this Marine captain. Captain Tartabull. And this Army captain. Captain Taylor, he's there as an observer. The Marines is showing the Army how they get it done. Some bullshit like that. We don't know who this Tartabull is. Nobody never seen him before. But he's acting like he's the captain and is out in the bush commanding us all day and night and backwards and forwards. Captain, he a motherfucker.

"He done get us all fucked up.

"There's twenty-seven of us, including the three officers. We go into the LZ—the landing zone—in two CH-46's. Alright. Everything's alright. LZ is cold. We're out of the Hueys. Hit the ground running, like Joe insists his boys do, and into the tree line. Form a perimeter. One, two, three guys out on the flanks.

"The two captains, Tartabull and Taylor, stroll outa the choppers, you know, motherfuckers trying to outcool each other. Like 'Look at me, I ain't 'fraid o' no NVA.' So then this Tartabull, he say we're going into this here valley, that's right in front of us, to the next valley, to find Charlie, 'cause we're gonna get some *bodies* today. Yes, sir, we're gonna get body count, take home some ears.

"You know what's comin', right. We all sees it comin'. Joe Broz, sergeant, he says, "Scuse me, Captain. That's ambush country in there. Don' go that way.'

"Captain says, 'Tha's where we going. Those are the orders.'

" 'Sir, that's a mistake, sir. Maybe if we went over on the left . . . left flank—'

" 'Sergeant! You afraid to go in there, in the valley there?'

" 'Yes, sir. Because that's what Charlie wants us to do—they waitin' for someone dumb enough to do that.'

" 'Sergeant, you are relieved.' Then he calls up the lieutenant. ''Lead your men, Lieutenant.' LT takes the captain aside, speak to him personal, but everyone can tell he's trying to say something about Joe and his experience and shit. Tartabull is all fired up and pissed off, because they's questioning his judgment in front of this Army captain. Just 'cause he's wrong and he's gonna get us killed, tha's not gonna stop him.''

Joe had expected dogs. You always did in the country. He had laid down scents that were supposed to lead the mutts away from the men. A bitch in heat, which was the best thing for males, and fox in case the dogs were females. It was hard for the men, who couldn't smell the packaged aromas—and if they could have probably wouldn't have appreciated them the way the dogs did—to have confidence in the product. So they froze when the dogs came out.

The dogs, two beagles named Ford and Nixon, came racing out of the house, clearly enthralled by exciting new scents. They raced in a circle trying to pick out the track to follow. They didn't seem dangerous, by themselves, but discovery certainly was. The three men were armed and on the property of a very rich celebrity. They could each imagine the arrival of the local and state police, cars, bloodhounds, and helicopters, turn the whole thing into some crazed John Landis film, like *The Blues Brothers*, cop cars in record-setting numbers roaring across California to converge on the Beagle vanity vineyard. Or turning into *First Blood*, maddened pigs against demented vets, *live at five, tape at eleven.*

Suddenly, Ford and Nixon put their twitchy black noses down close to the ground. Heads low, tails high, they ran like like little madmen, following an invisible line.

It took them right between Joe and Hawk and far from both of them.

Both scents, fox and bitch, led to a bunch of bones, meat still on them, which would keep the dogs busy once they got tired chasing smells that went nowhere. There was a little bit of sedative in the meat, the sort that they give dogs to make them sleep in their portable kennels during airplane flights.

Joe waited for the rest of the household to wake up.

Taylor checked in with the couple watching Beagle's house from their vantage point on the road. He asked them if they'd seen anything. They said no.

"Sure it was an ambush. We done lost five guys in the first minute, less'n a minute.

"They's dug in. We's pinned down. They in bunkers, with machine guns and mortars, they got the bunkers camouflaged. A B-52 strike ain't gonna blow them suckers outta their holes. We pinned down good. They done been preparing this for long time, and every night they say this prayer, Lord, send us some Marine dumb enough to walk through the Valley of Death.

"The captain—this Tartabull—is trying to call for air support. Anything, choppers, Puff the Magic Dragon, fuckin' B-52's if he can get 'em. But he cain't. Nothing available.

"The way we is, is like in a half circle. There's this steep mountainside on what was our right flank comin' in, but now tha's sort of our rear. What was our forwardly direction, that's now the right flank. We's got four guys there, Joe with Joey and two others, both brothers. I'm in the center with three other grunts and Taylor. Taylor got balls, pardon me, but no question about it. Man ain't no coward. And he's doing the best he can. The LT, he's on the left, what used to be our rear, the way out, if they is a way out. Tartabull, he's behind a fallen tree and some rocks, near the steep part. We got fifteen, sixteen guys down already.

"They's maybe fifty, sixty of them out there. If something don' happen soon, we gonna be overrun, we be dead meat.

"You never been in combat. I don't know how to tell what is like. I don'. It's loud, it's like being inside a barrel of noise, screaming and explosions and gunfire. Noise, noise, noise.

"Tartabull is screamin' into the radio and he's finally got through and they're gonna give him something. I don't know how Joe hears what Tartabull is doing. But he knows that the captain is fucking up. Captain giving the fly boys the wrong coordinates. Captain givin' them—I don't know this at the time, Joe tells me later—captain givin' the wrong coordinates. Captain calling in an air strike right on top of us.

Nanny took Dylan outside. They called for the dogs, but they didn't come. Dylan was disappointed. Nanny was more concerned with distracting the boy than figuring out where the dogs had gone.

At little while later Beagle and Jackie woke up. They waved from the window at Dylan. He held his little hand up, opening and closing it, which was his way of waving. It was adorable and his parents cooed. Then he saw a really great stone and needed to pick it up and throw it at Nanny.

Hawk had the best view of the front of the house and the road. It was Hawk that spotted the U.Sec. company car coming up the driveway. He whispered the news into the microphone that he wore on his wrist, the other two heard it on earpieces. Though it came from a different manufacturer, it was essentially the same communication system that the Secret Service uses.

"Joe crawls over to the captain. All the way over he's yelling, 'You're wrong, you're wrong.' Captain ignoring him. Yelling into the radio, same coordinates over and over. Wounded guys are screamin' what they're screamin'. Screamin' for a medic, morphine, their mamas. Screamin' and firing.

"Joe finally gets to Tartabull. Screamin' in his face. Wrong coordinates. Give me the radio. Calling him names. All that shit, everything he can think to say. Tartabull screaming back at him. Then Joe takes his M–16, he points it at the captain.

"This is weird, cause with all the screamin' and all the shit, suddenly everybody looking at Joe and the captain. Including me and Taylor, who's right next to me, practically. Joe holds the gun. Captain holds the radio. Clutching it. The LT, he's over there with them. Captain's got a .45. He points it at Joe. Somethin' comin' in over the radio. The NVA ain't stopped, they're still at it. Suddenly, Joey gets hit. Joe looks over there. Looks back, says somethin' to the captain. Captain says somethin' back.

"Joe shoots him. Once."

The man from U.Sec. stayed ten minutes or less. Joe guessed that he told Beagle that he was there to sweep the house for bugs, but that he was really there to pick up the day's tapes.

The three watchers waited patiently. Around nine o'clock Jackie and Beagle went down to the stable. It was clear that Jackie could ride well and thought that she looked good doing it. Beagle could barely stay on and just didn't have the knack of moving with the horse's movement. Rather, he moved against it, even at a walk, ensuring that his buttocks thwacked into the saddle ever other step the horse took.

They headed up toward the apricot grove. Hawk willed himself to invisibility. The horses smelled him and whinnied. They were not distracted by foxes and doggy bitches. But their riders assumed that the noises were over horsey business and yanked on the reins and rode on past.

Next to leave was the cook, for the market.

About a half hour after that Nanny put Dylan in a stroller and started walking up the road.

Unless there was someone they didn't know about, the house was now empty.

. . .

"Joe gets on the radio. He's screamin' new coordinates. Taylor screamin' at him. The LT gets hit. Stupid fuck is out from cover.

"Joe lays down smoke grenades, purple, maybe yellow too, I don't know.

"Not more than two, three minutes later, it seems like, the F-4's come screamin' out of the sky. And they're laying down napalm. It's one, two hundred yards from us. We can feel the heat. There's this wall of flame. Couple hundred yards we woulda been refried Marines. Barbecued. Turned into crispy critters.

"We use that, that's our cover, to run our asses out of there.

"Joe is carrying Joey. I catch up to him. Joey's dead. I tell him that. Then suddenly I'm hit. Joe is crying. I never seen Joe show nothin'. He's crying. I'm on my knees, somethin's wrong. It's all goin' away. Then Joe, he puts his buddy's body down and he lifts me up and he carries me on out of there.

"I don't know, firsthand, too much what happened after. But what I understand happened was this—we got ten men out. Ten of the original twenty-seven. Got the LT out. I think Joe went back for him, that's what someone tol' me. They also tol' me he weren't never gonna walk no more. Never again. Maybe tha's true. I don't know. Taylor got out."

Back at his motel, a Super 8, Taylor attached his scrambler to the telephone and waited for David Hartman to call him from the Washington office. In the waiting he thought about Vietnam, which he didn't like to do. It hadn't worked out the way it was supposed to work out, not at all.

He'd been in the top half of his class at graduation. High enough. Top of the class never meant a whole lot in the military. Top of the class turned into, more often than not, armed nerds, paper pushers, planners, think-tank types, never get higher than colonel. Also, Taylor

had lots of athletics—football, boxing, golf. Golf had been the difficult one, half the time with his hands swollen, his arms aching from
blocking punches, the other with that slightly concussed feeling when
his head hit the football field at full wallop. But there had been
generations of Taylors in the military. All officers. The live ones told
him boxing and football for respect, they'd get you an assignment.
However, no general was going to get in the ring with you, or let you
slam your shoulder into his thigh, wrap your arms around his legs and
toss him to the ground. If you wanted the sort of social association with
older men that could help you up the rungs of the ladder, you played
golf and learned to hold your liquor.

The good news was there was a war on.

It was a bit of a pussy war. Against a dip-shit little country. It
wasn't NATO against the Warsaw Pact, the barely subnuclear armored warfare—millions of men, tanks, the air filled with fighters and
bombers, across the plain of Central Europe—that military men on all
sides had dreamed of for so long. But it was a war. The military,
responsive to it's people and understanding the desire of every
ambitious officer to get combat time—far and away the most important single credit on any officer's résumé—had developed a quick
rotation scheme. Everyone was going to get a shot at combat, wear
the appropriate combat badge on their uniform and probably a
medal or two as well.

It was a bureaucratic response, the needs of the members of the
organization superseding the ostensible mission of the organization.
The organization never really considered the consequences to the
war, that they would lose it; or to the men, that more of them would
die due to always being led by inexperienced officers; or even to
itself, that being responsible for their own short term instead of for the
duration, any sensible officer would, almost every time, put the appearance of short-term success ahead of the hard news of what was
needed to ultimately win.

Taylor was well connected. His father had died in combat in
Korea. He had an uncle still active in the service, a colonel. He

instantly got posted to Saigon in a staff position. It was, for a young officer, heaven on earth, gratifying to every sense and to his sense of self-worth. He was bright, attentive, social, kept his uniform perfectly pressed, and very quickly got his captain's bars. Ambition and manliness both cried out for combat. So, at every opportunity, he pressed for combat. His superiors were not annoyed by that. Every young officer was supposed to press for combat. It was part of the shtick.

He finally got sent out to see some action. It was as an observer, but in the thick of things.

It was a weird war. Nobody had bothered to figure out what winning was. There was no bunch of guys in funny green uniforms and hard hats formed up in regiments and battalions that could be thrown back beyond the line of scrimmage. Nor were we going to march into the enemy capital, arrest the bad guys, find good guys, and teach them democracy. We weren't even going to put down insurrection. But if you have people working for you, you need to score and grade them. So they came up with body count and kill ratio. Which seemed to make some sense, since Westmoreland was operating on his theory of attrition.

Taylor's general, who had been up in I Corps, which was mostly Marine country, had run into some outfits with terrific kill ratios. Just terrific. Better than almost any Army group of similar size and makeup. There was Taylor, screaming combat, combat, combat, all the time. So his general said: "Here's some combat. Your assignment is to find out why they're doing so well." Then a nod and a wink. "If, of course, it's true."

The general's opposite number, in the Marine Corps, was hardly stupid in the ways and means of bureaucratic infighting. He put his own captain, who'd been screaming combat, combat, combat, on it. And said, "*Get him lots of bodies.*"

Guy named Tartabull. A total fuckup.

Taylor relived that day over and over and over again. It was the great *what I shoulda done.* I should have calmly stepped up to Tartabull and pointed out the error of his ways. But of course, Taylor excused himself, Tartabull wouldn't have listened. Well then, I was on the boxing team. One right cross. He goes down, out cold. I save two squads. Then I get court-martialed.

I shoulda stopped Sergeant Joe fucking Broz. Shot him between the eyes. Then told Tartabull he'd lost it and helped him through it.

"Taylor, he seen Joe kill the captain. First thing he wants to do is file charges. Killing a captain, tha's a pretty serious thing. Even in Vietnam.

"Meantime, the LT, Gelb his name was, Lieutenant Nathan Gelb, he puts in for a medal for Joe. Doesn't actually mention that Joe wasted the captain. But all 'bout how Joe called in the right coordinates, took over after the captain died and the lieutenant was wounded. Carried men out of the ambush. Went back and got Joey's body too. Now I know that he didn't do that thinkin' Joey was alive. That happens, guy is carryin' a dead man and he don't know. But I know that Joe knew Joey was dead, 'cause he put him down to pick me up. See what I'm sayin'."

There was a shit storm to end all shit storms.

Taylor put in his report. How the hell was he to know that Gelb also put in a report. Put in for a medal for Broz. Rumor had it that originally the sorry son of a bitch was so grateful to have his life saved he was going to put in for the Congressional Medal of Honor. Talk about a travesty. Put in for a Silver Star. Gelb's report didn't mention anything about Broz shooting Tartabull. Later on when Taylor had gone to the hospital to confront Gelb about it, Gelb said it didn't matter if Joe shot the captain, Tartabull would've napalmed himself to death in five minutes anyway.

Taylor should have prevailed. He had the rank, he was regular Army, he went to church on Sunday, not Saturday. But above and beyond all that was the principle: The military does not hold with shooting officers. No matter how wrong they are. This is basic to the existence and survival of armies.

But what he hadn't reckoned on was the media. Goddamn media.

His general had explained it to him. They would have to court-martial Sergeant Joe Broz, hero, who saved ten men from being napalmed by our own planes. His own lieutenant's going to wheel himself into the witness stand, in uniform, decorations on his chest, his mother, flown in from Atlanta, sitting there crying, telling the televisions all over America that Joe Broz did the right thing, sent her boy home alive to her, and the other nine boys home alive to their mothers. Including his accuser. "See, America doesn't like this war, son, and we can't afford this particular court-martial."

Taylor was certain of his own righteousness. Also, there was his name on a report that said he'd seen an enlisted man kill an officer. If that enlisted man was not prosecuted, it said something was very wrong with Mel Taylor's report. His first time in combat. So he pushed for a court-martial.

They found a place to hide Broz away. Some friend of his in the CIA wanted him. So the Marine Corps let him go. Not even a dishonorable discharge. Just signed him over or something.

Now the Army sort of wanted to hide away its share of the embarrassment, which was Mel Taylor. He never got his combat command. He never got back on the fast track. Or even the steady track. It took him a while to figure it out. No one ever confronted him or told him or even said a sad word about it. It just was. Then he knew he was never going to be a general. Then he figured out he wasn't even going to make colonel. Major was going to be his dead end.

Joe Broz, who had violated the most fundamental law of the military and of humanity and got away with it, was responsible.

The phone rang. It was Hartman in D.C.. Taylor switched the scrambler on. He reported what he knew: That everything at Beagle's house was quiet. That the tapes went on a shuttle flight from Sacramento to L.A. by ten-thirty every day and were being transcribed there. Broz had some people with him. He wasn't sure what it meant. There was no audio surveillance. But all the roads were being watched. "Plus," Taylor said, "I have an ace in the hole."

"What's that?" Hartman asked.

"Ace of spades," Taylor said.

"Tell you somethin' funny," Steve said to Maggie. "Joe, he says Taylor was right. He says you cain't have no Army with officers getting fragged. That's the end of the Army. Of course, it's up to the upper ranks to make sure that the lower-ranking officers are competent and remove the assholes. But it don't matter if they don't—man frags his commanding officer, they should fry his ass. That's what Joe says."

Steve laughed when he said that. A big knee-slapping kind of laugh.

His son grimaced. He was embarrassed around his father. The man tried hard, but he was hopelessly country. Twenty years of living in L.A. hadn't helped him at all. He should've stayed down in the cotton fields.

Another thing he hated about his father was his twenty years on the line at GM. Had a union. Big fucking deal. Because when GM shut down, that made his father a sucker, a patsy.

But at the same time, he envied his father's war. The *bloods* with M-16s! Fraggin' white fuckin' officers. Fightin' in the jungle. Now that was manhood. Come back from that no gangbanger gonna dis you, not with no M-16 in your hands and maybe some *souvenir* grenades.

People were casual in the country. A ground-floor window was left open. Joe put his gear through, then followed it.

Hawk and Dennis stayed outside, waiting, watching, ready to call Joe if anyone seemed to be coming.

Inside, Joe stood still. He waited and he listened. He took a directional mike out of his bag. He plugged it into an amplifier and from there to a headset, a high-tech, high-price version of a Walkman. With it he was able to pick up sounds down to about one-twentieth of what the human ear could hear. He swept it in an arc, listening for any human presence. He heard nothing except small scurrying feet. Mice in the wall or squirrels on the roof.

The room he was in was a reading room. Feminine, with a window seat, lots of books and magazine.

He took a CMS-3 out of the kit.

There was a microphone in the overhead light.

The reading room opened into the living room. It too was wired. That was good. It meant that Joe didn't have to put in mics, he could parasite, just find wherever U.Sec. was making its recordings and hook in ahead or behind. The question was where. Hidden well enough that no one would stumble over them by accident, but with easy access for changing the tapes and servicing. Most of the time that defined the attic or the basement.

CHAPTER

* * *

FIFTY-TWO

In the middle of making my installation the nanny comes back with Beagle's son. Hawk and then Dennis both warn me—whispers in my ear.

I decide to stay and do what I came to do. I've walked into hooches in Vietnam in the middle of the night, killed everyone inside, walked out without waking a soul.

There are five separate tape recorders. Fortunately, they're labeled. Bedroom, living room, dining room, reading room, bedroom 2. While I'm there, one of them comes on briefly. The living room. The nanny is passing through with Dylan. She tells him that it's a nice bottle and he will have a nice little nap, yes he will. She sounds like she knows what she's doing.

I tap into three of the lines. I put in broadcast units. Maggie's house is close enough to be the listening post. When I'm done, I use the directional microphone again. I can hear Dylan sucking on his bottle and the nanny murmuring to him. Then her breathing gets heavy and I thinks she's napping too.

I get out without any problem. Then the three of us make our way back. It's six miles as the crow flies, nine miles by road, about the same cutting cross-country if you don't want to be seen. We cross the road onto Maggie's land below a curve that hides us from U.Sec.'s watchers.

I send Dennis back to L.A. He has some business there. I don't need him for the moment. I keep Hawk, Steve, and Martin. I'm going to spend my time with headsets on. I won't delegate that to anyone except Maggie. I don't even tell the three guys what I'm doing or what I want. If they can guess, that's fine. If they can't, that's fine. Their job is to patrol the perimeter. To make sure Taylor's people don't get in. To protect Maggie. We have sufficient firepower for almost any nonmilitary situation. Not that I expect anything to happen. The way I figure it, it's my move.

CHAPTER

* * *

FIFTY-THREE

Listening to people, for the most part, is boring.

Surveillance is boring. Waiting in ambush is boring. It doesn't bother me. I'm good at doing nothing, having nothing happen. It makes me a good soldier, a good P.I. Whenever I do need a break, Maggie listens for me.

John Lincoln Beagle and Jacqueline Conroy seem to be making a go of it. She's acting real sweet. I say that to Maggie, that the gossip we've all heard in L.A. seems wrong. Maggie laughs at me. "She's faking it," Maggie says.

"I don't think so," I say.

"She's a terrible actress. If I ever have to play a terrible actress, I'll do what Jacqueline Conroy does."

I figure Maggie is being a little catty.

I'm certain I'm right that night when I hear them make love. Maggie wants to listen too. I hook up a second set of ears. We lay in bed and listen together. They even make love twice. Maggie is certain that she's right.

Martin is very impressed with Hawk. I can see him comparing Hawk to his father. The fancy clothes, the attitude, the whole thing. He's also very impressed with Maggie and this rich white people's world. I don't think about that shit much most of the time, but he is Steve's son and when I count on my fingers the number of people I trust in the world, I don't get much past Steve.

The next day Jackie and Linc snipe at each other a little bit.

He's playing with the kid and showing him things and he's enjoying it. In small doses with the nanny to help. I don't know about child raising. I think it's a woman's thing. They have patience and a different kind of love. I know I'm not supposed to think that, but I was raised by my father and it was shit. It wasn't even that he didn't know any better, it was that his makeup couldn't do any better, even if he wanted to do better. It just wasn't in him. The patience, or whatever it is that women have.

Linc's surprised at how well coordinated the kid is and how well he communicates, though all he says is "dis" and "wus" and howls almost to bust a microphone when he doesn't get what he wants. It's a happy surprise. You could use him in a Dad commercial. But Jackie, she uses it to nail him. That he wouldn't be surprised if he spent more time at home. If he spent more time with his only son. With his wife. This is a common song that women sing about men. Maybe she's right. I don't know how much time a man is supposed to spend at home. If Maggie gets pregnant and we have a child, are we going to sing this song?

But then they get past it and go back to sounding good together. Not like new lovers but not like they're going to get divorced tomorrow.

At dinner Linc tells Jackie that he's happy that they're trying and it's working and he thanks Jackie. "I love my son," he says. "And I loved you. We lost our way. I'm sorry. It's partly my fault, I know. We can find our way back. To loving each other. I'm starting to feel it."

"Thank you for saying that," Jackie says. "It's important to me too.

How things work out between us is very important."

There's silence for a while. I hear some small sounds. I can't figure out exactly what they're doing, then I realize they're smoking some reefer. Jackie giggles. Linc makes some smug noises. They leave the room. I pick them up again in the bedroom. Jackie urges him to take another toke. "I'm going to make this special for you. I'm going to put you in orbit." A little later she says, "No one knows you like I know you, John Lincoln, and no one can make love to you like I can." I only have audio, not video, but I think what she does is tie him up and then start to tease him and rub his body with oils. She announces that she is going to take a long time, so I ask Maggie to take over and I go downstairs and brew some fresh coffee. When it's done, I go back upstairs with cups for both of us and some brandy too. "This is very strange," Maggie says, "listening to them like people listened to us."

"Is it?"

"Yeah, we made some mistakes."

"We did?"

"We were too aware of the microphone. This is much more . . . incoherent. And boring. Those tapes we made, those are exciting. I bet there's a whole underground market for them."

"Does that bother you?"

"If they were real, maybe it would."

"It really doesn't?"

"That's what I do. I show parts of my body. I make orgasm faces and orgasm noises. That has to be included in the act. The trick is . . ."

"What?"

"I don't know. I've done different things at different times. I've always wanted to do the Jane Fonda scene. From *Klute*. Where she looks over the guy's shoulder at her watch."

"Why? Is that the truth?"

"If it were, would that confuse you?"

"Yes."

So Jackie does the kind of number on John Lincoln that you dream about getting in a good Bangkok whorehouse with the beads and the whole thing. And when he does make it, Beagle screams. A real howl. It's pretty impressive. Then there's silence for a long time. He's in outer space, floating. When he comes to, he says so, and how amazing it is.

Then he says, "What's this?"

"You have been served, John Lincoln Beagle," Jackie says. Which is what you're supposed to say when you serve papers on someone. We assume that she has just done so. It would be a comic scene if you could see it.

"Huh?"

Maggie's cracking up. She doesn't have to say, "I told you so."

"I'm divorcing you."

"What?"

"Do I have to spell it out?"

"Wha . . . Why? . . . I thought . . . Dylan . . . What . . . you just did."

"I wanted to be sure you knew what you were missing."

"Jackie—"

"Go to hell, John Lincoln—"

"What'd I do wrong?"

"What did you do wrong? What did you do wrong? Where the hell have you been for six months? Huh?"

"Working."

"On what?"

"A movie."

"What movie?"

"You know I can't tell you."

"Well then, you know I can't be married to you and you know you can't see your son."

"Can we talk about this in the morning?"

"Talk to yourself in the morning. I'll be gone. As will your son. And if you try to stop us or interfere, I will have you arrested for assault."

"Come on, come on, I'm not gonna assault you."

"Bye."

"Wait."

"What?"

"What can I do to make it right?"

"I don't know what the hell you've been working on, but is there a part in it for me?"

"Well, no, but—"

"Of course not—"

"Jackie—"

"That's OK, you don't have to put me in your mystery movie. But did you ever think of anyone but yourself? Did you ever pick up the phone to your friend Hartman and remind him that one hand washes the other. That if you want to put some other bitch in your movie, which is fine by me—you don't direct women very well, do you? That the other bitch's husband or father or whatever, might find a role for me?"

"What I've been working on—"

"So go to hell."

"If you understood—"

"Just remember, to see your son—"

"—what I'm really doing—"

"—you better be very, very nice—"

"—is reality. I'm planning a real—"

"—and very generous."

"—thing. A real thing."

"A real thing. Great," Jackie says.

"I am. A war. A real war."

"Just like a divorce."

Beagle picks up the phone and dials. "I'll prove it to you."

"Hello?"

"Kitty," Beagle says.

"Do you know what time it is?"

"I want you to remember . . ." Jackie says.

"I don't know," Beagle says. "You have to go to the office."

"Now?"

"Now," Beagle says.

"I want you to remember what you're missing."

"It's after eleven," Kitty says. "It's eleven-eleven."

"You have to go right now. In my desk . . ."

"And I want you to remember that what you're missing, the next guy is getting."

"Hold on," Beagle says. "I'm gonna prove it to you. I have a secret memo. Just wait . . . Kitty?"

"Yes?"

"Good-bye," Jackie says.

"In my desk. In my personal drawer."

"Your personal drawer . . ."

"Yes. In Correspondence. In letters from my mom."

"Letters from your mom?"

"Yes. You'll find a memo. It says 'YEO' at the top. I want you to go to the office and fax it here."

"Now?"

"Yes, now."

"Yes, sir."

She hangs up.

Beagle calls for Jackie. He goes through the house calling Jackie. I keep switching channels. I lose him, then find him.

Finally, he comes back to the bedroom. He dials the phone again.

"Hello?" It's Kitty.

"She's gone."

"Who?"

"Jackie."

"Oh."

"She had the car packed. Ineke and Dylan were in the car already. I guess. And they left."

"Ineke?"

"The nanny."

"Oh."

"So don't bother about the fax."

"I won't."

CHAPTER

★ ★ ★

FIFTY-FOUR

Katherine Przyszewski started to scream when the man with the rubber mask over his face pointed the gun at her. But then he said, "Please don't scream. We really don't want to hurt you." The voice belonged, definitely, to a white man, and that relaxed her. "It's just a movie," he said, and he seemed to smile inside his Ronald Reagan mask. Then she noticed that he was nicely dressed—clean jacket, neatly pressed pants, and very clean. Even his fingernails were clean.

There were three of them. Two of the novelty-store masks were presidents. The third was Dan Quayle.

The clock on her desk said 11:11 A.M.

"Show me Beagle's desk," he said. "Please."

She felt terribly disloyal doing it, but he had the gun and she had her children to support, so she did. One of the others came with them. He opened the drawers and found the correspondence file. He went to "M" and found "Mother." Kitty noticed that he had gloves on. He took out a single piece of paper and gave it to the man with nice fingernails.

"Thank you," he said.

They took her back to her office.

"No one's gotten hurt," the one with the nice nails said. "Think of it like a video for *Bloopers and Practical Jokes*. You can call the police if you want. But don't scream. That would create a problem."

"All right," she said.

She called the police when they left. But as she reported the crime, it seemed like there wasn't much of a crime to report. A piece of paper from a file marked "Mother." A detective came anyway because it was CinéMutt and the police were always excited to do anything that brought them in contact with the entertainment industry. He was an older man, in his fifties, and seemed very kind. She said the file might be important because Beagle had called her the night before and asked about it.

There was something simpatico between them. Either because he found her attractive or because he understood that she'd been traumatized, he asked her if she wanted to go out for a nice bowl of soup or something. It was lunchtime and she didn't have company for lunch so she said yes. It was a modest place. Suitable for a police officer on the city payroll. There was something wise and very tolerant in his eyes, so she decided to share something with him that had been bothering her. "Every time I look at the clock, every time something happens . . . I know it's silly. I mean, what would it mean, but what happens is that it's always eleven–eleven. One, one, one, one. It's like it's telling me something."

"It is," the detective said.

"It is?"

"But are you ready to listen?"

"Sure. I guess."

"It's going to sound strange," he said.

"That's alright."

"There were aliens . . ."

"Aliens?"

"Yes. They built the pyramids. And those strange shapes that you can only see from the sky in Peru. There's a lot of evidence."

"Yes. I saw that. On television."

"There's a lot of evidence. Things that just can't be explained away."

"That's what they said."

"I could give you books to read. If you want. *Chariots of the Gods?, We Are Not the First.*"

"If you just gave me the names, I could even get them myself. Through the office. We get a lot of material. Books, videos, for research."

"Some of them were left behind, some of the aliens, when the others departed. And they had children."

"Do you really believe that?"

"Yes. Yes I do," the police officer said.

"What . . . what happened to them?"

"In order to survive they had to mingle themselves with humans and eventually they lost most, almost all, the knowledge of the stars. But still they were different. Are different. There had to be some subtle way to make the children known to each other. And even to themselves."

"And the sign is?"

"The sign is eleven-eleven."

"You too? It happens to you too?"

"Eleven-eleven," the detective said.

Kitty told herself it was L.A. weirdness, New Age nonsense. Come on, *aliens?* She was a sensible person. Practical by nature. Yet the idea filled a void. It made her feel special. It explained so many things about why she was better than most people. The detective told her they had a group, a whole organization with their own place, like a church, but not a church. He gave her his card and said she could call and he would take her to the next gathering. She liked that, the sound of it, *gathering.*

Happy, she called Beagle and told him what had happened, the robbery, not about eleven-eleven. She couldn't believe how upset he was. Even after she told him that the robber had said to think of it like *Bloopers and Practical Jokes.*

. . .

A less arrogant man than Beagle might have tried to hide the fact that he had kept a copy of the memo, which he was not supposed to have done, and that it had been stolen, and would hope that the storm would never come. But to be a great director—possibly to be a major feature-film director of any sort—you need the ability to make big mistakes, mistakes worth a couple of hundred thousand dollars, a million or two, or even blow the whole forty million, and be able to say, "Yeah, so? What's next?"

Beagle immediately called Hartman.

Hartman didn't waste time getting angry at Beagle. John Lincoln was his director and he was going to need him. Hartman called Sheehan. Sheehan, who was much smoother than Taylor, said with great aplomb: "That's good news, sir. Now we've uncovered a weak spot and exposed an enemy. The operation is not concluded, but it appears to be functioning successfully."

"You knew this was happening?"

"We are very good at our job, sir," Sheehan said, shucking and jiving for all he was worth, which was quite a bit, actually. "Even Mel Taylor, though he could use more polish with clients."

CHAPTER

* * *

FIFTY - FIVE

I don't have precognition. I did not know what I would learn listening to Beagle. But it seemed reasonable that it might take me back to L.A. Once I was certain that Taylor was recording and I was listening live, I figured that would give me a twelve to twenty-four-hour jump on him. Especially if I could get past his watchers. Sun Tzu said: *Rapidity is the essence of war: take advantage of the enemy's unreadiness, make your way by unexpected routes, and attack unguarded spots.*

I leave Steve, Martin, and Hawk to guard Maggie. I go cross-country by mountain bike, across Maggie's property, across the neighbor's property, and then out on the county road that runs more or less parallel to the one that goes to our driveway. That way I evade the two guys in the van watching our driveway and I don't have to worry about the car cruising between them and the watchers near Beagle's property.

Once I'm out on the road, I have a ten-mile ride to a small local airstrip. There's a pay phone there. I call Dennis from the airport and give him my ETA, and he calls the other two, Hank Dressler and Kim Tae Woo, a cousin of Sergeant Kim. Dennis meets me at the airport. He has the masks and jackets for us to wear.

By 11:10 A.M. we're at CinéMutt. Woo walks up to the guard

and speaks to him in Korean. The guard is confused. Then Dressler marches in and starts talking to the guard. The guard tells Woo to wait and turns to Hank. Hank asks him where Kitty's office is. The guard tells him. Woo steps behind the guard, puts a hand on each side of the guard's neck and presses until the guard passes out. It is done very deftly. They slide the guard under his desk. Woo puts on the guard's hat and sits in his place. Dennis and I enter. All of us, except Woo, put on masks. We go into Kitty's office. It goes perfectly. It's all over by 11:20.

By noon we're at the airport. I'm certain that I've pulled it off before Taylor has a chance to react. But he will react. So I take them with me. With the three guys I already have, that will be seven of us against whoever Taylor cares to send—Otis and Perkins or Hartman's Ninjas. I think it will be enough.

By 4:30 we're five hundred miles away. Back in Napa. No need to hide our return. We go back to the house by cab. When we get inside, I find Steve lying on the kitchen floor. He's face down. There's blood on the floor and what looks like a bullet hole in his back. Martin and Hawk are gone. Maggie's gone.

CHAPTER

★ ★ ★

FIFTY-SIX

Steve is dead. When Martin comes back, he drops his bags of groceries. They split and spill. Dennis picks them up. Greens and smoked pork and yam and ribs and a bunch of other stuff. Steve was going to cook some soul food for everybody. Sent Martin away to do the shopping. Martin was embarrassed about that. When Steve talked about black-eyed peas and corn bread, Hawk talked about California wines versus the French, nouvelle cuisine and the better chefs on the Left Coast. He doesn't want to believe Hawk did it. He wants to believe one of us, the whites or the Korean, did it. But with Maggie gone, it sorts itself out.

"I'm gonna kill him," the boy says.

"Alright," I say.

"You know what he said?"

"Hawk?"

"No. My father. Is he really dead?"

"Yes. About half an hour, I think."

"You an expert?"

"Not a doctor . . . but yeah, I guess."

"That's what they call the entry wound?"

"Yeah. In the back. If we roll him over, the exit wound, it'll be bigger."

"Did I tell you what he said?"

"No."

"Never trust a nigger calls hisself Hawk and dresses like a pimp."

The phone rings. I pick it up. It's a woman. She asks for Maggie. When I say Maggie's not here, she asks if I'm Joe Broz. I say yes. She identifies herself as Barbra Streisand's secretary and wants to know if Maggie got her screening copy of *The Prince of Tides*. "It's under consideration for an Oscar in several categories," she says. "In a way, a vote for it is a vote for women in the industry. I know that's important to Maggie." I agree with her that it is, tell her we've received our copy; and hang up.

"Are you gonna help me?" Martin says.

"What?"

"Waste the motherfucker. Are you gonna help me or not? He was your friend, wasn't he? Or doesn't that matter with you people?"

"You really want him?"

"Fuckin' A."

"Can you do it? When the time comes; will you be able to do it?"

"You try me. I'm gonna waste the motherfucker, motherfucker gon' die."

The phone rings.

I grab the kid. "Listen to me, Martin. You answer it. I'm not here."

"What?"

The phone rings.

"Listen and listen good. I'm not here. If it's a man named Taylor, I never came back. You don't know where I am. You can ask him where Hawk is. Tell him you're gonna kill Hawk—"

The phone rings.

"—if you want. Find out where he is. If you can. Get it?"

He nods and picks up the phone. I go in the other room and get the extension. By the time I get it, I hear Taylor saying, "I know he's there. You tell him my people watched him come back."

"Fuck you. I want Hawk. You tell me where he's at."

"Put Broz on."

"I told you, asshole, he's not here."

"You tell him to get on now or Maggie Lazlo goes to Bo Perkins and Chaz Otis and they have a party from which she'll never recover."

Of course, I want to get on and tell him I'll kill him if he does that. But there's no point. He knows that. The point is he can't play his cards until I sit down at the table. Since he has a winning hand, the only hand, I don't want to sit. Sure, he's going to offer a trade, the memo for Maggie. And we'll all walk away and go home happy.

It makes Martin pause. He doesn't need to know who Bo and Chaz are to understand. He's got a crush on her and he's tempted to respond to the threat. But he's smart in spite of himself and just says, "I would if I could, but I can't. Man's not here."

"Who the fuck drove up, then?"

"Some other guys."

"What other guys?"

"I don't know. One of 'em's named Dennis. Don't know the other two."

"Where is Broz?"

"Who are you?"

"Tell Broz he's got one hour to call me."

"Where?"

Taylor gives Martin a number. Martin writes it down. "What if I don't see or hear from him?"

"One hour or she's dead meat. Like that bitch in Hué. Dao Thi Thai. Except we'll play with her first."

"You best think about that, man," Martin says. "What if I don't talk to him in a hour. And then you kill her. Then what you got to play with, dude? Then you got Joe Broz coming to kill you as well me coming to kill Hawk. You some kind of stupid, man."

"Shut up, boy. Don't you call me stupid, boy. As for you coming after Hawk, boy, go ahead and try. You just do what I tell you."

"I don't do what the fuck people tell me. Where the fuck you living, man, you think people do what the fuck you tell them. You tell Hawk, Martin Joseph Weston comin', comin' for him. And he's gonna die."

"Goddamn you, kid, put Broz on."

"You stupid or deaf? He ain't here."

Taylor slams down the phone.

I check the phone number. I recognize it. He's at John Lincoln Beagle's house.

"I need you to do what I say, Martin. If you do it my way, you'll get him. If you rush, if you go at him too soon, he'll get you."

"I'm gonna take care of business. I don't need you to—"

"You got a gun? Money? Backup? A plan? What are you gonna do with your father? You call the police, then you have to tell them who was here, where you were, and all of that. Then if you go after Hawk, they know its you. You need us, we need you. I need you to save Maggie. I need you to go up against Hawk, when the time comes."

"Alright," he says.

We have five 9-mm handguns, a rifle, and a shotgun. "Hawk, I want you to go buy another rifle. Something suitable for sniping. Scope to go with it. High-power, night scope if you can get it local. Get another shotgun. Pump action, something we can cut down. If you can get a spray gun, Mac-10, Uzi, anything like that, get it. Get four sets of body armor. Dennis, you've been to Beagle's, you're in charge of that. I want you to scout it. Take Kim and Martin. See if you can figure out how many men Taylor's got, their positions, how they're armed. See if you can figure out where they're keeping Maggie. Martin, don't do anything yet. Except gather information. You treat this like you're in the Marines and Dennis is your NCO. Taylor only wants one thing, for us to go in. It's an ambush."

The phone rings.

I point to Martin. He goes to the phone. I go to the extension and put it where we can see each other. On my signal we pick up the phone together. He says, "Hello."

"Put him on, boy," Taylor says.

"I told you, he isn't here," Martin says.

"Too bad," Taylor says. "Since he's not here, he'll miss hearing this." There is a pause. Then Maggie screams.

I gesture to Martin to hang up. He looks at me. I gesture again. *Hang up.* He does and I do simultaneously. He looks at me like I'm something different than he is. He says, "You're an ice cube. There's something dead in you."

Maybe he's right. Maybe I've just been here before. Steve would understand. I say, "We have to keep your father for twenty-four, forty-eight hours. Can you handle that, Martin?"

"He's dead," Martin says, being strong. "It won't make that much difference to him."

"No."

The phone rings again. I just want to let it ring. Or cut it off. But that will tell Taylor that I'm here and that I can't take it. Then he can say that he's cutting off her finger or her breast or taking out her eye and I better come quick. Whatever it takes to make me think that I have to try. Then we both die.

I gesture to Martin again. He shakes his head no.

So I say, "I thought you had balls?"

We pick up the phones simultaneously. Martin says, "Hello." This time it's a woman's voice. She whispers, "Is Joe there? Joe Broz?"

Martin says, "No."

She says, "Oh, God," like she's going to hang up.

"Wait," I say into the phone. "Bambi Ann?"

"Joe?"

"Yeah."

"Don't go, Joe. They're going to kill you. And kill her. I don't know what you've done and I don't care."

"Where are you?"

"At a pay phone away from the office."

"OK. I don't want you to get in trouble."

"Don't let them hurt her, Joe."

"I'm trying, Bambi Ann."

"You know what she did for me, don't you?"

"Yes."

"She had John Travolta call me. Me, personally. To advise me about Scientology."

"How do you know they're going to kill her?"

"I listen. I always have. I control the intercom. It makes me seem very efficient. Like Radar O'Reilly in M.A.S.H."

"Oh."

"Really. It does. I show up with things before they ask. They think I'm wonderful."

"And you are."

"But not how they think."

"Better."

"You really think so?"

"Sure. You're beating them at their own game."

"I hadn't thought of that."

"Tell me what you know," I say to bring her back.

"I've never gone against the company."

"I know. You're a loyal person."

"I am."

"And it's good."

"I'm doing this for her. For Maggie."

"I understand."

"Taylor's going to kill . . . kill both of you. I think. He and that Mr. Hartman person, they argued over it. It's the memo. You shouldn't have taken the memo, Joe."

"She wanted me to. Maggie. I did it for Maggie."

"Oh."

"Go on."

"That's all I know."

"Where did they argue over it?"

"On the phone. With Mr. Sheehan.

"Conference call?"

"Yes."

"Scrambled?"

"I operate the scrambler."

"Where was Hartman?"

"He was in his office, I think."

"He going to stay there? Or does he want to be in at the kill?"

"In on it. He insists."

"OK. Will you help me some more?"

"If I can."

"To save Maggie's life."

"Yes."

"If I need you, I'll call you at the office and say this is your uncle . . . you have a real uncle?"

"Arnold."

"Uncle Arnold. You'll be to busy to talk and you'll call me back. OK?"

"OK."

"Can I call you at home?"

"Yes."

"Thanks."

"There is something else," Bambi Ann says. "Mr. Bunker called about . . . about it."

"What did he want?"

"He said to be sure to get a copy of the memo."

"To who?"

"To Mr. Sheehan to tell Mr. Taylor. Oh, yes, Mr. Hartman that's why he wants to be there. To be sure he gets the memo."

"Do they know—Taylor, Sheehan, Bunker—do they know what's in the memo?"

"It doesn't sound like it."

"Thank you, Bambi Ann, thank you."

"Good luck. Save her," she says.

CHAPTER

★ ★ ★

FIFTY - SEVEN

I wait outside the dojo for Sergeant Kim to leave. It is evident now that I am not as clever as I think I am. Taylor had me under surveillance and picked up on my recruitment of Hawk. And if Hawk is working for Taylor the whole time, Taylor knows all about ROK.

Kim drives a Lincoln Towncar. I follow him. He lives twenty minutes away in a section that has become almost completely Oriental in the last ten years. He pulls into his driveway, gets out, walks to the curb, and waits for me. He invites me into his home. I've never been there before. I know that his wife is dead. A young woman, perhaps twenty, greets us at the door, in properly obsequious Confucian fashion. She and Kim speak in Korean. He does not introduce me. We go sit in the living room and she brings a bottle of reasonably good Scotch. Again, he says nothing about her, whether she is a daughter, a relative, a maid, a woman that he brought over mail-order from Korea. I tell him what has happened. She brings us cheeseburgers. They're excellent, thick and juicy, topped with sharp cheddar, sliced dill pickle on the side. "I hate kimchee," Kim says. "You like kimchee? I got some. You can have."

"This is fine," I say.

"Gourmet cheeseburgers," he says. "You want recipe?"

"No, that's alright."

"Hartman, he still have Sakuro Juzo with him?"

"Usually."

"Ahh . . . You want beer? Soda?"

"Same as you."

"Hartman the emperor. Juzo the dragon. Taylor the enemy general. Magdalena is the treasure. The memo is the Maguffin. That's what Hitchhock call it. You like thrillers? Hitchhock my favorite. Like a game."

"Sure," I say. Except that I love her.

"Sure," he says. "A game."

CHAPTER

* * *

FIFTY-EIGHT

At noon the next day a Vietnamese delivery boy brings flowers to Bambi Ann Sligo. In the flowers there is a note for Frank Sheehan.

Dear Frank,
Maggie for the memo.
Her house. 2:00 A.M.
Just Taylor and her.

Bambi Ann takes a late lunch, with permission, to see her Uncle Arnold. She doesn't like her Uncle Arnold, but she hopes to inherit something from him when he dies. I ask why she hates him. She says it's none of my business. She tells me there were several calls back and forth. Hartman is flying back to L.A. from Napa immediately. As I had hoped he would. They won't bring Maggie until later that night because they don't want to move her twice and have to find another place to keep her.

"They're very upset at you. That they don't know how to reach you."

"How is she?"

"I think she's OK."

"Good," is all I can say.

"She's a wonderful woman."

"I need one more thing from you. Did we do RepCo's security? And for Hartman at home?"

"I think so."

"Can you get me a copy?"

Dennis, Kim Tae Woo, and Martin meet me at Maggie's house at eleven-thirty that night. I bring every piece of equipment I have. They begin making preparations like they're getting ready for a siege, checking blind spots and vantage points and sight lines. I ask Mrs. Mulligan to prepare a pot of coffee and sandwiches. As soon as I am certain that she's called U.Sec. and told them how many of us there are and how we're armed, I send her away and disconnect the telephones. I wonder which side of her double game she's really on.

As soon as she's gone, Kim Tae Woo and I leave.

I figure that I have to leave two behind. Taylor will send someone to watch the house. I would. Anyone would. There has to be some activity. I leave Martin because he's the least well trained. The other has to be white to at least suggest that it's me to someone catching glimpses through a window.

The paper said overcast. It was right—the cloud cover is good, the night is dark, and we move quickly and easily down the beach. We have a mile to cover. When we come out on the Pacific Coast Highway, there's a car on the side of the road. The driver is changing a tire. He's a friend of Sergeant Kim's and he's been expecting us. He finishes quickly. We leave.

The names, addresses, and phone numbers of the regular security personnel are all in the material that Bambi Ann got me. She's made it a lot easier. If not for her we would have had to try a car intercept or something else that required us to act out in the street. As it is, Hank got to the guy who works the midnight-to-eight shift before he came to work. When we get to RepCo, Hank is sitting at the guard desk, watching the video monitors, controlling the front door. He lets us in.

"Hartman still here?"

"Yes."

"Is there anyone else here?"

"Kim's already here."

I look around. Kim, dressed in black, materializes from the shadows.

"One other agent," Hank says. "I think he's on with Japan. His phone has been lit up all night. And Hartman has his bodyguards with him."

"How many?"

"Juzo and two more. I think. There's no way I can be sure."

"Stay here," I say. That's three of us against four of them. But we have surprise on our side.

We move silently down the hall to the elevator. There are several possibilities. We can go up and possibly signal that we're on our way; we can try the stairs, though it's possible they'll be coming down the elevator at the same time; or we can wait and spring our ambush right here. I signal the other two to stop. I want to listen and I want to see what I can sense. I can't see Sergeant Kim, he's done his fade-into-the-darkness number again. It's almost magical. Kim Tae Woo stands on the opposite side of the elevator doors from me, holding his 9-mm, perfectly still, perfectly quiet. I can't tell if he's breathing or not.

The elevator makes a noise. It's operating. Upstairs. I grin at Tae Woo. Things have just gotten a lot simpler. We stand on either side of the elevator and wait for David Hartman and however many Ninjas he has with him to walk into our guns. The progress of the elevator is very clear from the sound. It gets closer. It grinds to a halt. The doors start to open. I feel a gun in my back. A hand reaches around and takes my gun from me. Another one of the Ninja, black outfit and all, is behind Tae Woo. "Drop gun," he says.

The elevator door opens. "Well done," David Hartman says. Sakuro Juzo stands beside him. He's got a sword. "Taylor's an idiot. But Sakuro said you would come here. The mind of a strategist. He

says you read Sun Tzu. But that you only understand it like a westerner. I hope you brought the memo with you."

"No," I say. "I didn't."

He sighs. He and Sakuro walk out of the elevator. He's close
enough for me to breathe on him. There's a gun in my back. They walk
out of the narrow hallway where we're standing and into the main
hall. The ceilings disappear into darkness they're so high up. There is
a fire, as always, in the fireplace. There is a bucket of champagne on
ice.

"That is a five-hundred-dollar bottle of champagne," Hartman
says. "I bet Sakuro that you wouldn't show. Not that I disbelieved
him, but it would be disrespectful, I think, to have given it to him as
a reward. Or a tip. The man is a genius."

Both Sakuro and Hartman look extremely pleased with themselves.

"I want the memo. Or I promise you that . . . well, I have you and
Maggie. One of you, Sakuro tells me, will break, to save the other
further pain and degradation."

Suddenly, a voice from the darkness calls out. In a language I
don't understand but recognize as Oriental. It's Sergeant Kim. I don't
know what he's saying. But I can hear that it is full of mockery and
derision. Considering the self-mastery that is required to rise to the top
of any of the martial arts, it must be very strong to get a visible reaction
from Sakuro Juzo.

Sakuro speaks back.

Then Kim.

Then Sakuro. Then Sakuro says something to his two Ninjas and
suddenly we are all facing the fireplace. Sakuro turns to Hartman. "I
am going to have a private battle. I will win. It will not affect this."

"Sure," Hartman says.

"Clear," Sakuro says to Tae Woo and me. Since he has defeated
us, we are less than him and we should obey. We do as he says and
pull the chairs and tables back away from the fireplace. When there
is a space, we step back. Sergeant Kim comes out from wherever he's

been.

To judge from appearances, this is a match that Kim is going to lose. He looks like what he is, an old soldier who's been more interested in money than fighting for the last twenty years and who drinks more than he should. Than I realize it's worse than that. Much worse. Unless Kim has a magic trick up his sleeve, he's crazy. He's going to fight Sakuro with his hands and feet. Sakuro is going to use a sword. This is a samurai weapon of which he is one of the living masters. Forget about the mysticism and ki and all of that. Just think about pro sports. Think about getting in the ring with even the a serious middleweight contender. Think about getting on the football field against the Detroit Lions. Or maybe on the tennis court with one of the top five men. Things are going to happen with a speed and a power that are beyond you. With tricks and in combinations that you can't imagine.

They face each other. Kim laughs. Sakuro, faintly, sneers. They stand still, but they are maneuvering. I see nothing, but I know that they are battling. Suddenly, Kim springs sideways, does a cartwheel and appears on Sakuro's right. Where Sakuro has already turned, his strike evaded before it was made. Everyone is staring at them. I move slightly to see if my Ninja has lost his awareness of me.

No. He has not. And I am a fool for testing him and failing, thereby increasing his awareness and attention. The glimmer of hope dies.

Sakuro, in a movement so fast I would not have seen it except that the fire glitters on the blade and flashes a reflection across the room, strikes and slices off Kim's hand.

Time stops. Sakuro stops and looks at his handiwork. The hand that falls from the man.

Blood begins to spurt from the stump of Kim's arm. He moves forward holding his arm at face height, blinding Sakuro Juzo with spurting blood. Holding the arm high so the blood spray stays in Juzo's face, Kim drops forward and down. Then he comes up with his good hand, with a driving blow into Sakuro's unprotected neck and kills him.

I draw the gun from my ankle holster and shoot the Ninja next to me.

Hank steps into the room, gun drawn, and points it at the other Ninja.

Kim thrusts his arm into the fireplace and sears the end on a flaming log. He must be in shock because he doesn't scream.

I turn on Hartman, gun drawn.

Kim turns from the fire, walks to the bucket of champagne, takes the bottle out, tosses it to Tae Woo, then thrusts his blistered flesh into the ice. Then he turns very, very pale and slowly sinks to the ground in shock.

David Hartman falls to his knees and vomits.

"Is he dead? Dead?"

I go over to Sakuro. I check. He's dead.

Hank makes the live Ninja lie flat and spread-eagled. They're dangerous people, even defeated. I have no desire to kill him though.

"You killed Sakuro Juzo. You're crazy, crazy," Hartman said. "You just killed a twelve-, a twenty-million-dollar investment. He was . . . He was . . . He was going to be, be, be, be a money machine. Money machine. Clubs. Toys. Movies. Clothes. A clothing line. Everything. He's shooting his first picture in two weeks. Two weeks. You're crazy, Broz. Crazy."

I slap him across the face. The hysteria stops.

"He's just dead. He understands that."

Tae Woo carefully picks up his uncle's hand. He looks for a clean cloth—he sees a napkin on one of the tables—and carefully wraps it. Then he opens the champagne. He cradles his uncle's head in his lap and gives him some of the wine to help him out of shock.

"Come on, David," I say. "We're going to exchange you for Maggie. Then I'm going to give you the memo. My only copy. Then we're going to pretend this never happened. None of it. U.Sec. will help take care of the bodies. They can do that. We're going to be friends. You'll help Maggie's career. I will keep your secrets. Forever.

If you break our deal, I will survive and I will come and I will kill you. Because that's what I do. I kill.''

CONSPIRACY

★ ★ ★

The scientific method has become the criterion and the underpinning for almost all contemporary thought, even casual, not particularly educated, man-in-the-street styles of thinking. It has become so pervasive, basically, because it works. And we can see that it works. A famous psychic once said to me that thinking thoughts at her was insufficient—"If you want to be sure to get in touch with me, try the telephone."

The scientific method begins with the objective observation of phenomena. Not what ought to have happened, or we hope happened, or might have happened, but what actually did happen in so far as it is possible for us to observe and verify it. Then we develop a hypothesis to explain why and how it happened.

We can invent many explanations for a phenomenon. How then do we decide which one to use?

By the way, and it's a subtle distinction, science doesn't really say which theory is true, it determines which one to use, as if it were true, because in the context in which you are using it, it will work.

The preferred way is to set up a controlled experiment that can then be replicated. This, very frequently, cannot be done with human and historical events. But there are other standards. If there are two theories, or more, which one best accounts for all the known facts?

Which one best fits the other things we know, and can demonstrate, about the universe? And which one is the simplest?

The famous example is the question, does the sun revolve around the earth or the earth around the sun? It is possible—or was, it may not be anymore—to build a model of the universe in which the sun revolves around the earth just as it sort of appears to from where we live, that is, if we have accepted the notion that the earth is round. The problem with it, especially as we observe more and more phenomena, like the moons of Jupiter, is that it becomes very, very complicated and so cumbersome as to be unusable. And then it begins to interfere with other concepts that work for us, including gravity and inertia and so on.

It is an observable phenomenon that Hussein invaded Kuwait and conquered it. That the United States and it's allies then sent troops and arms and fought a war that drove him out of Kuwait. And so on.

But it's legitimate to regard the official story about why and how it happened as a hypothesis, an unproved theory, just as many, many people regard the official story of the assassination of John F. Kennedy as flawed. The official story—that Saddam just up and decided to annex Kuwait and we just up and decided that not to oppose him, would be creating a new Munich Pact, an appeasement whose consequences would bring worldwide disaster—leaves a whole lot of moons around Jupiter to be explained.

Here is a list of at least thirty-three anomalies. There are many, many more. Aficionados of conspiracy theories will want to follow this in detail. If, however, like myself, you fell asleep during Oliver Stone's *JFK*, you should, at the most, skim this section and simply accept that the war does not make sense as it was presented.

1. Why was no one interested in this war except George Bush? The State Department didn't ask for it. The Pentagon opposed it more than supported it. There were no hawks in congress as there were, for example, in Korea and Vietnam. Even the Arabs initially opposed it.[117]

2. Why was Iraq a friend one day and not the next?[118]

3.   Why was Bush suddenly appalled by Iraq's civil-rights offenses when he hadn't been a few months earlier and even though they were little or no worse than those of many other countries whom the U.S. either ignores or calls friends?[119]

---

[117]". . . to judge form initial soundings, there was no great alarm in Washington, and no suggestion of an attempt to roll back the Iraqi assault. . . . Bush met with Scowcroft, Cheney, Powell, Judge William Webster of the CIA, White House Chief of Staff John Sununu, and other members of the National Security Council. The prevailing attitude among the group, according to one participant, was "Hey, too bad about Kuwait, but its just a gas station and who cares whether the sign says Sinclair or Exxon?"

". . . both King Hussein and King Fahd placed the blame for the invasion squarely on the Kuwaitis who were being exceptionally stubborn and difficult in their negotiations with Iraq. . . . 'It's all Kuwait's fault,' he (King Fahd) told King Hussein the morning after the invasion. 'They would be this adamant. They've brought this about.' "

Jean Edward Smith, (*George Bush's War* Holt, 1992)

[118]How friendly were we? In March 1982, Iraq was removed from the State Department's list of terrorist countries, making it eligible for U.S. economic aid. . . . said Noel Kock, head of the Pentagon's counterterrorism unit—"The reason was to help them succeed in the war with Iran. Later that year the Department of Agriculture agreed to guarantee $300 million in credits for the purchase of American farm products. By 1990, Iraq had received about $3 billion in farm and other loans.

[The U.S.] looked the other wasy . . . when an errant Iraqi jet launched an Exocet missile into the USS Stark, killing 37 marines. . . .

When the war with Iran concluded . . . Washington continued its tilt toward Baghdad. When Saddam directed his attention to Iraq's Kurdish minority, including the infamous gas attack . . . the U.S. more or less ignored it. The Bush administration . . . reviewed America's pro-Iraqi orientation and decided that there was no reason to change. A National Security directive to that effect was issued in Oct '89. . . . On 1-17-90, President Bush signed an executive order certifying that to halt loan guarantees to Iraq by the government's Export-Import bank would not be "in the national interest of the United States." Ibid.

[119]Jean Edward Smith makes this point, as very few do: "Iraq had long and legitimate grievances against Kuwait . . . Iraq, a secular, modernizing state stood four square against Khomeini-style Islamic fundamentalism. . . . Given the choice between a modicum of social progress in Iraq and the unrepentant feudalism of Kuwait, it was a tough call."

4.   Why did the U.S. arm and finance Iraq?

5.   Why did we do it with agricultural loans financed by an obscure bank?

6.   Why did the Justice Department subsequently try to impede an investigation into those financial manipulations?

7.   Why were the Kuwaitis "encouraged to hang tough in their negotiations with Iraq. On the other hand, the Iraqis were led to believe that the United States would not intervene if Kuwait were attacked. Ambassador April Glaspie was merely parroting official policy when she told Saddam that Washington had 'no opinion of Arab-Arab conflicts, like your border disagreement with Kuwait.' "[120]

8.   Why were the really big-time potential hostages conveniently out of town the day Saddam invaded Kuwait? April Glaspie left Baghdad two days before the invasion began. The Soviet ambassador left the same day. Harold "Hooky" Walker, the British ambassador was on holiday. The chief of Israeli intelligence was in Tel Aviv.

9.   Does the story that the president modeled himself on Churchill because he read a book ring true? Is the president known to have ever read another book or to have made any other policy decision in his entire life based on literature?

10.   How come the Soviet Union got on board so fast?

11.   Financing. Who ever heard of the U.S. getting it's Allies to pay it for military costs? Our whole history is exactly the opposite.

12.   Why did Saddam take hostages and go on TV with hostages, thereby enraging the west? "Bush's best ally was Saddam Hussein himself, who seemed to possess an unerring capacity for giving ordinary Americans reasons to detest him."[110]

[120]*George Bush's War*, not to be confused with *Mr. Bush's War*. The former is pretty balanced and more "factual" in the traditional sense. The latter is a polemic that sees the war as a kind of fraudulent political ploy and Bush as the heir to Reagan in a tradition of the corruption of truth.

[110]Most of these items can be found from a variety of sources. For convenience, mine and yours, all the direct quotations in this numbered section, unless otherwise noted, come from *Triumph Without Victory: The Unreported History of the Persian Gulf*

13.   Saddam threatened to use the hostages as human shields. This might well have been an effective tactic. Would Bush have given the order to kill Americans in order to destroy the military installations behind them? Would our pilots have been willing to carry out those orders? Saddam seemed almost to have gone out of his way to incur the onus of suggesting it, and then gave up the very real benefits of actually doing it. Why?

14.   Why did Saddam then release the hostages prior to hostilities even though the West had made it quite clear the release of the hostages was not going to stop the war?

15.   The Army did not especially like General Schwarzkopf. He was given Central Command probably because it "was considered a backwater [that] had no troops attached to it . . . it was widely known that Schwarzkopf would take his retirement at the earliest possible opportunity." Leading a war is the plum of plums—look what it did for Andrew Jackson, Ulysses S. Grant, and Dwight David Eisenhower. Who selected the less-than-loved Norman to lead it? Was he merely in the right place at the right time? Or was it, as was subsequently proved, a brilliant piece of casting?

16.   Why did the majority of Arab leaders, prior to the Gulf War— according to Gen. Schwarzkopf and others—say we did not have to worry about Iraq, they would never attack a fellow Arab?

17.   Why is that Central Command, which had never had plans for an Iraqi threat, suddenly started to plan for one just months before it happened?

18.   Why did Saddam take all of Kuwait. He could have taken just the Rumaila oil field, which would have solved his financial problems and occupied just enough of Kuwait to give him direct access to the Gulf, satisfying his other primary complaint? He "probably could have kept his ill-gotten gains at little cost except some short-lived international criticism."

War (1992) by the staff of *U.S. News & World Report.*

19.   Why did Saddam stop after he took Kuwait?

20.   Why did Saddam wait when American forces arrived and were most vulnerable?

21.   The original deployment of U.S. forces in the Gulf was egregiously represented as necessary to defend Saudi Arabia from Iraqi attack. But the Saudis were not convinced they were threatened by Saddam, and despite the elaborate spin control engineered by Washington, there is no evidence that they were.[122]

22.   Why did Saddam appear to dig in, but *actually* send his elite troops, the Republican Guard, to safety, and why did he do the same with the bulk of his air force?

23.   Why were the Iraqi frontline troops "almost without exception . . . poorly trained and poorly led, made up of the least educated men from the countryside and the cities. Many . . . created for the war . . . about 70 percent of Saddam's front line forces were Shiites, 20 percent Kurds . . . Saddam Hussein's 'throwaway divisions.' "

24.   Why did we stop when we could have driven into Baghdad?

25.   Why didn't the Kurds receive any support from the Allies. In August, Kurdish leader Jalal Talabani came to Washington. Although it's obvious on the face of it that a Kurdish revolt would have weakened Iraq and drawn troops away from the Gulf, no one wanted to

---

[122]*George Bush's War.* Obviously, there are people who would disagree. But it is certainly a fact that Americans went to the Saudis with aerial photographs and said, in effect, "Here, look, he's poised to invade you next." Then King Fahd said, in effect, "Oh my, you better come protect us." Aerial photographs are not home snapshots at which anyone can point and say, "Hey, that's your mom!" They are, to the contrary, rather hieroglyphic and require a trained expert to interpret them. So what they show is pretty much what the trained expert says they show. "The problem . . . was that there was no hard evidence that Saudi Arabia was threatened by Saddam. To the contrary, the Iraqi Revolutionary Command Council had just announced its impending withdrawal from Kuwait. But the defense team showed the Prince elaborate satellite photography of Iraqi armor deployed near the neutral zone that separated Kuwait and S.A. . . . it's not clear where else the Iraqi tanks should have gone. There was no need for them in Kuwait City, and Saddam's generals, just as President Eisenhower had done with the marines in Lebanon in 1958, ordered them into the countryside."

talk to him. " 'We were concerned about the violations of the Kurds' human rights,' a senior Bush advisor explained later. 'But we did not want to get involved in anything like the creation of a new Kurdish nation.' "

26.   Why did Schwarzkopf give Saddam permission to use helicopters, giving him exactly enough force to suppress both Shiite and Kurdish rebellions.

27.   Why even attempt to name Robert Gates head of the CIA when (1) it had been necessary to withdraw his name once before (2) there was practically a revolt by CIA analysts over his appointment, an unprecedented internal rejection (3) he has a track record of unbelievably incorrect projections, and misanalyzing almost every single important contemporary political event? Unless it's to reward him for something that we don't know about.

28.   Why was the press handled so very well here although it hadn't been in Grenada, Panama, and Vietnam?[123]

---

[123]There were a lot of complaints from the press about how the press was handled. But that's the point of view of apparently a minority of the press, and they seem rather whiny and moot and after the fact.

In fact, the media reported the war almost exactly as the government and military wanted it reported and made the government and the military look more than good, look terrific, doing it. It was a masterly presentation and not a true dissenting voice was heard. Including Saddam, who was not a dissenter but a fine and perfect goad.

The most prominent progovernment press distortion—as a film director from World War II or this one might have planned it—was the illusion that all our bombs were smart bombs that surgically destroyed only cancer cells. The media also helped set up the war: ". . . the administration began a concerted press campaign. . . . Both the New York Times and the Washington Post carried front-page stories on Sat. 8-4, that Iraqi forces were massing at the frontier, ready to invade. . . . Both had been leaked by the administration. They were designed to help make the case for American involvement. . . . The news had been deliberately doctored, despite the fact that at no time did either the CIA or the DIA believe it probable that Iraq would invade S.A. The president had decided to intervene, the government's elaborate public-relations machinery was preparing the way." *George Bush's War.*

"The news media did much to befog the atmosphere still further, defining the

29. "The size of the Iraqi army in the Kuwait Theater of Operations was probably much smaller than claimed by the Pentagon. On the eve of the war, Iraq may have had as few as 300,000 soldiers there—less than half of the 623,000 claimed by General Schwarz-kopf, or the 540,000 estimated by the Pentagon."

30. "Iraqi casualties were probably far lower than the 100,000 calculated by the Defense Intelligence Agency. In fact, the number of Iraqi soldiers killed in action may have been as small as 8,000."

31. The Pentagon had a war game on computer that played out an Iraqi invasion. "Its code name was Internal Look. . . . Iraqi forces were labeled 'red' and American forces were 'blue.' . . . Saddam's Republican Guard division . . . were acting just like the red force in the Internal Look computer exercise. . . . 'It was something like Twilight Zone,' said Major John Feeley. . . . 'I would brief the computer game,' Feeley said, 'and then I would turn right around and brief the real situation as it was developing. Sometimes I would get them mixed up. I had to keep thinking, Okay, the computer did that; no, *this* is the real thing over here!' "

32. The Pentagon, Powell, Scowcroft, Gates, and John Sununu opposed the United Nations role and felt it would hamper the president. Bush and Baker were for it. Baker has managed to garner most of the credit for it as he always does when anything near him works or almost works.

33. What happened to Saddam's threats to unleash terrorists on the West?

34. What happened to Saddam's threats to use biological and chemical warfare, and wasn't handing out all those gas masks great,

---

issues either as the White House framed them for the press or as they imagined them. The breathless commentator . . . spoke in an idiom that reflected a mind-set shaped wholly by the events of America's Vietnam experience and not of something so insignificant as Thatcher's Falklands war. Reflecting constantly on Lyndon Johnson when they would have done better to dwell on Ronald Reagan and his loyal disciple, George Bush, they missed the only story worth telling." *Mr. Bush's War.*

great video?

35.   What was that whole business with the Scuds and the Patriots? They both had terrific political impact and very little military impact.

36.   Why was Saddam given virtual carte blanche to suppress the Shiite and Kurdish revolts Bush had invited and inspired?

37.   The biggie. How come, if Saddam is another Hitler, we let him stay in power? Even over those people who are willing to die to get rid of him?

There are a few other items worth noting that don't quite fit into the format above or may not seem relevant in the alternate version of the story as told here.

First, there are the deals. In order to bring the world into line, the United States cut a lot of deals. This is not to suggest that they are wrong, but to remark on the style of them, which is frankly more that of motion-picture packager than of a conservative Republican president. Egypt got $7.1 billion in forgiven military debts. Colombia, chief target of the war on drugs, was quietly allowed to renounce its treaty agreements to extradite major drug traffickers to the U.S., the only effective tactic in that war and the only thing that Colombia had ever done that was serious enough to annoy a major member of one of the cocaine cartels. Malaysia, a member of the U.N. Security Council at the time, got a break on textile import quotas. Syria got taken off the State Department terrorist list and received billions in aid from Saudi Arabia. Turkey, which may have climbed on board primarily to be one of the European gang, something they desperately desire, despite a Third World economy, managed to get a little much-need cash out of the deal. They received long-sought permission to resell American F-16 fighters to Egypt for millions of dollars.

Second, there is the whole motion-picture, television-miniseries flavor to the war. As if we *got it* that some TV or film director was doing a quickie-cheapie sequel to World War II, *WWII-2-V*, even if we didn't actually *know it*. A perfect example is Stephen R. Graubard's book *Mr. Bush's War: Adventures in the Politics of Illusion*.

All the major American players in the nation's capital . . . had their war television debuts on the very first night of the fighting. General Colin Powell . . . at his own news conference . . . the mood was one of controlled elation; it was D-Day all over again, without the casualties and nothing like the disgraceful war conducted in Vietnam . . .

The political genius of the President lay in his insistence that it was going to be hard, exceedingly dangerous, but that he would persevere and win in the end. The truth was that it would all be relatively easy, and had to be, given the differences between the military equipment and the potential of the two adversaries.[124]

The unique achievement of the gulf war was . . . the enlistment of mass public support through the expert manipulation of one twentieth-century communications medium, television. The war began with aerial photographs of the bombing of Baghdad; it ended with a black American soldier reassuring an Iraqi prisoner of war that he was safe; all was well. *The war was a tale manufactured for television from beginning to end.*

Dunnigan and Bay in *From Shield to Storm* get a sense of it too: "From a purely television-*image* point of view, Saddam offered the hawks a perfect target." "Operation Desert Storm was also dazzling *international television.* . . . heady and enhanced by instantaneous local coverage of the attacks on Baghdad. . . . the first true 'videowar.' "

All of these things make sense if we believe the other story:

That Lee Atwater wrote a memo. He would have hardly been the only one to reflect on Maggie Thatcher's fortunes after the war in the

---

[124]This is a bit of a cheap shot. I have the feeling that if Mr. Graubard was writing about Vietnam he would castigate the Americans for their arrogance, for assuming "that it would all be relatively easy." That's how Mike Tyson lost the heavyweight crown to Buster Douglas. While I do believe that there was a great deal of "pre-game hype," that it was an uneven match, even that the fix was in, there's a level on which that doesn't matter to the guys on the ground, to the linebacker who loses his knee to an inferior team, to the champ in the ring against some Palooka.

Falklands and what they meant. On a certain level this book could be dedicated to Dan Quayle, who said on camera, "I reminded Mrs. Thatcher that there was another time she was very low in the polls, but she bounced back. And I asked her, do you have any advice for me. Turned out she did. Now I just got to figure out a way that I can invade the Falkland Islands." It is also a fact that they tried to replicate her success—Grenada, Panama—and failed.

That the fix was in. That Saddam's threats were carefully orchestrated—by a western media intelligence—to get and keep the West "fightin' mad," but were never carried out to the degree that would create the kind of hysteria that would force the western powers to remove him from government, incarcerate or even execute him.

The thing that really stands out and screams Hollywood is the financing of the war. This is exactly how movies are always financed. No war has ever been financed that way. Certainly, no American war. In fact, in the twentieth century we've financed all our wars exactly the opposite way, with the United States contributing money to it's allies to keep them fighting. It is difficult to imagine that radical a financial creativity in Washington.

The main argument for the official story of the war is our faith that *a president of the United States would not do the things suggested here. A president wouldn't hire film directors to tell him what to say and do. Presidents don't manufacture incidents to go to war. A president wouldn't make policy, life-and-death policy, just for the sake of being reelected. Our leaders are men who put honor over expedience.*